2605

By John P. Palmer
London, Ontario
Canada

*a*lea iacta est ("the die has been cast"), allegedly spoken by Julius Caesar as he led his army across the Rubicon River, setting off a Roman civil war.

> The phrase "crossing the Rubicon" has survived to refer to any individual or group committing itself irrevocably to a risky or revolutionary course of action, similar to the modern phrase "passing the point of no return". [Wikipaedia]

Fred Young had been successful in agricultural finance, based in Omaha, Nebraska, but his life was empty. He had been pretending his entire life, believing in and trying to live the Great Mid-American Dream.

When presented with the opportunity, he escaped his past life and embarked on a search, attempting to find what he really wanted.

2605 is the story of his escape and rediscovery.

According to most knowledgeable people, there were 2606 people killed in the attacks on the World Trade Center, September 11, 2001. Actually the correct figure should be 2605. This is the story of the one person who shouldn't have been included in that number.

Also from Amazon by John P. Palmer:
- **Three Murder Mysteries – Scripts for Mystery Dinner Theatre**
- **Susan's Story** (forthcoming in early 2020)

Version 6.0 as of 2020-02-02

Chapter 1 – *Facing the Rubicon*

I'm a human alarm clock. My body is programmed to wake me up at 6:30 am.

So that morning, the same as every other morning, I woke up at 6:30.

I rolled over, picked up my laptop from the hotel nightstand, and sent a quick email to my wife.

> 'morning, Love. Looking forward to meeting with Jordan Singer. I guess he's the point man for our project with Cantor Fitzgerald. I'll let you know how things go. Love to you and the kids.

I showered, got dressed, reviewed my notes for the meeting, and made a final check of my email messages, including the response from my wife.

> Hope it goes well! Call me when you're done.
> Love you!
> ~~Susan~~

I slipped my laptop into my shoulder bag, took the elevator to the hotel lobby, and started walking toward the World Trade Center.

I checked my watch again. It was 7:30 on the nose. My hotel was only ten blocks from the World Trade Center, and I figured that if I arrived at the North Tower by 8:30, I would have plenty of time to join the elevator queue and make my way up to the Cantor Fitzgerald offices on the 101st floor and be early, as I had hoped, for my nine o'clock appointment with Singer.

I had an hour to walk those ten blocks. I was a bit overweight, and I knew the walk would do me some good.

Because of my weight and some heart issues, I wasn't supposed to have pastries, but I couldn't resist them when I was away from home. I planned that I would stop at some small shop along the way for a quick pastry and coffee.

It was a beautiful morning: sixty- four degrees and not a cloud in the sky. I felt really happy, even excited about the prospect of working out a deal with Cantor. I needed this deal to go through to make up for some things that had gone wrong back home in Omaha, Nebraska, and I knew it was pretty much in the bag. That, and the great weather, helped me feel as if I was walking on air.

Well, almost.

New Yorkers walk fast. I don't know why they don't just leave a bit earlier and slow down. I felt rushed and jostled by the other pedestrians, and I resented it. Sure, I had a bounce in my step, but I didn't enjoy being rushed. I wanted to enjoy the stroll, take in the sights, and find a place to have coffee.

Just as I saw what looked like a promising little coffee bar, a little over a block away from the World Trade Center, I heard a loud roar overhead.

I remember thinking in that split second, "Wow that plane is flying awfully low!" And before I could finish that thought, the plane hit the North Tower of the World Trade Center.

An enormous ball of fire flew out from where the plane hit the building, followed by a cascade of debris --- broken glass, papers, fiery chunks of concrete, strips of aluminum, bits of luggage, melted plastic, and burning body parts.

People around me stopped in their tracks. Some screamed. Some yelled. Others stood frozen in stunned silence. The man closest to me, muttered, "Oh, my God!" and crossed himself.

My next thought was, "What kind of idiot pilot couldn't avoid hitting a World Trade Center Tower?" and it didn't take long for me to decide it wasn't an accident.

That scared me, but I assumed the pilot had been mentally ill. I had no idea what his real motivation might have been for flying his plane into that building.

I don't know why, but for some reason I felt drawn to the site. Maybe it was morbid curiosity. Maybe it was something else. Whatever it was, I was irresistibly drawn there.

As I neared the building, people began pouring out of it. Some were crying, but most were frightened or in shock. They seemed to know the building had been hit or something like that, but many of them assumed a bomb had gone off somewhere inside the building, like when the truck bomb exploded there in the underground parking garage eight and half years earlier.

Hundreds of people started gathering in the side streets, plazas, and other open areas, looking up at where the plane had hit the North Tower. It was both frightening and awe-inspiring to see so much fire and so much damage. And so much death and destruction.

Someone near me said, "Looks like it hit about the 100th floor."

"Damn," I muttered. That was just below Jordan Singer's office at Cantor on the 101st floor.

I looked at my watch. "7:53," I said. "I think it must have hit about five or ten minutes ago." That was how long it had been since I first heard the plane over head and made my way to the Tower.

"Look again, pal," said someone else near me. "Maybe your watch isn't working."

"Damn," I muttered again. He was right... in a way. My watch was working, and it did say 7:53, but it was on Omaha time, not New York City time. I had forgotten to reset my watch when I left home in

Omaha to come to New York City for the meeting with Cantor Fitzgerald. It was 8:53 in New York, and the plane had hit the tower at 8:48 (only later did I learn the exact time).

If I had gotten up on time and if I had made it to my meeting a bit early, as I had planned, I would have been in Singer's office on the 101st floor when the plane hit. I would almost surely be a dead man.

- - -

Then it hit me: I had a chance to escape my life.

I had been contemplating making an escape for the past few years but mostly in my daydreams, as a fantasy. I guess it was a sort of coping strategy; I never really thought I would be in a position to actually do it.

I stood in a recess, back away from the crowd, and kept my head down. I tried to think through what I would have to do if I really wanted to escape my old life, how to do it, and what it would mean.

I knew I could turn back within the next few hours if I changed my mind, but I decided to try to drop out of sight.

So far as anyone would know, Fredrick Robert Young was killed when that plane slammed into the World Trade Center. I was now Carl Benson Jacobs.

I hesitated for a minute or so as I contemplated my future, but I realized I would have to act quickly if I was really going to do it.

The first thing I did was turn off my cell phone. It had to be dead if I was going to be dead. I knew my family, friends, and co-workers would be calling, desperate to know how I was and whether I was safe.

It was a very long minute or two as I struggled with myself. I really wanted to call everyone and share with them my relief at being alive. I wanted to tell them about how my own incompetence in forgetting to reset my watch made me safe on the ground looking up at the horror of the plane crash instead of being up there, crushed and incinerated in Jordan Singer's office on the 101st floor of the North Tower.

But I didn't call them. Instead I took another step and waded into the Rubicon. I opened my phone and took out the battery and SIM card.

As I stood with the growing crowd staring up at the crash site, I thought about returning to my hotel to collect a few things. Nope, that wouldn't do. I had to leave everything there. I couldn't let anyone see me as Fred Young after the plane hit that tower. Also, leaving **all** my belongings in that hotel room would go a long way toward convincing people that Fred Young was dead.

My next step was to find a drugstore or variety store. Fortunately there was one just a couple of stores back from where I had stopped. Some people had rushed out of the store to see what was going on, but the clerks were still on duty, albeit in a state of puzzlement, asking, "What happened? What was that big explosion?"

"I dunno. Looks like a plane hit one of the towers," I mumbled, keeping my head down.

I bought a pair of scissors and a pack of disposable razors. I almost paid for them with my credit card, but I remembered just in the nick of time to pay with cash.

Whew. That was a close call --- the first of many.

I found the employee restroom at the back of the store and went into a stall, making sure the latch was secure. Using the scissors, I cut my longish hair and beard as short as I could. I saved some of the hairs but flushed most of the rest down the toilet along with the SIM card from my phone. And then I flushed the toilet again for good measure.... And I flushed it again to get clean water in the toilet bowl.

Using that water and a disposable razor, I shaved my head and beard as close as I could. It was a spotty job, for sure, but within five minutes or so I felt as if I looked pretty much completely bald and beardless.

As I stepped out of the stall, I saw myself in the mirror and was horrified. I hated my look, but honestly I didn't even recognize myself. I had read that shaving your beard and hair are a great way to make yourself impossible to identify, but I hadn't expected anything like this. I was sure that no one, not even my closest friends or family members would recognize me unless they heard me talk.

I touched up the shaving job in the mirror and prepared my wallet. I took out most of the cash and put it in my front right pocket, leaving forty dollars in the wallet along with all my Fred Young ID cards and credit cards.

Then I removed the false ID that I had prepared to make my daydream of escaping seem more real than I ever really expected it to be. I never thought I would actually use the new persona, but I carried a false ID hidden in my wallet mostly as a lark, something of a secret little fantasy I had developed. I put the false ID in my front right pocket along with the cash.

I looked at the photo of my two children, Timothy (15) and Liz (13), sighed, and closed the wallet, putting it into my left front pocket, where I usually carry it.

I took off my necktie and suit coat and then I cut the tailor's name and labels and tags out of them and stuffed them into the bag they gave me when I bought the scissors and razors. I hoped no one would come in, and then I shoved the bag into the wastebasket, pushing it under some messy paper towels.

 I took another long look in the mirror and shrugged.

"Here we go," I said to myself.

I unbuttoned the top two buttons on my shirt, and walked out of the drugstore. I kept my head and face down just a bit, in case they had security cameras they might check later, and hurried back toward the North Tower as quickly as I could, dropping the cellphone battery and the clothing tags and labels in different trashbins along the way.

By then, the second plane had hit the South Tower of the World Trade Center, and people were in a panic.

Hundreds were still streaming out of the North Tower, and the rush to evacuate the South Tower was just beginning.

Up above where the planes had hit, people were leaning out of windows, waving white material, begging to be rescued; others had gone to the rooftops, hoping to be airlifted to safety by helicopters.

Still others had no escape route. They couldn't bear the heat, but they couldn't get away from it either. Rather than burn alive, they jumped to their deaths. Hundreds of them! I still shake and cry when I think about that. Especially the young couple that jumped holding hands.

There was screaming and shouting. Everywhere. Such a din.

And the smell of fire and smoke. It was a smell I would never forget and hope I'll never smell again.

As people came out of the buildings, some of them would stop briefly to look at the carnage among debris. Others from nearby offices came to look at the devastation. I'm sure some came or stayed to gaze at the scene more out of shock than anything else. Others gawked at the scene because of a raw, ghoulish curiosity.

One thing you never saw on the news was that scavengers went to work almost immediately. More than just a few people had swarmed to the site and were going through the debris: the luggage bits, the body parts, and the clothing, stealing jewelry and money if they could find any. They worked quickly, undoubtedly trying to steal what they could before the areas were cordoned off. No foolin'.

I joined in.

Not to steal but to plant evidence.

I hadn't anticipated the scavengers, but they made my job so much easier. I could blend right in with them.

When no one was looking, I put my hair strands under some hot concrete chunks. I hoped the heat would singe the hair ends a bit so no one could tell they had been cut. And then I put my wedding ring under another chunk and my wallet under another nearby bit of building debris. I hoped my attempts to plant evidence wouldn't be too obvious then or later. I certainly didn't want people to see me planting the evidence. I hoped anyone who saw me would think I was scavenging, along with the other scavengers. I didn't like the image of being a scavenger, but it was great cover for me.

I also hoped I had done a good enough job that when my hair, ring, and wallet were discovered, people would assume I was dead, that the impact of the plane into the Cantor Fitzgerald offices had killed me and somehow knocked my remains right out of the building. And I hoped that if scavengers found my stuff and took it, they would take what cash I had left in the wallet and then throw the wallet and credit cards in the trash somewhere.

Fred Young was now dead and gone. I had become Carl Jacobs.

I knew I could concoct a story later if I changed my mind. But by planting my personal items among the debris, I had taken another significant step, wading a little farther into the Rubicon.

I was nervous and shaky, and yet calm. I had fantasized about and actually planned this identity change as a way to escape, but I honestly never thought I would be in a situation where I might be able to actually do it, much less have the guts to try to pull it off if the opportunity ever presented itself. Until that plane hit that tower, it had only been a way of escaping mentally and emotionally from the emptiness and the growing problems of my past life.

My next plan was to escape New York City with my new identity. I had about five thousand dollars in a bank account that I had opened as a part of my escape fantasy under the name of Carl Jacobs, a bankcard for that account, a false birth certificate, and a Social Security Number for Carl Jacobs; and I had my shoulder bag and laptop. Oh, and the scissors and razors I had just bought.

I felt for my wallet to check for sure how much cash I had but then slapped myself alongside my head. I had planted the wallet among the debris and bodies outside the North Tower, and I had already forgotten. I would have to concentrate and be careful if I was going to pull off the escape and the new identity.

It turned out I had about $240 in cash. I also had the bankcard that I could use to gain access to my secret bank account. That was it. I was going to start a completely new life with a small bit of money, no credentials, no education record, no job, no work history, no family, no friends, and no home.

I felt a cold thud as those bare facts hit me, but I had prepared myself. Or so I thought.

Amidst the screaming and the chaos and the smells of fire and smoke, I walked away from the Twin Towers, hoping to eventually find my way to the bus station or Grand Central Station. It turned out I'd walked east, but what did I know? I wasn't sure how far or even which direction to go. I hadn't thought that far ahead, and it didn't matter anyway because the smoke from the fires was blocking the sun and I lost track of which direction I was going.

And then the South Tower collapsed.

I was about two blocks away, and the paper and ash storm that rushed up the street was frightening. I ducked into a doorway to avoid whatever flying debris I could, but I could barely breathe because the air was completely filled with dust and ash. Building ash, dead body ash, paper ash. I had to pull my shirt up over my mouth and nose to keep the dust and ash from choking me and filling my lungs.

People were running past me as fast as they could, screaming and crying.

There was such a giant, panicky horde that if I had tried to join them, I'd have been trampled.

One young man dove under a parked car to avoid the mob that was hurtling down the street. Another stumbled as he neared where I was standing. If he had fallen, he would have been pulverized by the runaway herd of people. I grabbed his wrist as he was about to fall and pulled him into the doorway with me.

He promptly vomited against the wall. It was a strange kind of vomit – food bits mixed into a slurry of coffee with the ash that he had swallowed as he had been running.

He was really frightened. Then he looked at me, wiped his mouth, and panted, "Thanks, man. I could have been killed out there."

"Do you have any idea what's going on?" I asked.

"Yeah," he said. "Two big planes crashed into the Twin Towers and killed thousands of people. The South Tower just collapsed, and they're trying to get as many people out of the North Tower as they can before it goes too."

"Oh crap," I said. I wept openly. So did he. We actually hugged each other.

The screaming people, the constant rumbling as the South Tower settled down, and the wailing of sirens all combined were deafening. We were two blocks from what came to be called "Ground Zero", and we still had to shout to be heard.

Soon, the North Tower went too.

We heard it before we saw it. You have never heard a roar like the roars we heard as those towers collapsed.

And then the dust and ash storm came at us again, but we were prepared this time. As soon as we heard the North Tower collapsing, we took off our shirts and covered our heads and faces to filter out as much of the smoke and dust and ash as we could. We still gagged for fresh air, but we survived. And this time there were fewer people running because so many had already run away or been evacuated.

The sky was darker than night with all the ash and smoke. It was such an eerie, frightening thing. We could barely see, and there was noise and chaos everywhere.

As the air cleared a bit, we took our shirts away from our faces and stood out in the street. The young man who had dived under the car slowly edged his way out. He could barely breathe, but he stood up and slowly tried to regain his breath.

"Hi," I said to my doorway partner. "I'm …." I hesitated for just a moment and hoped he didn't catch on. "Carl Jacobs," and put out my hand to shake his.

"Bob Zuker," he said, shaking my hand. "You saved my life man. I owe you big-time."

Instead of responding I introduced myself to the young man who had regained his breath after riding out the smoke, dust, and ash storm under the car.

"Hi. Carl Jacobs." I wanted to say it often to get used to it.

"Tom," he said. He didn't offer a last name, but he shook our hands.

"Call me 'Zuke'", Bob said to both of us as he and Tom shook hands. The three of us had clearly bonded in that moment.

"What do we do now???" Zuke asked.

Tom said, "I'm really thirsty. How about we go for a drink somewhere?"

That made sense. We had been through a lot, and each of us had inhaled and ingested gobs of ash and dust. Washing it all down would really feel good.

So we headed for a bar Tom said was a block away, hoping it would be open.

A half block toward the bar, I saw a tiny soft-drink kiosk that amazingly had managed to stay open through all the chaos. It would do a land-office business before the day was over. I stopped to buy us all Cokes, and while we were buying them, I shouted over the din, "I'm not from New York City. I'm pretty concerned, and I want to get out of town. I think I'll skip the beers and head to the train or bus station."

"Don't bother," the kiosk owner shouted back. "They've cancelled all train, bus, and plane traffic from the entire area. You won't be able to get out. Everyone is just heading home or to a hotel or a friend's place. ..."

"You can stay with me," interrupted Zuke. "It's a seven-mile walk from here, but I have a couch you can sleep on until you can get away. It's the least I can do for you..." and then he snorted at himself: "Hunh! After what you did for me, you can have my bed, and I'll sleep on the couch."

"Thanks, Zuke. I really appreciate that. But there must be some way to get off the island and begin to make my way home." Actually, I had only a vague idea about where my new home would be, and so this felt pretty hollow as I said it. But mostly I turned down Zuke's offer because I was afraid to spend much time with anyone until I had my new life straightened out. I needed time to think ... by myself.

I repeated, "There must be some way to get off the island."

"Nah, I don't think so," Tom chimed in. "When the government wants things shut down, they shut 'em down."

"Not completely," said the kiosk owner. "As I was starting to say before you interrupted me, I heard on the radio that there's a massive flotilla of boats of all kinds taking people from Battery Park across the Hudson to Jersey.

"Battery Park? Where is that and how do I get there?" I asked eagerly.

"You're on Broadway now, Buddy! Just go that way and stay on Broadway 'til you see the park. You can't miss it!" He gestured toward the direction I assumed he meant I should go. "It's only about six or seven blocks."

I knew no one would recognize me, but I wanted to get as far away from the World Trade Center as I could as soon as I could.

I turned, waved, and shouted my good-byes to Zuke and Tom, and then I walked away quickly, very quickly, south on Broadway toward Battery Park.

* * *
**

Chapter 2 – *Jersey*

I walked quickly, almost running, down Broadway. The guy at the kiosk had been right -- Battery Park was right there, right at the end of Broadway. As I neared the park, the sound of sirens diminished slightly but the sound of motors was distinct.

Closer to the water the motors were louder. When I reached the waterfront, I could see them: dozens of boats taking on passengers and ferrying them to the Jersey shore. There were small, open outboard motorboats all the way up to some pretty decent-sized yachts. Most were small pleasure crafts, but a few were fishing boats or tugs, and the river was covered with them.

The people who had commuted to Manhattan that morning from New Jersey were desperate to get back to their families. The Holland Tunnel had been closed already, and so had the Lincoln Tunnel. The George Washington Bridge was closed to vehicles, and although people were allowed to walk across it and the other bridges, getting there and actually doing it would be nearly impossible from the southern tip of Manhattan.

Some people tried to rush the places where the boats were picking up the evacuees, but others seemed to have volunteered themselves to be traffic cops. I don't know who those people were, but they had taken control. They formed us into a massive snaky queue, reassuring us that the boats would keep coming as long as there were people waiting to be ferried to New Jersey.

I relaxed, but only a bit, and joined the queue.

As I stood in line, I thought some more about what I was doing. It wasn't too late to change my mind, and I hesitated. I knew I would miss my family, a couple of my friends, and some aspects of my job. If I continued with this escape, I would never be able to see or talk with anyone from my past ever again.

And yet, in most ways, I knew it was the right thing to do.

I shook my head, reached down and tapped my right knee, and turned my thoughts to where I should go. I certainly didn't want to go back to Omaha or anywhere in the Midwest where there might be even a remote possibility that I would be recognized.

I probably wanted to go someplace warm. Housing would likely be cheaper with no heating bills, and I wouldn't need a closetful of winter clothes, boots, and gloves. At the same time, I didn't want to go to California because I wouldn't be able to afford living there on a minimum-wage job. Texas is just too hot with no relief, and Dixie is too humid with no relief. That pretty much left Florida, where I might be able to make do in the summers with just a fan and in the winters with a light jacket and sweater.

But Florida has hurricanes, especially in the southern part. That was too bad because the Keys would have been perfect climate-wise. Miami and other major vacation meccas might be good, but too many people from Omaha who vacation in Florida go to Miami, Orlando, Tampa, as well as all the places where people buy time-shares or rent condos.

Pensacola might be good, I mused, but it too can be ravaged by hurricanes. Well that was silly. So can just about any part of Florida that is near the water.

So I began to consider Jacksonville. I had never heard of **anyone** who took a vacation in Jacksonville, and it is big enough to get lost in. Another possibility was Tallahassee, the state capital. It's in the panhandle and not too close to the gulf. It might be warm enough but not too hot and not too risky, hurricane-wise.

I was still thinking about where to go when the line started moving forward again as three more boats arrived at Battery Park.

The most desperate members of the queue were trying to buy or push their way forward, but with little luck. Others pleaded with folks to let them move up because they wanted to get home to their families. I wanted to get off Manhattan for sure, but I let a few really desperate-sounding guys go ahead of me in the queue.

"My daughter's school called. She's sick and needs to get home and my wife is laid up with chemo for her breast cancer. Can I go ahead?" was one story I heard. True or not, I didn't care. I let him move ahead of me.

"It's my son's birthday, and I promised I'd take him out for a special night tonight. Can I go ahead?" said another. I saw no reason for him to hurry home before noon when he wouldn't have made it until 6pm or so otherwise, but it didn't matter all that much to me. I let him go ahead of me too.

When it was my turn to board a boat, I asked, "How much?" and pulled out some bills from my pocket.

Right front pocket. I smiled with pride as I remembered -- no wallet.

I was expecting that all these boat owners had rushed over to Battery Park to charge exorbitant prices for helping us get across the Hudson River, but I was wrong. Nearly all of them were kind-hearted people who were so moved by the attack and the tragedy that they came out in droves to help however they could. Sure, some came for the excitement of being part of the rescue. Still others came to hear the stories of the evacuees.

Later I read that some of the boat owners farther up along the Hudson were charging people $20 apiece to carry them across the river. I would gladly have paid that much to get off Manhattan and on my way. I think most of the other people in the queues would have paid it, too. Some would have grumbled, but most of us would have been happy to pay that much or more.

The boat I was in was skippered by Barry. At least that's what the nameplate on the boat dashboard said in fancy script: "Your captain today is Barry." He looked like an older, retired guy who enjoyed having a small power boat and motoring up and down the river. He fit the stereotype: grey hair, white captain's hat, khakis, white polo shirt, and deck shoes. But his clothes were smeared with dirt and mud.

He took ten of us aboard even though he had only six life jackets. We didn't care. I can swim pretty well, so I didn't take one of the life jackets. Anyway, I was pretty sure that if we capsized in the Hudson, the pollution would take me before I drowned.

I tried to slip Barry some cash to thank him, but he seemed almost insulted.

"No! Nothing!" he shouted above the engine noise as he waved me away.

"Let me at least make a contribution to your gas expenses," I offered.

"Absolutely not!" Barry yelled, and then he turned away from me to focus on handling his boat. I read similar stories from others later. There was such a huge outpouring of goodwill that day.

I looked around the boat. Along one side two women were huddled together comforting and consoling each other. An older man on the other side was leaning back, head up with his eyes closed, almost as if he was enjoying the wind and sea spray on his face. Or maybe he was praying. It would have been a beautiful, even inspiring photograph.

One guy in a power suit and obviously tailored clothes was trying to pace despite the lack of room on the boat. He seemed really uptight, shouting into his cellphone, "Whaddya mean the market is closed?? I wanna short American Airlines! Find some way to do it for me!" He was the only passenger showing anything even approaching hysteria.

He wasn't the only person on his cellphone, though. Three of the others were calling family and friends, talking in quiet, reserved, and calming voices, reassuring them, letting them know they were ok, telling them where to pick them up. As one of them hung up, he offered me his phone and asked if I'd like to make a call.

"No thanks," I said. I pulled out my phone and showed it to him. "I've already made my calls." And then I added, "...just before my battery died. Whew!" I added that last bit because I didn't want anyone to ask if they could use my phone.

I thought about dropping my phone into the Hudson to get rid of it, but decided against doing that. I didn't think I could drop it without one of the other passengers seeing me or without making a big deal of having it slip from my hand as I leaned overboard. And even if I could do it somehow, I didn't know whether the phone would sink or float. I sure didn't want it to be found floating in the Hudson without its SIM card and then traced back to me.

Boats were constantly coming in at the harbor loaded with evacuees and going back to Battery Park to pick up more. I reckon they ferried thousands of us across the Hudson that day in just a few hours.

Physically, I was a mess, with ash and dust all over my skin and clothes. I tried to wash the worst of it off my face and hands as we were crossing the river, but I was reluctant to use much of that questionable water on my face. I splashed some water over my hands and then used them to wipe my face, but it was a lost cause. And when I used my shirtsleeve to wipe my face and hands, the dirt and ash on my shirt were so bad that it just made things worse. By the time we got to New Jersey, my face was streaked with dirt and ashes, my shirt had mud and ashes all over both the front and back, and my shoes and pants were dust and mud covered. Even my hands weren't very clean.

In no time flat, Barry pulled his boat into a slip at the Liberty Landing Marina. As he helped each of us out of his boat, he shook hands with each of us and gave us each a hug.

Now I knew why Barry's clothes were smeared and dirty: he had hugged all his passengers from previous trips, too. We all felt immensely grateful to be alive and so grateful to Barry for getting us off Manhattan and over to New Jersey. We wanted to do more than just perfunctorily shake hands and get a quick hug, but he quickly retook the controls of his boat and returned to the river, racing back to Battery Park for more evacuees.

Although most of the passengers had called ahead and were expecting someone to pick them up, a few of us were pretty much on our own. We sort of looked around, helplessly, as if to ask, "What do we do now?"

We didn't have long to wait. People from the marina, the restaurants, and three different churches or service organizations were there to help us. They had bottles of water for us and were arranging cars to take us where we wanted to go.

A woman approached me and asked, "Is someone meeting you?"

"No," I said. "I'm going to try to find a cab."

"Nonsense!" she said, in a no-nonsense voice. "Most cabbies are cowering at home watching the news on TV or else they're booked solid. And they'd rather stay in town than make an empty run out here to pick you up. So…. Where do you want to go? I'll take you there."

I hesitated, but she didn't have a clue why.

"Maddy Rush," she said and stuck out her hand. "I'm with the Episcopalian Church, and we're down here with water and sandwiches to help everyone we can. I have some in the car, and I'll be happy to drive you anywhere in the Newark area."

I was overwhelmed and started shaking just a bit, mostly inside, as I looked at her hand. The people here were doing so much to help those of us who wanted to get out of Manhattan.

I started to put my hand out; I didn't shake her hand though. Mine was too grungy. I just smiled and looked at my hand as I pulled it back. She understood. I could see it in her eyes and body language.

"Where are you going?" Maddy asked.

"Florida," I said, "but I gather the airlines all have their planes on the ground until further notice. What about the train station?"

"No way, José," she said. "The only trains in Newark are either coming from or going to New York. But they aren't moving today, and probably won't be moving tomorrow. By the way, what's your name? It's not José, is it?"

"Oh. Sorry. Carl Jacobs." Only a very brief unnoticeable hesitation this time. "What about the bus station then?"

"Well, you might be able to get a local to Trenton or Philadelphia and see what happens from there."

"Okay. Let's try that," and we went to her car, a champagne-colored Lexus. I hesitated along side the car.

"Come on. Get in," she urged.

"I can't. I'm filthy. I'll make a mess of your car."

"You're right," she said. "Here." She popped the trunk and took out a blanket.

"Put this on the seat, you'll be okay."

Another hesitation.

"Oh, don't worry! It's washable," she smiled.

So I leaned in and spread the blanket over the passenger seat. She opened the console and pulled out a sandwich and a thermos.

"I hope you're okay with ham and cheese on wheat," she said. "The thermos is martinis, but I have some bottled water here somewhere, too."

"I'd love a sandwich," I told her, "but I think the water would be best for me right now."

"Nice car, Maddy" I added.

She rummaged through the console, found a bottle of water, and handed it to me.

"Yeah. My husband has been pretty successful. I used to be a nurse, but when his business took off, I didn't need to work anymore, so I quit, stayed home, looked after the kids, and became a homemaker. Then as the kids grew up and left home, I started doing more volunteer work, including these things with the Episco-ladies."

She started the engine, and I unwrapped the sandwich. It was a thick slice of ham with Gruyere cheese on fancy whole wheat bread, and it looked delicious. I put the sandwich on its wrapper on my lap and opened the water bottle. I took a long drink and put it in the console cupholder.

"Episco-ladies?" I asked.

"Oh," she laughed. "That's my name for the group. I don't even remember the proper name. I just like to get out, do things, and help when I can. Where are you headed in Florida?"

I chewed on the sandwich as if I was busy eating while I made up a story. Then I took another gulp of water before I answered.

"Orlando", I answered.

And then, to keep her from asking anything else, I added, "I was there. I saw the first plane hit. What's happening? Is there anything on the news?"

"Anything on the news?!" Maddy hooted. "There's nothing but news about it on every station, even the all-music stations. They think some terrorists hijacked two planes and flew them into the World Trade Center. They've grounded all planes indefinitely, but there have been some rumours about some other planes being commandeered, too."

She turned on the radio, and we just sat there and listened to the news reports for few minutes.

"What's this world coming to?" Maddy wondered aloud.

***
**

Chapter 3 – *Transition at Liberty Park*

Before we started moving, Maddy looked over at me and said, "Carl, they're not going to want you on the bus looking like that. I know you want to get going and get home to your family, but you won't be going anywhere with all that ash and mud streaked all over your face and clothing."

She pulled up to the restaurant and said, "Go in there and wash up. They're expecting it. There have been lots of people ferried over here from Battery Park in your condition or even worse."

I was eager to get cleaned up but I was still a bit reluctant. I hated having to interact with any more people than necessary right now until I'd had a chance to think carefully about what I was doing. But the hesitation was for only a very brief moment. I knew she was right.

"Here," she said, handing me three twenties. "They have a small shop in there for all the yachters and visitors. Buy some clean clothes too." I started to object, but I could see it wouldn't get me anywhere. And I knew it was a good idea to change my clothes.

The restaurant staff were great. They pointed me to the restroom and told me there were some extra towels and napkins in the restroom to use for washing up and drying off. As Maddy said, they had already seen lots of people like me, and they were doing their bit to help out.

Before I went to the men's room, I stopped at the very small sportswear section off on the side of the entrance. Even though I had tried to wash my hands in the river, I didn't want to touch the clothing to check the sizes, and so I peered around the hangers to try to find something my size. I found some beige deck pants that were my size: 38-32, and an extra-large pale blue Lacoste shirt with an alligator where the pocket should have been.

I picked them up by their hangers and took them to the cashier. She looked at me, smiled sympathetically, and said, "We have a special discount for you folks today. Fifty-percent off. That'll be $60. And here's a bag for your clothes," she added. "If you want to keep them, that is."

I handed her the $60 Maddy had given me and smiled inwardly. I didn't know how many times she and Maddy had already done this, or whether it was just a coincidence, but I could see the prices would add up to nearly $120. "Oh well," I thought, "At this price they're probably still selling them to me for more than their cost." I felt jaded even thinking that way, but sometimes thoughts like that just poppeds into my head.

The restroom was very nice: brightly lit with soap dispensers, plenty of hot water, and large stalls. I began by washing my hands again, this time with hot soapy water. Then with my clean hands, I used a napkin to wash my face. I must have wrung it out two or three times to get rid of the grunge.

Without thinking, I started washing the dirt out of my hair, but then I realized I had shaved my head. I looked in the mirror again. I still didn't recognize myself.

It was clear I had drastically changed my appearance. What wasn't clear was whether I could change my life.

After getting my hands, face, head, and arms clean, I took off my shoes and washed the worst of the dirt and grime from them, too. I had messed up some of the restaurant linen and looked around. There was a bin with other dirty towels and napkins in it, so I put mine there, too.

I went into the stall to change and began to strip off my pants and shirt. I kept my old belt to use with my new pants and transferred my cash and new ID to the right front pocket of the new pants. Even though I had liked the suit pants and shirt, I crammed them into the bag the shop clerk had given me and dropped the bag into the garbage bin on the way out.

As I climbed back into her car, Maddy smiled. "You clean up pretty good."

"Thanks." That was all I said. I didn't want to encourage any more discussion. But after a moment I added, "How long will it take to get to the bus station?"

"Well, it sounds as if the traffic is pretty snarled on any highway that leads to the city, and the interstates are really moving slowly. I think we'll just head straight over the Hackensack River on the Lincoln Highway Bridge. It's usually only half an hour to get there this way, but with the weird traffic today, it might be longer."

I took another bite from the sandwich. As we passed I-78, I could see the traffic was moving pretty well going south, away from New York City, but it looked pretty jammed up going north.

Maddy had the radio tuned to one of the major news stations from New York City. We were beginning to hear that many of the first responders were killed when the buildings collapsed. Them and the people on the higher floors who couldn't or didn't try to get out.

At one point she looked at me and asked, "Where were you? What happened?"

I maintained a stiff demeanor and kept looking straight ahead. "Is it ok if I don't talk about it right now?"

That worked. No more questions.

"I'm sorry. I won't bother you about it anymore."

I kept my head up and continued looking straight ahead. "Thanks," I mumbled.

The streets were eerily easy to travel. People were staying home or going home to be with their families. We shot through Jersey City on Communipaw Avenue in no time.

As we passed the golf course, Maddy chuckled cynically, "I guess some of the people who teed off earlier still haven't heard the news. That, or they really don't want their golf games interrupted."

Most golfers I knew had cellphones and carried them while golfing. I was sure they had all heard the news. Frantic friends and family would have called them by now. Some of them, I was sure, decided to play their way back to the clubhouse and promised their families they would go home as soon as possible. I would have bet good money, though, that a few of them were determined to finish their round since they had already paid the green fees. I didn't say it out loud, but "Sunk-Cost Fallacy" was what I thought to myself.

We crossed the Hackensack and Passaic Rivers fairly quickly but were slowed down under the interchange in east Newark. Maddy slipped into the left lane and avoided the worst of the congestion.

As the enormity of the tragedy continued to sink in, I realized that most of the people on the road now were trying to get home. That hit me hard. I was still feeling an enormous sense of impending doom as I thought about my escape from being Fred Young and becoming Carl Jacobs. I didn't know what to expect, but I knew I could still make excuses and go back to being Fred Young if I changed my mind.

I tapped my right knee lightly with my right index finger, shook my head and murmured "Uh uh." I shook my head again. "Uh uh."

Maddy quickly glanced at me. I'm guessing she thought I was trying to shake off some tragic memories. She had no idea what I was going through.

And I wasn't about to tell her.

Finishing up business for the day would be difficult for most people. It was such a clear day that people could see the smoke from the burning and the collapse of the twin towers off in the distance. The other cars on the highways may have been business people, going to their next call. My guess, though, was that most of them were in shock and that business was pretty low on their list of priorities right then.

Communipaw Avenue had somehow become Raymond Boulevard as we continued west into downtown Newark.

Street traffic around the Greyhound Bus station wasn't too bad... yet. "Maybe you'll be lucky," said Maddy. "It looks as if most folks are still paralyzed by the events and haven't figured out that the bus is about the only way out of here. That, or maybe a one-way rental car."

She pulled into a passenger-loading zone. "I'll just drop you here and then park somewhere. I'd like to wait to make sure you get off ok."

"Thanks, but don't wait. I'll be ok. Please don't bother. I'll get on the next available bus going south, whenever that is." As I began to open the door, I forced a smile and said, "Thanks for the food, the water, and the clothes. You have no idea how much I appreciate everything. People have been so good." I half forced back a real tear and half forced back a fake tear for her benefit. I knew I was pretending and yet I felt it, all at the same time. It was a kind of limbo I had never experienced before. I felt all the emotions and gratitude, and yet I knew I was lying and deceiving.

Again I shook my head. Then I reached over and touched her arm before picking up my shoulder bag from the floor. I got out of the car, and went into the bus station without looking back.

***

**

Chapter 4 – *Newark*

I didn't look back at Maddy, and I didn't turn to wave good-bye. Those were important symbolic yet probably meaningless non-gestures for me. I had spent far too many retrospective hours in my life, especially during the past few months, contemplating "if only" or "what if I had," or worse: "what if I hadn't". At this juncture, I needed to look forward, think about who I was, and plan within reason for who I could become.

But not quite yet. I couldn't get ahead of myself. Right now my goal was to get on my way, heading south. I needed to focus on that.

"Delayed" and "Cancelled" were splashed all over the arrival and departure boards for buses to and from New York City. Hundreds of confused passengers were milling about the station. Some were on their cellphones; others were queued up to use one of the few remaining payphones. But most were trying to figure out how to get to New York City, or they were waiting for friends and family to arrive from New York City.

Separate ticket windows had been opened for people trying to get to New York City. They were frustrated, scared, in shock, and murmuring constantly with each other. The standard things I overheard were, "Well when do you think they'll let us go? I have a meeting there this afternoon." Or "I need to get to a wedding/funeral/birthday party." They should have gone to the marinas. There was plenty of space on the boats returning to Battery Park.

Some people just left the station when they realized there was no possible way to get to and from the city without walking across a bridge or taking a boat. Still others hung around with a myopic hope that things would soon change.

It took less than half a minute for me to survey the crowd in the station and figure out what to do. It looked as if a number of other people had had the same idea I did. If they were trying to leave Newark for any place other than New York City, they were going to have to scramble. The planes were grounded, and the trains were pretty much shut down as well. And of course all the express buses that originated in New York City weren't moving either. Greyhound buses were about the only things moving south or west from Newark, and I was concerned that spaces might sell out pretty quickly. I joined the lengthening queue for the remaining ticket windows.

The middle-aged man in front of me was trying to make the best of it. He turned to me, "Where you trying to go?" he asked.

"South Carolina," I said, trying to give away very little information. "You?" I guessed that if I turned the question back to him, he would answer and wouldn't ask anything else.

"South Carolina! Man, that'll be some trip! Flight cancelled?"

Well. That didn't work. I just sort of half-nodded, and tried again.

"What happened to you?" I asked.

"Same thing. Flight cancelled out of the Newark airport." He bobbed his head almost imperceptibly as he was talking. "I'm hoping to get to Toronto, up in Canada, so I need to find a bus route to Buffalo. Any ideas?"

"Oh, man...." I commiserated. "I can't imagine that'll be easy."

I kept looking straight ahead, though, at the ticket window. I didn't really want to talk, and I did really want to get going as soon as possible.

Slowly we inched our way up to the window. The guy in front of me took forever trying to find a route to Toronto or Buffalo. It turned out most of the buses going there are routed via New York City and Albany first. Eventually the ticket agent found a bus for him that would leave for Binghamton the next morning, and he was hoping to work his way onward from there.

Finally he was done.

"Good luck" he said as he smiled somewhat sheepishly and wandered off to look for some place to spend the night.

"Next" called the ticket clerk, and I stepped up. "Where to?"

"Jacksonville, Florida"

"Well, you can't take the express that goes there because it originates in New York," he said.

"Yeah, I figured. What do you recommend?"

"We have a late night milk run that goes to Philadelphia through Trenton. Let me see what I can do," and he started typing on his terminal, paused, and typed some more."

"The system is pretty jammed up," he apologized. "I can get you on that bus, leaving Newark at 10:30 tonight, I think. It's supposed to originate in New York, but it's not gonna get there from here, so they'll probably just take on what passengers they can from here. It stops at several towns and burgs along the way, so you won't get into Philadelphia until after 1:30 tomorrow morning. How would that be?"

"Sounds ok to me," I replied. "When's the first bus south out of Philadelphia after I get there?"

He looked at his screen and tapped some more… and then tapped some more. "The first bus I can get you on out of Philadelphia leaves at 6:30am. But you're in luck. The Philly station stays open all night, and as long as you have an ongoing ticket, they won't bother you if you try to snooze on a bench."

"How far does that bus go?"

"It's a shuttle to DC. You want me to book these two? I can't get you any farther from here, but maybe you can look after the rest in Philadelphia or Washington."

"Ok. How much?" I asked.

"$27.88 to DC."

I started to put my left hand in my left front pocket, but stopped myself.

"Right front pocket, dummy," I reminded myself silently. I pulled out some bills and paid the fare. The tickets were printed on a dot-matrix printer behind the clerk. He tore them off and passed them across the counter to me along with the change.

"Thanks," I said.

As I walked away from the ticket window, I heard him call out, "Next."

I looked at my watch.

"Argh", I muttered under my breath. I should have left it somewhere back at the Twin Towers. It was gold, and it was engraved on the back,

To Fred
Congratulations
Mom and Dad

I would need to get rid of it, making sure it couldn't be found anywhere. I took it off immediately and put it in my pocket. Left front.

It was 2:30 in the afternoon. I had nearly eight hours to kill before the bus left.

After wandering around the bus station for maybe five or ten minutes, I could see there were no shops there that I wanted to buy anything from. Instead, I decided to go out to walk around the area, hoping to find a dollar store or bargain-o-rama or whatever it might be called that would have a few things I would want to have with me for the next few days.

As I walked along, I realized how careful I had to be to get rid of my past. My cellphone and the laptop in my shoulder bag would have to go, along with my watch. I would have to find ways to dispose of them that they would not likely be recovered. Public trash bins were out. I had seen far too many street people and drug users who would love to find a cellphone, a laptop, or a gold watch in a garbage can. I decided to hang onto them for a while until I felt more confident about disposing of them.

Every store I went into had a radio or a television tuned to the news. Only then did I learn about the plane that crashed into the Pentagon and the other plane that was almost surely taken down by the passengers. I silently wept a bit more, thinking about the passengers sacrificing their lives to save others from lord knew what. I may have been silent, but I couldn't stop a few tears from running down my cheek. I tried to wipe or blot them away, but my Lacoste shirt had short sleeves and I couldn't reach everywhere on my face. So I just wiped the tears with my hands and went on.

One of the first shops I went into had lots of cheap digital watches. I found one for $14 that had big legible numbers and a few features I would probably never use, but I liked the blue light, so I bought it and put it on.

Three blocks away I found a discount store that had many of the types of things I could use. I had made up my mind that I wanted cheap pants and a cheap long-sleeved shirt instead of the yacht club garb. I also wanted an inexpensive larger bag to carry things in. I settled on a basic school-type backpack and put that into the cart along with a shirt and a pair of pants. I added a toothbrush and toothpaste, more disposable razors, antiperspirant, a new wallet, and a three-pack of socks and some grey briefs. I had always been a boxer man, but it was time for another change. I didn't need anything special; just enough to tide me over for a few days or maybe even a few weeks.

In the aisle on the way to the cash register, I saw some inexpensive multi-tool things. I picked up one that had two knife blades, a file, a can opener, and a couple of different screwdriver heads, all-in-one for three dollars. I knew it wouldn't last long, but decided to get it anyway, just in case I needed a knife or tool for something.

I really had very little idea what I was doing.

As I was checking out and putting things into the backpack, I nearly bought a two-pound milk-chocolate bar, but I stopped myself. Part of my plan to change my identity had to be to lose weight... a lot of it... and get in better shape. I weighed 210lbs and was just under 5'10". I wanted to get down to maybe as low as 150lbs very quickly. That's what I weighed when I was 20, so I knew it was possible. It would be almost exclusively salads, veggies, and protein for me. No empty calories.

I put my shoulder bag with my laptop on the bottom of the backpack, followed by the rest of my purchases and I left, wearing the backpack.

Next stop was a bank ATM. I had used the bankcard for my secret bank account several times back in Omaha, but I wanted to make sure it would work somewhere outside Omaha.

Whew. It worked. I took out three hundred dollars and put the twenties in my new wallet. Then I moved the cash and new ID from my right front pocket to the wallet, too. I now had about $500 in cash in my wallet, more than I usually wanted to carry, but I also didn't want to run out of cash.

I had always kept my wallet in my left front pocket in the past, and so now, as part of my new identity, I was determined to get used to having my wallet in my right front pocket.

I had a sense of relief as I started back toward the bus station. I had enough supplies to keep myself clean and presentable, and I was well on my way to adapting to the new me.

Once again, though, as I thought "new me" I had some fairly sharp pangs of guilt and twinges of regret. It felt melodramatic to have these feelings and yet I knew, or at least strongly believed, I was doing the right thing, and I consoled myself with that thought.

At the same time, I was developing a sense of paranoia. Someone bumped me slightly. My first thought was, "I have my hands in my front pockets. My wallet is safe." And it was. My pocket hadn't been picked.

My second thought was, "What's that about? Is someone onto me? After me?"

I took a deep breath and said to myself, "It's almost surely random, but don't slip up, and don't let down your guard…. Ever!"

I took a slightly different route back to the bus station. After walking a block or two, I came to a thrift store and realized I might find things there that I could use.

It was a nice but quaint thrift store run by a local church agency, not Goodwill or the Sally Ann. As I browsed through the store, I saw several pairs of pants and some shirts that I thought might suit me well in my new life. I was about to load up with them, but then I remembered I wanted to lose some weight and some bulk, and these clothes wouldn't fit me for long if I was successful. I also thought, "Geez, wake up, idiot. You have no idea what will suit you well in your new life. Besides, they have thrift stores everywhere. You can get more later; just get what you think you'll need for the next few days."

I ended up taking just one blue dress shirt and one pair of grey cotton slacks. I also bought a lightweight jacket in case it got cool at night over the next few days. Near the checkout, I saw a floppy bucket hat and bought that, too, because I realized I would need considerable protection from the sun now that I would be bald for the rest of my life.

Bald for the rest of my life!

Wow. Another impact. The thought of having to shave both my beard and my head nearly every day was overwhelming. Again, I pushed the thought aside. I put on the hat and put the rest of my purchases into the backpack.

Back at the bus station, I still had about 4 hours to kill before the bus departed. I went to the men's room and into a stall. I took the shirt from the thrift shop out of my backpack and put it on, and I put the yacht club Lacoste shirt into the backpack. That felt better.

I found a seat in the bus station and sat. I didn't know what to do with myself. I wanted to get on the way and begin working things out as Carl Jacobs. But I had to be patient, wait until I got to Jacksonville, and see what I could do *there*. Until then…. I finally let myself think about my past life. I needed to reconcile myself to leaving it and the people in it; and I needed to develop a plausible story about who I was about to become.

I sat and dozed and drifted and dreamed and contemplated.

***
**

Chapter 5 – *Omaha*

What I had done back in Omaha wasn't really illegal; it wasn't even unsound financially. But it certainly was controversial. It was probably even suspicious in the minds of many people. It was likely to get me fired or at the very least "reassigned", especially if the deal with Cantor Fitzgerald didn't go through.

And after the plane hit their offices, I could see that wasn't going to happen.

I had been a bond dealer, and I was being accused of having put together some fairly sketchy packages of packages … of packages … of packages of bonds based on farm mortgages, of having relabeled them as triple-A bonds, and of having sold off the re-packaged repackages of repackages to investment companies that were looking for higher yield AAA bonds than they could find anywhere else in the market. It wasn't unlike what others did several years later leading up to the housing boom and bust. It's just that I was a good six or seven years ahead of the pack in figuring out what to do and how to do it.

The problem was that as farm output prices crashed, so did the value of farmland. Farmers couldn't meet the mortgage payments on their land, and it was becoming clear that some of the financial paper I had repackaged and marketed as AAA was in reality high-risk junk. I could probably have covered enough of our losses with the deal that I'd had in the works with Cantor Fitz, but our firm's reputation wouldn't be completely saved and mine would be tarnished for quite some time: "Oh yeah, Fred Young. I remember him. He's the one who sold us junk labeled AAA." In fact the loss of reputation for both me and Klein-Staily were likely to be more serious than the actual problems with the bonds.

The handwriting was on the wall. It was only a matter of time before the wall itself came crashing down for me.

- - -

Like most farm boys, I went to a state agricultural university. In my case, it was Kansas State University in Manhattan, Kansas, where I was a quiet, respectable, top quartile student in agri-business. My parents, my siblings, and I all assumed I would major in farm management and then return to manage the family farm.

During the summers I went back to the farm in western Kansas and worked there, but it became pretty clear to everyone in the family that I was nowhere near as interested in the farm as they were in *having* me be interested in the farm. While I was home for Thanksgiving vacation in my junior year, Dad sat up with me for several hours talking about my future and the future of the farm. I could see the sadness in his eyes and hear the sadness in his voice, but he was reconciled to my not coming back to the farm after I graduated. In the end, he and Mom were very supportive of my doing whatever I wanted to do. They were terrific. I'm really glad he and Mom had already passed away before I began to have my career "difficulties".

I met Susan at a campus Christmas party that year. She was a home economics major, the typical pre-marriage major for women at many of the state colleges and universities back then. We hit it off pretty well, I guess. She acted interested in me, the farm, and my unsophisticated views on so many things; and I acted interested in her, her family, her coursework, and her somewhat more sophisticated views on politics, literature, and relationships. We saw each other pretty regularly all winter and seemed comfortable with each other.

"Sex was a natural dinner-table topic of discussion in our house," she told me one evening in the spring of our junior years. "What about yours?" she asked.

When I was younger, my aunt and uncle on the neighboring farm raised white-faced Herefords. "We talked about animal sex a bit, but mostly in practical, farming contexts. Which cows to breed when and with which steer. We never talked about sex between people."

The truth was, I told her, I was a virgin and knew next to nothing about having sex other than that masturbation seemed evil but felt good. Susan said she was a virgin, too, but that she had done some heavy petting with a boyfriend in high school. I pretended I believed her.

That night we went to a motel and had sex. I don't think it was all that great for her, and it didn't seem any better than masturbation to me. But we both enjoyed the fact that we had done it and that we had done it together.

We got engaged that summer and set a wedding date for the following summer, following graduation. We planned and expected to find jobs in the same city, somewhere, and start our lives together right after our honeymoon.

I think we both *wanted* our relationship to be a romantic, whirlwind affair, but in retrospect I can see it was mostly pretend. We liked each other, and we were comfortable with each other, but I was too reserved; and despite her organizational skills, she was in some ways a tad too scattered, especially when she got nervous socially. We were committed to each other, though, and we expected to see it through. I think we both took the prospect of our marriage vows seriously: "For richer, for poorer, in sickness and in health, forsaking all others, 'til death do us part…"

" 'Til death do us part!" Well… So much for that.

During the spring of our senior years, we began looking for jobs. I firmly believed that I would find a good job. I wasn't worried about finding one. I don't know why I thought that, but it just seemed obvious to me that I would end up with a good job.

My farming background with an agri-business degree meant I was able to land about ten job interviews with recruiters who came to campus. Susan did very well, too, with at least as many interviews. In less than two months, our strong degrees and good records from a reasonably good school in a specialized region made it possible, even inevitable, that both Susan and I would find decent entry-level jobs in the same city. They happened to be in Omaha, Nebraska. Susan was hired for a job combining her home-economics training and organizational talents working as an administrative assistant for a product manager at Arkero, a large meatpacking and food products firm. I was hired by the farm credit firm Klein-Staily in their farm mortgage assessment division.

About a month before the semester ended, Susan and I drove up to Omaha to spend a couple of days meeting with our future employers, filling out forms, and looking for a place to live. We found a very nice modern, scantily furnished, one-bedroom apartment about two blocks from Klein-Staily. From that place, Susan would have to drive to work, but she didn't seem to mind, and we had a reserved parking spot in the back of the building. We were set... well on our way to the Great Mid-American Dream.

We were married three weeks after graduation. It was a big church wedding with over two hundred people, cake, punch, tea and coffee, and not much else. That's the way we did weddings in western Kansas back then.

We honeymooned in Colorado Springs, along with what seemed like a thousand other young couples, and then we drove back to our respective parents' homes, picking up a rental trailer into which we threw a few discarded sticks of furniture and kitchen utensils from their homes, along with our clothes, a few personal possessions, and some of the more useful wedding presents.

When we reached Omaha, it took us only about an hour and a half to unload the trailer and return it to the local rental agent. Unpacking took maybe another hour. After that we went out walking to look for a local restaurant.

On the way back to the apartment, we stopped at a small grocery store to stock up on things we thought we might need for the next few days: milk, bread, peanut butter, Kool-Aid, coffee, sugar, juice, hot dogs and condiments. We laughed together as Susan said, "That should hold us."

We had a week before we started our jobs. We walked and explored. We quibbled about food preparation, and we did our best to indulge ourselves and each other while at the same time staking out emotional territories as we settled in. Overall, it was nice, pleasant, and unreal. I don't think either of us was honest with the other or even with ourselves. We had been raised to want the Great Mid-American Dream and we didn't really want to challenge it or each other's perception of it.

We drifted into a settled life style that seemed to suit us both.

- - -

Several years later, after we had both worked hard and saved all of Susan's income along with some of mine, we were ready for the next stage in the Great Mid-American Dream: buy a house, buy a second car, and start a family. We started with the house, a two-story four-bedroom two-and-a-half-bathroom two-car-garage suburban home. It was much more than we needed or wanted then, but we both agreed that we wanted to have two children and for them each to have their own room, plus we wanted a guest room for when our parents and others came to visit. We thought we were living in a palace and were more than contented.

Susan got pregnant about then and tested positive two months later. We were delighted. She gave notice at her work that she would be leaving five months later.

Meanwhile my career was progressing steadily at Klein-Staily. Early on, I was paired with Ben Gruvel, a no-nonsense farm appraiser. I thought I knew a lot about farms, but he taught me many more details to look for about each of the actual farms as we traveled together doing the appraisals: the age and condition of the equipment, the state of the fences, the health of the herds, the clay content of the soil, the family relationships, and on and on. Every appraisal took at least a full day of travel and research.

The farmers were almost uniformly kind and generous when we were there to do our appraisals. Ben would accept no gifts, making sure he avoided any appearance of a conflict of interest. His one exception was that we were always treated to a fabulous home-cooked meal at noon as well as coffee and refreshments during the day.

Ben's mentoring stuck with me in two ways. First, I would not accept gifts that even looked as if they might create a conflict of interest, and, second, I began to enjoy eating more food. I had been fit, trim, and strong until my mid-twenties, but the lack of physical work along with my enjoyment of food led to a bit of a weight and health problem. I dieted some and exercised some; and I played with the kids. So I wasn't in horrible shape, but my girth and flab continued to grow.

Susan and I had two children and a good life. The children, one of each – Timothy and Liz -- took swimming lessons, did well in school, played sports, learned a bit of Spanish, took music lessons, the whole suburban routine. Susan was a stay-at-home mom who looked after the house, the meals, the children, the pets, the household finances, and the chauffeuring. Her dedication to those tasks freed my mind so that I could work harder and more effectively.

We remained reasonably close. We talked with and about the children, and we discussed vacation plans as well as our financial situation openly, as a family. Slowly, though, I began to sense that our family life would be better if I were earning more money. I was doing well enough, but we frequently scrimped in little ways. We went to chain restaurants instead of fine dining places, we took our vacations on a tight budget, we bought lesser model cars with fewer options, we shopped at discount chains, and we donated less than we wanted to various charities.

When the opportunity arose for me to move into the mortgage bond business with Klein-Staily, I discussed the possibility with Susan. The diagonal promotion would require me to take some finance courses in night school, but the extra money would make things a lot nicer for the family. We were reluctant to have me gone two nights a week for classes and doing homework other nights, but we decided it would overall be a good move.

I thrived on the change. I loved the finance courses, and I loved trying to understand the mortgage and bond markets better. I also loved the break from family and work that the courses gave me.

***
**

Chapter 6 -- *Bonds*

Mortgage packaging had been going on for a long time. Farm credit firms would bundle up a group of mortgages, all with high credit scores, and sell bonds based on those mortgages. We did that at Klein-Staily, too. By packaging the mortgages that way, we were able to spread the risks, but we were also able to raise millions of dollars more from other investors, enabling us to grant even more mortgages.

Institutional investors loved our bonds because they were rated AAA and had a good yield. If one of the farm mortgages in the bundle went south, it was a small ripple compared with all the mortgages in the bundle, and so the AAA rating was clearly justified. The process didn't involve anything new, and it was no big deal by the time I got into the bond department and finally understood the process.

The problem with the bundling was that the mortgages that weren't scored so high still might be pretty good. Somehow it seemed to me there must be some way to cash in on the overall, average success of many of those mortgages.

One evening while the kids and I were sitting at the kitchen table, taking turns trying to float layers of cream on our mugs of hot chocolate, I figured out a better arrangement. Layers! We could package a bunch of mortgages into lower-rated bonds and then pool those bonds to create more AAA bonds.

I was so excited I could barely sleep that night. It took me a few days to work things out, but eventually I had it down pretty clearly, at least in my own mind. We had to be conservative and cautious in our layering and estimates to make the scheme work, but it was sound and solid.

I asked for a meeting with the bond group managers at Klein-Staily. I was so confident and so excited about the scheme I had worked out that I essentially insisted on the meeting. I spent hours developing computer pages and presentation slides for the meeting. I knew that what I was proposing was bizarre and unheard of back then, but I also knew it would work. We could make more money selling bonds to the institutions that were triple-A hungry, and they would be happy, too. We could even expand the operation by buying up and rebundling the cesspool of mortgages from other lenders. It was win-win-win.

I persuaded them all. Easily. They loved the scheme, and we worked with corporate lawyers to draw up the prospectus and offerings.

- - -

Klein-Staily made buckets of money from my idea over the next few years, and I earned enormous bonuses. Susan and the kids weren't all that happy with my being away so much, working on the mortgage bundles, but they loved the family room addition to the house, the fancier cars, and the nicer vacations (some of which I had to miss due to work). Overall, we were a happy, successful, upwardly mobile suburban family.

I had developed a passion for my work, and I loved the passion. Meanwhile, I began to feel an emptiness in my personal life, and it caught me off guard. We had money and things, but in my mind we were going through the motions. I wondered if I had been pretending about everything for my entire life. It was around then that I began dreaming about escaping from my life as Fred Young.

A couple of co-workers and I were at lunch one day when Steve wondered out loud if people ever escaped from a disaster, like a hurricane or an earthquake or an airplane running off the runway, but then they let everyone think they were dead as they started a new life. It was idle speculation, and I didn't let on that it intrigued me. I was pretty contented with my life, or so I thought. Yet as I thought about what Steve had said, I began to wonder about my own life and whether I really mattered to anyone. I loved my job, and I thought I probably loved my family, but it all felt as though I was going through empty, meaningless motions. I wondered if there was maybe a new or different life that I might enjoy more.

I kept these thoughts to myself, though. I didn't want to confront Susan or the kids with my sudden ennui or personal doubts, and to be honest I wasn't sure how real my sense of emptiness really was.

Maybe I was just going through part of what everyone referred to as "the mid-life crisis" or "male menopause". Apparently some men at that stage of life buy a motorcycle, and I toyed with that possibility. Others take up sports or have an extra-marital fling.

I didn't do any of those things. Instead, I started preparing for my escape. Inwardly I laughed at myself because I doubted whether, deep in my heart, I really wanted to escape; anyway I expected I would never have the guts to actually do it. I mainly hoped that making the preparations would help see me through the inner depression and listlessness that I felt.

The preparations helped some. I had a fantasy dream, and I enjoyed escaping to my fantasy world on rare occasions. I found a place that would sell me a fake birth certificate, and I had to decide who I would be. I chose the name Carl Benson Jacobs pretty much at random, piecing together bits from various friends and colleagues in my past. I made him about my age, and I was on my way.

Let me emphasize that all along as I was doing this, I fully expected it was pure fantasy, a means of emotional escape, and I believed that I would never actually do anything about escaping from being Fred Young. I never expected to be presented with the opportunity.

My next step was to get a social security number. I tried to apply for one online, but I needed an address, and so one day I stopped at a service that rented postal boxes. Using cash I paid for a post office box for a year in advance. I made sure the service used their street address and listed my postal box as a unit number so it looked from the address as if Carl Jacobs actually lived there. Still no problem. I had my fake birth certificate, and I got my social security number. I wrote my fake social security number on the fake birth certificate, shrunk and laminated it, and I carried it with me everywhere in a secret compartment in my wallet, just in case.... but mostly to remind myself of my fantasy.

48

The fantasy became more real for me when I received an unexpected $50,000 bonus check from work. I took the check to my bank and said I wanted to buy a $5,000 savings bond with it and deposit the rest into my checking account. For some inexplicable reason, that worked. The deposit to my (actually *our*) checking account showed up as only $45K. Susan would never know.

I took the savings bond to a different bank where I cashed it in and opened a new account. It wasn't completely untraceable. I knew that, but it was the best I could think of then.

Carl Jacobs now had fake ID, a post office box and address, and $5,000 in a bank account.

It was stupid, I knew, and yet it helped me cope with my perplexed inner confusion. It helped me escape from an empty reality that I didn't understand. All I knew was that I had the feeling that my entire life up until then was just one big game of "Let's pretend" and I was uneasy with it.

I felt more than a twinge of guilt about wanting to escape. I had always believed that I loved my wife and children. I had a great job and a good life. People looking at my life from outside would have said there was no reason for me to want to escape. Not really. Carrying the false IDs and bankcard in the inside pocket of my wallet made no sense. But it helped me participate in the fantasy that I could leave whenever I wanted to. Whenever something seemed to stress me unduly, I let my mind retreat into the reassurance that I had an escape option. Sorta.

I probably would have drifted on like this for years and eventually let Carl Jacobs fade from existence, but for two things. The enabling thing, of course, was 9-11. If the planes hadn't crashed into the Twin Towers of the World Trade Center and if I hadn't missed my appointment with Cantor Fitzgerald because I forgot to reset my watch, I would never have been in a position to decide to escape into my new identity. Heck, I'd be dead if I hadn't missed that appointment.

The other thing that precipitated my move was a bit more complex.

About two years before the terrorist attacks, I came up with a better scheme for repackaging the questionable mortgages, creating even more AAA bonds on the basis that some of the truly junk bonds would actually pay off. We just had to make sure we were conservative in our repackaging of those pools of bonds into AAA bonds.

The institutional investors loved these extra AAA bonds, and by creating the bonds, we were able to make buckets more money. I was made a managing partner, got a corner office and a big raise, and took home a half-million dollar bonus.

I'm not sure how I would have coped with my own inner unhappiness if I hadn't had this challenge and success on the job. Devising the scheme and implementing it was fun, exciting, and rewarding. I looked forward to work everyday, and I kept thinking about new ways to redesign the mortgage pools to make more money with the bonds.

- - -

And then the farm crisis hit. Things began to unravel for the MBBs, as we had begun calling the mortgage-backed bonds. Crop yields per acre skyrocketed, increasing world production of nearly everything as the so-called green revolution took hold, and food prices plummeted. I guess that was good for the poor people of the world, but it was really tough for midwestern farmers. They had borrowed against expected grain revenues that didn't materialize, and they couldn't meet their mortgage payments. The appraisers had all assumed that grain prices, and hence farmland prices, would just continue their upward trajectory. Were they ever wrong.

I should have paid more attention to the mortgage appraisals. Back when I was doing appraisals, Ben and I always assumed that farm prices could fall by twenty percent in any given year, but it looked to me as if the bozos in the field recently had been using nothing but straight-line extrapolation based only on recent historical trends to predict commodity prices. They had seen farm prices rise in each of the past five years, and they assumed the prices would just keep rising. Bloomin' idiots! And I was an idiot for packaging (and repackaging) these mortgages into bundles without examining the underlying assumptions more carefully.

Farms were failing left, right, and center. As the farmers fell on hard times, many of them considered declaring bankruptcy. There were liquidation sales everywhere, but no one was willing to pay more than about sixty percent of the appraised value for these farms and their equipment. The appraisers were going crazy because they had no idea how to evaluate the farms for re-mortgage and new-purchase mortgage applications.

I got a perverse kind of pleasure from watching all the politicians, country singers, and general do-gooders holding fund-raisers for the poor farmers. Nearly all the money that was raised didn't do much for the farmers, other than help them make more payments on their outstanding debts. The ones who were helped the most from all these fund-raisers were the lenders …. like Klein-Staily.

The farmers who were in dire straits used the money from fund-raisers to make payments on their loans, and we got the money. If they hadn't made the payments, they'd have gone into receivership, and we'd have been lucky to get fifty cents on the dollar, and then only five or six years later … if we were lucky. We'd have been out of luck and down millions of dollars. Thank you, Willy Nelson!

The upshot was that a lot of those AAA bonds we put together and sold to institutions turned out to be anything but AAA. Sure, half of all the mortgages out there were still good, but the bonds based on pools of poorer quality mortgages were much riskier than we had expected. Slowly, farmers were defaulting on their mortgages or renegotiating them, and there were many more defaults and renegotiations than the appraisers had counted on. The expected flow of funds from mortgage repayments simply was not there to cover the interest and principal on the bonds, and the institutions that bought the lower tranches of our AAA-labeled bonds were extremely unhappy.

Our clients weren't the only ones who were unhappy; so were the financial insurers like AIG, who had essentially sold insurance covering all our AAA bonds. For all AIG knew, we were a nice conservative midwestern farm credit financial firm that could be trusted with the keys to Fort Knox. The bonds we had issued had always been even more reliable than AAA debt, but suddenly AIG was having to cover losses on some of our AAA bonds. They were extremely upset with us and let us know about it to the extent that we had considerable difficulties issuing new bonds and getting them insured, regardless of the underlying credit-worthiness of the mortgagees.

As a result of all these things, Klein-Staily was hemorrhaging money; worse, its reputation was suffering, which was affecting all levels and all areas of our business. There would be no bonuses this year, and some of the middle managers were seriously looking for alternative career opportunities, a euphemism for planning to jump ship.

And the blame fell on me.

My scheme was a good one, so long as the appraisals were good. I blamed the appraisers, but my partners continually hammered that I should have had mechanisms in place to evaluate and assess the mortgages we were bundling and how we were bundling them. I tried to explain that we had been buying mortgages from all the lenders, and some of the other firms' appraisers weren't as good or reliable as ours. It was clear that I was spitting into the wind, though.

In a way they were right. I could see my days as a partner with Klein-Staily were numbered. I could also see that I would have to break it to Susan and the kids that our family income was about to plummet. And I could see that I would have to do a great deal to try to overcome this debacle. If I could do something reasonably good, not even spectacular, for the firm, I might be allowed to resign and not be driven out. But even that was a small chance. My career was pretty much over in agricultural mortgage bonds. I could probably go back to appraising, and my doing that would support the family, but certainly not in the manner to which we had become accustomed.

To try to improve my reputation a bit, I put together a package of bonds that others in the marketplace were overlooking but that seemed undervalued. For sure, no one in the market would trust a bond offering from Omaha's Klein-Staily, especially if I was involved. That was when I got in touch with Cantor Fitzgerald to work out financing for a joint offering.

***

**

Chapter 7 – *On the Bus*

When they announced the bus in Newark, there was a bit of a rush to queue up to get aboard. With the planes and trains cancelled, growing numbers of people were hoping to take the bus out of town. Greyhound did what they could, and put on extra buses, but more than just a few passengers were concerned that maybe the seats had been oversold.

I admit I was nervous. I wanted to get out of town, but at the same time I didn't want to stand out in the crowd by being too pushy or too obnoxious, especially since it looked like there were some hit-and-miss security checks being done by the police. I counted all the people at the gate whom I thought might be passengers headed to Philadelphia, and there were easily enough to fill three or maybe even four buses. There was only one bus in a bay, though, and that added to the general atmosphere of nervousness. I could see I was about 45th or more in line, and I doubted I would be able to get on the bus.

I began contemplating alternatives… maybe I could offer to share a rental car, if there were any left in the city, but not with my I.D., just me paying a share. I was about to suggest this option to a few people behind me when the second bus pulled in. You could sense the lightening of the tension in the queue. And then a third bus and a fourth bus pulled in.

I found a seat somewhere near the middle of the third bus and put my new backpack on the overhead rack. I was determined to keep it close to me because I didn't want my laptop stolen or even looked at by anyone.

You know what? This is weird, but I have absolutely no recollection of the person who sat next to me on that bus. Sex? Size? Hair color? Carry-on bag? Nothing. I think we may have nodded to each other and then settled into our respective anonymities. When I think back about this, I realize that even though I thought I was being careful, I wasn't. I must have been extremely tense, worried, nervous, even frightened about the future. I wonder if my seat partner noticed anything. Probably not. After the day's attacks, it made sense to be "extremely tense, worried, nervous, even frightened about the future." Everyone was, given the day's events.

The ordinary driving time from Newark to Philadelphia is about an hour. The scheduled travel time for the bus was three hours to allow for a number of stops along the way, but this trip took nearly four hours. The traffic had become horrendous as people began scurrying from place to place, even late in the evening. It seemed that everyone wanted to be with their friends and families.

I was in no rush. I was on the bus and on my way, and I knew that my continuation ticket to Washington, DC, was for a bus that wasn't leaving Philadelphia until 6:30 Wednesday morning. I had plenty of time.

I slumped in my seat and closed my eyes.

I hoped that I wasn't embarking on this escape just to avoid the sense of emptiness that I had been fighting in Omaha. If so, it was a big mistake, and I knew it. I would soon make a new life, and then the ennui would swamp my emotions again. I had that figured out back in Omaha, which is why I had thought of the escape more as a fantasy than anything with real possibilities.

What tipped the scales for me, what pushed me the rest of the way across the Rubicon, was the collapse of my schemes for mortgage-backed bonds. I had a good chance of losing my job, and somewhat dramatically at that. We would survive financially, but there would be glances and whispers everywhere. The church denizens would certainly have a heyday, as would the people in my wife's charities. Country club membership? Gone. Comfortable home? Gone. Luxury car? Gone. Vacation in Europe? Gone.

Deep in my heart, I knew I should suck it up and adjust to the losses, both financial and social. Even deeper in my heart I knew it would have been a good learning experience in responsibility and planning for our children if we all had to adjust. But I just couldn't bear the thought of the trauma and angst they would face if I (and we) were publicly ostracized.

The alternative seemed pretty good… to me, at least. In their minds, I would have died a hero. The firm would go all out to help the family, and my life insurance and pension savings would see the children through university and provide a comfortable living for Susan.

I expected Susan to have a nice nest egg of about eight million dollars, just based on our savings and the life insurance contracts we held privately and with Klein-Staily. Various so-called financial advisors would be falling all over themselves to offer to manage her portfolio. I was pretty confident that I had emphasized strongly enough the importance of having passive management and index funds. I hoped I was right. If I wasn't right, I hoped my former co-worker and mentor, Ben Gruvel, would provide the fatherly advice I would have wanted for her.

I had provided well for the family, and I had saved the family from loss of dignity, loss of face, and loss of material comfort. Little did I know that the life insurance policy with Klein-Staily would double the insurance payout because I had been in NYC on business, and little did I know that the various levels of government would kick in millions as well.

I expected that having me "die" in the terrorist attack on the Twin Towers would cause a sense of loss and perhaps even some grief for Susan and the children. At the same time, I also expected that in many ways they would have been worse off if I hadn't "died" in that attack. Still, it surprised me that I felt so comfortable with my decision.

After we pulled away from Trenton midway to Philadelphia I began to drift off, but the stops along the rest of the way kept waking me up. I turned my thoughts to my new life as Carl Jacobs. What would I do for money? Where would I live? What would I do in my spare time? What if I couldn't pull this off?

I would have to find a room in a rooming house, if possible. I didn't want a roommate who might be nosier than I could tolerate about my past. And I couldn't find a job involving agricultural business or bonds, especially since I would have no credentials, at least none that I could use; I would have to find some sort of minimum-wage job and begin slowly building credentials for some new career. I had no idea what new career I wanted to pursue or how to go about looking for one. That would have to come later.

We pulled into the Philadelphia bus station a little after 3am. I pulled my backpack down from the overhead rack, and followed the other passengers into the bus station. I was hungry again, and I hoped there was a diner open in the station or nearby.

Hungry again?? My eating patterns – actually, my over-eating patterns -- would have to change. Working with Ben, I had gotten used to eating a lot and eating frequently, a habit I carried with me when I moved to the bond department at Klein-Staily; and I was actually squeezing to get myself into my 38" pants. At 5'10", 210lbs, I was overweight and out of shape, and I knew it. I also knew that I would have to cut down… drastically. I wanted to change my appearance, and so I wanted to lose weight fast and keep it off. Also I would have to make my savings last. That was another reason I would have to watch my food binges and splurges.

Over the years on the farm with some cattle and then again around the office, I had learned about calories: if you eat more calories than you burn, you gain weight. I was living proof. Susan had done ok with dieting. We had both put on pounds and inches, but she gained much less weight than I did and had a pleasant too-young-to-be-matronly look about her now, more than twenty years after we were married.

I wanted to focus on nutritious food that was cheap and had very few empty carbohydrates or calories. That is next to impossible in a diner. About a block away from the bus station, I found an "All-Nite Eatery" that made the difficulty clear to me. The menu was loaded with starchy foods, and I inwardly drooled over the pictures of stacks of pancakes with gallons of syrup on them.

Instead, I decided on scrambled eggs and bacon with coffee, no toast, and no potatoes. I would have to get used to not having pancakes and syrup. Or potatoes. Or white toast with jam. It would have to be a permanent lifestyle change.

What on earth was I going to eat from now on? I loved pizza, pancakes, beer, ice cream, candy bars, and on and on. I would have to get used to carrots, celery, eggplant, zucchini, broccoli, and maybe a bit of rice or something.

There was a television going, rehashing the day's events: four planes, not just two. A third one was crashed into The Pentagon, and a fourth was apparently taken down by the passengers on it to keep it from flying into The Capitol building or The White House. I sobbed a little. Well, not really sobbed, but it moved me, and apparently that impact on me was noticeable.

"Yeah, honey, it's pretty horrible isn't it," said the waitress.

"Bastards!" I said. I almost went on to tell her I had seen it, but stopped myself in the nick of time.

"Never, never offer *any* information!!" I cautioned myself. "Never!"

By then, the area of The World Trade Center had been cordoned off, and crews were beginning the slow process of carefully sifting through the rubble, searching for possible survivors and looking for traces of the victims.

I thought, "I should have singed my hair clippings myself and not counted on the hot rubble to do that for me." I hoped that whatever happened to the north tower, the neatly cut ends of my hair clippings wouldn't give me away. Knowing the thoroughness of some insurance companies, I was pretty sure the recovered evidence and remains would be gone over pretty carefully.

The bacon and eggs arrived.

The waitress looked at me, a bit puzzled.

"Where you headed?" she asked, nodding at my backpack. I knew she wasn't flirting. Maybe she was angling for an extra tip, but she couldn't have been flirting. I was a bald overweight guy, and while I intended to stay bald forever, I didn't intend to stay overweight. I figured she was probably just bored and looking for some conversation.

"Atlanta," I replied. Again, offer nothing more. Keep your eyes and head down. Don't encourage or invite conversation or questions. I reached down the counter and picked up the early edition of The Philadelphia Inquirer. She got the message and moved back to her stool where she sat, watching the news on the television.

I read through much of the paper, but the reports there simply could not do justice to the horror I had seen and experienced. Nor could they do justice to the enthusiastic kindness and assistance by the legions of people like the yachter, Barry, or the Episco-lady, Maddy, or the clerk at the yacht club, or any of the others who must have helped so many of us evacuees and everyone else affected by the attacks.

I learned that nearly three thousand of the possible twenty thousand or more people in the Twin Towers had been killed and that many of those killed were policemen and firemen who were trying to rescue as many people as they could. I also read that apparently no one on the Cantor Fitzgerald floors survived the direct hit on their offices.

I dropped my head slightly as I read that. It made me sad, nervous, guilty, excited, relieved, and more. What a mess of emotions, but I controlled them.

"May I have some more coffee?" I asked to hide the sense of being overwhelmed.

"Sure, hon. Second cup is free." The waitress gestured vaguely in the direction of one of about twenty different signs on the wall.

"Thanks."

And I buried my nose in the newspaper again. I wondered how long Susan and Klein-Staily would have to wait before having me declared dead officially. Once my belongings were found under the rubble, they should have little difficulty. That is, they probably would not have to wait long IF anything much survived from the pile of rubble. I hoped the heat would melt things a bit but still leave them partially identifiable. The wedding ring would be the clincher if the rescuers found it. I really hoped that no one would steal the ring during the recovery efforts.

When I had sat at the counter as long as I thought reasonable, I took out my new wallet. The waitress came right over.

"That'll be three-ten, honey," she said.

I reacted with a hint of surprise. I had seen the prices on the menu, but they hadn't sunk in. It had been a **long** time since I had eaten a diner breakfast. All my breakfasts recently had been to entertain clients, and I don't think I ever paid less than fifteen dollars per person for those breakfasts. I had a lot of readjusting to do.

I dug three ones and three quarters from my pocket and handed them to her. She pushed one of the quarters back to me.

"That's nice, honey, but you're over-tipping a bit."

"That's okay. Keep it," and I scurried out of the diner.

It was 4:00am when I got back to the bus station, and my bus to DC wasn't due to leave until 6:30. I was tired. I knew I would fall asleep on the bench, and I knew I wouldn't be able to stop myself. I toyed with asking a security officer to wake me at 6, but I really didn't want to draw any attention to myself.

I looked at my watch. "Well, I'll be." I mumbled. The watch I had bought back in Newark was a dual alarm watch. Woo hoo! I played with the watch for about five minutes to figure out what each of the buttons did and then set an alarm for 4:06 to test it. It worked! So then I set one alarm for 6:05 and another for 6:07. I have no idea why I chose those times, but I wanted to be alert when it came time to queue up to board the bus.

I put my backpack on the bench next to me with the flap opening next to my body and I put one arm through the strap, wrapping the strap around my arm. I didn't want anyone to take what few possessions I had.

One of the alarms woke me in what felt like two minutes. I was lost at first. I had no idea where I was or why or what that constant beeping was. Finally I remembered my new watch and turned off the alarm. I had been asleep for almost two hours! Several people were sitting near me by then, also waiting for the bus, and a couple of them were shaking their heads and smiling. I guess the alarm had been going for more than just a few seconds.

I carefully turned off the second alarm and checked the big clock in the station to make sure I hadn't missed my bus. Whew again.

***

**

Chapter 8 – *On to DC*

I hate, absolutely **hate** using restrooms on buses because they always smell like outhouses. Besides, it is really hard to aim while the bus is moving, which I guess helps explain why they smell so bad. It was 6:07, and the bus wasn't due to leave Philadelphia for Washington, D.C., until 6:30. I went to use the men's room in the bus station.

I did a double take when I saw my reflection in the mirror. It would be awhile before I could get used to my new look. I relieved myself and checked my watch. 6:10. I still had at least 15 minutes, and it had been nearly twenty-one hours since I had shaved. I hated shaving, and now I had to keep both my beard and my head shaved. I dug out one of the disposable razors, and I looked around to make sure they had paper towels there so I could clean up my face and head after the shave. Using one of those hot-air blow dryers wouldn't be very convenient.

Liquid soap foam from public restroom dispensers makes a decent shaving cream. I used some sparingly on my head and face, shaved carefully, and then washed up using paper towels. It felt good. Clean. I hoped I would like this feeling for a long time and that I could get used to my new look.

When I went to drop the paper towels in the garbage, I saw an empty plastic Coke bottle there and thought, "Hey! Why not?"

I took the bottle back to the sink, rinsed it with really hot water for about fifteen seconds, and then filled it with cold tap water. I knew I would get thirsty now and then, and I really didn't want to drop a dollar or two on bottled water or pop several times a day. I now had a free sixteen-ounce water bottle.

The early morning shuttle from Philadelphia to D.C. is a popular run. It leaves at 6:30am and arrives at 10am with quick stops in Wilmington, Delaware, and in Baltimore, making it convenient for people going to Washington for the day. It was especially popular that morning because the trains were barely running and planes were still on the ground. As before, though, Greyhound contracted with other bus lines to put extra buses on the route, and there was no problem with seating. Those of us going directly to the nation's capital were put on separate express buses, and we went straight through with no stops.

I would have liked to sleep some more on the bus, but the two-hour nap in the Philadelphia bus station seemed to recharge me. I used the three-hour bus trip to take stock of where I was, where I was going, and what I needed to do.

I had pretty much settled on going to Jacksonville, Florida, but I would be open to reconsidering other options along the way or once I got there. I put the exact destination out of my mind for now, and turned my thoughts to other issues.

I had three things I still had to get rid of: my watch, my cell phone, and my shoulder bag with the laptop. I figured I could use that multi-tool thing I bought when I was in the bargain store in Newark to pry the inscribed back off my watch and dispose of the back and watch parts separately. But doing that would have to wait.

I also wanted to go through the shoulder bag carefully. Why hadn't I done this earlier? Geez, I felt stupid. Well, I couldn't do it now on the bus. I would have to wait until I had some time to consider everything in the bag. I could keep some of the unidentifiable pens and supplies, but everything else, including my keys, the laptop, and maybe even the bag itself would have to go.

I wanted to wipe the hard drive on the laptop, but I had no idea how to do that thoroughly. I decided that when I had a chance I would delete all the files and programs on the hard drive and then reformat it. I might also go so far as to take the hard drive out of the laptop and destroy it before getting rid of the laptop and hard drive separately. And for sure I needed to try to obliterate any serial numbers I could find.

These things could be done later, though.

I had seen enough dumpster divers in my day that I knew I couldn't just throw these things into the first trashcan or even dumpster that I came to. The odds were high that someone would find them and try to sell them, and eventually the items would be traced back to me. I had to dispose of them in a way that would destroy them or at least make them untraceable.

It occurred to me that I had never seen anyone dive into construction dumpsters. I could hang onto things, keeping them at the bottom of my backpack, until I saw a dumpster outside a renovation or construction site and then I could throw everything into that dumpster. It was an option worth considering.

How do you throw things into a dumpster without being seen? Maybe I could scout a dumpster site and then walk past it at three in the morning? That seemed like a good plan, for now at least, and I tried to just put those things out of my mind until I had more time to work on the details. I wanted to be prepared though.

I wondered what was happening with my family. Susan, along with my former colleague Ben Gruvel, would have been on the phone everywhere. They likely would have learned nothing yet. I pictured the uncertainty and the agony Susan and the kids must be going through, and I quivered a bit, feeling both guilt and sadness. I was convinced that in the long run they would be better off, but then again maybe I was just fooling myself, lying to myself, trying to justify running away from my problems instead of facing them.

I had to stop thinking about them. I had crossed the Rubicon and I was climbing up the opposite bank. I put my right hand on my right thigh and tapped my knee with my index finger, the way I had back in Newark in Maddy's Lexus.

Another "Oops". Tapping my knee like that was an attempt at thought-blocking I had developed when I was a teenager. I used it whenever I wanted to stop dwelling on something I didn't like. Susan had spotted it while we were still dating and laughed about it with me. The kids knew about it; Ben had noticed it, too. Actually, I was quite pleased about it, not only because it worked by helping me temporarily block out unpleasant thoughts, but also because it signaled people who knew about it when something was bothering me, giving them a silent message.

I needed to stop doing that. Poker players say it is hard to discover and then get rid of your "tell" or whatever you do when you are nervous or stressed. I expect it's the same with other habits. I reached up and lightly rubbed my neck behind my left ear, hoping that gesture would become my new thought-blocking trigger. I had my work cut out for me.

My thoughts turned to the more immediate issues: getting to Florida and conserving my nest egg. Taking the train the rest of the way would have had some advantages: comfort, convenience, nearly non-stop, the ability to get up and stretch on board, and food availability on board. At the same time, it would be more expensive than the bus, the food would be expensive, and it would limit my flexibility, compared with the bus, from which I could change my mind and go a different direction if I decided to. Besides, on the bus there would be stops at various places, where I could keep updated on the news and get less expensive food.

I guessed, correctly as it turned out, that Amtrak to Florida would be completely sold out for the next two days. At least that's what the news reports were saying as we arrived at the bus station on Massachusetts Avenue in Washington, D.C. The train was not even a possibility until after the weekend. I didn't want to wait that long unless there was no way to take the bus any sooner, and I didn't look forward to having to find a place to stay in Washington for several nights.

The bus had arrived in D.C. by 9 AM, about an hour early since we didn't have to make any of the intermediate stops along the way down from Philadelphia. I thought of immediately joining the queue at the ticket windows, but I had to pee after drinking so much water while I was on the bus. So instead I used the restroom again and refilled my Coke bottle with tap water. Then I joined the queue to buy my ticket onward.

It looked as if every ticket window was open, each with only a short queue. Again, people and businesses were responding quickly to everyone's needs. After only about a ten-minute wait, I was called up to the ticket window.

"Yes sir. How may I help you?" the attendant asked. That threw me off. I had expected something a bit more terse. I smiled and wondered if the terrorist attacks had temporarily pulled many of us together in a sense of closeness like what I had read occurred during the world wars.

I had to decide where I was going.

"I'd like a ticket to Jacksonville, Florida."

A smile back. "Sure." Clickety click on the terminal.

"I can't get you on the 1:30 bus, but there's room on the 4:30 express," he said with a bit of a question mark in his tone of voice, as if he was asking if that would be ok.

"That sounds fine. When does it get in?

"8:30 tomorrow morning. You'll have to change buses in Richmond, and there are stops along the way for meal and restroom breaks and to change drivers in Fayetteville, but it's pretty quick and pretty direct."

"Wow!" I thought to myself. "I can sleep on the bus and then have a full day to try to get somewhat sorted out and settled in Jacksonville."

"Perfect," I said. "How much?"

"We have a special today. Same as every other day," he chuckled. "$69."

I smiled and half chuckled, not knowing for sure why he chuckled, and pulled out my new wallet. I remembered again: right front pocket. And for good measure I touched my neck behind my left ear. I gave him $80 and took the change.

"They'll start boarding at about 4:15," he said. "You'll have a bit of a wait."

"That's fine," I replied somewhat deliberately. I was trying to avoid saying, "No problem" or "No prob Bob." I wanted to change that little personal thing, too.

"Thanks for your help!" I half-waved as I walked away from the ticket window.

I found a news depot in the bus station and bought the morning edition of The Washington Post. It was only 9:30, and I had nearly seven hours to catch up on the news.

* * *
**

Chapter 9 – *Washington, D.C.*

I looked for a comfortable place in the waiting area of the bus station to sit, relax, and read the paper. There weren't any. Not really. People were milling about, still talking almost exclusively about the terrorist attacks and how to get where they wanted to go. Here in DC, the talk was more about the plane that crashed into the Pentagon, and there was also considerable speculation about whether the plane that the passengers took down over Pennsylvania was headed for the White House or the Capitol building.

I put my backpack on the floor at my feet and put one foot through the backpack strap, forcing me to sit up straight but freeing both hands so I could read the paper. The awkwardness, the wariness I felt, plus the noise and the fact that I kept being jostled, all made it difficult to focus on the newspaper.

Security officers were out in full force, everywhere, randomly stopping people, asking them questions. I didn't see any officers ask to look inside anyone's bags, but it could happen. That only increased my anxiety. I decided to leave the bus station, but I didn't want to be obvious about it.

After about fifteen minutes, I stood up, slung my backpack over one shoulder, picked up the newspaper, and headed outside. It was a beautiful day, just like 9-11. The sun beat down, and I felt warm. I touched my head and remembered I could get sunburned pretty quickly if I wasn't careful. I dug out my bucket hat and put it on. I made a mental note to myself: buy sunscreen first chance you get.

I knew nothing about the layout of Washington, D.C. I had been there as a youngster on a class trip, but I didn't remember much about what was where, and I had no idea where to go to find a quiet, comfortable place to sit, rest, and read.

It didn't take me long to decide. As I exited the bus station I could see some office buildings ahead on my left, the Capitol building a few blocks straight in front of me, and maybe even a bit of the National

Mall in front of it. And there was parkland everywhere with walkways and benches.

I ended up in one of the parks, sitting on a bench under a tree. There was noise here, too, but it was just traffic noise, not people chattering and jabbering loudly in the bus station. No people jostling and bumping into me, and no cops stopping people and asking questions.

Again, I put my backpack down and put a foot through the backpack loop. I leaned back and began reading the paper.

I think the entire paper was about the attacks. The first section had a pretty full summary of what had happened, but with emphasis on the Pentagon, of course. I had to scour the middle pages to learn more about the attacks on The World Trade Center's Twin Towers. It looked as if they had lowered the estimate of the number of fatalities; maybe about 2800 people had been killed there. There were gripping stories of people helping others escape from the towers, of last minute phone calls from some of the victims, and of people who had stayed home sick yesterday and the guilt they felt.

But there was no mention of specific victims. I was frustrated not to see a victim list, but then I realized there was a lot of rubble to sift through to find body parts and personal belongings of the victims; besides, they had to wait for the rubble to cool off. The reports did confirm that the first plane had pretty much sliced into and through the Cantor Fitzgerald offices, though, and I felt a sense relief. I hadn't screwed that up.

And then, of course, I felt sadness and guilt. By all reckoning, I should have been killed by that plane, and yet here I was beginning a new and different life.

Suddenly the immense loneliness of my life hit me. I had no family, no friends, and no history. Nothing. I would be starting from scratch. It was an exhilaratingly lonely sensation. I was looking forward to being able to make new choices, but I hadn't banked on this loneliness. I should have, but I hadn't. I was determined to make haste slowly, though, in my new life. Very, very slowly. I didn't want to make choices that would set me back on the path to re-becoming the person I was trying to escape from having been.

I had a strong urge to find a way to go online to try to find Omaha news to see what, if anything, had been said by and about Susan, my kids, and my co-workers at Klein-Staily. What did they know? What had they done? How long would it take before I was officially declared dead?

I wondered about finding a public library to use one of their computers, but it seemed to me this area of Washington D.C. was all museums and government office buildings. I had no idea where to look for a public computer.

By the time I finished reading about how the terrorist attacks had affected baseball games and baseball players, football games and football players, the opera, schools, workplaces, and every other walk of life covered by The Washington Post, it was nearly noon. The enticing aromas from food trucks were beckoning me, and so I started back toward the bus station, stopping along the way for a Polish sausage in a bun with plenty of fried onions. It was **good!** But I would have to learn how to cut back if I was going to change my size and shape.

I really wanted to get rid of my watch, cellphone, shoulder bag, and laptop. I knew I was in little danger of being discovered while they were with me at the bottom of my backpack, but they were, to adapt a phrase my mother always used, "burning a hole in my backpack."

There were plenty of garbage receptacles around the bus station, and I probably could have put the items in one of those receptacles and been fine. I just didn't know, though, and so I held onto them for the time being.

I had over four hours to wait before my bus south was going to leave. I was tired and wanted to stretch out on one of the park lawns. Others were sitting around in small groups at various places, eating their lunches, and I might have fit right in. Instead I forced myself to do some walking. I thought, "No better time than right now to start trying to get into better shape."

I went back toward the National Mall in front of the Capitol building and walked all the way along the north side of the mall up to the Washington Monument. It was an inspiring location. Tourists weren't allowed to go up the elevator because of safety and security concerns about possible further terrorist attacks, and we weren't even allowed to go inside on the ground floor. I slowly walked around the monument, looking back east at the Capitol building, looking north to the White House, grateful those buildings had been spared, and looking west toward the reflecting pools and the Lincoln memorial.

"I cannot tell a lie," George Washington supposedly said to his father after cutting down the cherry tree. Hmmmph. I snorted out loud. I was going to be telling lots of lies the rest of my life. I felt squeamish at the thought. I hoped it was the right thing for Susan and the kids, and I hoped it would work out for me.

I tapped my neck behind my left ear. "Go on, Fred." I said to myself.

Nope. Groan.

"Go on *Carl*," I corrected, and tapped myself behind my ear again. "Walk to the Lincoln memorial. Just put one foot in front of the other. It's probably no more than a three-mile walk in total from here to the memorial and back to the bus station. You have plenty of time. Do it!"

So I started off, walking along the north side of the reflecting pools. I made a detour and walked along the Vietnam memorial, which saddened me. So many lives lost for what seemed like no good reason. Much like yesterday.

When I reached the Lincoln memorial, it was eerily empty. Schools were closed for the day because of worries about possible further terrorist attacks. Kids who had been in DC on class trips were taken home early; other class trips were cancelled. In general, tourists were few and far between. I climbed the steps and stood in the shadow of the great statue of Lincoln, set my backpack down, took out the Coke bottle, and finished the water. I should have done that earlier and refilled it. I reminded myself that I would have to be more careful to stay hydrated.

I thought about taking Constitution Avenue back toward the Capitol building, but I opted for a route on the south side of the reflecting pools and Mall, going near and through the trees to protect myself a bit from the sun. I needed to start exercising more, but I didn't need to be a total idiot about doing it.

I was used to walking fast. Well, fast for Omaha, slow for New York City. But I had to force myself to slow down and amble along the sidewalks. It was cool and pleasant in the intermittent shade. I began to relax a bit, mentally and emotionally, and I sighed a heavy sigh when I realized I was relaxing. It felt good.

In addition to the trees, the south side of the National Mall is lined with museums. Some were closed because of the fear of additional terror attacks, but I found one where I could use the public restroom without paying to get in, and I refilled my Coke bottle from the chilled drinking fountain after gulping some water directly. I sat on the steps, rested for a few minutes, and sipped some more water. When I was ready to move on, I struggled to resist the food vendors, but I made it. So far, so good.

It was after 2:30 by the time I arrived back at the bus station. I had walked more in the past few hours than I had in the previous few months. I was a bit hot and sweaty, and I wanted a shower. I wondered when I would be able to shower again. I was trying to avoid having to pay for hotels and I had no idea how else to get a shower. I would probably just wait until I got to Florida.

I was tired from my walk. Fortunately the station was clearing a bit, and I found a comfortable place to sit. Again I felt drowsy and started to drift off. I don't know why, and maybe it was because someone sat down next to me just as I was falling asleep, but I awoke in a panic. I didn't want to miss my bus. I looked at my watch: 2:45pm. I set one

72

alarm for 4pm and the other alarm for 4:05, and settled back to try to rest and maybe sleep.

I couldn't sleep, though. I think my body was jarred and my nerves were jangled by my panic from having started to fall asleep. I just sat there with my eyes closed and thought some more.

Who did I want to become? Why was I doing this? I didn't want to be famous or popular, but I wanted a good, fun, exciting life. I also wanted a quiet, calm, comfortable, serene life. I knew these were conflicting goals. In the past, it seemed I had a mostly comfortable life at home and had the fun and excitement on the job, especially once I developed the mortgage-backed bond schemes. I wondered whether that separation had led to my overall sense of ... what was it I had felt? Isolation? Not really. Ennui? Maybe. Depression? Why? I had no reason to feel depressed. A sense that something was missing from my life? What was missing? I really did not understand, but it had been a growing feeling for sure, and I hoped I could figure out how to lead a new life that would help me avoid those feelings.

Despite the intensity of my feelings and questions, I must have drifted off. The watch alarm woke me again. This time I heard it sooner than I had in Philadelphia and was able to turn it off quicker than I had there. I turned off the second alarm and slowly stretched and then got myself up slowly. ... Another trip to the men's room to relieve myself, wash up a bit, and refill the Coke bottle.

I hadn't queued up early for the bus to Richmond, Virginia, because after my experiences in Newark and Philadelphia, I was confident there would be plenty of room and enough buses for everyone. It turned out that Greyhound slightly miscalculated, and the extra buses I anticipated seeing didn't show up right away. I managed to get a seat on the second bus that was brought in. It left Washington, DC, only fifteen minutes after the first bus left.

* * *
**

Chapter 10 – *Richmond, Virginia and Onward*

The bus pulled into the station in Richmond only five minutes behind schedule. I had an hour before my connecting bus left at 8:15, and for that bus I wanted to be near the head of the queue to select a window seat a few rows from the front. I would be on that bus for the next 12 hours, the rest of the way to Jacksonville, and I wanted a good seat so I could sleep most of the way; at least I hoped to sleep as much as possible.

The Richmond bus station is in the heart of a light-industry and warehouse area, nowhere near any decent place for shopping or eating. There was a café of sorts in the station, and so I decided to check it out. Check it out? Nonsense! I was hungry, and I wanted something to eat. I hadn't eaten much in the past forty-eight hours, other than Maddy's sandwich, the bacon and eggs in Philadelphia, plus the sausage dog in DC. I went in and found a seat at the counter.

The menu was the standard bus station café 3Cs: carbs, calories, and coffee. Everything looked really tempting, but I lectured myself quite sternly and stayed away from those items. They had a julienne salad on the menu that had ham, chicken, cheese, tomatoes, and a hard-boiled egg in it. I hated hard-boiled eggs, but I knew deep in my heart that they don't kill you if you eat them. I ordered that salad along with just tap water to drink. I didn't want to pay for the coffee, and I didn't want the caffeine to keep me awake on the bus.

The salad was perfect. It had loads of lettuce, cheese, and ham, along with a bit of chicken and two halves of a hard-boiled egg that had undoubtedly been boiled more than twenty-four hours earlier. In fact, the entire salad had probably been prepared long ago and stored in some cooler, which explained why it was brought to me so quickly after I ordered it. But it was exactly the right thing for me, with lots of decent healthy food and not too many calories.

I ate the egg first. I knew it would seem more palatable when I was hungry. I had eaten a hard-boiled egg once before in my life, just a few years after we moved to Omaha. Susan and I were at some work-related party of hers, and the hostess forced a deviled egg on me in such a way I felt I couldn't just blurt out, "No, no! A thousand times, no! I hate those things." I ate the deviled egg and then washed it down with some wine. I felt as if I had somehow ruined the wine by using it that way. I also felt a sense of relief and accomplishment: I had eaten a deviled egg, and by some miracle I hadn't choked to death.

This time I bit into the egg and actually chewed it before swallowing it because I wanted to accustom myself to new flavors and new foods. I had decided to try to change my old patterns and tastes as much as I could, and changing my food tastes was another place to start making changes.

Hallelujah, I didn't die! I didn't much care for the egg, but I didn't die. I knew I could get used to it. I drank some water, ate some more egg, drank some more water, finished the egg, and then asked for more water. It would take some time, but I knew I could do it.

The rest of the salad was standard assembly-line food: strips of processed ham, cubes of processed chicken, factory-shredded cheddar cheese, and two wedges of an under-ripe tomato, all on a bowl of shredded lettuce. I dug in, and it hit the spot.

The salad came with a roll and butter. I really tried to resist them, but I couldn't. I would get there eventually and be able to refuse the cheap calories, but for now I was hungry and tired. I did, however, manage to avoid the candy bars at the cashier's counter as I paid for the salad.

It had been a good stop, and I still had twenty minutes before boarding would begin for the bus to Raleigh and points south. I used the restroom again and refilled my Coke bottle. When I returned to the station waiting room, I checked to find out which gate my continuing bus would leave from, and went there to join the queue. Boarding wouldn't begin for another fifteen minutes, but there were already about ten people ahead of me in the queue. That suited me. I wouldn't stand out, but I could still get a seat that would be okay for me.

The driver looked at my ticket and seemed only a little surprised that I was going so far but didn't have a suitcase of any kind. Apparently there were others who had turned to riding the bus when their flights were grounded, and some of those passengers had only a carry-on bag. I think I may have been one of only three or four going as far as Florida, though. And just in case there were any others who might be getting off in Jacksonville, I just kept my head down and looked nobody in the eye, trying to remain as incognito as possible.

I had plenty of choices for a seat. I took a window seat four rows back on the driver's side of the bus. That would be about as good a place to sleep as any other seat on the bus. But I wasn't sure about what to do with my backpack. I could maybe fit it under the seat in front of me, but then I wouldn't have much room for my feet and legs. I could hold it on my lap, which would be safer for sure, but doing so would be uncomfortable and might look suspicious. Or I could put it in the overhead rack, which would mean I could sleep more comfortably but it could possibly be taken from there by someone else, either on purpose or by mistake.

Choices and risks and costs. I had studied these concepts in my finance courses, and I couldn't stop thinking that way. After about three seconds of contemplation while others were boarding and trying to get past me in the aisle, I opted for the rack and hefted my backpack up onto it, pushing it as far back away from the aisle as I could. I decided that having better rest when I disembarked in Jacksonville would be worth taking the possible miniscule increased risk of losing my backpack. It was the same type of risk assessment and decision I'd had to make on the previous buses all the way down from Newark.

The trip to Raleigh was uneventful. Quiet seatmate, quiet passengers, and a smooth ride.

It had been a day and a half since the terrorist attacks. By then my family and friends would have begun the process of accepting my death at Cantor-Fitzgerald. For my family, I was pretty sure it would be confusing and difficult. I expected they would want "closure", but for some reason I didn't think they would necessarily grieve very much.

I had a sneaking feeling that more than a few of the people at Klein-Staily were actually hoping I had died and that they could dump some of their own garbage on my reputation. Any bad decision one of them might have made? "Oh yeah, Fred did that." Or "Fred recommended that. We should have checked more carefully." Within the firm, for sure, I would be blamed for the mistakes many others had made.

I trusted and hoped, though, that the scapegoating would primarily be boardroom and water-cooler gossip. My former co-workers might leak a few hints about other things, trying to deflect the blame from themselves, but for the most part, they would stand united in their apparent sorrow at my death and would offer ongoing support for Susan and the kids.

At least that would be the public façade. I hoped they would be discreet in their scapegoating and let Susan and the children remember me in a good way, as the hard worker and good provider I had strived to be.

With those thoughts, I drifted off to sleep for the next two hours. We pulled into Raleigh a little after 11pm, and the driver announced that for those of us going on, there would be a 25-minute break. About half the bus emptied out here. It looked as if there was a regular, thriving business between Richmond and Raleigh, two state capital-tobacco-university towns.

The driver recommended for those of us going on that we leave something on the seat to claim it for re-boarding. I got my pack down, took out the jacket I had bought in Newark, and put it on the seat. I figured I might actually want the jacket at some point if things cooled off much more, and I probably should have had it out of the backpack before I boarded the bus in Richmond. I was about to put the backpack back up on the overhead rack, but then I realized I didn't really want to leave it on the bus while I was in the station. I slung it the over one shoulder and went into the station.

There was a snack bar there and a bevy of vending machines. The machines sold soft drinks, candy, chips, and other snack food. I walked past them, determined not to give in. The snack bar wasn't much better. It had coffee, cookies, and pre-made sandwiches on thick white bread with very little between the slices … none of which interested me. Then I saw little done-up plastic bags of cut-up celery and carrots. I bought three of them even though the carrots were looking a little old and the celery was a bit soft.

After a quick trip to the restroom where I relieved myself and refilled my Coke bottle, I re-boarded the bus, putting my backpack back up on the overhead rack and settling into my seat.

The woman who ended up sitting next to me for this leg of the trip was what we used to call a "Chatty-Kathy". She wanted to talk all about the terrorist attacks and tell me all she knew and thought she knew, including some wild conspiracy theories. At first I smiled politely and nodded or made other noises or gestures, as if I was dealing with a client and was trying to keep things rolling. But then I realized I didn't have to be like that. I didn't want to keep things rolling; I had really hoped to get some more sleep during the next one-hour leg of the trip, to Fayetteville. After about five minutes of her ramblings, I yawned a few times, closed my eyes, and leaned against the window. She got the message and stopped yakking.

A few years earlier, as one of our vacations, Susan and the kids and I took the train from Kansas City to Chicago. We had lovely seats facing each other across a table, where we ate the sandwiches we had brought with us, played games, and had a great time. It would have been even lovelier, but a person behind the children was on her cellphone, whining about her love life for what seemed like hours on end. I think her battery must have given out, thank goodness, because she stopped eventually.

I was reminded of that incident when Chatty Kathy started talking to me. I hoped she wasn't disturbing the others around us too much, and I was relieved when she quit talking. When I realized that I had actually encouraged her to keep talking, that confirmed for me that I had to rethink what I was doing as a person, who I was, and whether I wanted to keep doing that sort of thing in my next life.

I dozed lightly off and on for the rest of the trip.

They changed drivers in Fayetteville, where we had a nearly one-hour rest stop. Again, I left my jacket on my seat and took my backpack with me into the station, with a slight smile and nod to Chatty Kathy, who, it seemed, was being met by someone there. Whew. I hated social confrontations, and I had hoped I wouldn't have to ask her to stop talking. My yawning had worked at first, but I was relieved to see the end of her since I wasn't sure if I could get the tactics to work with her the rest of the trip.

The Fayetteville bus station is good-sized, but there wasn't much happening in it between midnight and 1am. The coffee shop was essentially closed, aside from selling day-old donuts and basic coffee. I found a discarded newspaper, took a seat, and started reading some more, nibbling on my carrots and celery sticks and drinking water from my Coke bottle as I read.

The rest of the world's leaders were aghast at what had happened, especially in New York City. And politicians were weighing in with how unacceptable this terrorist attack was, calling for "strong measures" whatever that meant. There was wild speculation, also, about how many had died in the attack, and whether it was appropriate to include among the dead the terrorists who had hijacked the planes and flown them into The World Trade Center and The Pentagon.

My own speculation about the number of deaths was way too high initially. I had guessed there were more than twenty thousand people in the two towers at the time of the attacks and that at most only fifteen thousand had been evacuated. Fortunately I was wrong. Some people on the higher floors of the North Tower had managed to escape down a stairwell before the Cantor-Fitzgerald floors were completely impassable. Also many people began evacuating the South Tower even before it was hit.

Judging from the reports, the stairwells of both buildings were jammed with evacuees going down and rescue people, later referred to as "first responders" going up. Wow! Imagine trying to climb a hundred floors in full rescue gear. Those poor guys. Doing their best to help others, hoofing it up the stairs as fast as they could, and then being crushed when the buildings collapsed. It didn't seem fair. I wept a bit for them, trying to hide my tears from others who might be looking at me.

After the South Tower collapsed, the first responders were pulled from the North Tower, to the extent possible. Apparently some made it, but many didn't, and those who did make it to safety felt both lucky and guilty. The total number dead was estimated to be somewhere between 2700 and 3200, but some of the higher estimates included deaths at The Pentagon and in Pennsylvania.

The new bus driver stepped inside the terminal and announced he was ready for us to board. I put down the paper, refilled my Coke bottle at the water cooler, and joined the lineup to get back on the bus. Next stop, Savannah, Georgia, in about four hours.

* * *

**

Chapter 11 – *On to Jacksonville*

I put my backpack back up on the luggage rack, picked up my jacket, and retook my seat. My seatmate for the next leg turned out to be a large man who wheezed as he walked down the aisle and plopped heavily into the aisle seat next to me. "Oh great," I thought. I was big and he was big. I was out of shape, but he was even more out of shape. I edged closer to the window, but there was no escaping the fact that our bodies would be in contact for the next four hours.

I pulled my right elbow back against the seatback, and he rested his left elbow on my forearm. There was nothing else to do, but I wished he had sat somewhere else, like next to a skinny person maybe.

His breathing was heavy and labored. I was a bit concerned, and started to look at him more carefully. Then I remembered: head down, no eye contact. For all I knew this guy could be an insurance investigator. At this point, I was probably just being overly cautious, but it could easily have turned into serious paranoia if I had let it.

Fortunately, his breathing cleared after just a few minutes.

It was as if I was in a cocoon, sitting there, pinned in by my seat partner. Slowly I leaned against the window, closed my eyes and drifted off.

The next thing I knew, the bus was slowing and pulling into the Savannah bus station. I checked my new digital watch. 6:45. We were a bit ahead of schedule.

It was another twenty-minute scheduled break, just long enough to call it a restroom break, a stretch break, or a cigarette break for the smokers. As before, I left my jacket on the seat and pulled my backpack down. I got off the bus, used the restroom, and topped up my Coke bottle with water from the drinking fountain.

I was becoming emotionally attached to that Coke bottle. I laughed at myself when I realized it. I determined at that moment to find a different bottle soon to use as my water bottle.

There was a small variety store across the street from the bus station, but it wasn't open yet. I had hoped to buy some more fruit and vegetables, but then I realized they would just add to the weight I was carrying around in my backpack and sighed. I was hungry, and I had no idea what I was doing ... not about anything. I knew I needed to lose weight and get in shape, but I also knew I wanted something to eat.

The bus station had vending machines. I bought a small bag of salted peanuts, hoping they were among the healthiest of the options available. I would have to think more carefully about what might be right for a diet for me, but that could wait a few days at least, until I was closer to being settled.

Settled. That word made me feel uneasy, not because I didn't want to be settled, but because I did, and I had no idea what I was going to be doing the rest of the day, much less the rest of my life. Thinking about being settled seemed more than a little premature.

Fortunately my former seatmate found a different seat for the short trip to Jacksonville. For the first time on the entire trip, I had two seats to myself. I stretched and sprawled and thought I might sleep some more, but I couldn't. My mind was racing, contemplating various plans and options, worrying about the future, trying to prepare myself mentally, trying to anticipate potential problems and how I might be able to cope with them, and trying desperately to keep myself open to various possibilities.

Where would I stay? I could burn through my nest egg pretty quickly if I stayed in a hotel. Ideally I wanted a small efficiency apartment with a private bathroom, a refrigerator, a bed, and maybe a microwave or hot plate. I certainly did not want a roommate or a shared apartment. A bed-sitting room might be ok, with the bathroom down the hall if it had even a bar fridge, sink, and microwave oven, but an efficiency apartment might be better.

When I got to Jacksonville, I would buy a newspaper and check out the classified ads for an apartment or room. With no references and no job, I might have to pay a couple of months rent upfront plus a security and damage deposit, and that would limit my options. I was confident that within a month or so I could find a semi-permanent job paying minimum wage, but with a job like that, I would not be able to afford much.

Nuts. I should have withdrawn more cash from an ATM. How could I put much money down on an apartment if I didn't have a checking account or credit card. Change in plans again: first stop in Jacksonville would be an ATM.....and maybe a bank soon after that to set up an account.

I couldn't do much more about finding a place to stay while I was on the bus. I was glad I would have the entire day when I arrived to try to get things set up. If nothing worked that day, I would find a cheap hotel room for a night or two.

I turned my thoughts to what type of job I might look for. With no references, no credentials, and no job history, I would be lucky to find anything. I might have to establish some history by taking temporary jobs through a temp agency, but I wasn't even sure they would find work for me, what with my having no background.

I had so much to learn so quickly. Housing, apartments, banking, jobs, bus routes, cooking, shopping, laundry, safe neighborhoods, the list was endless. Clearly I had relied on Susan much more than was apparent at the time, and I missed having her with me to discuss options. I hoped I wouldn't make too many mistakes on my own.

When the bus pulled in, I said a silent good-bye to my old seat. It had been my home for the past 12 hours, and I wrenched myself away from another emotional straw. Again I laughed at myself, even a bit out loud, this time. I was becoming morbid and stupid in my anxiety and loneliness. I touched my neck behind my left ear and reminded myself yet again of my new thought-stopping gesture.

My first stop wasn't an ATM after all. Instead I went to the men's room where I checked myself in the mirror and decided I needed another quick shave. I brushed my teeth and tried to wash up a bit, including my armpits. After that, I changed shirts, back to my "old" Lacoste yacht club shirt that Maddy had bought for me up in Newark. I wanted to look presentable when I went to a bank and went apartment shopping.

There was a bank right across the street from the bus station. I had only vaguely heard of Everbank, and maybe that was good. Maybe they hadn't bought any of the MBBs put together by the late Fred Young. They had a tall building downtown, and so I figured they should be fine for my limited banking needs.

My first plan had been to try to transfer the money from my secret account in Omaha to a new account. But I didn't really want to leave an explicit connection between me in Omaha, albeit as Carl Jacobs, and me in Jacksonville. Instead, I just went to the bank's ATM and withdrew the five hundred dollar daily maximum from my Omaha account. I put the currency in my wallet and thought about going for breakfast while I waited for the bank to open so I could see a teller to open an account.

Well I certainly wasn't planning as carefully as I wanted. I would need an address to open an account, and I would need an account to write checks for an apartment. I really needed to think more clearly.

I recovered in a few minutes. I went back to the bus station and asked the person at the information desk where I could rent a mailbox. She said there were several business service places, including Fed-Ex and UPS over on Hogan Street and gestured.

I looked puzzled.

"Hogan is two blocks that way," and she pointed straight out the bus station door.

"I think one of them has postal boxes for rent. Just go out those doors and over two blocks," she said as she gestured toward the revolving doors. "They're up a block or so from here," and she vaguely waved left to indicate I should go left when I got to Hogan Street.

Head down, eyes down, I mumbled "Thanks," and went in the direction she indicated.

I came to the Fed-Ex office first. "Do you have any postal boxes for rent?"

"Yes, we do ordinarily," replied the woman at the front counter, "but they're all rented out right now. I think some are going to expire this month though if you want to try again next month."

I looked at my watch. It was Thursday, September 13th, 2001.

I sucked in my breath, and hoped it wasn't too noticeable. I thought, "Forty-eight hours. So much has happened." However out loud I said, "That's more than two weeks from now. I would rather find something today, if possible."

She smiled. "Why don't you try the UPS Office across the street?"

"Okay," I mumbled, head down. "Thanks."

The UPS office was across the street and up a short block. The guy at the counter seemed a bit distracted. He looked up and half-suppressed a scowl, raising his eyebrows as if to ask "Yeah?" but he said nothing.

"Do you have any postal boxes for rent here?" I asked, somewhat timidly.

"Yeah. Hold on," and he finished writing something and then said, "What size?"

"The standard letter size will be fine," I replied.

He dug out a form and shoved it over the counter to me. "Twenty dollars a month tax included, three months in advance," he said. He was not a terribly communicative or friendly guy. "Fill out this form."

I had seen a similar form back in Omaha, and so I pretty much knew what to expect. I used my new name, Carl Jacobs, and wrote in a fake business address and a fake phone number. I assumed there was a Main Street and just wrote in some four-digit number for Main Street. For the phone number I looked at his number and saw 904-355-xxxx. I used those same first six digits and made up four new ones.

I took sixty dollars out of my wallet and handed the money to him along with the form. He looked at the form and then looked up at me. Undoubtedly he had had many people rent mailboxes who didn't want to reveal anything about themselves. This was nothing new for him.

He took the cash and put it in a drawer. Then he went to a locked cabinet and took out a key for me. "Box 744," he said as he handed me the key. "Make sure it works. We get rid of everything in the box if you're more than two weeks late."

"That'll be fine," instead of "No problem." I found the box. Bottom row, which meant I had to bend over a bit to open it and look into it. I opened the box easily. "What address do I give out?" I asked.

"Here." He handed me a card:

> 221 N Hogan St,
> Jacksonville, FL 32202
> Box _____

"We can print up cards for you in several designs, if you need some. We'll call it 'Suite 744' to make it sound better." That was the most he had said my entire visit.

"Sounds promising," I said. "I'll think about it. Do you have a price list?"

He handed me a list with some sample designs.

"Thanks," I said as I was leaving his storefront. "I'll take this along and consider it." I put the key in my front left pocket. I had to get used to the new system: keys on the left, wallet on the right.

I passed a couple of credit unions on the way back to Everbank. I had tried some credit unions in the past, and while they seemed concerned about customer service, they didn't have anything like the up-to-date internet banking options that I thought I might eventually want. These may have, but I decided not to take a chance.

I looked at my watch. 9:15am. I had accomplished a bit already and still had the day ahead of me.

I hoped Everbank had a branch somewhere near wherever I ended up living, but if they didn't, I would just open another account with a different bank. That might be a good idea anyway, just to lengthen the distance between Omaha and the new me. There was a coffee urn in the lobby of the bank. I hadn't had any coffee for several days, and I wanted some now to help me stay alert through the rest of the day. I also needed some food, but that could wait. I went to the urn and poured some coffee into a styrofoam cup. It smelled good, and it was hot. I sipped some of the coffee and imagined I was feeling a jolt already.

I joined the line to see a teller, but then I saw a sign that said "New Accounts" and went to that desk. A pleasant young man stood up and welcomed me.

"Good morning. I'm Ted Fry," and he put out his hand.

"Carl Jacobs." I shook his hand, but kept my head down just a bit. "I'd like to open a checking account."

He gestured for me to sit down. I put my backpack down beside me and took a seat.

"Do you have any other accounts here Mr. Jacobs?" Ted smiled a receptionist-type smile.

"No, I don't."

"Why are you opening the account, Mr. Jacobs?" Ted asked, still smiling, trying to make it look as if he was making small talk when really he was collecting information.

"I've just moved here. I hope to find a job and stay here."

He looked a tad skeptical.

"I see," he said. "How much do you want to put into the account to start?"

"I'll need to keep some cash for now," I replied, "But I can put $400 into the account to start and add more soon." That would leave me with only about $500 after the money I had spent getting down to Jacksonville. I could get another $500 tomorrow, but I wasn't sure $500 would be enough for today.

"Wait a minute." I added. "I'll probably need more cash to get around and maybe make a payment on a room. How would it be if I start the account with only $200?"

"Sure," Ted answered. He seemed eager to sign me up. I wished I had said only $100. "Do you have any other assets we should list, Carl?" I noted the subtle shift from 'Mr. Jacobs' to 'Carl'.

"I have some savings on deposit in another bank to tide me over. I'll transfer those funds slowly into this account." I was purposely vague.

I almost pulled out the receipt from my earlier withdrawal at their bank, showing I had nearly five thousand dollars on deposit in another bank. I knew that the receipt didn't show the original bank, but I also knew he could trace it if he wanted to. I would be taking a chance if I showed it to Ted. Fortunately he didn't ask about it.

"Excellent," said Ted, and he began to complete some forms on his computer.

"What's your full name, Carl?"

I pulled out my birth certificate and set it in front of him.

"Okay. Carl Benson Jacobs", he said as he typed my name.

"May 8th, 1958," he said, but he typed 1958-05-08.

I gave him my new address, and he didn't bat an eye. I told him I didn't have a local phone number but I would be getting one in the next few days.

He suggested I might also want to apply for a credit card, but I said I needed to get settled for a month or two, but then I almost surely would apply for one. I didn't tell him this, but I wanted to transfer more cash from my Omaha account slowly to this new checking account before I applied for a credit card.

When Ted asked about my employment, I reminded him, "I don't have a job right now, but I have a bit of a cushion to see me through while I search for something that I might like."

Ted tapped some more on the computer keyboard.

I took $200 from my wallet and handed it to him. I was about to flash the other money, to prove to him that I did, indeed, have plenty of other cash, but then I stopped. Don't give out any more information than is necessary. I reached up and touched my neck behind my left ear.

He counted the money and asked me to wait while he deposited it. That left me with about $700 for the day. I figured I should be okay with that.

He took about five minutes. I began to get a bit nervous, wondering what was taking so long. "Here we are," he said cheerfully. He handed me a receipt for the $200 and some blank checks for the account.

"Thanks for choosing Everbank, Carl. May I ask what you did before? Where you're from? How you ended up in Jacksonville?"

I had been dreading questions like these but I knew I would have to deal with them time and again. I needed a good response.

"Oh, I've done different things in different places." I added, "I chose Jacksonville because I wanted …." I hesitated. I almost said I wanted a warmer place to live, but it dawned on me that I'd be giving away that I had lived in a colder climate before. No reason to give away any more information than necessary, I reminded myself.

"… I wanted to live in a place that has a lot of growth potential, and I think Jacksonville has that."

Ted smiled. "It sure does! And as you get settled here in town, let us know if there are any other banking services we can provide for you."

"Sure thing, Ted," I smiled. "And thanks for your help." I stood up and we shook hands. I liked the idea of getting settled. I wasn't sure I would end up in Jacksonville, but it seemed like as good a place as any.

I put the blank checks into the little plastic check wallet the bank provided, and I put the check wallet into a pocket on my backpack.

I had a checking account and an address already, and it wasn't even 10 o'clock yet. Now I was ready to look for an apartment and a job.

***

**

Chapter 12 – *Apartment Search*

But first I really wanted something to eat. Yes, I knew I needed to drop about 60 pounds, and I wanted to do it fairly quickly, but I was hungry. I hadn't had much to eat since the terrorist attacks, and in the past 16 hours I had eaten only carrot and celery sticks. I cautioned myself to stay away from starch and empty calories, but I really wanted an Egg McMuffin …. or two or three.

I stopped myself. I would not have an Egg McMuffin until I had dropped a lot of weight.

I remembered having passed several restaurants when I was walking up to the UPS office and then back to the bank. I picked one of the restaurants, went in, and sat down. I found a discarded newspaper, called the ***Florida Times-Union***, to look through while I waited to order something.

"Hi," said the waitress as she handed me a menu. "Coffee?"

"Sure," and I put down the newspaper and picked up the menu. I knew I needed vegetables and some protein, so I ordered a veggie omelet, but I asked for tomato slices instead of hash browns, and no toast.

While I was waiting for the omelet, I looked at the newspaper again. It was really tempting to spend some more time reading about the attacks, the victims, and the survivors, but I picked up the Classifieds Section instead. For some reason I was less worried about finding a job than I was about finding a place to stay. Actually, I needed a place to stay, and every day that I didn't have an apartment or room to stay in was a day I'd have to pay for a hotel to stay in. The sooner I could find a place to stay, the better. Once I had that settled, I could look for a job.

"Looking for an apartment?" It was the waitress with my omelet. She was looking over my arms at the newspaper spread out on the table.

"Yeah. I just got into town, and I need a place to stay ... and then a job."

"My boyfriend is looking for a roommate," she said. "He's quiet and clean and the rent would be cheap."

"I think I need a place of my own," I smiled. I didn't want to encourage her. "No matter how small it is. But thanks."

"Sure. Be careful about renting a trailer, though. Those things blow away in hurricanes."

"Good advice," I said. I hadn't even considered a trailer rental. If they were cheap, clean, and safe and near a bus line, I would probably be just fine in a trailer for a few years.

"But I don't have much stuff of any value that I couldn't take with me," I replied, "and there's always plenty of warning for a hurricane, isn't there?"

"I suppose," she pondered a moment. "But if one hits, then you gotta find a new place to live. I wouldn't wanna have to do that."

"Yeah," I agreed, "but it might be worth the risk for a year or so while I'm getting settled here in Jacksonville. Besides, I can't afford much, so a trailer might be good for me."

As I finished my omelet, I circled some of the ads that appealed to me.

"More coffee?"

"Thanks. Yes, that'd be nice. Is it okay if I sit here a few more minutes to finish looking through the ads?"

"Of course," she said. "Let me see what you're looking at. Maybe I can steer you away from the slummy areas."

She poured more coffee and slid into the booth next to me. It felt good and uncomfortable at the same time. I edged away every so slightly, not wanting to signal any interest in any way.

"Oh NO! You can't stay there." She pointed to one of the ads I had circled. "It's a buncha drug dealers and welfare people." She took my pencil and Xed out that ad.

"Hey, this one is right around the corner from my boyfriend. I know this place. It's ok, but the managers charge for everything, so be careful about the rent."

It turned out that "...the managers charge for everything..." was a good warning in general.

"What about this?" I asked, pointing to an ad for a two-bedroom trailer for only $300 a month, everything included. It was more rooms than I needed, but I expected the total space was pretty small.

"It's next to a cemetery," she said. "You okay with that?"

"Sure. We used to play hide and seek in a cemetery when I was a kid." Too much information. Stop doing that, Carl! I touched the fingers on my left hand to my neck behind my left ear. I needed to stop volunteering *any* information at all.

She went back to work, and I looked through the ads again, circling a few more. I liked the idea of private renters. The corporations that owned or managed apartment buildings would likely require their building managers to get references, and I had none. But private renters might be ok if I offered a larger-than-required deposit. I focused on those ads in my search of the classifieds. The trouble was that privately sponsored ads could be for real dives, and I didn't have a way of driving around to check them all out.

Before leaving, I used the restroom and refilled my trusty Coke bottle. I really would need to find a new bottle soon. I needed to get rid of those trivial emotional attachments that I had seemed to develop so easily.

When I paid for my omelet, I asked the waitress if I could have some dimes and quarters in change and where the nearest pay phone was.

"Payphone?" she asked, almost mocking me. "Everyone has a cellphone nowadays."

"Yeah, I should get one in the next day or so, but I need to make some calls about possible apartments."

She was right. Searching for an apartment and looking for a job would all go much easier if I had a cellphone. I really wanted to find a place to live first, but if that was too hard, I would have to see about getting a phone. I wondered to myself, "How do people with no nest egg get by? How do they make or receive calls? How do they look for jobs or anything? I guess that's why we have charities," but I was determined I would never have to use one if I could possibly avoid them.

"They might have a payphone in the lobby of one of the banks around here," she offered as she gave me the extra change for two of my dollar bills: six quarters and five dimes. It had been such a long time since I had used a payphone that I didn't know how much it would cost. I half assumed the price had gone up to a quarter, but I wasn't sure.

On my way back down Hogan Street, I passed a government office building that had two payphones just inside the front door. Yup, a quarter per call.

The first place I called had a semi-furnished efficiency apartment for $400/month upstairs over their garage. It sounded private and like something I would be able to settle into for a year or more. The woman on the phone said they had internet, cable, and all the utilities were included. It sounded great to me.

After I got the address, I hailed a taxi to take me there. There would be no messing around on my search for an apartment. I wasn't going to try to save a few dollars by riding public transportation since my search time was important. It would take me hours to figure out bus routes and then to ride the bus, but I wanted to look at several places that day, if possible. What I spent in taxi fares would be more than made up in savings later if I could look at several places without having to spend money on a hotel.

I asked the taxi driver to take me to the address I had received from the woman on the phone. Ten minutes and fifteen dollars later, we pulled up in front of what would charitably be described as a dump. I didn't like the looks of it at all, but I thought I'd take a look since I was already there.

I knocked on the door and a woman who looked to be in her late forties answered.

"Hi," I smiled my best I'm-a-decent-kind-of-guy smile. "I'm Carl Jacobs. I called you awhile ago about your apartment."

"Hi, Carl," she smiled back. "I'm Meg-Ann. Let me get the key." And she ducked back into her house, emerging with a key in her hand a few seconds later.

"Where are you from Carl?" she asked as we walked around the back of the house to the stairs leading up to the apartment.

I had already decided to try to avoid the question whenever it came up. "I just got into town today and need a place for a few years," I answered.

I looked critically at the stairs and railing. They were pretty dilapidated.

"Yes, I know that step is a bit wobbly. I'll get someone in to repair it if you take the place," She offered. Hmm. That implied to me that there was no one living there right now.

She opened the door and a rush of mustiness emerged. The apartment clearly had not been rented for some time.

We stepped in and I waited a few seconds for my eyes to adjust to the darkness. I looked around. "Where's the bathroom and kitchen?" I asked.

"Oh," she said, "You get full privileges using the house."

"Well, I was sort of hoping for a private place of my own." I added, "I think I'll look for something else," and turned to go back down the stairs. It was basically an above-garage storage room that had been very slightly gussied up. I felt insulted.

"What if I lowered the rent a bit, Carl?" she asked.

"I don't know," I replied. "I think I'll see what else is available. This is the first place I've looked at."

"Okay. But keep my number handy in case you decide you might like it."

"I will", I said as I left, trying not to seem too eager to get away. I felt very uncomfortable there and didn't want to stay any longer than necessary.

Actually, I was extremely angry! I couldn't imagine I wouldn't find something better. The fact that the room seemed to have been vacant for so long strongly suggested that other potential tenants agreed.

I thought I could maybe remember how the taxicab had brought me to her place. I hoped to find my way back to a major street where I might come across another payphone or a taxicab that could help me out.

I had learned my lesson: ask first on the phone if there's a private bathroom with at least a shower, a refrigerator of some sort, laundry nearby, etc. Ask more questions up front and save the time and cab fare. "Oh well. Live and learn," I actually said out loud as I was walking away.

I took a long drink from my Coke bottle and headed toward a major street.

***
**

Chapter 13 – *Finding a place to stay*

I was about a block from Meg-Ann's dump when I saw a green plastic 7UP bottle lying along the side of the road.

"Perfect," I thought as I reached down and picked up the bottle. "Next chance I get, I'll clean this up and get rid of my Coke bottle."

I looked at my watch as I got to a major street. It was already well past noon.

It was also September 13th. I had been in town only about four hours, and it had been only two days since the tragedy at the Twin Towers.

Suddenly I felt a very strong sense of exhaustion. I had walked more in the past twenty-four hours than I had for a long time. Also, I hadn't slept much in the past 48 hours, and the sleep I'd had was fitful and uncomfortable. I wanted to force myself to go on, but I had no idea where I was going on *to*.

My sense had been that Meg-Ann's place had been north of downtown Jacksonville. I looked up to find the sun and headed in the direction of the sun, trying to go back toward downtown. I was dead tired, and I needed to sleep and shower before going on. I hoped to find a cheap hotel or rooming house as I went in that direction.

From the street signs, I learned that I was on was Sibbald Road. As I walked down the street, I wondered how long I could go on. I kept putting one foot in front of the other, but I was overwhelmed with exhaustion. I had expected to be able to keep going, but of course I had walked more in Washington, D.C., than I had in years, and now I was expecting to be able to walk even more? Nonsense. I was no longer a twenty-year-old Fred Young. I had to adapt to who I was and what my body was like right now. I needed more realistic expectations.

I really wanted to hail a cab and say, "Take me to the nearest inexpensive motel," but I also didn't want to spend all my money on a motel room and on cab fares.

As I walked along, I reached up and touched my neck behind my ear. This new thought-stopping technique was working well. Part of my thought-stopping involved not dwelling on the negatives. Instead I reflected on how lucky I had been so far. I hadn't been killed at The World Trade Center. I had been able to get out of Manhattan and on my way. I had changed my appearance dramatically. I had an address, a bank account, and some cash. I was ok.

I also expected that I could not count on both the luck and the generosity I experienced in Manhattan and Newark. It was time to think about hard slogging and the long, lonely times that lay ahead of me.

Soon I walked past a park. There was a high, spiked wrought-iron fence along the side of it, but I didn't understand why it was there because there were gates and openings everywhere. A sign at one entrance said "Miller Park".

I couldn't resist. I set my alarm for 2pm as I walked into the park. I looked for a shady place that was well away from the street and somewhat protected from possible interruptions by onlookers or police officers, but I needed to lie down somewhere.

I was remembering an experience my friends and I had had at the State Fair in Topeka after our last year in high school. Four of us had climbed into Jason's crew cab pickup truck and headed to the fair, but we had very little money and no idea what we would do or where we would stay. The first night there, we tried to just stay in the parking lot and sleep in the truck, but the officials rousted us and wanted extra money for overnight parking. Rather than pay, we left and drove into town.

It didn't take long to find what looked like a dark alley, and we pulled in there to park. An hour later we were awakened by a very bright spotlight and a policeman with a loud voice threatening to run us in because we were vagrants and were loitering. We apologized profusely and drove to a different part of town where there was a park.

We managed to catch another hour of sleep there before the sun rose. Of course with the sun beating down on the truck cab, it was as hot as the machine shed back on the farm in the Kansas sun, even with the truck windows down, and so we piled out and went to sleep on the lawn of the park. We all found shady places and crashed immediately. But about two hours later, the shade had moved, and the sunlight woke us up. We stretched, looked around, and were more than a little embarrassed as we realized we looked pretty grungy to all the people walking by, staring at us.

At that point we decided just to drive home and not stay for another day at the fair.

I was remembering those experiences as I looked around the park, and so I sought out a place that would remain shady for the next hour and that would be shielded from the sidewalk and Sibbald Road.

As I lay down, I swore at Meg-Ann for having wasted my time and cab fare. And then I swore at myself for not having asked the right questions on the phone and for the time and money I had wasted by looking at her place.

I was determined to improve my search strategies. To do that, I needed more time to understand the Jacksonville housing market and to make a list of questions and priorities.

I took my jacket out of the backpack to use as a pillow, stretched out in the shade, and promptly fell asleep.

I woke up to the beeping of my alarm again. I was both annoyed and grateful. As I stirred, I realize with some urgency that I needed to renew my search plans.

I was resolved to find a place that would rent me a room for a week so that I could use the time to search more carefully and with more leisure. I also wanted to get a cellphone so I could carry out my search on the phone more easily and begin a job hunt as well.

I knew that various mission services would put people up. My understanding, though, was that those services were for people who were down-and-out and homeless, and I wasn't. I also had read about the theft and violence in some mission accommodations. The risk of staying in one just seemed too high.

Then I remembered that in many cities, the YMCA had short-term rooms for rent. I decided to try to look into the Y next. If they didn't have any rooms available, they might have a list or know of some places I could stay for a week.

I looked up and down the street next to the park. Just to the south there was a big drugstore, so I headed there to use the phone.

As I walked in that direction, though, I saw a grocery store across the street. I knew I would be taking time from my search but I decided to go there instead. First things first though: I found their restroom in the rear of the store and washed out my 7-Up bottle, filled it with cold water, and ditched the Coke bottle. Whew. I didn't want meaningless attachments.

I bought some green peppers, celery, and carrots. When I had a place to stay, I would get some peanut butter and rice cakes, but for now these would have to do.

I smiled at the cashier. "I'm new in town and I need a clean, inexpensive place to stay for a week or so while I look for an apartment. Can you suggest anything?"

The cashier looked at me blankly, then got a horrified look as if I had just propositioned her. I was chagrined. That was the farthest thing from my mind.

"I mean like the Y or some short-term residential hotel." I hastily added.

"No," she answered, looking away from me. "I don't know of nothin' like that."

I grimaced both inwardly and outwardly. "Ok. Thanks. Do you have a payphone here I can use to call a few places?"

She didn't look at me as she muttered, "No, but there's one at the corner of the parking lot out there."

"Oh yeah. Thanks." I should have seen it on my way in and remembered it. Now she'd be even more suspicious.

I paid and put my vegetables in my backpack, which was getting pretty full.

The payphone booth was in bad shape. There was no directory where there was space for one, and the plastic sides had graffiti scratched on them. I lifted the receiver and put a quarter in the coin slot.

A dial tone! I felt lucky. I dialed 411, hoping to speak to an operator, but got a voice message instead, asking me what number I wanted to call.

On the off chance it might work, I pressed "0". It worked! I got a real person!

"Operator." Not, "How may I help you?" but at least it was a person.

"Hi," I said, rushing a bit, as I often did for some strange reason when speaking with an operator. "I just got into Jacksonville today, and I'm at a payphone, and there's no directory here. I need an inexpensive place to stay for a week while I search for a job and an apartment."

I took a long shot. "Can you recommend anything?"

"Listen, Pal," she said. "Do you know how many times a day I get propositioned like this?"

"**Don't hang up**!" I yelled into the phone. "I'm serious. I need a place. Can you at least give me the number of the YMCA or some place like that that might be able to help me?" I was scared she'd hang up. At least my quarter had been returned.

She hadn't hung up.

"Sorry, Pal." She actually chuckled a bit. "I think the Y and some of the local churches might be able to help. Let me connect you with the Y first."

"Okay," I replied as the phone went dead at her end. Then I heard the beeps of the call going through.

Again I hadn't thought ahead and prepared: I had no pencil or paper handy. There were some in my shoulder bag, but it was at the bottom of my pack. I set it down and dug out the shoulder bag just as someone answered.

"Jacksonville Y. How may I direct your call?"

Nuts. I should have anticipated this. A receptionist. But maybe she'd connect me with someone who could help.

"Hi." I tried to slow down my spiel just a bit from when I had spoken with the Information Operator. "I'm new in town, and I need a place to stay for a few days or even a week. Does your Y offer short-term stay rooms?"

"No sir, I'm sorry. We no longer do that. We focus more on community outreach programs and fitness. But Ms. Alberts keeps a list of inexpensive places for people to stay. Let me put you through to her."

"That would be great. Thanks." I said somewhat flatly, hiding my excitement. I was thrilled to be on a positive roll again.

I managed to get my shoulder bag out of my backpack while I was being connected.

"This is Thelma Alberts," a voice said.

"Hello," I said. "My name is Carl Jacobs. I just got into town today, and I need an inexpensive but clean and safe place to stay while I look for an apartment and a job. I was told you might be able to help me find something."

I have no idea why I gave her my name. It just came out, maybe because she had said hers. The good thing was that I gave her my new name, not Fred Young.

Gotta stop thinking like that. Just push the old name out and don't even think about it.

"Well, yes, we do have list of mission places..."

"I can pay for something," I interrupted. "I'd rather have a private room with a door that locks. I just can't afford much right now, that's all."

"Oh. I see," she said. "We do have a list of residential apartments and hotels. One of those might suit you. We drew up this list when we stopped providing residential living spaces for young people at the Y some years ago. I'm not sure how up-to-date the list is, though."

"Would you be able to give me the names, addresses, and phone numbers of a few that you might particularly recommend?" I asked.

"Well...." She hesitated.

"Please," I begged. "It'll probably cost me a night's stay in cab fare if I have to go in to your office to write these down. It would be a great help to me if you could give me just the names and phone numbers of a few places that you've heard decent things about...." I tailed off, hopefully.

Well...." Again she hesitated. "There's The Alameda Residences. They're on Atlantic Boulevard, just off U.S. Highway 1, south of the river but real convenient to lots of places. We've sent people there before and have had no complaints. But they did have a knifing there last month, so keep your head low if you go there."

"What was the knifing about?" That would affect my decision about going there.

"A domestic quarrel, the police said. I think they'd been drinking and got riled up. But there hasn't been any trouble there other than that, so far's I know..."

"Do you have any idea what they'd charge?" I asked.

"Here's the good part," Thelma said. "They like referrals from the Y because you folks who use the Y are generally decent people. So you tell 'em Thelma at the Y sent you, and they'll give you a room with a private bath for only $30 a night, or $180 for the week. Can you afford that?"

I tried to take that in. $180 would set me back a bit, but it would give me a solid base to work from and probably would save me money in the long run. Tomorrow I could see about getting a cellphone and a bus pass and then look for an apartment.

"I think so. Do you know if the rooms have air conditioning or any other amenities?" I bit my tongue as I said, "amenities". Too fancy. Ugh.

"Amenities!" she laughed. She'd caught it. I was glad she couldn't see me blushing. "They have window air conditioners that sometimes work. They aren't the Hilton, after all!" She laughed again.

I laughed along with her, but I was upset with myself.

"Just make sure you check the air conditioning before you agree to a room. Here's their number, and she told me all ten digits. Groan. I knew I couldn't remember all ten.

"Hold on," I said. "Let me get a pen and paper and write that down. I have some here in my pack."

"Ok." She waited a few seconds. "You ready?"

She suddenly sounded rushed. I dug out the pen and paper as fast as I could. "Ok. Shoot.

She rattled off the phone number and address so fast I barely got 'em down.

"You'll have to excuse me," she said. "I gotta go now. Bye." And she hung up before I could even thank her.

I thought for a moment. If the Alameda had been reasonably safe and clean until that incident last month, maybe it would be okay. I knew better than to expect a super-clean, super-safe place, but all I really needed was a place that would be acceptable while I was looking for an apartment and a job.

So I called them.

"Alameda," droned the voice at the other end of the line.

"Not too welcoming, but, here goes," I thought.

"Hello," I said. "Thelma Alberts at the YMCA said I should give you a call. I need a place to stay for the next week or so. Do you have anything available?"

"We got two units," said the voice. "Y rates."

"Huh?" I thought. And then it hit me they were saying "Y", not "Why". They were used to the referrals from the Y. And given the way Thelma rushed me off the phone, I wondered if she got a kickback for all the referrals, but didn't want others there to overhear what she was saying.

I didn't care. If she put me onto a decent place to stay for the next few days, I was happy and wouldn't begrudge her making a bit on the side. Besides, she likely wasn't being terribly dishonest all if she seemed tentative about the place and was warning me about the knifing they'd had there last month. That, or she was a good liar. Or maybe she just hustled me off the phone for some other work-related reason. It was good to be skeptical, I reminded myself, but not overly so.

The person on the phone at the Alameda confirmed that both of the two units available had private baths and that the air conditioning worked. They seemed a bit defensive when I asked about the air conditioning, but I didn't really care about their feelings. I just wanted a place to settle for the next few days.

"I'll be there in about a half hour," I said. "I'm up north in the city right now, and I need to find a cab."

"No rush," said the voice, and the phone clicked down, followed by a dial tone.

I had no idea when a taxicab might come by to pick me up, and with no telephone directory in the phone booth, I'd have to call information again if I wanted to call a cab. But then I remembered seeing a dedicated phone line for a taxi inside the door at the grocery store.

I went back to the store to use that phone.

"It'll be 10 minutes," the voice at the other end said right after I picked up the phone. No greeting, no question about where I was going, nothing. They obviously knew where I was and what I wanted.

"Thanks," I mumbled and hung up.

While I waited, I thought for a moment or two and then, with the full expectation that I would end up staying at the Alameda for a few days, bought a package of rice cakes and a jar of store-brand peanut butter to go with everything else I already had in my backpack.

"W̶   ̶to?" the cabbie asked as I got in.

"The Alameda on Atlantic Boulevard," I said, remembering the address Thelma had said on the phone.

"Ok, Mac. It'll setcha back at least $20, though. It's on the other side of the river. You got that much?"

"It's nice to be trusted," I thought sarcastically. I pulled out my wallet, hid it down where he couldn't see it, fumbled a bit to add some uncertainty about it all, and pulled out a twenty to show him.

No acknowledgement. Nothing. He just took off.

"It's on the other side of the river," he had said. Thelma had also mentioned it was south of the river. I didn't even know Jacksonville HAD a river. I should have expected that, though.

So the Alameda was across the river. I needed a map of Jacksonville. I hoped they had one at the Alameda.

* * *

**

Chapter 14 – *The Alameda*

It wasn't even 3pm yet. I sat back in the cab and tried to anticipate more of the issues and problems I would be facing over the next couple of days, making a mental list of things to consider.

First things first: I wanted to shower and sleep in a bed. I hoped the Alameda would provide these for me. I could tolerate something that wasn't spiffy so long as it wasn't too grungy.

"But what about tomorrow?" I wondered.

I wanted a map of the city. I should have gotten one from the information person at the bus station. I almost asked the cabbie to stop there on the way to the Alameda, but decided it could wait until tomorrow. I could go there first thing in the morning, and at the same time I could withdraw another $500 from my Omaha account to deposit in my new checking account at Everbank.

I also needed a cellphone; I couldn't search for an apartment or a job very easily without ready access to a phone, and a cellphone seemed good because I would have it with me all the time. I thought I had seen cellphone shops near the UPS office and the bank, but I wasn't sure. I knew there would be something downtown, though. I would put off my apartment and job searches until I had a phone.

And I needed to look into the public transportation system in Jacksonville. I'd seen trolleys and buses and something overhead, but I had to get a pass and a bus route map. Maybe that would be the way to go, a public transportation map if the bus station information desk didn't have any city maps. At any rate, I knew I couldn't afford to cab it everywhere for long.

Something I had put out of my mind was the need to dispose of my old cellphone, my laptop, my watch, and any other personal effects from my shoulder bag. I would have to start looking for construction dumpsters.

Eventually, too, I wanted to get a new laptop. But that would have to wait until I had a longer-term place to stay and a job.

The driver had gotten us onto an interstate and was moving quickly. After going through a spaghetti-like interchange, his route took us across the river to the south side of downtown Jacksonville. From the river, it was only a minute before he pulled up in front of the Alameda.

"We made good time," said the cabbie. "Almost no traffic. Let's call it $20 even."

Until then I hadn't noticed that he hadn't put the flag down. He was planning to keep all the money and not pay a percentage to the cab company. Probably not a wise decision, given that he had picked me up on a call from a direct line, and they'd wonder what happened if he didn't report the fare and the trip. But that was going to be his problem.

I handed him a twenty. He looked at me questioningly.

"Thanks," I said, opening the door.

He hesitated, clearly expecting me to give him a tip, but I saw no reason to tip him if he was going to cheat the cab company. I closed the door, and I would swear he sped off before it was completely closed.

"Well, that went well," I muttered. But at least I had saved a few dollars, and I might need that money. "So long, buttface," I added under my breath.

I turned around to look at the Alameda. I stood there for nearly a minute, studying the place, but then shook myself slightly and forced myself to touch my neck with my left hand. This was not going to be my forever home; it was a place to spend a few nights. I didn't really need to soak it all in.

Nevertheless, I did wonder about the place. It looked like one of the first two-level motels that had been built in the 1950s. Apparently it had been converted into short-term residences. That would suit me if it was clean and safe. It was L-shaped with an outside balcony running all along the upper level – probably no inside hallways, I guessed. On the ground, there was a dirty, scrubby square sort of enclosed by the L where undoubtedly there had once been a swimming pool.

I consciously touched my neck again as I realized I had been standing there, looking around, mostly to put off going to the office, dreading what might not work out and unenthused about continuing the search if I had to. I knew I had to plunge onward, though, and headed to the office.

"Yes?" said the person behind the desk. I had no idea that someone could make such a short word sound monotonous. Not just monotone, but monotonous. This had to be the person I spoke with on the phone. She or he, I couldn't tell for sure, was overweight with stringy hair and a deep contralto voice.

"Hello," I offered somewhat tentatively. "I called a little while ago about a place to stay?" I wasn't really asking, but I let my voice ride up at the end as if to ask, "Do you remember?" and to plead, "Please let this go well."

"Yeah." That was it. Nothing more.

"Well, would it be okay for me to look at a room to see if I want to stay here?"

The person slid two keys across the desk. Clearly s/he was prepared and was expecting me. That gesture, by signaling that they wanted to rent the room, put me at ease a bit. It also made me a bit nervous in case it just meant they were too eager.

"207 and 224 upstairs. Take your pick." Still with a monotonous, flat tone. "Stairs to the left outside."

"Thanks," I said, trying not to mimic the monotonous drone too obviously.

I scooped up the keys from the desk, hoisted up my backpack, and left the office.

The stairs were solid, I noted, remembering the disaster at Meg-Ann's dump that morning. The balcony felt solid, and there were no broken windows, at least none that I noticed.

Unit 207 was about halfway down the first leg of the L-shaped balcony. I took a deep breath – apprehensive but also laughing at myself for feeling so overly dramatic.

As I opened the door... Nothing. No stench. It was too warm inside the room, but that was all. So far, so good.

I turned on the light to look around. It looked like a standard room from the 50s. A slightly sagging double bed with a worn, faded chenille bedspread, a marred blond wooden desk, a beat-up wooden chair, and a floor lamp that doubled as a desk lamp. I checked the bed, and while it was soft and maybe a bit lumpy, it would probably be okay.

Next I turned on the air conditioner. It was pretty noisy. I let it run while I checked out the bathroom. Again, straight out of the 50s – turquoise ceramic toilet and pedestal sink, a basic turquoise tub with rubber stopper, and a basic chrome showerhead.

No grunge! Well, maybe a bit in the grout, but nothing serious. I was more than relieved. The shower worked, and the toilet flushed ok. The towels were threadbare but would be acceptable. Things all seemed well-worn, but there were no signs of serious mold or grime. I was pleasantly surprised. So far it seemed like a place that would have received the very basic two-diamond AAA rating twenty years earlier but hadn't been updated; it would suit me fine. I checked to make sure there was soap and plenty of toilet paper, and then walked back into the room.

The air conditioner was pretty noisy, but it was spitting out some cool air. Spitting, not pumping for sure.

I was about to accept it without checking any further, but instead I left the air conditioner running and went to check out room 224.

It was about the same. Old, worn, clean enough, and everything working. The only difference that I could tell was that the air conditioner seemed quieter and smoother, but it wasn't putting out much coolth.

I smiled to myself. Susan and I used to say "coolth" all the time. The kids grew up using the word, thinking it was a normal word. Reluctantly I told myself to drop it. And then I touched my neck again. No reason to get maudlin and teary at this point. Wait 'til I was alone and had some time to work through it a bit.

I left unit 224 and went back to check on 207. It was cooling off nicely, so the air conditioner was working fine. Then I went back to 224, which was not at all cool. The air conditioner seemed to be working, just not very well. I turned off the air conditioner there, turned off the lights, and locked the door.

On my way back to 207, I heard a lot of screaming and yelling from one of the units on the lower level. I couldn't make out the content, but words like "bitch", "asshole" etc. peppered the exchange. I half-expected something like that from what Thelma had said about the knifing, but I hoped the neighbors on either side of me were quiet.

And then it dawned on me. There were no televisions in the rooms. Since I didn't expect to be watching much television during the next few days, I saw this as a plus – no loud TVs in the neighboring rooms seemed like a good thing to me.

I checked in on 207 once more, just to make sure the air conditioner was still working, ran water again to make sure the drains worked ok and to make sure there was hot water for shaving; and I made sure there was a lightbulb in the floor lamp. There was, albeit only 40-watt.

Back in the office, I handed the key for 224 back to the person. It turned out the person was a woman, Ellen Smith, according to the name badge I should have seen earlier.

"207 looks fine," I said and reached into my left front pocket for my wallet. Left hand to my neck as I silently reminded myself: right pocket.

As I was pulling out my new wallet, Ellen asked, "How long?" Not, "How long will you be with us?" Not, "How long will you want the room?" Just, "How long?" Ellen was a woman of few words.

I learned long ago to answer a question with a question, and with my changing identity I didn't want to offer any more information than necessary.

"What are the rates?" I asked. "You said something about 'Y' rates."

She looked at me and my backpack. I guessed she was sizing me up. The yacht club shirt wouldn't help get me a lower rate, but the wrinkly clothes might help. At the same time I probably looked like someone who wouldn't cause any trouble.

"Is that all you have with you?" she asked.

"Does that affect the rate?" I asked. Answer a question with a question.

"Is it?" She was good at answering a question with a question, too.

I smiled at her. "I don't like to answer many questions." And I smiled a bit more.

I honestly believe I saw a hint of a smile from her, but I'm not sure.

"Twenty-five dollars a night," she said. "One-fifty for the week if you pay in advance."

That was less than Thelma had said, but I didn't say a thing. I turned away slightly so she couldn't see my wallet and took out $150. When I handed it to her, she said, "Five hundred a month if you pay in advance."

"Hmmm," I pondered for a second. It was tempting to have a settled base for the next month, but I really wanted a place with a refrigerator and some way to cook.

"How about I try it for a few days and then if I end up thinking I should stay for a month, you give me that rate then?"

"That'll do," she said. "Let me know by Tuesday if you want longer. Fill this out." More words than she had said in all her previous utterings put together.

"Well, here goes," I thought to myself.

I put "Carl Jacobs" where it wanted my name. But after that? I had no phone, no car, no other address, and so I left the rest blank. That was easy.

"Here," I said as I handed the card back to Ellen.

She didn't bat an eye. Didn't even look at me. She just wrote "207" at the top and "$150 pd wk" after that.

"Thanks. Is there a 7-11 or some sort of convenience store nearby?"

"Bill's. Two blocks west." She almost imperceptibly nodded in a direction I took to be west.

"Thanks again," I said as I left the office.

I went straight to the room. It was nice and cool, so I turned off the noisy air conditioner. I would let it run while I was away but it was so noisy I would try to avoid having to use it much while I was there.

I locked the door and began "unpacking" what little I had. I set the vegetables on top of the air conditioner. Then I looked around. No dresser, but there were two drawers in the desk. That would work. I put the underwear and socks in the top drawer and refolded the pants and shirts to put in the bottom drawer. I took off the pants I was wearing and looked around. Sheesh, no closet either. Just a shelf by the door with a couple of wire hangers on hooks under the shelf. I swore at myself again for not checking for a closet. Then I swore at myself again as I touched my neck. I didn't need a closet for a short-term stay, and there was no reason for me to get down on myself for that.

I hung the pants on a hanger, used my fingers and hands to smooth out some of the creases, and stretched out on the bed. It was okay but far from great. It would do for now.

My mind was racing with things I wanted to do, and I had had a nap just two hours earlier. I knew I couldn't sleep right away, but I needed to calm down and relax after everything I had been through for the past two and half days. I took a long, soaking shower and lay back down on the bed. I closed my eyes and thought about my family, wondering how they were doing. I missed them, and I began sobbing quietly.

* * *

**

Chapter 15 – *Reflections*

I remembered the shock and horror that friends and relatives had felt when someone close to them died suddenly in an accident, and I could recall the grief and sorrow Susan and I each felt as our parents got sick and died.

I was overcome with guilt for having dropped out of my old life, leaving Susan and the kids to face the uncertainty of my death and having to cope with it suddenly.

At that point I almost wished I had been on time for the Cantor-Fitzgerald appointment. If I had died then, what they must be experiencing wouldn't be the result of a lie.

Maybe I could go back to my old life after all. Maybe I could claim I had suffered from post-traumatic stress syndrome and had run scared.

I didn't want to do that. I didn't think I could pull it off, and I'd be too embarrassed to try. I reminded myself that I was doing all this to discover a new life, a new me.

I consoled myself by knowing that Susan and the kids would be well-looked-after financially and by knowing that if I had been on time for that appointment, I would in fact be dead. I convinced myself that it was okay. Fred Young was dead, as he should have been, and I had been reborn as Carl Jacobs. I knew I was lying. But it was a lie I could live with, for now anyway.

Susan had been wonderful our entire marriage. She had supported me when I was struggling emotionally with my job transitions, unsure of myself. She had comforted me when my parents got sick and died. We had had disagreements and conflicts, of course; what couples don't? But we worked through the ones we could and accepted the others. As I thought about it, though, I had to admit that I pretty much gave in most of the time when we had a disagreement. I hated when she was upset, and so I just capitulated. Maybe that was one of the reasons I had been depressed?

Overall, though, our marriage had been a good one. Susan was the standard, sensitive, devoted, "good wife and mother". I knew I would miss her, her support, her insights, and her love. I sobbed some more. I let out a muffled shriek as I cried, "Why? Why?"

It surprised me and saddened me to realize I didn't feel nearly so connected to the children. Timothy ("Not Tim!" he would say) was 15, a sophomore in high school. He was a good student when he did the work, and he was a decent athlete. He was on the soccer team at school and had played reasonably well in some matches, but he never really stood out. He had lots of friends and seemed strong, inwardly. I worried about his work ethic, but I had seen him rise to the occasion when he had to.

Timothy and I had never really bonded. We talked sports some, and we talked a bit about his plans for the future -- maybe go to the University of Nebraska? He wasn't sure. But we never really talked much about relationships. Actually, I had no idea how to talk about relationships. I had counted on Susan for all the relationship stuff between us. I knew Timothy would feel a loss, but I expected he would find other father figures along the way. Ben might fill that role for now, and maybe one of his favorite teachers would, too, later on. He would have down periods, of course, but I was fairly certain he would end up happy and successful. Despite this cold analysis, I knew that if I saw him again I'd break down in tears. I regretted not having tried to be closer with him.

Our daughter Liz was more of a concern to me. We had named her Austen Elizabeth. It was sort of a requirement in Susan's family that she use the name Austen, her sister's and aunt's name. Neither of us was thrilled with the pressure we faced to use that name, but we went along with it. And you know what? I would do it again. Now that I had no family and no history, I could see how important and valuable these historical connections might be.

Already it had hit me. If you had asked me last week, I would probably have said we should have resisted using Austen. Now I was glad we had used the name.

We raised our daughter with the name Lizzy, but we made it clear early on that she could choose some other short form of Elizabeth if she wanted to. She seemed happy with Lizzy when she was young but dropped the "zy" later, becoming Liz for school and friends. I still thought of her as Lizzy, though I tried hard to call her Liz, since she seemed to prefer that.

Liz was 13 and in 8th grade. She, too, was a good student. She sang well, was in a choir, played various sports, and seemed socially well-adjusted. Maybe it was the machismo in me, but I worried about how she would deal with love and boys as she grew up. Again, though, I trusted that Susan would be a good, solid anchor for Liz. With that thought, I realized I probably wouldn't have imagined this escape if I hadn't trusted that Susan would carry on and raise the children to be strong and independent.

The four of us had been happy together, most of the time. There was no clear, obvious reason for my unhappiness or my feeling of emptiness. I knew I had those feelings, though, and they were intensified as my career began to fall apart. The pure and simple truth was that I felt as if I had never really connected with anyone in my family, much less outside the family. I had never been honest with myself, and I had never explored my feelings about anyone or anything.

It slowly dawned on me that I had not anticipated the immense sense of loss I would feel at not being with my family ever again, and that loss hit with a thud. I felt stupid and uncaring.

Escaping like this seemed a good way out. I'd die a hero (of sorts) in the minds of my family and neighbors, and I could decide what and who I wanted to be. The sad part was that I fully expected I would still feel empty. The best I could hope for would be to try to follow their lives through the news. But that wouldn't relieve my feelings of emptiness.

I felt so alone. And I knew it was my own doing, my own choice. I kept thinking about my friend John's adage when he was feeling angry back in college: "It's okay to have the feelings. It's what you do with them that's important."

And with that, I fell asleep.

It was my first real sleep in a bed since I'd spent the night in the hotel in New York City. And it was traumatic. I had intermittent nightmares.

People were screaming, Timothy and Liz were leaning out of a window up high looking at me, waving. There was vomit everywhere. Trucks were washing away the vomit and the ash, but there was more and more of it. Co-workers who had resented me were grinning at me through airplane windows. Susan kept repeating, "Call me." "Call me." There was a cascade of hair from the sky.

And the smells. I didn't know you could dream smells.

* * *
**

Chapter 16 – *More and More Search*

I woke up drenched in sweat, partly because I had turned off the air conditioner and partly from whatever I had been reliving during my sleep.

I looked at my watch. 7:00. But was it AM or PM? I forced my eyes to focus on the watch. It was 7:00 AM, and it was Friday.

I had slept for nearly fifteen hours!

What's more, I hadn't eaten in nearly a day, and I was famished. I rubbed my eyes and looked around. When I saw the veggies on top of the air conditioner, I remembered my plan to lose a lot of weight quickly. I groaned, but I knew it was necessary.

As I picked up some celery, I turned on the air conditioner to cool the room. I used the multitool knife I'd bought in Newark to cut the ends off the celery. ... Hunh ... I looked around for a place to put the ends and had to use the wastebasket in the bathroom.

I started eating a stalk of celery, but I knew that wouldn't do it for me, and so I opened the package of rice cakes and the jar of peanut butter and made two open-face peanut butter sandwiches.

I was still hungry, but I also wanted to get a few things done that morning, and so I put the lid back on the peanut butter jar and washed off the knife. I showered again, shaved, brushed my teeth, used antiperspirant, and put on the clothes I had bought at the thrift store in Newark. They suited me well – not too baggy, not too tight; not too flashy, not too drab. They were going to be fine, especially for today, when I would continue my apartment search and maybe begin my job search.

I knew it could be a stressful, busy day, and since I still had some time, I decided to cut up some more celery and some carrots to take with me. I also made some rice-cake peanut butter "sandwiches" and put the food in the rice cake bag, leaving the rest of the rice cakes on the desk. Then I washed and refilled my 7UP bottle.

I looked at my shoulder bag. It would be perfect for carrying my lunch, but there wasn't enough room in it for my laptop, my other personal effects, my lunch, and my water bottle. I considered leaving my laptop in the room, but that just seemed too risky. I had no idea how safe things would be there, and I really didn't want to take a chance that someone would steal or even look at these things.

So I scrunched and pushed and fit the rice cake sandwiches and veggies into the shoulder bag, and I put the water bottle in the front pocket of my pants. Well I could see that wouldn't work, and so I put the computer in the shoulder bag at the bottom of my backpack, put the food on top of it, and put the water bottle in a side pocket. I was ready to go, and it was barely 8:00AM.

I slung the backpack over one shoulder, turned on the air conditioner, and locked the door as I left the room. Key in the left front pocket, along with my mailbox key.

It was pretty cool this early in the morning, but I expected it would warm up during the day. I stopped at the office to ask a few questions and met "Bubba", who was apparently just finishing the all night shift at the desk.

"Hi there," he said. "You the new guy in 207?"

"Hi. Yes. I'm Carl," I answered. "I was wondering if you can help me out with a few things."

"Sure 'nuf," Bubba said. "What can I do ya for?"

I forced a smile and a half chuckle.

"Well, first, I need to get to downtown on the other side of the river. Is there public transportation like a bus or something I can take to get there? I hope there's some place to get bus tokens or passes or something, too, because I don't have much change."

"Well, shucks, Carl." Bubba smiled. "There's a Skyway tram goes across the river. Ain't no charge. It leaves reg'lar from the station just a few blocks north of here."

"That's great news!" I said. "Do you happen to have a map or, even better, a spare map of Jacksonville? I have no idea where I am and I really need to find my way around over the next few days."

"Shucks, no, Carl," said Bubba. "But they might have maps showing all the streets and bus routes up to the Skyway station. We usually try to keep a few here, too, for folks like you, but we're plumb out right now." He smiled apologetically.

"Geez, thanks!" I looked at his name badge and added, "Thanks, Bubba. How do I get to that Skyway station?"

"Just go west..." He pointed to his left. "...'til you get to Hendricks and turn right. When you cross the highway but before the interstate, look right. You'll see a big hotel. There's a walkway to the station from the huge parking garage behind the hotel."

"Let's see," I repeated carefully. "West to Hendricks, turn right, look for the hotel across the highway on the right and head for it?"

"You got it."

I thanked Bubba and left with a sense of relief and anxiousness. As I walked toward Hendricks, I passed Bill's Convenience store and remembered that was the place Ellen had mentioned last night. I had fallen asleep before going out for any supplies, but that was probably just as well; I wasn't sure I'd have been able to resist buying a bag of cookies or some candy bars.

Along the way up Hendricks, I stopped for breakfast even though I had just eaten some food an hour earlier. Once again I decided to have a veggie omelet – and again tomatoes, but no toast and no potatoes. I felt as if I had shed at least five pounds already, but there was such a long way to go.

I bought a paper as I was paying the check so I could look for apartments and a job later in the day after I had a bus pass and a cell phone. I continued my walk north to the Skyway station and quickly realized that "a few blocks" to Bubba was more like about eight or ten blocks.

The Skyway station was full of people commuting across the river. There were no ticket booths, no paper maps, no nothing. Just turnstiles to count the passengers, most of whom seemed to have parked in the large parkade near the interstate.

It looked to me as if the Skyway had been put in to avoid having to build another bridge for all the auto traffic going back and forth between the north and south sides of the river. To the extent that it relieved some of the congestion, it made sense I guess, but a bridge could handle thousands more cars a day than could fit in a parkade, so I thought there must be more to it than that. It probably also increased bus ridership to and from the Skyway.

There was map on the wall that I had to fight the crowds to stop and study. "Well I'll be," I said under my breath. The Skyway was the overhead system I had seen yesterday morning while I was walking around downtown. It didn't go very far though… just to the downtown and to the community college that's on the northern edge of downtown.

"Well, I'll be" was another phrase I'd have to change. I uttered, "Well sock it to me." Nope that wouldn't do. I decided to try to make more use of "Nuts" instead.

It turned out that one of the places to buy bus tickets was the very UPS office I'd been in yesterday. I felt stupid for having been so single-minded about renting a mailbox and not having realized that, but I consoled myself that I wouldn't have been able to take it all in then anyway. I took it as a reminder that I was still a long way from understanding much about anything.

The ride across the river on the Skyway was pleasant, though crowded. I just stood in the aisle and held onto a strap, being jostled and jostling back. Aside from the fact that I wasn't wearing a suit, I fit right in with the rest of the commuters – freshly shaven, showered, clean clothes, backpack over one shoulder with a laptop, etc. I was feeling ambivalent about fitting in. I was glad I felt as if I could fit in, but at the same time I knew I needed a different type of life. Finding that new life would be a challenge.

I got off the Skyway at the Greyhound bus station, followed the crowds into the station and made my way over to Everbank, which was just opening. There I withdrew another $500 from my Omaha account, walked over to the teller and deposited $400 in my Everbank account. As I was leaving, I nodded a "hello" to Ted, with whom I had opened my account the day before.

"Good morning, Carl." He remembered me and my name. He struck me as a quintessential networker who would likely go as far as he could using networks. I didn't begrudge him that; I just hoped there was more substance to him than the networking.

I smiled back, nodded again, and went over to pick up one of his business cards. We exchanged pleasantries, and then he went back to looking at his computer screen. I was willing to bet that he was looking to see what I was doing with my account. Networkers collect information for later use. I had to keep that in mind.

I helped myself to another cup of Everbank coffee and headed out to the UPS Store. Mr. Gruff (a name for him that popped into my head as I walked in) was there again today. This time he looked up and actually smiled.

"Hi. What can I do ya for?" Huh? Was that a common greeting in Jacksonville or had I just been unlucky? Oh well, at least he seemed more friendly this time.

"Hi," I said as I smiled back and faked a minor chuckle. "I was in here yesterday to rent a mailbox. I should have bought a bus pass while I was here then."

"Sure." I wondered what had accounted for his apparent mood change. I was guessing he had been in the middle of some sort of conflict when I was in the previous day.

"What do you want? Tickets? A week? A month?"

"I think I'd better start with a monthly pass," I started to say, but I stopped myself. No reason to get chatty and give out any more information than necessary.

"A month," I said, keeping my voice flat.

I paid for the pass and was about to leave when I saw a big sign that I had completely missed until then:

Ask About "Our" Cell Plans

How could I have missed it, especially with the quotation marks around "Our"?

So I turned back and asked Mr. Gruff about their cell plans.

He said, "Yeah. We carry Nokia phones and can hook 'em up with any of the major services – T-Mobile, Verizon, AT&T, you name it. But if you're not gonna travel much, we recommend a local service, Kazzoo. They'll really nail you if you use 'em out of the region, but they use AT&T towers and they're dirt cheap for local calls."

I thought about it for a few minutes and looked over their collection of Nokia and other phones.

"How much?" I asked.

"Twenty dollars up front and twenty dollars a month on a two-year contract with unlimited local calls," he beamed. "That's about half what it'd cost you with one of the majors. But ya gotta sign up for automatic payments from your bank to get this deal."

I figured that arrangement would be worth taking a chance on. I had no plans to travel much, if at all, and I expected I'd be using the phone for at least another two or three years. I had never heard of unlimited local calling, and I had never heard of "Kazzoo", but I had a general sense that Mr. Gruff was right about the price being half that of the majors. I hoped they weren't fly-by-night. I filled out the paperwork and attached a blank check with "Void" written across it. Mr. Gruff activated the phone, and I walked out a happy man with a phone in my pocket and a charging cord for it in one of the pockets of my backpack.

I realized that I probably could have saved myself a ton of headaches if I had been more observant yesterday. I could have bought the bus pass and the cell phone then and done more of my search more effectively.

I reached my left hand up to my neck. I had to stop beating myself up for past decisions that really weren't all that awful. After all, I had an acceptable base and was doing ok as it was.

I started to open the newspaper to look for apartments again. Oops. I needed a city map, and I needed a place to sit and spread out the map and paper. I thought about going back to the restaurant I'd been at yesterday, but I had just eaten…. twice… I wasn't hungry, and I needed to save money; also, it occurred to me that I didn't want that waitress to think I was going in to see her again, even though her input might have been helpful. I decided to find a library. There had to be one somewhere near downtown.

I turned around and went back. Mr. Gruff had his head buried in his computer doing some work.

"Sorry," I clipped briefly. "A coupla more questions," trying to use a tone that resembled some of the clipped tones I'd heard the day before.

"I need a map of the city," I added. I could find the library once I had a map.

"Don't have any here," Mr. Gruff was reverting to being Mr. Gruff. "Try the store down at the corner." He half-nodded to his right.

Figuring that was the end of our conversation, I went to my mailbox and checked it. It had a signed contract for the mailbox in it; I left the contract in the box and left the store.

The shop Mr. Gruff undoubtedly had in mind was a stationery shop at the corner, and it did indeed have city maps. I bought one in book or atlas format, hoping it would be easier to carry around than a full fold-up map, even though I hated not having the whole big picture at once.

I leafed through it a bit and felt very awkward because I had very few reference points.

"Can you help me find the library?" I asked the clerk.

"Sure," she said. "Just go over to Laura Street and up to Monroe." She saw the puzzled look on my face and realized I had no idea about streets or locations or anything.

She took the street atlas from me and leafed through it. "Here," she said, pointing to it. "It's right next to Hemming Park," and she showed me that on the map, too. "It's just a short two-block walk from here," and she pointed to where we were. It was so close it was almost embarrassing.

"Thanks," I smiled and headed off, keeping the street atlas open and looking up at street names as I walked along. I was there in less than five minutes.

The library was exactly what I had imagined: tables, chairs, a few computers, and a front desk. I decided to go to the front desk first.

"Hi," I said and this time I remembered to keep my head down a bit. "I'd like a library card."

They had me fill out a form with my name and address, typed up a card, and laminated it. "We'll have you come back in a month for a permanent photo card," the woman said. "I don't know why we don't just take them now, but I guess they want to wait to see if you're still interested in a month."

"Thanks," I replied as I turned to find a table. I had to force myself not to even consider looking at the computers because I was really curious... more than that, I was super-curious ... to know what was happening with my family in Omaha. But I wanted to spend the day productively getting on with my new life, not dwelling on my old one.

I found a table to sit at. I wanted one that had plenty of space where I wouldn't bother anyone sitting near me when I spread open my newspaper while using the street atlas at the same time.

* * *

**

Chapter 17 – *Finding a Place to Live*

I went through the classifieds again, circling ads just as I had the day before, only more carefully this time. I circled maybe twenty different ads and went back to look at each one to check on whatever details I could find. Even though I had a few days and could afford The Alameda even longer if necessary, I wanted to organize my search better than I had before.

First I determined how much I thought I might be able to afford. My short-term goal was to find two jobs and work 80-90 hours a week. I knew they would be minimum-wage jobs with no benefits, but with no job references I couldn't hope for anything else. I'd be lucky to find even these jobs, and I had no idea how long it would take to find them.

I was also realistic enough to assume that at first the best I could do would be to find part-time work. I roughly estimated I could earn perhaps $150/week initially, but I hoped to push that up to over $300/week within a few months with extra hours and a second job. I knew my clothing and food costs would be minimal; nevertheless with these expectations, I didn't want to look at any apartments that were priced more than $550/month.

I narrowed the list to six different ads, hoping that I could check them all out that day, if necessary, but also knowing I still had six days to stay at The Alameda, so I didn't have to panic if I didn't find something the first day. I wanted ads that said a stove and fridge were included (no more Meg-Anns, please!), but I was willing to look at either efficiency units or one-bedroom apartments. I wanted an efficiency unit if it would be cheaper, but I also wanted a separate living/eating area if I thought I could afford it.

After yesterday's disaster, I was determined to do my initial searching by phone. This time I would ask more questions on the phone before wasting time riding the bus to various places.

I didn't want to disturb the other library patrons, and so I stepped out into the foyer to make my first call. I took the classified section of the paper, my backpack, and the street atlas with me but left the rest of the newspaper spread out on the library table to unofficially stake a claim to my spot there.

The ad for the first place on my list made the place sound too good to be true – high-rise, great view, convenient location, modern efficiency, etc. etc. $575/month, but I'd try to stretch myself if necessary and if it worked out. So I called.

"Remington Arms," said the voice at the other end of the phone. "How may I help you?"

I smiled to myself, thinking about the name of the place. "Remington Arms! Hah!" but I didn't say anything about it. Instead, I answered, "Yes," and I immediately felt foolish for having said "Yes" when she hadn't asked, "May I help you?"

I quickly went on, "I'm calling about the efficiency apartment you have advertised in the paper."

"Yes?" she replied. "Which one is it you're interested in?"

Huh? I had just said "efficiency". Oh well.

"The efficiency unit for $575." I said.

"Okay. What can I tell you about it?"

"It has a stove and refrigerator, right?"

"Yes. But the bathroom has only a shower. No tub."

"That's fine with me. What utilities are included?" I asked.

"Water."

Dead silence.

"Just water?" I asked.

"Yes. You pay for your own electricity, cable, and phone."

"I see. Thanks. I'd better keep looking then," and I hung up.

I saw no reason to waste much more time with her. The apartment already would have been a stretch for me at $575 if the electricity had been included but the electricity for air conditioning, cooking, the fridge, lights, and heat would probably cost me somewhere between $30-$50 a month, and I hadn't even confirmed that the unit **had** air conditioning.

I walked back to the library table feeling just a bit disappointed even though I knew I shouldn't be. I had shot too high and had to get real with my expectations.

"That's okay," I consoled myself. "I sorta figured some places wouldn't work out. Just as well that I called first."

The next call was to a $500/month one-bedroom sublet, all appliances and utilities included. I probably should have called this one first. The woman who answered the phone sounded quite pleasant.

"We're moving to Texas," she told me, "and we need someone to take over our lease. If you like it, then you can continue at $600/month when our lease expires in five months."

Oops. That sounded very tempting, and I realized I might very well be able to afford $600/month after five months, and so I pursued it with another question, "Are all the utilities included in that higher rent under the lease?"

"No," she said. "Our utilities run about fifty to seventy dollars a month."

Muted groan.

"Well, I think I'd better keep looking, then." I said. "I don't really want to commit to spending that much. Thanks anyway."

I hung up quickly, once again pleased and relieved that I had called and gotten all the information I needed without wasting a lot of time traveling to see the place. Back to the classifieds.

Next up: a $450/month one-bedroom apartment. Not much information about it in the ad, but something about it caught my eye .... Ah, yes, "...convenient location, utilities included..." appealed to me.

"Four-Star Apartments," said the woman who answered the phone.

"Hi," I said. "I'm interested in the one-bedroom apartment you have advertised in the paper."

"It's $450/month including heat, water, and electricity" she said. "Let's see...." The sound of clicking a keyboard. "That unit comes with a small four-burner stove and a small but full-sized refrigerator. We need first and last month's rent plus a $200 damage deposit."

So far so good, and I was pleased that she offered so much information.

"I'd like to come by and look at it," I said. "Is it available to look at now?"

Hesitation..... some keys clicking. "I can show it to you this morning," she said. The current tenants are leaving next week, but they're both at work this morning."

"Great!" Perhaps I was a bit too enthusiastic? "Where are you and what's the nearest cross-street? I'm new in town, and I'm using a street atlas to figure out locations and the bus routes."

"New in town, huh? Do you have any references you can provide us with?"

Oh, oh! I was dreading this.

"Not really. I'm paid up for the next week at The Alameda, though, and I can give you post-dated checks for the rent for the duration of the lease."

"I'm sorry, sir." I noted the cold formality in the tone. "But we need some references."

I just hung up. Didn't say good-bye or anything. I was upset, and yet I understood their position.

As I had thought earlier, I figured that maybe if I could talk to the landlord or supervisor in person, I might have a better chance. So, no more telling people I was new in town, at least not on the phone.

It was only 10:30 in the morning. I told myself there was no need to panic. I still had six days that I had paid for at The Alameda and I could stay there longer, if necessary. I had $600 in my checking account, over $600 in cash, plus over $3700 left in my nest egg.

I stepped outside for a few minutes. I really needed to calm myself down. I didn't know when I had ever had so many failures in a row in my lifetime – four straight places that didn't work out for one reason or another.

I'd had better luck looking for a date for the senior prom in high school.

I went back inside. Someone was sitting in my chair, reading my newspaper. Grrrr. A bad omen, I thought, even though I don't believe in omens.

I convinced myself it didn't really matter. I had the classifieds with me, along with my street atlas and my backpack. I told myself to relax, and I sat at a different table, re-opened the classifieds, and renewed my search.

The next place on my list sounded just about as good as the last one, so I called and made an appointment to see it at 11:30. When I got the address, I looked it up in the street atlas. Frig. It was on the south side of the river.

Oh well...I figured I could start by taking the Skyway back across the river and get help from the transit office back there. There's a Skyway stop at Hemming Park, just a block from the library through Hemming Park, and the street atlas was pretty good about showing bus stops. I just didn't know for sure which bus to connect with and where.

Skyway. Help from the transit office. Bus. No problem. In no time, I was on a bus headed down Phillips Drive.

There seemed to be lots of businesses along Phillips Drive. I took that as a good sign – increased odds for quickly finding a job nearby.

I made it there by 11:20. The apartment building was just off Powers Avenue, near University Boulevard --- a large, sprawling three-story walk-up building, with the manager's office just inside the front door on the main floor.

"Hi. I'm Carl Jacobs. I called awhile ago about the apartment you have for rent?" Again, I let my voice rise at the end, questioning just a bit, indicating that I was a bit unsure whether I was in the right place and (horrors) whether the unit was still available.

"Hi, Carl," said Louise. At least the name plaque on the desk said that was her name. "I got the key ready here, so we can go on up now to look at the apartment. It's on the third floor. Are you okay with that?"

She looked at my physique, or lack thereof, as she asked.

"No prob,..." I started to say, but tried to stop myself. At least I didn't add "Bob".

"That should be fine." I added, touching my neck with my left hand. And then to myself, "C'mon Carl, this will be great for conditioning and weight loss."

I tried to hide the fact that I was a little out of breath after going up just two flights of stairs. Either Louise didn't notice or she was politely pretending not to notice.

It was pretty much what I'd been looking for: bedroom, full bath, and combination living room and eating area with a kitchen at one end.

"This is just what I was looking for," I told Louise. "What's the rent again?"

"450," she replied. "You'll have to pay for your own cable and phone, if you want those. Twenty dollars extra to rent an air conditioner and to cover the extra electricity for using it, but we'll install it and maintain it for you."

I tried the faucets, flushed the toilet, made sure the refrigerator was cold and made ice cubes, looked out the windows, and checked out the closets.

"Are the curtains included?" I asked.

"Not from us, but you can probably buy the curtains and maybe even some of their furniture if you're interested. She's been transferred overseas, and he's going with her. They've gotten rid of most of their stuff by now, and this is pretty much all that's left."

I looked around again. It was pretty sparsely furnished. That suited me. I wasn't thrilled about the $20 add-on for air conditioning, but overall the place seemed pretty good.

"What about laundry?" I asked.

"There's a 24-hour laundromat just two doors up the street," Louise said. "If you want the unit, you can't move in until next Wednesday.

They're moving out this weekend, and we always like to clean up and go over the place before a new tenant comes in."

That would be perfect. I was paid up at The Alameda until next Thursday.

I looked around yet again and imagined the apartment as my new home for the next how-many years. I liked the feeling. I also liked that I had passed hundreds of businesses on my way there and should be able to find a job in the area.

"I'll take it," I said.

"Great," said Louise. "Let's just go back downstairs and complete the paperwork. I can give you the phone number of the people who will be moving out, too, so you can call them about buying their furniture and curtains, if you're interested in those items."

It was a standard lease form. Louise filled in the rent as $500/month plus a requirement that I pay the first and last month's rent plus a $300 damage deposit plus the rider for $50/month for the air conditioner.

I was stunned and angry, but I tried to hide it.

"These aren't the numbers we agreed to upstairs," I objected somewhat tentatively.

"Oh, I'm sorry!!!" she replied. "Those are the rack rates for someone who is renting month-to-month. The rates I quoted upstairs are for a one-year lease." And with that she looked at me questioningly, as if to ask, "You do want this on a one-year lease, don't you?"

"Oh, I see," I nodded. I didn't like that approach – quote me one price without specifying what it meant. But then I probably should have asked, too. "Yes, I'd like a one-year lease," I added. I looked at her skeptically. How does one do that? I don't know, but I felt it, and I'm sure she did, too. I cocked one eyebrow slightly.

Louise ripped up the old form and filled out the new one correctly. I noted that the lessee was Geneses Properties and wondered who they were and why they had such a weird, plural-sounding name. Lots of startups, maybe?

The bottom of the form asked for my phone number; I had to turn my phone on to copy it. Then it wanted previous addresses. I probably shouldn't have done this, but I said, "Louise, I'm new in town. I'm staying at The Alameda. I can list that address if you like. And I can give you the address of the mailbox rental I have set up."

She hesitated. "Well…. I'm not sure."

And then I saw the lines for names and addresses of references. My stomach churned a bit. I just drew a diagonal line through that section.

"You can't do that!" Louise said. "We need the references or else Head Office won't approve the lease!"

"Louise," I smiled, priding myself for not saying 'Geez Louise.' "I told you, I'm new in town. I have no references except Ted Fry at Everbank and Bubba Smith at The Alameda, and they don't know beans about me. I can give you their names and leave you with post-dated checks for the rent for the entire year, if that will help."

She looked extremely wary. It suddenly dawned on me that she was less worried about me and whether I was a scoundrel than she was about what would happen to her if she didn't follow the outlined company procedures.

"I can't do that," she said. I think she was genuinely sorry, but she adopted a very formal bureaucratic tone as she said it.

I was both frustrated and livid. I had wasted a couple of hours, and I was right back where I had started. I stormed out of the office and strode angrily toward the bus stop.

As I reflected, I knew it hadn't really been a complete waste of time. I had learned that $470/month for a decent one-bedroom air-conditioned apartment was actually within the realm of possibilities. I had also learned, after two mishaps, not to say I was new in town. I would also, from now on, list my mailbox address as my current address without saying it was a rental mailbox, and I would list Ted and Bubba as references, expecting that most places wouldn't bother to check references anyway.

There were several park-like areas along Phillips Drive. I found a bench in the shade in one of them to settle down, eat my rice-cake-peanut-butter sandwich and vegetables, and drain my water bottle. The stress of not knowing where I would live was getting to me, and I had to control that stress. I had been in town for only a little over a day, and I was making good progress. Part of the search process, I reminded myself, involves considering things that don't work. I was learning. Things would work out.

I actually laughed to and at myself: "After all if I had found a place to live on my first attempt, I probably would have missed lots of opportunities and lots of information."

I felt like stretching out on the park bench and dozing again, but I resisted the urge. Instead, I opened the classifieds and began my rental search with a slightly different perspective. I'd had the right idea initially when I went to look at Meg-Ann's place – rent from someone private, let them look me over, and be nice. In my hopes of finding a modern anonymous place in a modern anonymous apartment building, I had forgotten that strategy.

I looked back over the classifieds and was intrigued by the trailer ad I had seen the previous morning. Two bedrooms, all included, only $300/month.... and located next to a cemetery according to the waitress I showed the ad to at breakfast yesterday. I wondered if it had been rented yet, and if not, why not. I figured it would be iffy, but it might be iffy in ways that I could accept.

I called the number.

"Hello?" said a woman's voice. Good. A private rental. Otherwise the woman would have said the company's name when she answered.

"Hello," I said. "My name is Carl Jacobs and I am calling about your trailer for rent."

"Oh, good," she said. "What can I tell you about it? It's only eight by 36, and the second bedroom is more like a crib-sized room or really a storage room. I don't want to mislead you about it."

I liked what I heard, and I liked the way she said it. I loved her honesty and under-selling of the trailer, but it made me wary, too.

"That sounds ok so far. What about the appliances?"

"It has a kitchenette at one end of the living area with a big under-counter fridge and an eighteen-inch oven and stove. It's ok for one or maybe two people, but I wouldn't want to raise a family there."

For some bizarre reason, it occurred to me to ask, "Where's the hot water heater?"

"It's in a cabinet in the bathroom. The tub is trailer-sized – less than four feet long. It's fine for bathing a child, but otherwise you just use the shower."

It was still sounding ok.

"What about air conditioning?" I asked. "I gather trailers can get pretty warm in the sun."

"You're darned tootin' they can get warm in the sun. The trailer's mostly in the shade, but it still gets mighty hot. There's a small air conditioner included for now, but if it ever gives out, you'll have to buy your own after that."

"You'll" not "You'd". The switch from the subjunctive seemed significant to me, as if she was assuming I would rent it.

It all sounded okay to me.

"It sounds as if the place might be what I'm looking for. Would it be okay if I have a look at it today?"

"Sure. I can't be there before three, though."

I looked at my watch. It was 12:30.

I started to say, "No problem" but caught myself with only a very slight hesitation. "That should be fine," I said instead. "What's the address?" I just wanted to confirm the address that was in the ad.

She said that the trailer was on Main Street, North, and gave me the address of the trailer park. The address amused me since I had listed Main Street as my address when I rented the mailbox the previous day.

"The trailer is on lot 27 at the back," she added. "Actually it's closer to Hubbard Street," she almost half-giggled it seemed, as she said that.

"That'll be fine." My new phrase, I guess. For now anyway. "I'll be there by 3pm for sure."

She asked for my name again and said, "I'm Evelyn Krochuk. I'll see you at 3. Thanks."

She seemed awfully pleased that I was interested in the trailer. I figured there must be something wrong, but I couldn't imagine what. Maybe loud neighbors? Maybe no parking? Maybe broken windows and doors? After all my previous failures, I could conjure up all sorts of potential problems.

I caught a bus along Phillips Drive and took it back up to Atlantic Boulevard, where it was just a few blocks walk to The Alameda. There I showered again and changed back to the clothes Maddy had bought me up in Newark. I wanted to look presentable in my khakis and golf shirt. Then I thought maybe the golf shirt was too much, so I put on the cheap sport shirt I had bought at the bargain shop up there. It was clean and looked ok, but not too spiffy.

I thought about leaving my backpack at The Alameda, but decided not to risk it. There was just no good reason to take a chance that someone might nose around and find the old cellphone, the watch, and the laptop. Before leaving, I refilled my 7-up bottle and checked my hair and face.

My hair! As if I had any. I touched my neck as I corrected myself: I checked my head and face. I figured I still looked okay and set off.

I walked up to the Skyway and took it back across the river to downtown, where I caught a bus going north on Main Street.

* * *
**

Chapter 18 – *The Trailer Park*

All along Main Street, North, there were chain and non-chain restaurants, auto supply stores, health specialty clinics, and myriad other small businesses. As the bus neared the address of the trailer park, we passed monument shops, funeral parlors, and a couple of small religious chapels. And there it was, on the right: the trailer park. It seemed crammed with older trailers, but that was just an impression I got as we went past it.

It was only 2:15, so I stayed on the bus for a few more blocks, checking out the businesses and the neighborhood. The housing I could see looked like what I had seen in middle-to-lower-middle-class neighborhoods everywhere: extra cars, some dumps, but mostly well-cared-for lawns and small homes.

A few blocks later I saw a shopping plaza with a good-sized grocery store. Bonus! There was some shopping available within a few blocks. There had also been at least two different laundromats in the past few blocks, so things were looking up. I got off the bus at the plaza and walked over to look at the shops. There was a pizza place, the grocery story, a pet food shop, a Dollar Bill, … standard for small shopping plazas. I took a brief walk through the grocery store and had to control myself. I didn't want to buy things I couldn't carry easily, especially since I had no idea whether I would actually like the trailer or when I might be able to move in if it did work out. There was also a school and a huge discount store across the street, so shopping should be pretty good in general.

I walked back south along Main Street toward the trailer park, passing a liquor store, a convenience store, an apartment complex…. It all looked fine. Well, it looked as if it would be okay, anyway, but probably not "fine".

I turned in at "The Palm's Trailer Park." No Foolin'. The sign had an apostrophe there. I briefly entertained myself with thoughts about what the conditions would have to be to make that apostrophe correct. "Maybe someone nicknamed The Palm owns it," I mused.

Holeeee Crap! It looked like stereotypical trailer park environs: old, junky cars, rust stains on the trailers, unkempt lawns, etc. I was unimpressed. And then I reminded myself: "Carl, you are unemployed, you have no good job prospects, and you will be lucky to get a job earning minimum wage; also, you're a run-away, a deserter, and a liar. Don't ever think you are too good for something like this."

I swallowed. Looked straight ahead. Kept walking toward the back. Yup, the cemetery did indeed back onto the trailer park, and Hubbard Street seemed more like a car path for the cemetery than a real street. That explained, maybe, why Evelyn half-giggled when she mentioned it.

The trailer on lot 27 seemed to be in decent shape. It had very little rust on it, and the concrete step by the door seemed to be solid. I walked around it, and there were no broken windows and no obvious holes in the sides. Like most of the other places in the trailer park, the lawn was more dirt than lawn, but unlike most other places, the trailer had no skirt going to the ground. In fact it still had what looked like a functioning attachment to hook it up to a car or pickup, and the tires seemed to be in pretty good shape.

I wandered back to the cemetery to look around but turned back as I heard a car pull up and park alongside the trailer. It looked like a three-year-old Chevy of some sort, but I had no idea for sure.

"We don't pay for long-term parking," said the woman who got out of the car. "But parking here every once in awhile is okay."

She looked to be in her late 40s or early 50s, desk-job type probably. Nicely dressed, slightly touched-up hair, minimal but decent makeup.

Before I could ask what she meant about the parking, she put her hand out and smiled, "Evelyn Krochuk. Hi. Are you Carl?"

I smiled back and said, "Hi. Yes, I am." Slight pause. "Thanks for meeting me."

She started speaking a bit too rapidly, as if she wanted to get everything out and convince me, all at once. I was open to being convinced, but I was also somewhat reserved, at least inside. I still thought I might like the place, but I wasn't sure, and I didn't want to seem too eager. I also wondered why she was so eager to convince me.

"As the ad says, the rent is only $300 a month, and that includes everything except phone and cable, but it does include the lot rental and fees. I see you've been looking around. Shall we go inside and take a look?"

Before I could answer she had unlocked the door and gone in. She turned on the lights and then went straight to the air conditioner and turned it on.

"Well, here it is," she babbled as she turned toward me.

The trailer was warm, but not musty. It was clean, and there were no apparent problems that I noticed anywhere near the entry door or living area.

I didn't have much of a chance to take it in before she continued. " What do you think?" She asked too eagerly.

I didn't answer right away. Instead, I turned to the right to look at the kitchenette. It had a small sink, some cupboards, and the fridge and stove, as she had described them. I checked the fridge; it worked. The freezer had ice cubes in it. I checked the stove; it seemed to work, but it was electric, so I couldn't tell right away. The water worked, and the drain worked. It was a functional eight-foot kitchen area against the front wall of the trailer, with a tiny curtained window over the sink. There was a small microwave on the counter, leaving not much workspace, but I liked it.

She was standing in the living area, clutching her hands nervously as I turned around.

"Nice, huh?" she asked.

"I like what I've seen so far," I answered cautiously. "Let's take a look at the rest."

"Sure," Evelyn said. "The air conditioner should have things cooled off soon." It was just a window air conditioner in the living room, but it was doing a decent job already. "The hallway goes down the left with the storage room on the right, then the bathroom, and the bedroom at the end."

As I walked down the hall, she continued, "You could maybe fit a crib or child's bed in the first room. It's only about six by six. I know, I know, we called it bedroom in the ad. That's because we thought maybe a young couple looking for a nursery might be interested in this place. Do you have any family, Carl?"

I side-stepped the question. The room was indeed about six by six. It had a window and a working ceiling light but no closet. It did, however have a closet rod that ran along one side. There was also a small dresser with three drawers in one corner.

"I might use this room as an office," I said. "Or maybe storage at some point."

Evelyn took the hint and didn't press me about family.

I moved on and looked at the bathroom. It was clean and tiny. A towel rack, a tiny pedestal sink, a small toilet, and the tiniest tub I had ever seen. I actually burst out laughing.

"I know, I know," Evelyn said. That seemed to be a phrase she liked. "The tub is weird and tiny. It's really just a shower. And I've seen bigger sinks in airplane restrooms."

I smiled. I liked the comparison. I flushed the toilet and noticed there were no stains in the bowl. I ran the water in the sink and shower and noticed the shower had a hand-held showerhead. In fact all the fixtures seemed to be pretty good quality. There was a small, mirrored medicine cabinet over the sink. I turned to move on to the bedroom.

Evelyn was standing in the doorway, blocking it, and I couldn't leave. It felt just a bit awkward, but after all it was a small, efficiency trailer.

She smiled, and I smiled back, feeling a bit embarrassed.

"How about I see the bedroom now?"

"Oh, yeah." She seemed flustered, but she had the presence of mind to back up toward the living area to make room for me to get out of the bathroom and move on to the bedroom.

I was surprised by the size of the bedroom. It was the full width of the trailer, eight feet, but it was also about eleven feet deep. It had a queen-sized bed against the back wall and a big dresser just inside the door. It wasn't cramped, but it was over-full, with not quite two feet of room on each side of the bed. There were matching nightstands on either side of the bed, and a big curtained window over the head of the bed.

The place would have suited Susan and me perfectly when we first got married. I wanted to call her and tell her to come down right away.

I made sort of a quiet grunt and touched my left hand to my neck behind my left ear.

"No closet?" I asked, remembering my discovery of no closet at The Alameda.

Evelyn was apologetic.

"I know, I know," she sighed. "Actually we used that second room as a walk-in closet. You probably noticed the closet rod there."

I caught that. She had said "We". She and someone else had used this trailer.

She had gone to the opposite side of the bed, leaving the way clear for me to leave the bedroom. I left the room and headed back to the living area.

"Let's sit in the living room and talk about it," I said.

I could sense she was tense and nervous.

The living area had a loveseat and a matching easy chair. Behind the loveseat, next to the kitchen area, was a small table with two chairs, one at either end.

I sat in the easy chair. I wanted a higher position, if possible, and it worked. She sank onto the loveseat.

I looked around again and smiled. I really liked the place, and for only $300/month, all included, there had to be something wrong. I wanted to know what it was, but I didn't want to come right out and ask what it was. So I eased into it.

"You used to live here yourself?" I asked.

Evelyn nodded.

"This was our getaway place, Don and me. He bought the trailer when he was married and we'd come here for our getaways." She tried to be matter-of-fact about it, but she seemed uncertain and maybe just a bit embarrassed.

"Then when he and I got married, we towed it all over the south. We loved taking the trailer to a park for a week or two, whenever we had a chance. But we're just getting too old to be hauling ass all over creation." She blushed a bit.

"Don's retired, and living here would be perfect for us, but he doesn't want to leave the house, especially with the steps here. I guess I understand. Downsizing enough for us to fit in here would be too much for him to deal with. But he doesn't want to sell the trailer, either, and I understand that, too. We both have a pretty strong emotional attachment to it since it was sort of our first home together. So we thought we'd try to rent it out while we take our time, trying to decide what to do."

"I see." I paused some more. I didn't want to rent a place that would be sold out from under me. But I had other questions, too.

"Evelyn, your trailer seems pretty nice. I hate to ask this, but why haven't others been knocking down your door?"

"Did you look at the other places here in the park, Carl? There are lots of run-down places in this park. In another park, we'd ask $500 and have them lined up to take it."

"Hmmmm." That made some sense. But it couldn't possibly be the entire story.

She could tell from my 'Hmmmm' that I was still doubtful.

"Also there's the cemetery," she said. "It's right there, and it spooks some people."

She looked at me with a hint of a question in her eyes.

"I see," I said again. "Is there a laundromat here in the park?"

"Yeah," she was getting dejected, "but you won't want to use it. There are at least two others within two blocks of here, and one of them is open 24 hours. ... Now that I think of it, maybe both are."

"It still seems okay to me," I smiled. And then a wild-guess thought occurred to me.

"Is the furniture included in the rent?"

Evelyn gulped a tiny bit. Then full-speed ahead: "I can include all the furniture and linens and kitchen utensils for another ... ten dollars a month."

"That's fine," I said, trying to conceal my excitement, and I gestured weakly around the living room. "Beats the heck out of what I have." Which was nothing, but it was okay if I didn't say that so long as she didn't press me on it.

She relaxed. But before she could ask me anything about my background, I continued, "Evelyn. I don't want to have to move again for a while after I move in here. Would you be willing to give me some sort of lease that would provide me with some protection? It would also guarantee you the income from the trailer."

"I think so," again she looked a bit nervous and confused. "I don't really understand all this, and Don doesn't want to be bothered."

She paused for a moment, and then seemed almost inspired.

"Maybe I can download a standard lease form from somewhere on the internet and print it out."

"Great," I smiled some more. I was really pleased. "How about I move in tomorrow?"

"Sure!" she was enthusiastic. "I can meet you here any time before ten. I can have the lease and the keys for you then. Don has physio at eleven."

From that, I inferred that Don had had a stroke or heart attack or maybe had been in some sort of accident, but I didn't want to ask.

She hadn't asked for references or anything about me. I prepared myself that maybe she would tomorrow and would have second thoughts.

"How would you like me to pay the rent?" I asked. I headed off the request for first and last month's rent and a damage deposit by taking out my temporary checkbook. "I can write a check for the first month's rent now and give you eleven post-dated checks for the rest of the lease tomorrow."

What was I saying? I wasn't sure I had enough checks. I may have promised something I couldn't deliver.

She seemed hesitant. I was beginning to suspect she had little idea what she was doing. I hoped Don was okay with whatever was going on.

"Will Don be coming with you tomorrow? I mean, if he owns the trailer, he'll have to sign the lease I think."

She shrugged that away, "Oh don't worry about that. He signed it over to me last year as part of our estate planning. I can sign the lease. And just to put your mind at ease, I don't really want to sell it... At least not yet. Maybe in a few years, but not now."

"Well, that all sounds good," I said. "Why don't we meet here tomorrow at about 9:30 to settle things up?"

Evelyn visibly relaxed. I got her to spell her name and wrote her a check, dated the next day, September 15, 2001, for $310. As I handed it to her, it occurred to me that this could be one big con job, and I probably twitched just a bit.

Evelyn looked confused at first. Then the light went on. "Oh, yeah, ten dollars a month for everything that's in here."

Bingo. I smiled again and nodded.

"Well, I'm glad this is working out," I added on top of my nod as I stood up.

Evelyn brushed against me and touched my elbow as she stepped past me and reached out to turn off the air conditioner. I realized then that the air conditioner, while small, was quiet and was good enough to do the job. At the same time, I wondered whether she had brushed against me on purpose. I wasn't going to think about that, though, and pushed the thought from my mind.

As we left the trailer, Evelyn looked around and then looked up at me. I hadn't really thought about it when I first met her, but she was likely only about five feet, two inches tall. I think I must have been as nervous as she was, not to have noticed it when we were both in the trailer.

"Carl, I don't see a car here. And you didn't ask about the long-term parking situation. I have to tell you parking's another ten dollars a month, and they'll get nasty about it if you don't pay."

"I don't have a car, Evelyn," I said with just a touch of sheepishness. " I have a bus pass and took the bus here." I hoped that my saying I had a bus pass would add a hint of stability.

She looked at me strangely and then smiled ever so slightly with a hint of coyness. "I'll bet there's a story or two in you to be told," she said. "What do you do for a living?"

"Here we go, again," I thought. "Get used to it, Carl."

"Well, I've done lots of different things, Evelyn." I added hastily with what I hoped was a reassuring smile, "None of them illegal."

She squinted her eyes at me slightly, "That's no answer, and you know it, Carl. But that's okay. I can tell from your check that you've just opened this account at Everbank. I'm sure there are stories and explanations there. I want to get this taken care of, though, so I sure hope you're not in trouble and not gonna cause me any trouble."

"Don't worry, Evelyn." I put on an accent of sorts. "I don't wahn no trouble, ma'am." and laughed, hoping to put her at ease.

It didn't really work. But she also didn't seem to care all that much. I opened the car door for her. Suddenly she reached out and touched my hand. Her eyes glistened a bit. I expected there were lots of stories in her, too.

"Thanks, Carl. I really need this."

I had no idea what she meant. I could make some guesses, but I hoped I wasn't being scammed.

* * *
**

Chapter 19 – *Preparing to Move*

It was nearly 4pm when I waved good-bye to Evelyn as she drove down the gravel laneway out of the trailer park. I ambled back toward Main Street, trying to take stock of the "neighborhood" I had just decided to live in. Some parts looked pretty seedy – rusty trailer sides, broken windows taped together, a dusty car with four flat tires, doors that looked as if they wouldn't close, screaming kids and screaming parents...

But other places were ok. Across the road from lot 27 was a twenty by sixty double-wide with a shed and a nicely manicured lawn. Next to it was a ten by sixty single-wide with an entry foyer added on. Others had added rooms here and there to their trailers, and nearly all of them had skirts, some with hinged doors and locks. I guessed that lots of people had lived here a long time, and they used the space under the trailer to store stuff. I couldn't imagine ever getting to that condition, given where I was at that moment, but maybe putting on a trailer skirt would be a good idea anyway, just to keep vermin from nesting under the trailer. I'd ask Evelyn and Don about that tomorrow. They seemed like the type of people who would have a skirt on the trailer, and so I surmised that they had stopped "hauling ass" with the trailer only recently and hadn't gotten around to putting a skirt on it.

On the way out, I looked in at the laundry facilities. There was water on the floor near one of the machines, and there was laundry stacked and piled everywhere. Apparently people would start their laundry and go back to the trailer but then not come back to remove the laundry right away so others could use the machines. I had seen that happen in the dorm at Kansas State. Anyone who wanted to use a machine that had someone else's clothes in it just took the stuff out and put it on a ledge or table if there was space available, but here it looked as if some had been thrown on the floor. That would be more than annoying, but not the end of the world. What would be even worse would be if people stole your clothes. I would have to ask Evelyn about that tomorrow.

On the bus back downtown, it occurred to me that the bank might not be open tomorrow, Saturday. Oh, oh. I would check to see if it, or any other branch of Everbank, would be open tomorrow. I really wanted to transfer another $500 into my checking account.

Checking account! How many checks did I have, anyway? I took out the plastic check holder Ted had given me. I had only eight checks left, and it would probably be weeks before my pre-printed checks arrived. I would have to explain that carefully to Evelyn. I would offer five more post-dated checks, with a promise to mail her the other six when I got the rest of my checks, in plenty of time to reassure her the rent would be paid. She already knew I was new in town and had just opened the bank account, and so she shouldn't be surprised by my situation. If she balked, I could give her as much as $930 in cash up front plus my eight checks, but she seemed considerate enough that she wouldn't force me to use up my checks now and not have any for the next few weeks. I didn't want to make this offer, but it would be a gesture that would probably help allay any concerns she might have. For my backup plan to work, I would need to keep another $400 in cash *if* I could find an open branch of Everbank tomorrow.

I got off the bus downtown and walked to the bank. The branch was still open. I looked for a sign with their hours. Whew, sort of. The branch I had started with was open until 8pm on Friday nights but it was closed Saturdays; however, the sign said there was another branch only five blocks away that would be open tomorrow.

I took a chance and stopped to see Ted Fry. He was just closing up, as I approached him.

"Hi, Carl. How are things going?" he said right away.

"Pretty well, Ted. I've hit a minor snag, though, and I wonder if you can help me with it."

Before I could continue to explain the snag, he interrupted with, "Sure. I'll do what we can."

"Well, I've found a place to stay,"…

"Great!" Another interruption. If Ted was going to network successfully, he'd have to learn not to interrupt so often. I tried to hide my frustration, but it probably came through to some degree.

"…and I've told them I'd give them post-dated checks for the year. I did that to reassure them that I'll pay the rent and that I intend to stay here in Jacksonville."

"Good plan, Carl. What's the snag?" He smiled. I was beginning to want to punch him. I couldn't take a half-breath without his interjecting something.

At the same time, I was glad he had interrupted me because I was talking too much. I didn't need to offer any explanation to Ted. "No more information than is necessary," I reminded myself as I touched my neck with my left hand.

"Well, as you probably know, Ted, I got only ten checks when I opened my account with you, and I've had to use two already, so now I'm down to eight. Is there any way I can get a few more blank checks for my account?"

Pause. He was new and he seemed nonplussed. I could see it, and I hated having to waste his and my time while he tried to recover.

"If you can't do it easily," I said, "Then let's just skip it. But if you have some kind of machine that can print more of them with my account number, I'd love another five or six."

I could see the light go on after I offered that suggestion.

"Let me look into it, Carl," he said. "Do you have one of the checks with you now?"

I dug one out and gave it to him. He looked at it carefully.

"This check isn't numbered. There's just a blank there for you to fill in the check number up here at the top. I think we can do this," he said. "I was just about to close up this desk, but let me talk to someone in the back office. I'm pretty sure we can take care of this right now. I'll either be back in a minute or in ten minutes," he smiled.

Ted was doing pretty well after all.

He was back in about a minute. I groaned inwardly, taking this as a sign that it couldn't be done.

"We'll have another ten for you in just a few minutes," he said, beaming broadly. "We can just run off a few on our two-sided color copier."

"That's wonderful, Ted," I said. "Thank you for your help and for sticking around to help get this taken care of. I really appreciate it."

"No problem, Carl. That's what we're here for."

I smiled both outwardly and inwardly. Outwardly because I was glad this was working out; inwardly because he had said, "No problem," which used to be one of my stock phrases.

I didn't know what else to do while I was marking time, so I picked up a brochure from the table next to his desk and leafed through it somewhat disinterestedly.

"Now that you have a place and expect to be here awhile, Carl, why don't we get you started on an Everbank Visa with us? We have a really good special now. You can get a Visa with a five thousand dollar credit limit AND you get a great rewards program."

I expected that a credit card application would need more information than I wanted to provide, and so I demurred. "I think I'd like one eventually," I said, "but not right away."

And then, in part to be nice to him and in part to see what they wanted to know about me, I added, "Why don't I take one of your forms with me, though. And just so you get the credit, when I am ready, I'll bring it back and give it to you."

"Thanks, Carl, but you don't have to do that."

"No..., that'll be fine, Ted," I replied. "And at some point, I should also probably get a bank card so I can withdraw cash or pay with the card." I couldn't believe I hadn't asked for one or been offered one when I opened the account, but I would look after that on Monday, after I was settled.

He went back to get the checks and returned with them. We compared the new ones with the ones he had given me yesterday to make sure the copies were acceptable.

It occurred to me that maybe I could put the trailer park address on the checks that were being ordered for me, but then I really wasn't sure. I hadn't met Don, and I hadn't signed a lease. Furthermore, I saw no reason to give Ted my address, and so I let it drop.

"While you're here, Carl, in just a few minutes, I can get you that bank card you mentioned. You'll be able to use it right away in stores and at ATMs to access your checking account. Let's do that while you're here. It'll save you a trip later and might come in handy over the weekend."

"Okay," I hesitated. "I guess that would be a good idea."

He put a blank card in a machine, typed in some numbers, and handed me the card.

"It's just a temporary card," he said. "We'll mail out a permanent one soon."

We said our good-byes and shook hands, and I walked to the central bus station. I wanted to celebrate, I was in such a good mood. Things had gone pretty well, so far, all things considered. I had a place to live that I could afford even if I didn't find a job right away, I had a phone, a bank account, and a bus pass. The only thing missing was a job, and that kept me from splurging on a celebratory dinner.

I sat back in my seat on the Skyway and relaxed a bit, probably more than I had since the first plane had hit the North Tower. I knew things weren't really settled, but I was finally confident that things would work out. Maybe in the next day or two, I could spend some serious time thinking about who I wanted to be and what I wanted to do with the rest of my life.

As I was walking down Hendricks Avenue toward The Alameda, I passed a small sub shop and went in. I had been moving a lot during the day, and I had seriously restricted my caloric intake, and so I ordered a deluxe foot-long sub with extra lettuce, peppers, olives, and tomatoes. This would be my splurge, my celebration for having made this much progress.

"Anything to drink?"

"Just some tap water, if I may."

In the past there had been a few times when I had replied, "Just water," and found myself paying for bottled water, so now I often said "tap water" to avoid that situation. I sat on a stool at a ledge along the wall while I waited for the sub and water, and then I sat there to eat it, too. It felt good to chomp down on a huge mouthful of bread, meat, cheese, and vegetables. Really good.

Maybe because I was excited, maybe because I was tired, maybe because I had already cut down on the amount of food I was eating.... Whatever the reason, I could tell after three bites that I wouldn't finish the sub there at the sub shop. So I wrapped up the rest, jammed it into my backpack, and walked back to The Alameda.

Ellen was back at the desk when I arrived. I knew it was a bit of a gamble, but I figured I'd give it a try:

"Hi, Ellen," I said. "I'll be checking out in the morning. I've found a place where I'll be moving. I was wondering whether since I'll be staying only two nights if I can get a bit of a refund on the amount I paid for the week." "Whether…. If". It conveyed my uncertainty and I hope some modesty.

In my mind, she had no reason to give me a refund. I'd paid for a week up front to get a discount. Also, I thought my asking now was a bit dicey since I didn't really have the trailer yet. I probably should have waited until after tomorrow to suggest it, but assuming things would work out with the trailer, I wanted to take everything with me tomorrow and not have to come back to return the key.

Ellen scowled. Surely she had dealt with requests like this in the past.

"Well, I can't give you a full refund," she said. "Here's sixty bucks." And she pulled three twenties out of a drawer and slid them across the desk to me. I wondered if I should negotiate for more, but decided against it.

"Thanks, Ellen. This'll be fine. I appreciate it."

I started to add that I'd need the money, blah blah blah, but then reminded myself to keep my mouth shut. Actually, I was delighted. I had thought it was a long shot, and I wouldn't have been very upset if she had said "no". Now I really did want to celebrate, but instead I went to my room, showered again and then ate some more of my sub.

It was Friday night, and the terrorist attacks had been on Tuesday morning. Even though I had been alone with my thoughts on the bus down from Newark, I really felt alone now.

As I sat in my run-down room in The Alameda, I was once again overcome with loneliness and grief. I had been so wrapped up in my escape and my journey that I hadn't emotionally anticipated all the loneliness ahead of me, even though I knew it would be there. I had known, intellectually, that I would be lonely, and I had tried to prepare for it several times over the past few days, but it hit me solidly now. I was feeling it, not just thinking about it. And contemplating the loneliness to come was overwhelming. I knew I would be busy tomorrow, but Sunday? I probably couldn't do much job search on Sunday, and I would be in the trailer, all alone.

"Well, Carl," I said to myself. "You thought this was what you wanted. Now make the best of it." And I forced my left hand up to my neck behind my left ear.

My family hadn't heard from me for three and a half days. I tried to imagine the grieving and the uncertainty they were going through, and I wondered how they were doing.

I decided that if everything went well tomorrow and I had the lease for the trailer signed, I would buy some groceries and then I would find a nearby library so I could use their computer to see how my family in Omaha was doing.

I set my watch alarm for 6:30 AM and went to sleep.

* * *

**

Chapter 20 – *Moving to the Trailer Park*

After years of waking every morning, at 6:30 Central Time, my body's schedule had really been thrown off over the past few days. Back in Kansas and Omaha, I'd had to adjust twice a year to the changes to and from daylight savings time, but those transitions went smoothly. The past few days had been different, though.

I had set my watch alarm just in case my body tried to sleep late. I wasn't sure how my body would work now, and I worried that I might have more nightmares that would interrupt my sleep. I wanted to get back to the trailer park early, if possible.

Good thing I set the alarm. I had a fairly solid sleep and woke to the beeping of my watch alarm at 6:30AM. No nightmares; at least none that I remembered.

I got up and ate some celery dipped in peanut butter. Then I showered and shaved. Ugh. It was such a bother to have to shave so much so often. Oh well, I would probably get used to it. I finished off the rice cakes with peanut butter and cut up the green pepper, carrots and the rest of the celery and put them in the rice cake bag.

The clothes I had worn to see the trailer yesterday were still in pretty good shape so I just put them back on.

Packing up for the move was straight-forward. Shoulder bag on the bottom of the backpack, clothes folded neatly next, then toiletries, then food, then re-filled 7UP bottle in a side pouch with the check wallet and cellphone in the front pocket. I was off by 7:15.

I gave the key to Bubba as I left The Alameda and thanked him for his help yesterday. Out front I turned slightly to say a silent good-bye to the place. It had provided me with a sense of security for two days, and I was grateful for that, and I was grateful as well to Thelma Alberts at the Y for having recommended it. But now it was time to move on... I hoped.

The walk to the Skyway wasn't bad, even with my backpack; after all, up in Washington I had walked several miles with it, and I had "hauled ass," to use Evelyn's phrase, with it all over Jacksonville the day before. I certainly had been getting used to walking more these past few days, and I was determined to keep that up. I could already tell my walking and dieting were helping because my pants fit better and I didn't have to struggle so much to get the belt to the second hole.

The Skyway was less crowded on Saturday morning, but it was still busy. This time I took it all the way to the end, the community college. From there, I walked to the Everbank branch that would be open later.

I shook my head and grunted at my stupidity. I now had a temporary ATM card. I didn't need to find an Everbank branch that would be open to withdraw cash from the Omaha bank; in fact I never did. Well, maybe I wasn't stupid after all... I could use any ATM to withdraw cash from the Omaha account, but I didn't really want to use even an Everbank ATM to deposit that cash. I probably could have, but I had always felt uneasy about depositing cash that way; I preferred making cash deposits in person.

At the ATM, I withdrew another five hundred dollars from my Omaha account and put it in my front pocket next to my wallet. I already had almost $600 in my wallet, and I didn't want to struggle to fit more cash in it.

Fortunately, this branch of the bank would open at 8:30; nevertheless, I was still left cooling my jets for the next twenty minutes or so.

I did some financial reconnoitering. According to my withdrawal slip, I was now down to $3357 in Omaha. I guessed the extra $157 was interest I had earned over the past few years, but I hadn't really paid much attention to the account. Susan had looked after the family finances for years, but I had pretty much ignored this account until September 11th. It was time for me to start paying more attention.

With today's withdrawal, I had nearly $1100 in cash. That realization made me very uncomfortable. I couldn't wait for the bank to open so I could deposit a bunch of it. I figured I would need only about $300 in cash from now on, assuming the trailer rental went through, and I could use my bank card to pay for larger purchases, like groceries and supplies.

There was a Dunkin Donuts next door, so I got a coffee there, and forced myself not to buy any donuts. I sure was tempted though! Also, I started drinking my coffee black. Every little calorie would help, I told myself. The place wasn't too busy this early on a Saturday morning, so I had a table to myself. I pulled out my check wallet and made out eleven more checks to Evelyn Krochuk, dating them on the 15th of each month, starting in October. I didn't sign them, though; I would do that in her presence, after we signed the lease.

At 8:25, I went back to the bank and joined the other two people waiting to get in. I was third in line, I guessed. And when the doors were opened, I stayed third in line as we queued up to see the only teller who was on duty that early. She still had some setting up to do, and I began impatiently shifting my weight from foot to foot. The way things were going, I feared I'd be lucky to get to the trailer by 9:30.

I was relieved: the two customers ahead of me were quick, and all I wanted to do was deposit $800 in cash to my checking account. Done and out of there by 8:45. Over to Main Street, North. Catch a bus ten minutes later, and at the trailer park by 9:15.

I strolled back to Lot 27 along the second laneway in the trailer park, again taking stock of the neighborhood. It seemed pretty much like the other side of the park. Kids were playing in the road; some trailers were in excellent shape, others weren't; and there were cars of all types from small Fords to a BMW at one place.

When I got to the back, two things struck me.

First, there was a funeral taking place on just the other side of Hubbard "Street", not more than about forty feet from Lot 27. I stood and watched for a few seconds, contemplating how I would feel with that going on frequently; and then I wondered if maybe they were burying the remains of someone who had been killed on 9-11, as it had come to be called. Hand to the neck. I was getting pretty self-centered and needed to stop.

The other thing that struck me was that Evelyn was carrying a box from the trailer to a big Cadillac. That concerned me. I wondered what she was having second thoughts about leaving for me.

So I called out, "Hi Evelyn!" and so as not to show my concern, "Can I give you a hand?"

She was clearly embarrassed.

"Oh. Hi, Carl," she recovered. "I'm just taking some of our personal belongings from here…so they don't clutter up the place."

I cocked an eyebrow slightly but didn't want to seem too suspicious. I just looked at her, waiting for her to explain.

She did, of course.

"Look, it's some cookbooks, a radio that Don bought when we first started coming here, and some of our cleaning and cooking supplies. Our agreement didn't include those, did it?"

I glanced in the box and smiled.

"No, of course not," I said. "As I said, can I give you a hand?"

"No, I'm okay. I'm just gonna throw this in the back seat, and then we can get to the paperwork."

I looked at the car. There was a person in the passenger seat, sort of slumped and looking straight ahead. I looked at Evelyn with what I hoped wasn't a nosy, questioning look but just a hint of a question.

"Don had a stroke three months ago," she said. "His mind is good most of the time, but he can't get around much, and he sleeps a lot. He's happy to doze there in the car while we finish up."

"Oh. I'm so sorry," I said, and I meant it for her sake. Now that I knew this, as I reflected on her demeanor yesterday, I could see that she had a lot to cope with.

"I turned the air conditioner on when I was in there, so let's go in and sit at the table to go over this stuff," she said as she picked up a thin briefcase from the car.

And then she added quietly to Don, "I'll be right back, Hon," closing the car door quietly.

And to me, "I know, I know. I like to say things like that to him, but I don't like to wake him, so I just say them quietly."

She was wearing very nice clothes – good-fitting slacks and a loose short-sleeved white blouse. I was wearing the same things I had on yesterday – khaki slacks from the sailing club and sport shirt from the discount store, all from Newark.

When we got inside the trailer, she stopped in the living area and turned to face me, closer than necessary I thought, as I reached back and pulled the door closed.

"Before we sit down to sign all this stuff, Carl, I want to tell you a few things. You've probably guessed that I have no idea what I'm doing. Don used to look after everything, but I've had to take over so much lately. His brain seems ok most of the time, but other times I'm not so sure. So I'm glad in a way that we did some retirement planning when we did.

"And as you maybe could see, Don is fifteen years older than me. For a 71-year-old, he was pretty fit when he had his stroke, but he can't really do much exercising these days. I have a sense that he is giving up."

I didn't know how to respond other than in my usual way. "I see," with what I hoped was a slight nod of concern and understanding.

It was a good response usually because it encouraged people who were nervous to continue talking, and Evelyn did."

"So you can do the math. I'm 56." Then she smiled a bit and posed. "Not bad for an old lady, eh?"

I smiled back, but felt a tad wary inside. I had no idea what was going on in her mind. She was right that she looked good, quite good in fact, but I didn't want to pursue anything. Pause. I nodded approvingly but resisted staring. Instead, I turned toward the table.

She went on quickly. "Well, enough of my sad tale," she said. "Let's get this done."

She took two copies of the lease from her briefcase and set one copy at each end of the table. The table was a cozy two-person table. It would certainly be good for me, and I pictured her and Don having breakfast here when they were younger. She sat down at the far end and gestured to the chair across from her.

The lease was perfect, specifying that she was responsible for all the existing utilities, trailer park lot fees, taxes, and maintenance, and that I was to pay her $310 per month. It also said the trailer was being rented furnished but that she would not be responsible for replacing any furniture as it wore out or broke. That was fine with me. There was no mention of requiring a deposit of the last month's rent as a security deposit, and no mention of a damage deposit. It had a nice clause that said we would talk about renewing the lease during the 60-90 day period before it expired. I didn't know what that meant, but I liked that she had included it because it indicated to me that she intended to lease the trailer to me for more than a year.

The lease copies had her name as lessor, her phone number and home address at the top, and she had already signed and dated both copies of the lease.

I dug the checks out of the pocket of my backpack and put them on the table.

"I'll sign the lease," I said, "and then I'll sign these checks for you."

I filled in my full name as lessee at the top of each copy, and by some stroke of sheer luck, I remembered my cellphone number and filled it in. She fidgeted a bit while I did all the signing. She put the checks and one copy of the signed lease in her briefcase and handed me two keys, but she didn't stand up to leave. She just sat there, slowly looking around and then at me.

It made me uncomfortable. And so, uncharacteristically, I spoke.

"I think the bank will take all the checks and hold them for you," I said. "Then they do the deposits automatically – nothing more for you to do but just check your bank statements to make sure everything is okay." I smiled. Reassuringly, I hoped.

She nodded a bit but didn't say anything. I felt awkward, and so after a moment I added, "Do you think Don is okay out there in the car?"

She had left it running so the air conditioning was working, but I was feeling uncomfortable again.

"Oh, he'll be fine," she said. "And he's got plenty of time yet before his physio."

Pause. No movement. She looked around a bit more.

"Carl, we never had a coffee maker here. I just want you to know I'm not cheating you. We always used a strainer with a paper towel filled with coffee grounds, sort of a poor-man's Melitta," she laughed.

I laughed too. Susan and I had done the same thing when we were first married, but of course I didn't say that. Instead I said, "Been there, done that. Two saucepans. One to boil the water, one to hold the coffee."

Nope. Still too much information. Also I didn't want to encourage her.

We smiled at each other. Then Evelyn looked at my backpack.

"Carl, I thought you were moving in today. When will you be bringing the rest of your things?"

"This is it," I said, somewhat shyly. "What you see is what you get."

"Good grief," she said. "What about clothes? Groceries? Supplies? Stuff?"

"I have some clothes in the backpack," I said. "But," and I stared at her very significantly, "I have no past. No stuff."

And then I relaxed my stare as I continued, ".... I'll get groceries and supplies when we're finished here."

She wilted under my stare. I think it frightened her.

"Okay, I know, I know," and she stood up.

She touched my shoulder as she went around me. I wondered if it was out of habit, the sort of thing she used to do with Don when they used the trailer. I stood up after she passed me.

"Well, thanks for everything, Evelyn," I said as she got to the door. "I know I will be very happy here for quite some time."

She put her hand on the door latch but didn't open the door.

"Carl," she looked up at me, "this means a lot to me, too. I know I'm clutching at the past, but I really don't want to sell the trailer, and I don't want to rent it to a young family who would do God only knows what to the place. And to be honest, I don't know what we'd do with all this stuff if you didn't want it. So it's working out real well for me, too."

She began to push the latch but stopped, pulling her hand back.

"My phone number is on the lease, Carl. Call me if you need anything, okay?"

"Sure thing," and I reached down and opened the door.

I walked her to her car.

"Oh. One more thing," I said.

She stopped quickly and had a panicked look on her face as if to say, "Oh no, don't do this to me."

I smiled again, hoping the smile was reassuring.

"Do you know where the nearest library is?" I asked. I started to explain that I wanted to use a computer there, but stopped myself.

"Sure!" Her relief was obvious. "The Brentwood Branch is just a few blocks that way," and she gestured sort of southwest. "Well, it's over on Pearl Street... that way," she pointed to the west, "and then it's actually about six or seven blocks south from there. Would you like a ride? We'd be happy to drop you there."

"No thanks," I smiled again. "I'd like to get settled here first and then go pick up some groceries and supplies," and I nodded slightly as I said, "... and supplies" and even got her to smile and chuckle lightly.

"I know, I know. Well, thanks again, Carl. I'm glad you're the one who answered the ad."

"Me, too!" I said with sincere enthusiasm.

I reached down and opened the door. It was cool inside the car. Don slowly turned his head, smiled a bit, and maybe even nodded ever so slightly. I nodded back.

"Hello," I said. "I'm Carl and I like your trailer very much."

Don half-smiled and mumbled something.

"Remember to call me," Evelyn said, emphasizing 'call', "if I can do anything for you," emphasizing 'any', and she reached out to touch me before she got in and closed the door.

I guessed that I could only begin to imagine the turmoil in her life. She was coping, but she seemed to be looking for something, too.

I waved as they drove away. She saw it in her mirror and waved back.

* * *
**

Chapter 21 – *Settling In*

I sighed after they were gone, and I paused for a few seconds. I stood where they had been parked and mentally marked the moment. I didn't want to pause too long though; I was eager to get started in my new home.

"My new home." Again, I felt melodramatic about it, but it was, after all, another big step on my way to discovering and rediscovering myself.

Both of the keys Evelyn had given me looked old and well-used. I assumed she had kept a key for herself, too. I'd be surprised if a landlord…. landlady in her case… didn't keep a key.

I felt as if I should somehow make a big deal about going back into my new home, my new beginning, but I didn't know how. I opened the door, stepped in, and closed the door. That was it.

I put my backpack on the table, took out the veggies, and put them in the fridge. It was an old-style, under-counter, apartment fridge – about fifty percent wider than a standard bar fridge. I checked, and the ice cube tray was still there, filled with cubes. I silently laughed at myself: apparently, Evelyn hadn't considered the ice cube tray "supplies".

Now where would I put the peanut butter? I opened the cupboard door on the right, over the fridge.

Well bless Evelyn and Don. In the cupboard were six plates and bowls on the middle shelf, some serving bowls on the top shelf, and some glasses, including four wine glasses, on the bottom shelf. The other cupboards were empty, and I put my peanut butter on the bottom shelf of one of them.

The stove was on the far left and it was mighty narrow. It had just two big burners, and it had a narrow oven, too. I'd never seen anything like it, and I hoped I would never have to replace it since I didn't know if such narrow stoves were still being made.

Next to the stove was the sink, which was also narrow, leaving about five feet of counter space to the right of it, some of which was taken up by the microwave oven.

There was a cupboard under the sink. It had a dish rack and draining-mat to go with it, but that's where I would keep supplies, too.

Between the cupboard and the fridge was a stack of drawers. The top drawer had what looked like six basic place settings of silverware in a container designed to hold the pieces, plus some serving spoons and forks. The second drawer had a spatula, a wooden spoon, measuring spoons, a hand-crank eggbeater, hand-crank can opener, a couple of old knives, and some measuring cups crammed together. The third drawer had a tea strainer and a larger "Melitta-sized" strainer. I smiled when I saw that.

I looked at the counter again. I knew that eventually I would end up leaving the dish rack and drain board on the counter most of the time, leaving very little space on the counter with the microwave oven there, too. I guessed that meant the table would be my workspace much of the time. I contemplated whether at some point I might want a small appliance cart to hold the microwave and maybe other appliances I might acquire, but I had no idea how I would fit it in. Or maybe I could build a small shelf under the cupboard to hold the microwave and free up some counter space. Anyway, for now this would do.

"Where are the pots and pans?" I wondered out loud. I looked in the drawer under the stove, and there was a stovetop griddle there, but no pans. I made a mental note to pick up a pan or two in the next few days.

And then as I turned around, I saw the shelf hanging from the ceiling over the table. How had I missed it earlier? I really needed to be more observant and aware of my surroundings. From the living room, it looked like a room-divider type of beam, protruding down from the ceiling about a foot, and I hadn't looked back at it from the kitchen. From the kitchen side, it was a shelf with a toaster, an old model crockpot, a large Dutch oven, two different sizes of frying pans, and three different saucepans. They were all old and without the modern no-stick coatings, but they would certainly be fine for now. I wondered how Evelyn reached them, even standing on one of the chairs, but I guess it worked for her.

I sat at the table and rested my head on my hands. I had been SO lucky. Even if things weren't perfect here, Evelyn and Don had provided me with things that would have set me back hundreds or probably thousands of dollars and numerous days of shopping time. Although some of the other apartments I had wanted to rent might have been nicer in some ways and more modern, this trailer was perfect for me at this stage of my re-emergence.

I leaned back and closed my eyes. I thought about the prospect of living here for the next 30 years. It suited me.

Next stop, the small bedroom/office/walk-in closet; I hadn't really thought much about what that room would be. Bless her. Evelyn had put a few hangers on the closet rod. They weren't there yesterday; at least I didn't remember seeing them. They were flimsy wire hangers, but they would be just fine for now. I didn't need fancy colored plastic hangers at this stage of my life. I would, however, want a few nicer hangers for my pants, and I made a mental note to pick some up when I had a chance.

I took the few clothes I had out of my backpack and hung up the grey cotton slacks I'd bought at the thrift store up in Newark, along with the cheap pants I'd picked up at the bargain store there. Those were my only other pairs of pants. Then I hung up the golf shirt Maddy bought and the blue dress shirt I had bought at the thrift shop. Those were my shirts. I had a bunch of dirty socks and briefs in the bag, and I threw them into the bottom drawer of the small dresser that was there, and I put the clean ones I had left in the top two drawers.

Mental note: buy pants hangers, briefs, socks, t-shirts, laundry detergent, and garbage bags. And as I thought about it, I'd also need dish detergent, bar soap, toilet paper, paper towels, butter, and lots

of low-calorie veggies plus meat and eggs. I took out a pad from my
shoulder bag and wrote everything down.

The bathroom was as it had been yesterday. There was soap at the
sink and in the shower, and a fresh roll of toilet paper. Evelyn must
have arrived quite early to go through the trailer and make it so
welcoming.

I put my razors, toothbrush, toothpaste, and antiperspirant in the
small medicine cabinet over the sink. In the corner of the bathroom
inside the door was a narrow cabinet. The bottom portion housed a
small water heater, and the top had open shelves where I would
store my paper supplies, extra towels, and backup toiletries, if I ever
acquired any.

The bedroom was almost exactly as I had left it. The only difference
was that there was a box of Kleenex on one of the nightstands that I
didn't remember from the day before. I looked through the drawers
of the dresser and found an extra blanket, another set of towels, and
an extra set of sheets in one of the bottom drawers.

I lay on the bed and closed my eyes. If I had been a praying man, I'd
have given thanks for being alive and for having had the good luck to
end up there. This "attitude of gratitude" would see me through, I
was sure, no matter what problems arose.

I looked at my backpack. It was time to take the shoulder bag out
and leave it behind. I hadn't detached myself from it since I had left
the hotel in New York City. I took out my watch and put the rest of
the shoulder bag under the bed. I used the multi-tool to pry off the
back of the watch. Then I took out the mechanism. I would drop the
back in a waste bin at the grocery store and the mechanism at some
public trash bin along the way. I wrapped them both in Kleenex, so it
would be less obvious that I was throwing away watch parts, should
someone be watching me. I would get rid of the case and strap later.

I took another look at the empty backpack. There was no way it
would hold all the things I wanted to buy. I decided to take it along

anyway. If I bought more than I could carry in the backpack and with my hands, I would take a cab home.

"Home." That had a nice ring to it. The trailer didn't feel like home. Not yet. But I did feel as if I was well on my way toward developing a new life for myself.

I looked around, left the air conditioner running but turned out the lights. I made sure I had my wallet with me (right front pocket) and one of the trailer keys (left front pocket along with my mailbox key). I closed the door, and walked up to the major shopping store, across from the grocery store I had strolled through the previous day.

As I neared a trash bin along the way, I took the Kleenex with the watch mechanism from my pocket, blew my nose into it, and dropped the watch mechanism in the trash bin. Outside the store, I repeated the procedure with the watch back.

It turned out the "major shopping store" was a discount store, but it didn't carry much in the way of groceries. I picked up quite a few supplies there though. It was difficult to resist the lower per-unit prices for many of the larger-quantity packages of things, but I didn't buy them: I couldn't carry them home easily, and I had no place to store them anyway once I got them back to the trailer. I had always known that "the poor pay more" because they don't have ready access to cheap storage and transportation; now I felt it. At the same time, I knew that renting a larger place with more storage space and paying for cab trips would cost me a lot; I was more than just okay with the higher per-unit prices and the small trailer for now.

With all the supplies I had bought, I had a full backpack plus four plastic grocery bags. I made it home on foot, but the plastic bags had cut into my hands and they hurt. Back when I was working on the farm, my hands were tough, and I could have carried a lot more without a problem. My hands were soft now, though.

I unpacked the supplies, drank two glasses of water, and took the vegetables out of the fridge to eat. It was only 11:30. I was now officially moved into the trailer and I was out of food. I had to kick myself, figuratively, or else I would loll about the rest of the day. I needed groceries, and I wanted to go to the library.

So I made the trek back up north along Main Street, this time heading straight for the grocery store. I loaded up on bacon, eggs, cheese, ground beef, and pork. I never could understand why pork is so inexpensive, even more so today when the good pork loins were on sale for less than ground beef, so I put the ground beef back. I also bought some plastic freezer bags and boxes for storing food in the fridge, and then I picked up a few cans of soup, some canned diced tomatoes, canned tuna, flour, sugar, butter, cheese, and a lot of vegetables. Oh, and two bananas.

It was a very different "first shopping" from the one Susan and I had done in Omaha the day we moved there. The comparison made me smile but also brought up some more painful loneliness.

I put the heavy items in my backpack and still had two plastic bags to carry home.

I had bought too much food. I separated the package of pork loins, put them into separate freezer bags, and put them into the freezer. After I put the groceries away, I realized that if I was going to use the crockpot much, I would want some milk or cream and some other really cheap cuts of meat. I would also want a basket to hang onions and garlic in. But those things could wait. I started another list on a sheet of paper: chuck roast, garlic, milk, rice cakes.

I started to fry some onions. Oops, I needed to use a saucer as a butter dish. I could keep that on top of the microwave maybe. Next to the dish drainer was a rolled up plastic sheet that I decided must be a cutting board.

Well, nuts. Where was the wastebasket for the stuff I wanted to cut off and throw away? I thought I remembered seeing one in the bedroom, but I couldn't find one in the kitchen. I'd have to get one, but where would I keep it? On the floor on the far side of the table behind the chair would be fine now, but where did Evelyn and Don keep one? I looked behind the dish drainer, and sure enough, there was a small wastebasket there. So they had probably kept the dish drainer on the counter most of the time, too, I guessed, and they kept the narrow wastebasket in the cupboard. I put a grocery bag into the wastebasket – it fit perfectly. I should have known.

I cut up an entire onion and an entire green pepper and put about two-thirds of what I had cut up in a plastic storage box in the fridge. I put the rest in the frying pan, into the butter I had melted there. After the veggies fried awhile, I broke two eggs into the mixture and added some cheese. People have always liked my scrambled eggs like this. The secret? Lots of butter and no milk.

I ate the mixture straight from the pan, standing at the counter. When I was ready to clean up, I ran the water, but it was tepid at best. I hoped it was warm enough and the pan was cool enough that it would be okay to soak the pan then rather than later. I found a nylon brush hanging inside the cupboard door and decided to just go ahead and wash out the pan. There were no towels for drying dishes or my hands, so I set the pan upside down on the corner of the sink and wiped my hands on my pants. I'd have to look at the towels in the bedroom dresser to see if there were any kitchen towels mixed in there.

Now I really needed a rest, even if I didn't sleep. I had walked quite a bit, and I had made more strides toward becoming a new me. I was nowhere near being completely emerged from the old me yet, but I was getting there.

* * *

**

Chapter 22 – *News from Omaha*

The bed felt good. Once again, I reflected and felt grateful for how things had worked out for me. I closed my eyes and may have dozed for a few minutes, but mostly I just lay there. I sensed an unsettledness underlying my gratitude. I knew I was moving awfully fast and hadn't really thought about who I wanted to be or what kind of life I wanted, but I still had so much to do.

After lying down for about an hour, I decided I didn't want to lie there forever. "Get up, Carl," I said. "Keep moving. Do something." And the something I had planned to do was to finally let myself find out how things were with my family in Omaha. I was grateful for how things had worked out for me, but how were Susan, Timothy, and Liz?

I looked up the library in the street atlas and decided to strike out down Main Street and then cross over to Pearl farther south. It dawned on me about then that a lot of internet search traffic coming from Jacksonville, especially from one location in Jacksonville, looking for information about Fred Young in Omaha might look suspicious, should anyone choose to look at browsing patterns and website hit patterns.

I decided to reduce this risk in several ways. I was already wearing my floppy bucket hat to protect my head from the sun, and I would make sure it was pulled down over my face. As I passed a variety store, I stopped in to buy a cheap pair of not-too-dark sunglasses, too. I liked the look, and with the hat on I was barely recognizable even as Carl Jacobs.

But I would have to be careful how I carried out my search, too.

First, I would open a yahoo email account. Then I would spend time on many different Midwestern newspaper sites but I would cut, copy, and paste articles from the Omaha paper to send to myself so I could read them more slowly, at my leisure, from any computer, without having to revisit the Omaha sites any more than necessary.

The Brentwood Library Branch was a busy hive on a Saturday afternoon. Children were there for some story-time activities, teens were there to work on projects (and to socialize, of course), and some older adults were there reading newspapers. There were only three computer stations in the back corner, and they were being monopolized by some young people who were pointing, gasping, and giggling with each other.

I approached the desk and asked the young man what the policy was for computer use.

"You just use your library card number. It's first-come, first-served," he answered.

"Is there a time limit? I mean how long do you think I will have to wait before I can use one?"

"Oh," he said, "It's pretty much the honor system. But those kids have been on the computers almost since we opened this morning. Let me speak to them."

"No, no," I hastily replied. "I don't want to intrude on their fun," meaning I didn't want to be seen as the adult who made them stop.

"Don't worry. Just have a seat over there and start reading a paper or something." He clearly understood what I meant and gestured toward the newspaper rack. "I'll let them know that they should be moving on just because it's library policy. Too many people are afraid to go up to someone on the computer and ask when the person using it will be finished, and so we try to sense when it is time to ask some users to move on, especially when it's teens who are probably just searching porn sites."

Sure enough, a few minutes later, after having spoken at his desk with several other customers who had various questions, the attendant went back to the computer area and spoke with the teens.

They seemed slightly embarrassed and not at all defiant. I gathered he had been through this routine with them and others many times in the past. They all knew what to expect.

The teens took their time, but over the next few minutes they shut down whatever they were doing, logged off the computers, and left the library. I waited a couple of minutes to make sure it didn't look as if I might have been the person who asked the attendant to move them out, and then I wandered back to the computers.

The teens had turned the three screens so they could all see each screen. I turned the one I was using back so it faced the wall and no one else could see what I was doing. There were instructions on a laminated sheet of paper on how to turn the computer on and how to log on.

I logged on and entered my library card number. It looked as if the library disliked Internet Explorer as much as I did. The computer gave me a choice of Netscape and Mosaic. I had not enjoyed Netscape at times in the past, but I preferred it to Mosaic.

First step. Create the Yahoo email account. Done. CarlBensonJacobs@yahoo.com.

Next step: Read the St. Louis Post-Dispatch, then the Des Moines Register, followed by the Omaha World-Herald. I lingered over the St. Louis and Des Moines papers to try to make it seem I had spent the same amount of time on all the papers. Starting with the Wednesday morning editions, their papers were filled with stories about the attacks. Generally, the local-interest stories were on pages two and three of the Wednesday papers: people from those cities who had seen the planes hit, seen the buildings collapse, or lost a relative in the attacks. I read the stories fairly carefully; they were filled with speculation because nobody knew for sure who had died. They had feel-good stories about people who were still alive, who had made it down the stairs, and in one case had missed her flight to New York City. But it was clear that identifying and confirming the dead would be a long, tedious process.

When I moved on to the Omaha paper, I kept my email tab open with a message to myself already started. Because I had already read the major wire service stories about the attacks and collapses, I just quickly scanned those and looked for the local interest stories, especially but not exclusively stories about Fred Young.

There, on page 2, was my photo and a story, saying that I had been at an appointment at Cantor Fitzgerald and the last anyone had heard from me had been an email to my wife before I left for the appointment. The community was shocked and horrified. My firm, Klein-Staily, issued a release saying they were all devastated and were praying and hoping for the best, that I was a valued partner, and that their thoughts and prayers went out to my wife and family.

Susan, bless her heart, refused to be interviewed and refused to let the children be interviewed. Ben acted as a family spokesperson, saying quite pointedly that there was no news about my fate and that there would be no family interviews until there was.

I block-copied the text and pasted it into the email. Then I block-copied other articles that might involve me and pasted them as well.

Thursday's paper moved me to page 4 with no photo. Essentially it said there was no news and that people (Who? Which people?) were fearing the worst. Once again Klein-Staily issued a formal statement about how valuable I had been to the firm and how much I would be missed. I noted the tense. It appeared that by Thursday most people had already accepted that I was dead. Ben added that he had called my hotel and they had confirmed that my belongings were still there and that their computer lock system showed no one had entered the room until the maid went in to clean later that morning. Man, was I glad I hadn't gone back.

Again, I block-copied that text and a few other stories and pasted them into my email.

Friday's paper said that multiple officials from multiple agencies were beginning to comb through the rubble of the buildings now that it had mostly cooled off. They were starting the process of finding body parts and personal effects to help identify the dead. I block-copied those articles, too, and then moved on to the current day's paper.

The Saturday morning paper really upset me. I saw a photo of Susan and the kids. Block copied everything that looked pertinent into my email, and then moved on to the Kansas City Star, where I spent another fifteen minutes or so reading various articles.

Then I went back and looked at my email and sent the whole thing to myself.

The article in that morning's Omaha paper was by a journalist I had never much cared for, Jeremy Hall. He was always probing people's personal lives, looking for dirt. Somehow, he had managed to isolate Timothy to ask him about me:

> Choking back tears, Tim [sic] said he didn't know how he would get over his father's death.
>
> "We all have so many great memories of things we did together – playing soccer in the park, singing Christmas carols together every Christmas Eve..."
>
> And he broke down, "What'll we do this year for Christmas?" he sobbed.

I wanted to punch Jeremy Hall. I put my head in my hands and used every muscle I had to control my sobs.

"Leave him alone!" I shouted in my mind. I actually muttered it, and then looked around. Fortunately nobody else was using the computers, and so no one heard me.

I wiped my eyes and read on.

The article also quoted a few of my former co-workers at Klein-Staily. They all said nice things, to a person, about how I had been innovative, creative, and a source of inspiration. A couple of them, especially Johnson, it seemed, made none-too-subtle comments about how "...we'll all have to pull together now to help the firm get over some of the holes Fred has left behind." Outsiders would think he meant my death would be a loss for the firm. Insiders would notice Johnson said "holes Fred has left behind," not "holes Fred's death has created in the firm." They would know that "the holes he left behind" was a reference to the mortgage-backed bond mess the firm was having to deal with. I guessed that Johnson had sought out Jeremy Hall, rather than the other way around.

Once again Ben spoke on behalf of the family. He berated the journalist who intruded on the family while it was grieving, he spoke about my dedication to my family and my work, and then he dropped a bit of a bombshell:

> "At Klein-Staily we have a generous life insurance plan for our younger senior executives like Fred. Fortunately, if it is appropriate to use that word at all in this situation, the life insurance is double-indemnity, meaning the benefits are doubled if someone is killed while traveling on work for us. Fred's family will be well-looked-after."

Holy Cow! I leaned back in the library chair to take this in. The life insurance policy with Klein-Staily was a declining-benefit term policy, meaning that while it would pay a lot if I died young, the amount it would pay would be much lower for people who died at older ages. At my age, the policy would pay Susan five million dollars ordinarily, which was plenty for her and the family for the rest of her life. But now she would receive ten million dollars! Wow! Prudently invested, those life insurance benefits alone would keep the family in excellent shape financially for the rest of their lives.

I was both shocked and pleased for their sake. We had other insurance policies, too, in addition to our retirement savings, all of which would help along the way.

Ben then added,

Of course establishing Fred's death for the sake of the insurance company might be a bit of a problem, as it will be for the all the grieving families of everyone killed in the terrorist attacks on the World Trade Center. We are confident, though, that because he wrote the email at 7:40am New York City time to Susan that he was going to meet with people at Cantor Fitzgerald, and since nobody but the maid entered his room after the attacks, there should be no difficulty in having him declared dead at this time.

Way to go, Ben! I smiled through my tears. He was already making the case on our behalf. "Our behalf?" Well, specifically on behalf of Susan, Liz, and Timothy. But also consistent with my plan, so on my behalf as well. And likely on Ben's behalf, too. He would be generous with his time and his advice, but I expected he would take at least a quarter of one percent for managing the funds when they were paid.

Ben concluded,

We at Klein-Staily are a close-knit family. We will make sure that Fred Young's family is well looked after no matter what delay they might have to endure before receiving the life insurance benefits.

I knew that would be the case, but I was relieved to read it.

Our local church had been very solicitous in trying to help. The schools made special arrangements for Liz and Timothy. The memorial service was scheduled for that afternoon.

I sat back and took a deep breath. Things were unfolding pretty much as I had anticipated they would. Susan had been more tight-lipped herself than I had expected, but when I thought about it, her stance made sense: it was her and her children's grief that had to be dealt with, and it was nobody else's business. I was sure she was furious with the journalist for having persuaded Timothy to say anything. At the same time, I guessed she was both upset with and proud of Timothy. Upset because he didn't tell the journalist to take a hike, proud because he said really heart-warming things. I hoped the same journalist would be knee-capped before the memorial service.

I felt sad that Susan had to go through all this, and yet I knew she could handle it all better than most people could. Over the years during our marriage, Susan had shown a powerful protective instinct for the family, especially the children. Part of that instinct included a desire for privacy. "Leave them alone, you jerks!" she would often shout at newscasts on television during which reporters shoved microphones in the faces of people who had suffered a recent loss. Knowing this made me love her more and miss her intensely. It also made me confident that the family would come through this okay. It was as if I had actually died.

I pictured Ben running interference for the family. He and I had always gotten on well, and I was delighted that he was stepping in to help as much as he could. I knew I could count on him. I could see him answering the door and explaining to Jeremy Hall, among others, that no, they couldn't just have a quick word with Susan. He might even have hinted at various forms of physical harm that lay ahead for them if they persisted.

At the same time, I pictured Johnson and his jealous crony creeps acting pious for show and then heading to the bar to exchange stories about how I was to blame for everything that had gone wrong at Klein-Staily in general and with their own sad careers specifically. They were jealous of my creativity and my success, and they cheered the farm mortgage crisis secretly even though it was hurting them and everyone else in the firm. Their jealousy was worse than annoying. I hoped Ben would shut them down and maybe even get rid of them.

It was four o'clock when I cleared the browser history. Holy crap, the things that were in there! Oh well, I shouldn't have been surprised.

The memorial service was taking place, right about then! Even though I hadn't been declared dead officially, it was clear that everyone in Omaha assumed I had been killed when the plane hit the north tower.

I would want to go to a different library tomorrow to read about the memorial. I stopped at the desk on my way out to pick up a flyer about the library system and nodded my thanks to the desk clerk. The brochure said that a few of the branches would be open tomorrow, Sunday, at 1PM, and so I would have to wait until then to get access to a computer again.

I decided to return to the trailer by walking straight up Pearl Street to check out that part of the area and then stop at the discount store and the grocery store for more food and supplies.

The walking helped some. It was so odd reading about myself in the past tense; and it was so lonely: I wanted to talk to Susan and the children, I wanted to be with them, I felt so dumb for having wanted to get away. I began sobbing, quietly, as I walked along.

While I was walking, my feet were getting hot inside my shoes, indicating I was getting blisters.

"Oh, oh," I thought. "I should have expected this."

I had been wearing my dress shoes constantly ever since I left Omaha on Monday. I had tried to be careful about not wearing any pair of socks for too many days in a row, but I really needed to get a decent pair of walking or running shoes. I hoped the discount store would have some good ones, not just cheap ones. And while I was there, I should get more socks, briefs, shirts, t-shirts, and maybe pants. And sunscreen; I had nearly forgotten sunscreen.

As I was walking up Pearl, my cellphone rang. It shocked the bejesus out of me. I hadn't heard or set the ring tone, but I think it was the standard marimba ring.. The caller had to be Evelyn. She was the only one who knew my number..... well the only one other than Mr. Gruff at the UPS office or the Kazzoo cell service, and I had no reason to expect a call from either of them.

I answered on the third ring. "Hello?"

"Hi Carl, it's Evelyn. I just wanted to see how things are going and if there's anything you need."

Evelyn needed to be needed apparently. So long as that was it, I was okay.

"Oh, hi, Evelyn. I think things are ok. I made lunch and didn't burn down the trailer," I laughed. And then I scowled.

"I gotta stop saying things that give away information about me," I thought. This attempt at a self-deprecating joke implied I didn't have much experience with cooking, which for the past ten years or so was pretty much true. But I didn't really want people knowing that or anything else about me.

Fortunately, she just laughed along with me.

"There are a couple of questions, though, Evelyn." I waited.

"Sure," she replied somewhat cautiously.

"I'm wondering about cleaning equipment," I said, hoping my mentioning this would reassure her that I would be an excellent tenant. "I mean something like a vacuum, a mop, a broom, a bucket?"

"Oh my. I never thought about those things when we were talking, Carl. I'm sorry. We usually just hauled along our stuff from home when we traveled. And I'm afraid we don't have any of those things to spare…."

"That's okay," I quickly reassured her. "I can pick things up as I need them. The trailer is in great shape now, so I can probably wait a bit and pick things up over the next few days or weeks."

Okay…," she seemed hesitant. "Are you going to be okay with that?"

"Of course I am. Evelyn, I'd have had to get these things pretty much any place I might have ended up living. You've provided more than enough for me already."

Again, I felt a wave of gratitude. I was glad Evelyn couldn't see me right then. I had stopped and leaned against a tree along the way, and was choked up a bit. I knew that the main reason I was choked up was that I had just been reading about, and trying to read between the lines about, my family. I missed them, and I cried for them. Evelyn's generosity just tipped me over the edge emotionally. I tried to hide that from her. I think I succeeded.

"Well, thanks, Carl." And then out of the blue, "And be sure to stay out of that strip club down the street."

She had a playful laugh. It would have been fun in the office, but it renewed my concerns.

"Geez, I hadn't even seen it," I lied. "Don't worry, though. I'll behave… Mom." I tried to shift the tone a bit.

Evelyn laughed good-naturedly and said good-bye.

* * *

**

Chapter 23 – *Exploring*

I walked on, making that my second trip to the discount store in less than four hours. From there I would go to the grocery store for a second time as well. I was really getting a workout.

I made a beeline for the shoe section at the back of the store. According to the measuring device that was hanging on a hook there, it looked as if I took about size 10 ½ or maybe 11. That's what my dress shoes were, too. I took a shoe off and looked inside to check. Yup, 11B. The odds of getting anything narrower than a D width at best were slim in a discount store. I'd have to try both 10 ½ and 11.

It felt good having my shoe off, so I took off the other one, too, and began walking through the aisles of the shoe department in my stocking feet, looking at the racks of men's running shoes. I grimaced. I didn't recognize any of the "brand" names, and I was not all that enthused with the apparent flimsiness of the shoes they had. I wanted something that would last reasonably well, but I had learned as a teenager on the farm that it was really important to have good-fitting shoes. I kept that in mind as I looked through the shoe racks.

I found six different pairs of shoes that might fit and took them to the end of an aisle where there was a stool to sit on. Trying on shoes after you've been walking and when you have the beginnings of a blister is dicey business. I tried to take these conditions into consideration, and finally settled on a pair of size 11 red "Excell" shoes with white trim. $19.99. I doubted if they were very good, but at least I could put in additional cushioned inserts, if necessary, to make them more comfortable. At least I hoped so.

I left those shoes on and put my dress shoes into the shoebox.

Next stop was the pharmacy section, where I picked up some store-brand versions of Band-Aids and some sunscreen; then on to the housewares section for some black shoe polish, Mr. Clean, and small packages of dishcloths and dishtowels. I knew I would want a broom, mop, and dustpan, but maybe those could wait a day or two when I would have fewer things to carry. But I'd want a bucket soon, so I picked up a rectangular one that could maybe double as something I could use now to carry my things home and use later as a wastebasket.

I also wanted to have at least one more shirt as well as more socks, briefs, and t-shirts. Off to the men's department, where I picked up a jumbo pack of a dozen pairs of socks, half black and half grey. I also threw a six-pack of grey boxer-briefs and six white t-shirts into my shopping cart. As I bought a white dress shirt and looked at the slacks, I remembered fondly some of the clothing I had seen in the thrift shop in Newark, and I wondered where the nearest thrift shop might be so I could pick up more clothing and maybe a few other items, like a used vacuum cleaner, a knife sharpener, and, it just occurred to me, some books.

I could barely fit all the things from the discount store into the bucket, but I made it, so long as I carried the shoebox in a separate bag. With any luck, I could maybe handle a grocery bag or two as well. I went across Main Street to the grocery store to see how much more I could buy and still carry home without too much difficulty.

I limited myself to buying only so much as would fit into one grocery bag, since I had my hands pretty full as it was. I didn't really want much from the grocery store anyway: just a pint of half-and-half, some garlic, more rice cakes, a small pork roast, and more peanut butter. And an orange. I had a hankering for an orange, no matter what the calories were.

They fit into one bag easily, and I was on my way home.

The concept of home for a place I had been renting for only a few hours still amused me and perplexed me. I had no idea how long I might last there, but at this stage I could readily imagine living there the rest of my life. At least I imagined I could imagine that. I hoped I wasn't lying to myself. Still, it felt strange to make such a dramatic change after living with a family in the suburbs for nearly two decades.

I unpacked my purchases, put away the groceries and clothing, and put the bucket on the far side of the dresser in the bedroom, the only place it would fit. The sunscreen, bandage strips, and shoe polish fit in the medicine cabinet in the bathroom, just about filling it.

It was nearly suppertime, and so I slowly cut up some lettuce and tomatoes for a salad. I fried up some vegetables in butter with a bit a pepper, and put the salad in a large bowl.

Then I sat down at the table to eat.

There was no conversation.

There was no radio, no television, no laptop.

Nothing. Just me and my food. I had never experienced such aloneness.

I tried to slow myself down. I had no reason to rush through my meal. I began to think about what I wanted to do next. I wanted to find out about the memorial service in Omaha. I also would like to find some more used clothing and maybe a vacuum cleaner. And I needed a job. I wouldn't let myself buy a computer or sign up for the internet until I had been on the job for a few weeks.

The next day would be Sunday. I would find a library branch that was open and use the computer there to read about my memorial service. With any luck, I might pass a thrift store, too. Job search would begin in earnest with the morning paper before I left for the library.

The more I thought about jobs, the more I realized I wanted a job where I could slowly move up, based on my performance. I realized I might have to start with just about anything I could find, but I didn't want to be stuck working several part-time minimum wage jobs for the rest of my life. I was probably dreaming, but that was my goal.

I looked at my feet. I couldn't really wear my new running shoes on the job search, at least not as I approached anyone about a job; and yet, even with bandages on, I didn't want to wear my dress shoes to walk any great distances during the next few days. If I wore my running shoes, I would have to carry my dress shoes with me. But my dress shoes were pretty messy and scuffed. I would have to polish them before I went out to visit potential employers. I would save a section of tomorrow's paper to put my shoes on while I polished them tomorrow evening.

As I was still slowly eating and planning, letting my thoughts wander, I remembered that I had the brochure from the library and looked through it to choose which branch to visit tomorrow.

Well phooey. Most of the library branches were closed on Sundays. There was one branch way down across the river that opened at 1pm. I decided I would go there. But how to get there?

Aha! I pulled out my bus pass and there was a phone number on it to call for help with bus routes.

"Now's as good a time as any," I said to myself, and I called the number listed.

"JTA," said a voice at the other end. It sounded bored.

"Do people actually work at cultivating bored voices for jobs like these?" I wondered, albeit to myself and not into the phone.

"Hello," I said. "I live at 40th and North Main and I want to get to the Southeast Branch of the Library tomorrow afternoon. Can you give me the best route to take and a guess as to how long it might take?"

"Tomorrow afternoon, huh?" the voice said. "We don't have a lot of buses out there running on Sunday afternoons, but you can do it. What time do you want to be there?" The voice was sounding much more helpful now, almost as if it enjoyed the challenge of helping someone.

"Well, I'd like to be there when they open at 1pm," I said.

"Okay...." Pause.... Pause. ... Pause some more with some keyboard clicking in the background. "I got two routes you can take, but either way you gotta catch the Main Street bus at 10:56. It's a long trip with several long waits unless you get lucky."

I had my atlas open, and my pencil and paper. I wrote down the two suggested routes and thanked the voice. And then,

"I know this might be a long-shot," I added, "but do you know if there are any thrift shops near that library branch that might be open tomorrow?"

"None that I know of," and then the voice sounded downright friendly, "but if you take the second route I mentioned and leave at 9:56, you can get off in the San Marco district. There are some good ones there that might be open. Oh wait, it's Sunday tomorrow. They might not be open tomorrow morning. Maybe you could leave the library early, then and get off the bus on your way back by 4pm to check the places out. There's some good stuff in a couple of them."

I thanked the person again and was about to hang up.

"Hold on a sec," said the voice. Pause again. Clickety-click. "Yeah, the St. Vincent de Paul Thrift Shop is on Atlantic. That bus route goes right past it. You can maybe leave earlier in the morning and check them out in case they're open. I like them. Their prices are good, and the ladies who volunteer there are nice. They don't always have the stuff I'm looking for, but they're good if they do. Wear old, grungy clothes, and they'll cut the prices for you."

"Great plan!" I said, and thanked the voice once again and hung up.

It was 7pm. No radio. No newspaper. No television. No books. Nothing but me and my thoughts. I puttered about the trailer, to the extent that puttering was possible in that limited space. I washed the dishes and dried them and put them away. I had never done all that before in my entire lifetime. I had shared doing the dishes with Susan, often, especially when we were first living in Omaha, but I didn't remember doing them all alone. Then as I reflected, I realized that of course I had done the dishes by myself, and often. It just felt different now that I really was alone.

I went to the bedroom and sat on the bed, leaning back against the headboard. I wondered what was going on with Evelyn and Don, but didn't ponder that too long. I knew they had saved me weeks of time and thousands of dollars I'd have had to spend shopping. I was really pleased about that.

I looked at the massive dresser and mirror at the foot of the bed. I could see that I had a lot of storage space there that I wasn't using. I had pretty much by default decided the small bedroom would be my walk-in closet and dressing room because I could hang my clothes there and I didn't have enough other clothes to run out of space in the small dresser that was in that room. So I figured I would store extra supplies in the bedroom dresser. For now anyway.

I was lonely. I was also bored. I think, too, that maybe I was afraid to go to sleep. Afraid of the nightmares I'd had my first night at The Alameda.

I got up and walked back to the kitchen. It was as if I was trying to escape from all the thoughts and feelings that had come from trying to escape my past life. "Weird," I thought. "Escaping from an escape."

Out of habit, I guess, I opened the fridge. There was nothing in it that I wanted to eat, not really, but I took out a stalk of celery to nibble on anyway. Good thing I hadn't bought cookies or nuts or ice cream.

One time when the kids were little, I stopped on the way home and bought some Joe Louies, figuring we'd have a treat on the weekend. But they came in a box of six, and there were only four of us, so I ate one right then. In the car. And then another, leaving four – one apiece. And then I ate another and another…. And another… and another. They were all gone and the wrappers disposed of before I left the parking lot. For some inexplicable reason I wasn't very hungry at dinner that night. I smiled with self-derision as I remembered the incident. It reinforced my determination not to buy any candy or cookies, knowing my severe lack of will power when it came to sweets.

I was still restless, and it was only 8pm. I decided to go for a walk outside to try out my new running shoes before tomorrow.

The trailer door had a spring lock, not a deadbolt, so it locked every time you closed the door. I would have to remember to take a key with me whenever I left the trailer. I wondered if Evelyn and Don had ever hidden a key outside anywhere in case they got locked out. I would try to remember to ask her the next time she called, as I was fairly certain she would.

At some point I might get a copy made and put one under the corner of a gravestone in the cemetery. I liked that idea, so maybe I wouldn't ask Evelyn about it after all. No reason to suggest I might hide a key. I wondered if anyone else in the trailer park hid a key under a gravestone. I wondered if maybe I'd find out, picturing the amusement I'd feel if I found someone else's key where I was trying to hide mine.

I put one of the two keys Evelyn had given me under the silverware tray in the kitchen and made sure I had the other one with me, putting it into the zipper compartment of my wallet.... Nope, not a good idea: if I'm mugged, I lose my key, too, meaning I can't get back in and also meaning someone else would have a key to the trailer. So I just moved it to my... let's see... left pocket. Keys on the left, wallet on the right.

Keys? Hah! I had two friggn keys: one for the trailer and one for my rental mailbox. I smiled as I stepped down, outside the trailer and shut the door behind me.

I wandered down the gravel lane. It was both more pleasant and less pleasant at night. More pleasant because I couldn't see the grunge, rust, and clutter at some places; less pleasant because I didn't feel particularly safe. I would have to get used to it.

I stopped in at the laundry facilities to check them out again. There was a young couple there using three washers at the same time. They smiled and nodded to me, and I smiled back. I had no idea how to break the ice with new neighbors. Susan had always looked after that for us.

There was a bulletin board near the door with lots of hand-written ads, so I spent some time looking at them. Some offered baby-sitting services, others offered cleaning services... hmmm, maybe that would be a good idea. Nope. I didn't want anyone going through my stuff, especially not until I got rid of the laptop and cellphone.

There were seven thousand ads for churches and a few ads from people who were selling things. I looked through the "For Sale" ads carefully to see if there was anything I might want.

Lego sets! I missed Timothy. I choked up a bit and almost had to leave the laundry room right then.

Mostly baby clothes, baby toys, and baby furniture. Used tires. A used television was tempting, but not yet. Not 'til I had a job and was better-settled.

I had walked north on Main several times already that day. So I went south.

Maybe I was drawn by the strip club, but I don't think so. Anyway, it was a Saturday night, and the place was alive with activity. I was curious, but not so curious that I was going to go in. I hadn't had much experience, sexually. I had been a virgin when I met Susan, and I had remained monogamous and faithful to Susan. We had tried different things and had enjoyed exploring possibilities with each other, but I hadn't really seen any naked women, except in some magazines as an undergrad and in some films at Chuck Frame's bachelor party. Man, what a bust that party was! It was not fun at all, but everyone seemed to think it should be fun, so they all whooped it up. I left as early as I could.

I'm not a prude. At least I don't think I am. I just felt as if lusting after other women was something I shouldn't encourage during my marriage, and I wasn't ready to start yet.

It was dark along the east side of Main Street walking south past the cemetery. But there was a visitation in progress at one of the funeral parlors, so I didn't feel unsafe. Even better, the running shoes seemed fine so far.

This time I tried to force myself to walk a bit more slowly, trying to take in what I was seeing. There were lots of businesses along Main Street. I wondered if any were hiring and wouldn't care about my lack of experience, credentials, and references. Finding a job could be pretty tricky; I would need a lot of luck. I kept an eye out for "Help Wanted" signs but didn't see any.

I walked under the interstate and kept walking. Forty-five minutes later I was on the northern outskirts of downtown. I realized I should have brought along some water and kicked myself for not thinking about it. I sure wasn't going to buy any bottled water for a dollar or whatever they might charge at some convenience store along the way.

It was nearly 9pm as I turned around and walked back toward the trailer, this time on the west side of Main Street. There were no places along the way that had drinking fountains, so I just kept putting one foot in front of the other, plodding homeward. Well, not really plodding, but walking steadily.

One good thing was that the inexpensive Excell running shoes seemed to be working out well. I would still probably want to get some sort of arch support at some point, especially if I ended up in a job requiring me to be on my feet much of the time. But now I had two pairs of shoes that were decent enough.

I didn't like being out after dark in an unfamiliar area, but walking back up Main Street after 9pm on a Saturday night turned out to be okay. It was reasonably well-lit and had a constant flow of traffic along it, so I felt reasonably safe as I walked along. I passed two different places that advertised "Keys Made". I would want to visit one of them early and soon if they weren't open the next day, Sunday.

Back at the trailer, I remembered to pull my key from my left pocket, unlocked the door, and went in. The little air conditioner was doing its job. The place was even perhaps too cool, so I turned the temperature control up a bit. But I left the fan on what passed for "high" just to keep blowing the cooler air around, hoping some would continue to make it back to the bedroom.

I drank a big glass of water and then sat at the table with another big glass of water. I pondered a bit. I would have to take my laptop out of my shoulder bag tomorrow to make room for lunches and water. I wouldn't want to head off to the library or on a job search without taking food and water. I could leave the laptop in the trailer in the meantime, until I found a way to dispose of it.

I took the orange out of the fridge and peeled it carefully. I ate only half of it, though, saving the rest for the morning.

I looked at my watch. 10:30. I went to bed.

* * *
**

Chapter 24 – *The Memorial*

I'm a human alarm clock. Well, I used to be, but the turmoil of the previous five days had upset my body, my mind, and my metabolism.

Saturday night was the first night in my new home. I slept pretty well, all things considered, going to sleep about 11 and waking about 5:30am. Again, no nightmares that I remembered, but I had a very unsettled feeling about everything I had seen at the World Trade Center. I must have dreamed about it some more, but I probably just didn't remember the dreams.

I knew I wouldn't go back to sleep, and so I got up and showered. The shower worked pretty well. It had enough pressure and plenty of hot water, but it felt strange stepping inside a small tub to take my shower.

Then I shaved. My face and my head. I was trying to get used to that. Maybe after a few months or a few years I would get used to having to shave so much all the time. And I had to make sure I kept an adequate supply of good razors around.

I made breakfast. It would soon become my standard: bacon, fried vegetables, and cheesy scrambled eggs. That morning I splurged and ate one of the bananas, too.

After washing up, I pulled the crockpot down and plugged it in. I had no idea what I was doing, but I put the pork roast, some garlic, some water, salt and pepper, cut up onions and green peppers, and about a cup of half-and-half into the crock pot and set it for low. I knew it would probably be overcooked if I didn't get back until 6 or so, but I guessed that overcooking a cheap roast in a crockpot would just make it more tender, so I was fine with that possibility. I looked at the mess and decided it needed some thickener for the sauce, so I sprinkled what was probably less than a quarter cup of flour over everything. If the liquid didn't boil away, I could add more flour later to make a sort of cream sauce. Or so I hoped. I'd had so little experience cooking anything in the past fifteen years that I was mostly going on hope and vague memories. Too bad Evelyn hadn't left a cookbook or two.

My supper was prepared and cooking. My next task, which I probably should have done first, was to make two more peanut butter rice cake sandwiches and to cut up some carrots, celery, and green peppers to take along on my trip to the library. I ate the remaining half of my orange, refilled my water bottle, and was ready to go, but it was only a little after 8am.

I left everything, checked my pocket for my key, and went out to get a Sunday paper from the convenience store that was just a couple of blocks north of the trailer park.

I was back in twenty minutes. I glanced through the main section. It appeared the federal government was giving millions to the families of those killed in the terrorist attacks. Susan would be **very** well-looked-after financially. My rough estimate was that she would have a tax-free nest egg of nearly nineteen million dollars, counting all the insurance, retirement savings, and government payments.

Ben would likely be well looked after financially, too, if he was the person Susan relied on to manage her portfolio. I hoped she would.

I opened the arts and culture section, put my dress shoes on it, and polished them. Liquid polish; wax was always too much work. They could dry while I was out for the day.

I glanced through the classified ads section and took out only the pages that had job listings. I folded those pages up and put them in my shoulder bag along with the street atlas, hat, sunglasses, sunscreen, water bottle, and my lunch, and I left to catch the bus.

I was an hour early at the bus stop, but I took that bus anyway. I got off downtown and withdrew another five hundred dollars from my Omaha account. With all my spending the previous day, I had gotten pretty low on cash. After that withdrawal, I had only $2857 in my Omaha account and about $550 in my wallet. I didn't want to carry that much cash with me, and so I decided to take a chance and deposit another $300 into my Everbank account, using their bank machine. I also would start using my temporary Everbank bank card for purchases now whenever it was possible.

The next bus took me across the river and down along the highway. I got off at the next stop after we passed the St. Vincent de Paul thrift store and walked back to the store. They wouldn't be open until 1pm, as I expected, but it was fun window-shopping anyway. I saw some furniture that might have been nice if I had ended up renting an unfurnished apartment. There were also lots of outdated electronic things, like tape players and old black-and-white television sets. It looked as if they had several aisles of men's clothing in the back, and so I would be sure to stop there on the way home.

I walked for a few blocks instead of catching the next bus. It wasn't even 10am and the library branch wouldn't open until one. Maybe I would walk the rest of the way, just following the bus route I had been given the night before.

When I came to a coffee shop, I went inside, bought a coffee, and sat at a table where I could spread out the newspaper to look at the job ads.

Now I had to decide what I would look for:

- There were lots of ads for temporary labor to do yard work. No thanks. Only if I became desperate.
- A car wash attendant. Maybe.
- About ten ads for places looking for overnight help at convenience stores. Quite possible.
- Several local manufacturers looking for skilled tradesmen. Nope. No skills, no references.
- Banking jobs. I probably couldn't get one without references, and I didn't really think it would be smart for me to go back into the banking or related businesses.
- Auto mechanics. Nope, didn't have the skills.
- Delivery drivers. No car, no driver's license.
- Line cook. Maybe.

- Warehouse night shift; quite a few jobs it seemed. Possible.
- Sales jobs. I doubted it, but it would depend on the product and the market; certainly not if the job required bonding or driving.
- Cleaning, janitorial work in buildings. Another good option maybe.
- Construction helpers. Maybe, but likely not permanent.
- Lifeguards. Hah! No chance.
- Busboys. Maybe as a second job.

It looked as if the best options would be night shift work. Understandably, most people didn't want to work nights, meaning more of those jobs might be available for me. That would be okay for now. Also, the night shift usually paid better. I could maybe supplement with work in a restaurant or as a custodian somewhere. I circled the ads that looked most promising and walked on from the coffee shop, following the bus routes toward the library.

It was still early and so I just kept walking. About forty minutes later I saw another thrift shop, the Hubbard House. Like St. Vincent, it wouldn't be open until 1pm, but also like St. Vincent it seemed to have a lot of potentially useful things. I would stop there on my way back, in addition to my planned stop at St. Vincent.

While I was there, I looked at my street atlas and saw that I could save about a half mile or so by taking a diagonal road on my walk. This route took me past a park, too, where I sat on a bench and ate my rice-cake-peanut-butter sandwiches and vegetables. I finished the water from my water bottle and hoped I could find a drinking fountain before I got to the library. If not, I would rehydrate there.

I sat for awhile after eating and then plunged on toward the library. My new running shoes were doing fine. And I was pretty sure I had already taken an inch or two off my waistline. I put on some sunscreen, adjusted my hat, and put on my sunglasses. I was eager to read the news from Omaha.

I arrived at the library branch about five minutes before it opened. There was a group of about fifteen teenagers busily talking about a project they had due the next day. They all agreed that they had been able to do most of the work for the project from home using the internet, but they needed some hard copy sources to satisfy the requirements of "Mr. Trouthead," the moniker they had apparently assigned to the teacher. I breathed a quiet sigh of relief, knowing they wouldn't be tying up the computers.

The setup was pretty much the same as at the other library branches. Tables and chairs in an open area surrounded by shelves of reference works, and a nook back in one corner for the computers. This branch had six computers, and I sat at one where, again, what I was searching for would be less obvious to those who might glance in my direction.

I repeated yesterday's strategy but in a different order and with two different papers: The Denver Post, The Minneapolis Star-Tribune, The Omaha World-Herald, followed by The St. Louis Post-Dispatch.

Both the Denver and Minneapolis papers had stories confirming the federal government's plan to provide sizeable compensation to the victim's families, depending on the victim's expected lifetime income. Rumors were that the government would pay out an average of about a million and a half to each family, mostly to head off lawsuits against the airlines and against the airport security contractors. Both newspapers also carried follow-up stories about local connections to the tragedy, including the fact that some of the terrorists had taken flying lessons in Minnesota. But not landing lessons. Sheesh!

I was nervous and eager as I opened my yahoo email account and then looked at the Omaha paper. The story about my memorial service was on page 3, three columns under my Klein-Staily photo, about thirty column inches in total. The first part merely mentioned I was believed dead, having been at a meeting with Cantor-Fitzgerald when the plane hit their offices in the north tower.

The bulk of the memorial seemed to involve talks by Ben, Timothy, and Liz, all extolling my virtues as a financial genius and as a father.

Ben took great pains to avoid any hint that my genius had led to financial difficulties for Klein-Staily.

Then Susan spoke. She began with "I didn't have a chance to say goodbye."

The snippets reported in the paper were about what a loyal, loving, supportive husband I had been. And then she thanked everyone for their support and for their continuing offers of comfort and assistance.

I had to stop for a moment. I couldn't stop the tears from flowing as I read what they said. I sat with my head in my hands and wiped my eyes. I had to wipe them again, this time on my sleeve. I ducked down behind the computer monitor in case someone was watching, and wiped my eyes again.

Then I remembered to copy and paste the article into my email and then move on to the St. Louis Post-Dispatch. I sent the email to myself and opened it.

The next portion of the article summarized my life and my career. Jeremy Hall wrote the article, and I was surprised he hadn't included anything about the recent difficulties with mortgage-backed bonds. He did, however, manage to get a dig at Ben and the family, saying they were aloof and isolated in their attempt to deal with their loss, but his observation was just transparent whining that they wouldn't talk to him. Comparisons were made with Jacquie Kennedy, which pleased me and seemed appropriate. After all, Susan was pretty special.

The last few paragraphs mentioned that there was no physical evidence as yet of my actual death. Ben made it clear that the evidence of my having been killed when the plane hit the tower was overwhelming and compelling: I had written Susan that I was going to the meeting, my cellphone died when the plane hit, and no one had been in my hotel room after the plane hit; furthermore, I hadn't turned up anywhere, and no one had seen me. He was determined, and I knew he would win. Even if it took seven years to get a death certificate, I knew that Ben would make sure Susan and the family were looked after by Klein-Staily and their insurers, but I was fairly confident Ben would have a death certificate for Susan within a month or less.

My confidence on this point soared when I read an article in the St. Louis paper in which an insurance executive from Salomon Smith Barney was quoted as saying,

> "The insurers say they expect to rely on the word of employers and family members that people now missing were last seen in the trade center, or on their way there [in deciding to pay out claims]."

Ben would have a strong case that I was dead. He would have the bulk of the payout from the insurance company within the next month or two.

I cleared the browser history and then went to the New York Times site to see if they had anything to add to what I had already read. There were lots of details about the lives of the first-responder victims, and more details about the recovery efforts. There were armies of forensic specialists sifting through the rubble. I was sure they would find remnants of my wallet and would either find or steal my wedding ring. I wasn't sure about the hair I had left there; I almost hoped they wouldn't find the hair because it might be obvious that it was cut.

It didn't really matter, I kept reassuring myself. In seven years or less, Susan could have me declared dead legally and could collect all the insurance. And I knew that Ben would make sure Klein-Staily looked after my family.

* * *
**

Chapter 25 – *Thrift Shops*

I was exhausted. I had walked a lot already that day and I was emotionally drained from reading about and thinking about my family and my plans.

I found an armchair, and I sat there with my street atlas open, trying to look as if I was intent on something, but really I was just resting. Actually, I dozed off for five or ten minutes.

It was after two o'clock when I woke up. I drank a lot of water from the water fountain, and refilled my 7UP bottle. I had plenty of time to get to the thrift stores, but I was too tired to walk back that far, and so I just dragged my tired body out to the bus stop.

It looked as if I would have to wait maybe twenty minutes or so for the next bus. I'd wait. I sat on a wall and just mused while I was waiting. I was still a bit worried about being found out. I had to make sure that no one would ever have any reason to suspect what I had done. Even if the insurance investigators were skeptical about the evidence of my death, they would have to pay off eventually so long as they could not find and identify me.

My mind was going in circles. I had to stop worrying about the insurance companies.

I turned my mind to the thrift shops. What treasures might I find? Back when we first moved to Omaha, I had bought a cashmere overcoat at a thrift shop for only five dollars. It was a great coat. Too bad I "outgrew" it.

Well, I sure didn't need a cashmere overcoat now. I could use a sweater, though, and maybe a heavier jacket. It would be fun to browse.

I got off the bus first at The Hubbard House. It had lots of nice clothing, but not much else that I could use. I picked up another very nice pair of khaki pants and tried them on. A 38-inch waist was about right. I had been really cramming my gut and butt into my 38s in the past, and these felt as if they fit well. I was pleased... for now. I clearly had lost some weight and girth.

Weight! I wondered if they had any bathroom scales.

I looked through the dress shirts and found two more that were my size and in good shape, one yellow striped and one pink. I remembered to check to see if they were perma-pressed; they were. I also picked out a black necktie and a grey-blue regimental striped tie as well.

On the way back to the front of the store, I saw a really nice-looking cream-coloured cable-knit sweater from Scotland. Seven dollars? A bargain! I hoped it fit. I pulled it on, and it was a tad snug, but I knew I had to slim down, so I added it to my cart.

As I was checking out, I asked if they had any bathroom scales.

"Not that I remember," said the lady who was ringing up my purchases. "At least I don't remember ever seeing any that worked."

"What about a vacuum cleaner?" I asked.

"The last one we had in didn't work very well," she said. "We've had a few good ones now and then, though, so you might want to check back next week."

"Good idea," I said, avoiding "No prob, Bob," and paid for my clothing with my bankcard. Using my new bankcard was another step to resettling myself in Jacksonville. It was a trivial milestone when I thought about it, but I liked it.

Outside the shop, I had to wait only about five minutes for the next bus to come along. I got off at a corner near St. Vincent DePaul.

The shop was loaded with utensils, furniture, knick-knacks, crappy appliances --- many of the things I'd have needed if I had ended up at the apartment I first wanted. I rummaged around and picked up a grater. Then I spoke to the young woman who seemed to be the only person there.

"Do you have any bathroom scales?" I asked.

"Is your name Mr. Lucky?" she asked. "We got a nice old set in yesterday afternoon. They ain't electronic or nothin' but they seem pretty good."

And she led me to a shelf of odds and ends.

"Go ahead," she said with a challenging smirk. "Try 'em out. I won't look."

I smiled back. I was proud of the weight I had probably lost in the past five days, but I wasn't about to say anything about that. I set my shoulder bag on the shelf, pulled the scales down, and stepped on them.

204.

That was with my clothes and running shoes on and midafternoon. A week ago I had weighed 210 naked. I was ecstatic, but I tried to hide my pleasure.

"They seem to work ok," I said somewhat stonily. "I'll take them."

"Geez they don't have a price tag on 'em yet. How's five bucks sound?"

I wasn't sure if I was supposed to negotiate or even if that was a good price. I started to say I had no idea whether that was fair, but stopped myself. No reason to say too much.

Still stonily, "That sounds okay to me."

I then smiled a bit and added, "What about a vacuum cleaner? Can I get lucky there, too?"

"Shucks. They don't stay around long if they work. We got one, but it belongs in the garbage. I wouldn't letcha buy it."

"Okay. Thanks." I started looking around at the other stuff they had. There was a great cabinet that would be perfect for a tv and stereo system… if I had those things. I hesitated, wondering whether I should buy it just to have it for later. Nope. I didn't want to go that route, at least not now. And where would I put it anyway?

There was a plastic juicer for a quarter. I picked it up. I had no idea whether I'd want this, but it seemed like something that might be useful. And a steel rod knife sharpener. Fifty cents. And a Melitta coffee filter funnel thing. Also a quarter.

"I don't suppose you sell any coffee to go with this thing, do you?" I half-laughed as I asked.

"Nope, but there's a shop just two blocks north of here that might still be open, and they sell good coffee."

"That sounds good. Here. I don't think I'll need a bag." I paid for my purchases using my bank card again, put the scales in my shoulder bag, put the other things in the Hubbard House bag, smiled a good-bye, and walked north to the coffee shop.

"The woman at St. Vincent DePaul says you have good coffee," I said to the clerk as I walked in. "I'd like something medium-dark if you have it."

"Oh, Lois! She's a regular. And yeah, we got just what you want, our House Blend. Five ninety-five a pound. How much you want?"

"A pound will probably be good. I don't have a grinder, though. Can you grind it for a filter?"

I put the coffee into the thrift shop bag and caught the bus back across the river and then connected with a bus home. It was only about four o'clock, and I began thinking my pork roast would just about be ready when I got back to the trailer.

I was feeling pretty good as I walked up the gravel laneway toward my trailer. "My trailer" struck me as odd, but I guess it was mine since I was renting it.

Oh oh. What's that?

I became concerned when I saw that the Cadillac was parked there. I hoped Evelyn and Don hadn't changed their minds. I hoped they hadn't gone in. If they had, we would have strong words.

Evelyn got out of the car as I walked up. She was smiling as she walked toward me.

"Hi, Carl. We did have a spare vacuum cleaner so I thought I'd drop it by."

I swallowed all my unuttered swear words and suspicions. I hoped my embarrassment didn't show.

"Geez, thanks, Evelyn!" I said enthusiastically but not quite gushing. I still wondered why she or they were going so far to help me out.

"Here," I said, handing her the thrift store bag. "Can you hold this bag while I get my key out?"

The smell of the roast as we entered the trailer was faint but terrific.

"Oh, my, Carl! What are you cooking? It sure smells good."

"I thought I'd try a pork roast in your crockpot. Let's see how she's doing."

I set my shoulder bag on the loveseat, and she put the thrift-shop bag there. We both went into the kitchen, and I lifted the lid of the crockpot. Evelyn leaned against me, ever so slightly, as we checked out the roast.

"I gotta admit," I smiled. "It sure smells good."

I almost added, "Not bad for my first attempt," but stopped myself. I really did have a tendency to volunteer too much information, and I really did have to work on those urges.

She reached out and touched my arm. "Why don't I bring the vacuum in while you put away the things from your shopping trip?" Evelyn suggested.

"Great idea. Thanks!" I said as I picked up the thrift-shop bag and the shoulder bag and went to the dressing room, where I hung up the shirts and pants. I took the scales out of my shoulder bag and put them under the sink in the bathroom, and I put the sweater in a drawer in the bedroom dresser.

I went back to the living room just as Evelyn was returning with the vacuum.

"This sure is nice of you, Evelyn." I looked at her somewhat seriously. "I want you to know I really do appreciate it."

She started to talk but I put my hand up to stop her, maintaining my serious look.

"Why are you doing all this for me? You don't even know me. Not really."

"I don't know, Carl. Something about you seemed ok to me. Clicked, I guess. And we really do have more than we need, so I'm glad to share it in a way."

"Well, thanks."

I took the vacuum from her.

"Where would you have kept this?" I asked.

"Oh, we never kept this one here at the trailer. We had a smaller one that we kept in the closet," she said, indicating what I was thinking of as my dressing room. "This one should be okay in there, too."

I took it into the room and put it in the corner, just to the right inside the door.

"Perfect fit," I said and smiled.

There she was again. Sort of half-blocking the doorway, smiling up at me. I couldn't get out.

"Well, thanks again, Evelyn," trying to indicate I wanted to leave the room.

"Oh don't mention it," she said as she went back to the living room and plunked in the loveseat.

"Evelyn, I just remembered something I wanted to ask you. Did you and Don keep a spare key anywhere outside the trailer in case you got locked out? That door has a spring latch, and I can see me locking myself out if I'm not super careful."

She looked slightly embarrassed.

"I forgot all about it! We keep one under the steps."

I noticed the present tense in "we keep" not "we kept". I was glad I had asked. I would move it right after she left.

"But I hope, like a good landlady, you have another copy at home in case you need to get in."

She nodded vaguely, "I think so. I'll look when I get home."

I went back to the kitchen and picked up my shoes that had been sitting on the newspaper all day.

"Well, I guess I'd better finish cleaning up and putting things away before I figure out what to do about this dinner."

"I know, I know. Carl, I'm sorry," she said. "I can see you're busy and have things to do."

And she added, in what seemed almost like a rationalization afterthought, "Besides, I probably should get back to Don."

I walked over and opened the door to indicate that it would be fine with me if she left. Once again she reached out and touched me. She left her hand on my arm long enough for it to be pleasant, but not so long as to be too suggestive.

"Carl, I like visiting with you. Thanks."

Noncommittally, I replied, "You're welcome." And I smiled.

I used to say, "Anytime" in a situation like this, when someone was thanking me for my having done something nice; that, or "No prob, Bob." This time, though, I wasn't going to encourage her by saying "Anytime" and I was well on my way to expunging "No prob, Bob" from my speech patterns.

After she drove off, I looked behind and under the step. Sure enough, there was a key. I made sure it worked, and then I wandered into the cemetery. Three rows back, I found an older grave marker that looked as if it was rarely, if ever, visited. I examined its base. Yes, there was a gap at the bottom near a corner where the key would fit nicely.

I took my bearings: Northwest corner of the marker. John William Fellows. 1897 – 1954. "Nice name," I thought. I looked around and there seemed to be no one in sight or who could be watching me.

I bent down to examine the spot more carefully. The key would fit there perfectly and be well out of sight, but could I retrieve it easily if and when I might need it? With a pen or pencil or even a small stick, I could fiddle it out pretty easily, so back it went into its hiding place.

I stood up and put my hands worshipfully in front of me and bowed my head slightly. From that pose, I tried to look around and couldn't see anyone. After about ten seconds, I slowly raised my head and did a very slow two-seventy turn, scanning the horizon. Still no one in sight. Good. As I made my way, slowly, through the cemetery, I decided I should visit Mr. Fellows' grave at least twice a year to pay my respects and, more importantly, to check on my key.

Back in the trailer, the pork roast smelled great. I had felt as if Evelyn had wanted me to invite her to stay for dinner and coffee, but I also had a sense she wanted more from me than I was prepared to offer right then. I didn't want any entanglements, and I pointedly chose not to encourage her. She seemed quite nice, though, to a fault, and I certainly didn't want to offend her. To be honest, I liked her.

The roast turned out to be great – a slightly creamy sauce and enough food for at least four suppers. I would do this often with different cheap cuts of meat or maybe some chicken or something. I could also see myself making stews or very thick soups in the crockpot. Exploring and relearning how to cook would be both interesting and fun.

After I cleaned up the dishes, I cut up the rest of the pork roast to store in my various plastic containers, ... some in the fridge, some in the freezer compartment. I sat back down at the table and took the job ads back out of my shoulder bag.

OH NO!! Shoulder bag! I don't know why it hadn't occurred to me sooner, but I dashed into the bedroom and looked under the bed to see if my laptop was still there. Whew! It was. I looked around and it seemed that nothing had been disturbed. The shock and the fear made me realize that I must have been suspicious of Evelyn and what she wanted, at least in some ways. I pretty much trusted her, but not completely.

I looked around for a hair I could place on the laptop. I didn't have any of my own, of course, and Evelyn had cleaned the place pretty well before she turned it over to me. No hairs in sight. She had even emptied the vacuum cleaner, so there were no hairs there either.

The tub stopper! It was a goldmine of hair and grunge. I took the longest hair I could find there and stuck it over the side of my laptop, near the back, where someone opening the computer would be less likely to see it. I really needed to get rid of my laptop and my old cellphone.

I breathed a sigh of relief as I cleaned off the tub stopper, and then I went back to the kitchen table to look at the job ads.

* * *
**

Chapter 26 – *Job Search Planning*

I looked at the job ads again. I realized sometime during the previous few days that having no references meant I would be lucky to get any job at all. That really concerned me.

I had never really had to apply for a job before. Not in my entire life. I'd worked on the family farm all through school, from when I was a toddler right up through college. And then from college it was so different with ten places interviewing me as a prospective employee. It was almost as if I was interviewing them to see which job I wanted.

Things were going to change now, for sure.

I asked myself, "What type of employer is most likely to hire a person with no references?" and I quickly realized the answers were similar to the answers to the question, "What type of landlord would rent to someone with no references?" I had been lucky in my search for a place to live, but I didn't think it was all luck. It was also the result of learning from my mistakes during the previous day. I expected this learning should be transportable to my job search.

I had learned enough that I expected big organizations with regular human resources departments to require references and a list of previous landlords, or in the case of jobs, previous employers. I would have to look for something involving small-time businesses, most likely private entrepreneurs.

I had also learned that it helped if, for whatever reason, the person on the other side was desperate. It might help to show up just when someone quit, for example.

For most jobs, I wanted to look presentable but not artificial if I had a chance for a job interview. The neckties might help with some jobs, but not with others, and so I decided I would carry one with me.

At the same time, for this initial week of searching at any rate, I wanted to focus on jobs that had some potential upward mobility. Could I work hard enough and be smart enough and be reliable enough to end up moving to a supervisory position or a lower-management position eventually? I didn't want to do limited-skill, minimum-wage jobs all my life. Also, I wanted to be able to save for my retirement. Health care benefits would be nice eventually, too, but in the meantime I just hoped I could stay healthy.

With these thoughts, I turned to the want-ads again.

Yard work? Maybe I could eventually become a crew chief, and then maybe move diagonally into a supervisory role in a different firm. Yeah, but I'd have to do yard work, and I simply wasn't physically fit enough to do that. Maybe in the spring I would be in better shape and would reconsider if I hadn't found anything else.

Car wash attendant? Unlikely I could move up farther than maybe being a crew chief. But again, diagonal movement might be possible, but to what? Working in a car wash seemed like hard, unpleasant work; nevertheless, I thought I might prefer it to "lawn-care professional".

Night shift at a warehouse? Worth considering, depending on the fitness level required. I could probably build up some serious fitness working in a warehouse. And with my background in assessment and management, I could probably use the job as a stepping-stone, moving onward. I liked the idea. The problem was that I might be wasting my time applying for a warehouse job if they required references. I couldn't just go in and apply for a job without them, especially if they had forms and an HR department.

Night clerk in a convenience store? This was probably a job I could do. The main concern would be robbers and murderers, not to mention dealing with shoplifting. Judging from the number of ads for this type of job, the employer might well be desperate enough to give me a job, and I could probably use the job to move up to store management or even regional management, again especially if I moved diagonally through different organizations.

Busboys, line cooks, dishwashers? There were two types of jobs in these ads: institutions and restaurants. The institutional jobs would likely pay better and might even have benefits but would probably require references and a work history. Restaurants might be better, especially non-chain restaurants. I couldn't really cook, I knew, but I could probably work in the kitchen somehow. Again, these types of jobs wouldn't provide much opportunity for advancement, though.

Janitor, custodial services, cleaner? There were lots of ads for these types of jobs, but most of them were from households wanting people to come in and clean their homes once a week or something like that. Again, if I became desperate, I could piece together a bunch of these and eke out a living, and I suspected the households often employed people with no references. But it was a dead end. No benefits, and little opportunity for advancement, even diagonally. I might do better with a small company that cleaned buildings at night. I could certainly wash windows, mop and sweep floors, and empty wastebaskets. Unfortunately, these jobs were often through larger companies, as in "Apply with a resume and references to some stupid post office box number."

I actually laughed out loud when I saw one ad listing its address for resumes as 221 N Hogan St, Jacksonville, FL 32202, Suite 743. Their mailbox was right next to mine at the UPS office!

I had forgotten to ask Evelyn about mail: address, zip code, how and where it was delivered. Oh well, I could wait a day or two before calling to ask.

I thought about my experiences with landlords and building supervisors and worked out several ways to deal with potential employers who might want references.

One option was to hope they didn't ask. That solution worked with Meg-Ann and Evelyn. I was lucky with Evelyn, but not so lucky with Meg-Ann. That experience made me wary of looking for a job with someone who was desperate. Sometimes employers were desperate to hire someone and wouldn't ask for references because their business was failing or because they were difficult to work for. I needed a better strategy than "Maybe they won't ask for references."

Another strategy was to confront the issue head-on with the person doing the hiring. I could tell them straight out I had no references but that I would work for them for a month. If I didn't last a month without missing a day of work, they could keep my pay and if they had any reason at all not to like my work after a month, they could pay me for the last two weeks and let it go at that. It was a strategy that would convey to them my wish to demonstrate reliability and eagerness for the job. It was also a strategy that might fail if the business was failing; they'd get free labor for a month, stiff me, and I would have no recourse. It was a strategy that was fun to think about, but it probably wasn't very practical.

Likely the best strategy in my case was to lie, to make up past jobs and references. I knew that many firms relied more on interviews than references to judge the suitability of potential employees and never bothered to check references, especially if the references were out of town. I also guessed that if anyone checked my references and found out they were false, they wouldn't make a big deal about it – they just wouldn't hire me.

So I turned my thoughts to fabricating some references. I had to have a list, depending on the type of job I might be applying for, and I had to make the list plausible but such that employers would be unlikely to check on them.

I jotted down some ideas for past jobs:
>Produce Assistant, Red Giant Grocery, Mankato, Minnesota
>Telemarketing Operator, Zibo Sales, Salem, Oregon
>Car Porter, Sampson Brothers Autos, Houston, Texas

No, that wouldn't work. I had to have a plausible history, and having my last three jobs scattered all over the place was scarcely believable. The jobs would have to have been in the same general region. I decided on Houston because I had at least been there a few times and could converse a bit about the place if I needed to.

Starting a new life without a past was going to be difficult. I needed a job history that would seem plausible for someone my age but yet not be very easy to check up on. Same with education. I'd say I graduated from Hughes High School in Houston in 1976. I didn't even know if there was such a school, but I doubted if many people would check.

So a new history:

> Graduated from Hughes High School, 1976

> Last three jobs, in reverse chronological order:
> Produce assistant, Kroger, Houston
> Telemarketer/Opinion Surveys, Zibo Energy, Houston
> Automobile Porter/Assistant, Sampson Auto Sales, Houston

I had to make sure I didn't talk about this history if I didn't have to, and certainly not at all beyond a job interview. I wouldn't make up a resume because I wanted to be flexible about the lies I would tell. Also, I didn't want to go to some resume service to formalize all this. I figured I would just fill in the information on a job application form and try to get by with that.

It was 9:30, and I was tired. Tired from walking and tired from thinking. I went to bed.

I was afraid of having more nightmares. To deal with my fears, I thought more about how lucky I was to be alive, and I thought about happy times with the family. Two summers ago, we had revisited Colorado Springs, where Susan and I had honeymooned. We spent a wonderful week, hiking, shopping, sightseeing, throwing snowballs at each other on the mountaintops, and just plain enjoying each other. Just the four of us. And I drifted off to sleep.

* * *
**

Chapter 27 – *Disposing of the Laptop*

In my sleep, Susan and I were in one of the World Trade Center towers and Timothy and Liz were in the other. We were waving to each other. Then throwing snowballs at each other.

Like the day before, I awoke again on Monday morning at 5:30. Do two days in a row make a routine?

As I lay in bed, it occurred to me that I had seen several construction dumpsters behind the discount store. Some kind of big construction project was underway, and I was determined I would get rid of my laptop and cellphone there.

I got up and dressed, putting on the darkest shirt I had, along with dark grey slacks, my dark dress shoes, and the bucket hat. I put the laptop and cellphone on the floor, opened them, and stomped on both of them a few times. Then I put each one in a doorframe and slammed the door on them a couple of times.

I put the dented and damaged units in one of the thrift store bags and then emptied my garbage into the bag, covering the laptop and phone. To make sure it wouldn't fall apart on the way, I put that bag inside another plastic grocery store bag.

I checked my pocket to make sure I had my wallet and key, and stepped outside. With some effort, I lifted the concrete step again and dropped it on the bag, causing more damage to the phone and laptop. It wasn't foolproof, but the odds were good this strategy would work.

I walked up to the discount store and arrived just as the sky was beginning to lighten a bit. I took a quick look to see if there were any security cameras and didn't see any. Just in case, I put on my sunglasses, pulled the hat down over my face a bit farther, walked right up to one of the construction dumpsters, threw the bag in, and turned around.

All that worry, and it was over in about five seconds. But of course it was the worry that had led me to think about and plan the disposal of the phone and laptop. They were damaged to the point of being useless, and they were in a dumpster that was unlikely to attract dumpster divers. It would take a massively talented professional to figure out what was on the laptop if it was even possible, and I really doubted the laptop and phone would ever be found.

So far as I could tell, no one had seen me, but as I was walking away past the front of the discount store, a couple of cars showed up, probably with workers for the construction project. They didn't stop, and neither did I; in fact, I didn't even look in their direction.

On the way back to the trailer, I stopped at the convenience store for a newspaper. I looked at the situation there and wondered what it was like to work the night shift.

"No time like the present," I thought.

To the cashier, a short young Latin-American whom I had seen on my previous visits there, "What's it like working the night shift here?"

"It's okay, I guess. I don't get to sleep on the job here because of the traffic, but I work from eleven to seven. That means I can do my other job in the morning when I get off work from here and still get some good sleep."

I was impressed and hoped my face showed it.

"What's your other job?" I asked.

"It's only part-time, but I work a few hours a day moving cars for a car dealer."

"Thanks," I said as I paid for the paper. Car porter wasn't a job I could take because I no longer had a driver's license. But I liked the idea of having a job and a half. I hoped I could work it out.

As I walked back to the trailer, I calculated. Twenty hours a week at six dollars an hour would give me a gross of only $120/week, maybe a net of $100/week after taxes. I could survive on that, but barely. Forty hours would be much better. I wouldn't buy a computer or get the internet until I had a job or two, working at least thirty hours and netting close to two hundred dollars a week. That cashier was probably averaging fifty hours a week and netting close to three hundred dollars a week. I didn't want to count on it, but my goal was to do at least that well after the first month or two.

Three hundred a week and I thought that was good?!

That was only fifteen grand a year! A week earlier I had a job paying twenty times that much, and in previous years, with bonuses, I had cleared a hundred times that much. I marvelled at how much and how quickly my standards and expectations had adjusted.

Back at the trailer, I showered and made breakfast. There was one big change in my breakfast today: I had a Melitta filter holder! Using a technique that Susan and I had perfected in our first apartment, I filled the small saucepan with water to measure how much coffee it would hold, dumped the water into the larger saucepan and turned on the heat. I folded some paper towels to make a filter, put some ground coffee in it, and set the funnel on top of the small pan. It was pretty good, but I needed to make the coffee a touch stronger from now on. Also, on my next visit to a thrift shop I might look for Melitta-type coffee carafe.

While I was cleaning up and making my lunch for the day, I kicked myself. I'd have loved to take some coffee with me in a thermos. I should have bought one or two thermoses while I was at the thrift shops. I was sure I had seen some.

I packed my lunch and the 7UP water bottle in my shoulder bag. I rolled up my striped necktie carefully and put it in one of my dress shoes, put them in the shoulder bag alongside my lunch, and sat down with the want ads.

Today, according to what little I knew of chaos theory, I could end up making decisions that would affect my career path for the rest of my life. I snorted with self-derision at these melodramatic tendencies. I had been making potentially life-altering decisions all along; today would be no different, and in that sense it was nothing special.

The job ads were pretty much the same as they had been on Sunday. I would start with three warehouse night-shift job vacancies, continue with the convenience store night-shift jobs, and move on to the custodial and restaurant jobs. Applying for a job was different from looking for an apartment because I could apply for a whole lot of them in several days and then take the best offer or at the very least not worry if I had to turn down some jobs because I had already taken one. I guess I could have done that with apartments, too, but not if I'd had to put down a deposit for one while looking at others.

All the warehouse jobs said to apply in person and gave the addresses. I wondered why they made such a point of "apply in person". The details of some of the ads gave some indication: "forklift experience an asset", "some heavy lifting". They probably wanted to assess applicants for strength and skill. Well, of course. Why had I not anticipated this? Duh. At least I could plan my trip.

Out came the street atlas again. I would need to make sure I had it with me in my shoulder bag. The shoulder bag was getting too full, though. I crammed the 7UP bottle into one shoe as much as I could, and put the bag of veggies in the toe of the other shoe, keeping the necktie up where the shoe was open. Overall that helped.

I wondered if the employers used "apply in person" to discriminate against applicants from various groups. I sure wouldn't have wanted to be a Muslim with the name Muhammad applying for a job during those first few days after the terrorist attacks. I wouldn't even want to look like what an employer might assume to be a Muslim.

Two of the jobs that appealed to me said to phone for an appointment and gave phone numbers, but a third one seemed to be saying to just come by and apply. It wasn't even eight o'clock yet, and so I would start phoning the other two after 8:30 while I was on the bus, going to the first one.

I had zero experience with a fork-lift, but I could tell them I had driven tractors on my ... family's... strike that ... uncle's farm .... strike that.... ranch in Kansas.... strike that ... Texas – uncle's ranch in Texas – that would probably work. I figured I could learn the basics of handling a forklift in less than an hour and be a pro in a few days. I needed to add that work experience to my mental list of past employment.

"Some heavy lifting" had me a little concerned, though. I used to be fit, and I knew that if they let me ease into the heavy lifting I would regain my fitness. I had already dropped at least six or seven pounds and was eating healthy foods and walking more. We'd just have to see how my arms and upper body could adjust and redevelop.

As I made up my travel plans using the job ads and the street atlas, I saw that all three jobs were in the same general area, out on the western side of town, near some major interstates. That made sense to me – businesses would want to have their warehousing located where it would be convenient to major trucking routes. I would go to these sites first, and if necessary I could consider going to others in that region or to another one up near the airport. But at this stage, I would try to apply for as many jobs as possible in as short a time span as possible, which meant limiting the time between job application visits.

It took me nearly forty-five minutes to get to the first warehouse. On the bus while I was going there, I made calls to set up appointments with the other two warehouses where I would apply for a job.

The first place I called said for me to come in at 11, or earlier if I could make it. I said I thought I could probably be there early. I'd try.

And then the woman who answered the phone asked me if I was certified to drive a forklift.

"No, ma'am," I replied, "But I drove and operated a tractor on my uncle's ranch for many years. It can't be a lot different."

"Wellllll…" she hesitated. "I'll schedule you in for an interview, but don't getcher hopes up. We train too many forklift operators who then just move on when they're certified and get offered more money somewhere else."

"I understand," I said. But in fact I didn't. What kind of place trains people and then pays them less than the going wage rate for their new skills? I'd seen this kind of hiring behavior before, and while maybe it worked well enough when unemployment rates were high, it seemed wasteful now that the economy was coming out of its recession.

The second place I called had a message to call back after 9 o'clock.

My first visit, though, was to Smith & Bros Warehousing. I was there before 9am and the place was jumping with people coming and going and trucks lined up to get to the loading docks. If the line-up was caused by bottlenecks in the warehouse, I could see why they might be hiring more staff. But if the line-up was due to insufficient loading dock space, hiring more staff wouldn't help much.

I went in the door marked "Visitors" and looked around. A receptionist took a break from dealing with phone calls and forced a half-smile.

"Yes?" Clipped, and not at all like the monotone of Ellen Smith at The Alameda.

"Hi," I smiled. "I'd like to apply for a warehouse job."

"All we have available is night shift. You okay with that?"

"Sure."

"Leave your resume and we'll get back to you."

"I don't have a resume. I had hoped to complete an application form," I frowned a bit.

"Okay, here," and she dug out a form while answering another phone call.

I looked around for a place to sit while I filled out the form. I didn't see any chairs or even anything to put the form on while I completed it. I looked questioningly at the receptionist, as she kept up her streams of conversations with at least two different people on the line. When I finally caught her eye, she looked a bit confused but then quickly regrouped and gestured to a door on her right.

I nodded and waved my thanks and opened the door. It was basically a cubbyhole with a couple of school desks – plastic chairs with arms to put a paper on. I sat down and started with the application.

I got my name right and filled in the phone number without looking. I was on a roll! I smiled to myself.

Address: Hmmm. I wanted to write in the trailer address, but I didn't know the zip code there and I couldn't remember the street number of the trailer park. All I could remember was lot 27 and North Main Street, so I gave the UPS box address.

Date of birth: That was easy! I had selected it because it was funny and would be easy to remember: 5-8-58.

Social Security Number: I copied that down from where I had written it on the back of my laminated birth certificate and returned it to my wallet (front right pocket).

Job: What did they want on this blank line. I wrote, "Warehouse Employee, any shift".

Skills: I wrote, "quick learner, reliable, good reasoning skills," knowing full well that wasn't what they wanted. Then I added, "Drove and operated large tractors on ranch for 15 years." Okay, I actually did drive a tractor when I was only five, but the truth was closer to seven or eight years.

Education: Hughes High School, Houston, Texas. Graduated 1976.

Work experience: I listed being a ranch hand and driving a tractor first, mentioning extensive use of the loader, since I figured that would indicate skills most like operating a forklift. I followed with each of the jobs and employers I had concocted the night before, embellishing the actual work I had allegedly done only slightly. I left the dates blank, hoping it wouldn't matter. If someone asked me about the job dates, I could make up a few years for each job.

References: I wrote "Please contact above supervisors." And I added Ted Fry at Everbank. If they even bothered to check, he'd probably be okay. I considered listing Evelyn and Don, too, but I wanted check with them first. I decided to wait a few days, though. I kind of hoped Evelyn wouldn't call for the next couple of days, and then I would call her about the mail and about being a reference.

When I was done, I took the sheet of paper back to the receptionist, who was still busy on the phone dealing with people who seemed to need dealing with. She held her hand up, nodded at me, and said into the phone, "Hold on a minute," followed by "Just a minute ma'am." I hope she was well-paid for dealing with that stress.

She looked at the application and winced a tiny bit. "I'm not sure," she said, "but your experience with tractors should be good. We'll get back to you this afternoon if we can use you."

I smiled and thanked her, but she was already back on the phone. "I'm really sorry about the delay sir. We're working on it right now as we speak…" she said, glancing at me as I left the office.

Everything about the operation looked as if it was going great guns with more work than they could handle. The line-ups of trucks, the constant phone work, and the fact that there were several warehouse jobs available in the area made me think that the uptick in business had not been fully anticipated by the companies or else they thought it was temporary. Either way, I thought I would have a good chance at a job paying more than minimum wage. One of these places would surely take a chance on me because they needed the help.

It was 9:30 when I left Smith & Bros., and I called the place that said to call after nine.

"Hexley," said the harried-sounding voice.

"Hello," I said. "I'd like to make an appointment to apply for a job on the night shift in your warehouse."

"Can you handle a forklift?" the voice asked.

"I expect so. I drove a tractor for years on my uncle's ranch. I figure I can learn a forklift in no time."

"Yeah, yeah. We're desperate for certified forklift operators to get stuff ready during the night, but we need people with experience. We ain't got time to train people."

"Maybe you're not paying enough for trained operators," I ventured, "and maybe you're being short-sighted in not training people like me. I have a lot of related experience, and I might even stick around for a year if I were promised a hundred-dollar bonus after each six months of the first year."

I couldn't believe their idiocy. You need workers? You need to pay more to attract them, and you need to pay more to keep them. The firm was desperate for short-term solutions. And I didn't care if I offended them.

"Wise ass," said the voice. Click. The voice hung up on me.

I thought my suggestion was pretty solid, based on what little I had heard, read, and seen about the warehouse business in Jacksonville. The idiots should hire me to advise them.

Or maybe I was completely wrong. Maybe they just wanted trained bodies for an uptick in business over the next month or two and that was all. I should probably keep my mouth shut from now on. Oh well, at least I hadn't told them who I was.

It was only four blocks to the next employer, Wharfhousers, Inc. I liked the name.

I hoped that getting there before 10am would be a plus since they had said they'd like it if I could go in earlier than 11.

As with Smith & Bros., business seemed to be booming at Wharfhousers. There were trucks coming and going, but mostly queued up, and there was a traffic director in the back parking lot. I was walking around the block-sized warehouse when there was a lull in the truck traffic just as I was near the traffic director.

"Is it always this busy here?" I asked.

"Sometimes," she said, motioning a truck through narrow gate. "But not usually like this."

"Why is it so busy?"

"Dunno. Word is the Feds are stockpiling everything they can get their hands on. They don't want to be caught short of anything if the terror attacks continue."

"Thanks. Where do I go to apply for a job?"

"The office is through that door there," she gestured. "They'll be happy to see you."

"Why's that?"

"They can't keep up with all the flow inside. I've heard there's about a two-week backlog right now. Once they get that taken care of, things will smooth out a bit. Oh, excuse me...." and she blew her whistle and held up her hand to stop a truck from backing up.

I went over to the office. There was one other person ahead of me to speak with the receptionist. She was going nuts and didn't seem to have the cool to deal with all the demands of her job.

"I don't know," she whined into the phone. "I just don't know. I'll leave a message for Mr. Pedley to get back to you as soon as he can," and with that she hung up and scrawled a name and number on a Post-It and stuck that onto an inch-thick stack of other Post-Its. From the looks of things Pedley wouldn't get back to them for quite some time.

The person ahead of me sighed in exasperation. Finally he blurted out, "I've been waiting here for half an hour! Where the heck *is* Pedley? My stuff is in there somewhere, and it's been ten days since I was told it would be shipped."

"I know," said the harried receptionist, almost crying. "We made an arrangement to have everything computerized but the system just isn't working right. Mr. Pedley is out there trying to get things moving again while the computer firm tries to clean up the mess. All I can tell you is that we're doing the best we can since we discovered that system isn't working for us. I really don't think Mr. Pedley will be able to see you today. Please," and again she seemed near tears, "try to be patient."

"Well this lost shipment is costing me a thousand dollars a day in interest costs and penalties," he said. "Tell Pedley that! I'll end up owning this stupid Wharfhouse if he doesn't get things going soon, and when I see how it's being run, I really don't want to own it. I don't want the headache." And with that he stormed out of the office.

"Wow," I said as I turned and watched him go out the door.

I turned back to the receptionist and smiled. "Hi. I'm here to apply for a job?" The question mark again. Was I asking? Pleading? Wondering? Apologizing for interrupting?

"Can you drive a forklift?"

"I'm the person who called. I drove a big tractor on my uncle's ranch for years. I'm sure I can learn a forklift in no time."

"Oh yeah." She pressed an intercom button. "Jack, a job applicant."

A few minutes later, a big man with "Jack" on a patch over his pocket came in. He looked at me somewhat critically.

"Can you drive a forklift?" he asked.

I repeated what I'd told the receptionist, "I drove a big tractor on my uncle's ranch for years. I'm sure I can learn it no time."

"Maybe," he said. And then he looked at me critically. "How are you for heavy lifting?

"I used to be in really good shape when I was a ranch hand," I said, not mentioning that it was really a farm and had been over twenty years ago. "I know I'm not in great shape anymore, but if you're patient with me and let me do a little at a time, I'll get there."

"We don't have time for patience," Jack said. "We need people who are strong and who have experience, and we need them right now."

And with that he turned and walked back out of the office. I bit my tongue and decided not to open the door and yell, "Yeah, with an attitude like that, you'd better start offering a lot of money." Sheesh.

I was discouraged but not deterred, and so I asked the receptionist if I could fill out an application form anyway, just in case they got desperate enough they might need me.

"Sure." She sounded almost enthusiastic. She seemed to have a good handle on the desperate position the firm was in. It looked like she didn't want to throw away the possibility of what might turn out to be a good hire even if I didn't meet the criteria that were being set by the supervisor.

And so I filled out the application, pretty much the same as the one for Smith & Bros. and left.

* * *
**

Chapter 28 – *Frustration and More Job Search*

Like most loading docks, the one at Wharfhousers, Inc., was like a long, deep, covered walkway. I leaned against the wall, took out my 7UP water bottle, and drank all of it.

Before leaving, I looked around. Every available opening had a truck in it, leaving it, or entering it. But there were about ten drivers just sitting on the concrete and waiting. Some were smoking, others drinking coffee, others chatting.

I stood there for maybe ten minutes and saw one forklift loading one of the many trucks. Just one. It looked to me as if they needed forklift operators for the day shift, not just the night shift.

I went back into the office.

"It looks to me," I said to the secretary, "as if you need forklift operators for all shifts. … But then," I added hastily, "what do I know?"

She smiled faintly.

"May I use your restroom?" I quickly asked before she had a chance to reply.

"Sure. It's over there," and she pointed to a door with a sign that said "Restroom".

"Thanks."

After using it, I refilled my 7UP bottle and left.

I walked south on Huron Street, back toward Commonwealth and Beaver Avenues. My plan was to stop in a park somewhere and make some calls about other jobs. But then I passed the Westbrook Library branch, right at Huron and Commonwealth. Since it was only 10:30, I decided to go in to look at the Omaha news.

I pulled my hat down, put on my sunglasses, and went in.

I was greeted perhaps a tad too effusively by the woman at the desk.

"Everyone's in the Seneca Room," she announced and pointed to her right.

I had no idea what she was talking about, but I assumed it was some community or group thing. I stopped. My hesitation must have told her I wasn't there for that group.

"Oh!" she said. "Aren't you here for the Heritage Club?" She seemed dejected when I shook my head "no".

"No, I'm not. I just came in to use a computer to read some news."

"Oh. Okay. The computers are back over there," and she pointed to a back corner and before she finished what she was saying, she was back to whatever she had been doing before I arrived.

I wondered why all the library branches had their computer stations tucked away in some back corner. Maybe to provide some privacy for the users? Nah. More likely it was just easier to network them back in the corner near some electricity sources.

At the computers, again I took one where I expected I would have the most privacy. I logged on and went first to the NY Post. There was nothing new there; the rubble sifting was still in progress. And of course the front page carried the non-news that the US really meant it this time when telling the world they wouldn't stand for such an outrage. Right.

I decided to check the Omaha World-Herald second this time, just to mix things up. There was nothing new about me specifically. The paper reproduced some wire service stories and noted that there was no news about the fate of Fredrick Young. I copied the article and pasted it into a new email message to myself.

Then on to the Kansas City Star and the Topeka Capital-Journal. Nothing new in those papers either, but I browsed around in both papers just to make sure it wasn't clear what I was looking for. I knew that if someone seriously wanted to trace all this action, they could see that it was Carl Jacobs who had logged onto these computers, so mostly I was just trying to avoid leaving an obvious trail. Next time I wouldn't look at the Omaha paper.

After about forty-five minutes in total, I logged off, clearing the browser again as I did so. I took my shoulder bag to a table and spread out the job ads to reassess my situation. A warehouse job might be good for me and while I believed I would be a good hire for an employer, I accepted that I wasn't likely to land a warehouse job without forklift experience and a stronger upper body. I hadn't given up hope completely, but it was time for me to look for something else, too.

Next up, I would try to find a night shift job at a convenience store. Why night shift? I think I had two things in mind. First, I was guessing and hoping that employers would be more eager, even desperate, judging from the number of ads – to hire someone for the night shift; my chances of getting a job soon would be better for the night shift. Second, I hoped that the night shift paid better, and I wanted to earn more money so I wouldn't have to rely on my nest egg much longer. I actually hoped to start padding it, building it up soon.

There were quite a few convenience stores advertising night-shift openings, and so I went to the lobby to call them all to set up appointments for the afternoon. Kwiki-Mart had an opening. Two different 7-11s had openings. There was a Mini-Mart, a Minamart, and a Q-Mart that had openings. There also seemed to be a few others with names like "Kangaroo" and others that I'd never heard of. With this kind of job availability, I expected I could find a place that would give me at least six or seven shifts per week.

I sat with the street atlas as I called the various places for appointments, expecting I would have to make sure I allowed plenty of time to get from one place to another. Most of them didn't really want appointments, though. They just said things like, "Yeah, great. Come on in and drop off your resume or fill out an application form."

I wanted to apply in person, so that suited me; but I really wanted to talk with the owners or managers in person if possible. I wanted the potential employers to see that I was clean-cut and well dressed, that I spoke well, and that I looked reliable. I didn't want to just "drop off a resume" or in my case fill out an application that could easily get lost or just put onto a pile with nothing to distinguish it.

The first two places I planned to visit were out in the west end. Kwiki-Mart on Edgewood, North, was less than a mile from the library, and there was a 7-11 farther down along on Edgewood, South.

I drank some water and ate one of my "sandwiches" and some veggies. I went back into the library to refill my water bottle and began walking toward the Kwiki-Mart. I was still wearing my new running shoes and was surprisingly happy with them. I had seen no reason to put on my dress shoes to apply for a warehouse job, but I decided I should change my shoes and put on the striped necktie before I got to the Kwiki-Mart.

It was a bit over a mile to the Kwiki-Mart. When I saw it, I stopped in a doorway and changed my shoes. Tying the necktie without a mirror was difficult, but after a struggle, it seemed ok.

I checked my reflection in a window to make sure I looked presentable and went into the store.

To the clerk, "Hi I'm here to apply for a job?" The question mark in my voice seemed appropriate again.

"Yeah?"

"Well, I called earlier and was told to stop by."

"Yeah, well, we're looking for someone to work two nights a week. We got the nights covered otherwise."

"I really wish I'd known that. I wouldn't have come all this way if I had. I really need more work than that."

"Here. Fill this out. We get a lot of turnover."

And she handed me an application form that was pretty much the same as the others I had seen with one big exception. It said, "If you are under the age of 18, you must have the permission of your parents to apply for any position that requires working between 8pm and 8am." I liked that.

I stood at the counter and filled out the application. She looked at the application, reading upside down, and asked, "How old are you," she looked down at the application again,… "Carl?"

"Forty-three. Why do you ask? Testing my math skills?" I smiled.

"I don't get why someone your age, dressed neatly, wants a night job here."

"I've just moved to Jacksonville," I said. "I've gone through a lot, but there's no good reason to go into all that. Hire me for six or seven nights a week, and I'll be here for at least a year."

She raised her eyebrows at that. "Don't try to con me, Carl. Nobody stays at a job like this that long."

"Try me." I half-smiled, half-glared at her, challenging her to take a chance on me.

"Well, believe me, I'll keep you in mind."

"Great! Thanks!" and I left the store and turned south.

That was just what I had hoped for. Even if I wasn't able to land a job on the spot, I wanted to make an impression so they might call me first if something came up.

Bonus! There was a thrift store along the way on Edgewood. I took a quick detour to browse through it, but told myself to stay away from the clothing. The clothing I had was plenty and it probably wouldn't fit me long if I kept walking this much and eating sensibly. There was no reason to buy any more until I lost a lot more weight.

I did, however, find a metal thermos that looked ok that would hold maybe two cups of coffee. I searched briefly, but couldn't find a glass coffee pot for my Melitta filter holder. The thermos was two dollars, which seemed a bit high, but my own shopping costs in terms of travel time were so high I took it anyway.

And a cookbook! Better yet, a Better Homes and Gardens cookbook. I would need one of their bags to carry the thermos and cookbook, but I wanted to get them.

My next stop was one of the two 7-11s that were hiring.

Me, to the clerk, "Hi, I'm here to apply for a job. I called about an hour ago?" still the questioning tone.

"Ok, leave your resume with me and we'll get back to you."

This was the second time the clerk seemed to be the manager. It puzzled me. Maybe in larger operations there would be someone in some office somewhere, but for these first two places, the day clerk seemed also to be the manager. I asked.

"Are you the manager?"

"Yeah, sort of. I look after most stuff for the owners. You got a resume?"

"No, I'm sorry, I don't have one. Do you have an application form I can fill out?" and I thought to myself, "I may have to figure out how to use the software and printers in libraries and print out a bunch of resumes if this was the way to apply for a job."

He said, "Hold the fort while I go look for one."

What?? He's going to just go off and leave me alone in the store? He didn't even bother to lock the cash register! Oh well, not my problem.... Yet.

He was back in about twenty seconds, so it was probably no big deal. He had undoubtedly sized me up and didn't expect me to grab twenty cartons of cigarettes and run off with them. And maybe they had hidden security cameras so he could check on me from the office.

Again I completed the form, noting that it also had the parental-signature-required statement for young applicants. I approved. I wouldn't want Timothy working the night shift in a convenience store, and certainly not Liz.

"When can you start?" he asked.

"As soon as possible."

"Okay, Carl," he had looked at the application to get my name.

And then he looked again.

"Where is Hughes High School, Carl?" he asked suspiciously. "I lived in Houston for three years, and I never heard of it."

Should I bluff, admit it was a lie, or just leave?

Bluff. "It's a small school on the west side. Howard Hughes donated the land for it."

"Oh." He seemed to accept that and nodded. "What are you doing here, then?"

"I needed a change, a fresh start," I said, "and ended up here in Jacksonville."

And then to reassure him I added, "I've already signed a one-year lease on a place to live in, so I'm not going anywhere soon, if that matters to you."

"It does, Carl. Look, I can't make any hiring decisions on the spot without checking with the owners, but I'll get back to you within the next two days, okay? And don't take any other jobs without checking back with me, okay?"

"That'll be fine," I said and touched my neck behind my ear with my left hand. He seemed eager. "What would the pay be?"

"Minimum plus fifty."

"$5.65?" I asked. "I'll keep you in mind before I take anything else, but I'd like to do better than that."

"If we work something out," he said, "and if you last, we can talk about when you'd get your raises."

"That sounds a lot better," I smiled. "Thanks so much!" and I left the store.

The next stop was back toward downtown at Post and McDuff, a Thane-Mart, a store name I had never heard of. The quasi-Shakespearean reference amused me: "Lead on!" I said to my feet, knowing full well that I was misquoting Shakespeare but I didn't care because I liked "Lead on" better. Too bad the cross street wasn't MacDuff instead of McDuff.

Along the way there, I finished the remnants of my lunch and drank more water. I was still wearing my necktie and my dress shoes, but the walk was less than a mile according to my street atlas, and the Band-Aids seemed to be protecting my feet pretty well.

When I neared the convenience store, I realized it was larger and more comprehensive than the last two I had visited: it had four self-serve modern gas pumps and a lot of action. I smiled to myself when I saw the sign over the door: Thane's Q-Mart, wondering if the franchise was owned by someone named Thane, or whether the owner was making a play on McDuff.

Inside, there were three cash registers. Right then there were two people working the tills, and a third was rearranging the shelves, moving items to the front on each shelf to fill in the spaces left where things had been sold.

I looked around and was hesitating. I had no idea who to approach. The person who was working in the aisles was a man about my age. He looked up asked, "Can I help you find something?"

"I'm here about your night-shift job," I said. No question mark in my response this time, and I have no idea why not.

He hesitated a split second as he looked me over and then said, "Sure. C'mon back to the office," and he led me to the back of the store. "Let's see your resume."

"I don't have a resume done up yet. I was hoping to fill out an application form."

"Okay, let's start with names. I'm Dick Thane. Who are you? And why should I hire you?"

I wasn't expecting a job interview. I usually liked to prepare for important things. Oh well, into the breach.

I reached out my hand to shake his. "Carl Jacobs. And you should hire me because I'm a quick learner, a good decision-maker, reliable, and willing to work nights."

With that, Dick stood up, shook my hand and said, "Tell me your background, Carl."

I was applying for a schlock job, not a management position, and his manner puzzled me. Suddenly it hit me that he was sizing me up to be a night manager eventually.

I rattled off my work experience and high school. "You can check with them if you want references."

"You know what, Carl? I'm skeptical about it all, but I have no interest in checking out your past employers or references. I want you to do something for me, Carl."

"Sure."

"Go back into the store and outside. Look around for a few minutes. Don't take forever. Then come back in and we'll talk."

"Okay," I nodded. What was this about?

"Tell me your thoughts," Dick said when I returned to his office.

"Well, you have a thriving business that is well set for peak period business if you can figure out the peaks and hire part-timers for those peaks. I didn't see any security cameras. Either they're well-hidden or you must have more than just a few gas-and-goes from the pumps and some fairly regular robbery attempts. You have a huge convex mirror over the door, which may help deter shoplifting a bit. The store is well-lit, which makes customers feel good, and the aisles are clean and inviting, which is great. The snacks are near the front, making them easy to pick up for people who have the munchies and tempting for everyone else. And you have enough other stuff to make it pretty close to providing the basics that people might be willing to pay high prices for when they feel they need them. The coolers and freezer have a great selection. The restroom is clean and well-stocked, too. Overall I see a lot of attention to making the place attractive so customers will want to come here, not resent it."

"Carl," Dick said, "good observations. I could hire you here for this store, but we just opened another Thane's Q-Mart up north last week. My wife is running it now and working the night shift there. I think it might be better for us to have you working up there, not here. Is there a chance you could go up and chat with her later?"

"Well, yes, I guess so. But tell me more about what you have in mind."

"Carl, have you ever worked in a convenience store cum gasbar?"

"No. I told you the most relevant work experience I've had."

"Be honest. Have you ever worked in retail?"

"No," I repeated slowly. "I told you the most relevant work experience I've had." .... And then I smiled.

"Okay, smart ass. You clearly have some smarts and skills and I think we can work things out between us. You're lying about your past, and I'm sure you have your reasons, but my gut feeling is that we'd be making a big mistake to let you slip through our fingers. I sure hope I'm not wrong."

"Thanks, Dick. I've only recently arrived in Jacksonville, and I appreciate your confidence in me. I want to assure you that I've never been charged with or even investigated for anything illegal. And as you can tell, I am discerning and I will be a quick study. Where's the store up north? That might actually suit me better anyway, depending on where it is."

"It's at the southwest corner of Pearl and Beechwood, near 39th. You know where that is?"

"I think so," I lied. I knew right where it was, just a few blocks north of the Brentwood Library and convenient to the trailer park. In fact, I had walked right past it on Saturday afternoon. I had no idea why I lied, but I saw no reason to be open about a lot with Dick. Maybe I just didn't want to seem too eager.

"What time should I get there?"

"I'll call Alicia as soon as we're done here and suggest she go in early. She's usually there at 6 each evening. Why don't you try to get there by 5:30 to have chat with her?"

"That's sounds good, Dick, thanks. I hope things work out."

We shook hands again, and I started to leave.

As I got to his office door, I hesitated.

"Dick, was this a test?"

"What do you mean?" He seemed genuinely confused.

"You have no information about me: phone number, address, what-have-you, and you haven't asked me to fill in any forms. Were you testing me to see how thorough I would be? How careful?"

"Not at all, Carl. It's more an indication of how careless I can be at times. You can give us all that information this evening when you're done talking with Alicia, my wife."

"Okay, but just in case something comes up, I think we should at least exchange phone numbers now. Here's mine," and I wrote it on the back of one of the business cards that were in a holder on his desk. "Is this yours?" I asked as I picked up a second card from the holder.

"Yes," and he reached out and took the card from me. "And here's Alicia's," he said as he scrawled it on the back of the card.

I thanked him again and went to the restroom to wash my hands and refill my 7UP bottle before I left to catch the bus.

* * *
**

Chapter 29 – *My First Job?*

I was delighted with how things seemed to be shaping up, but I was more than a little concerned. Dick seemed to accept me with almost no good reason. On the plus side, I guessed that he had had several applicants who had not looked particularly impressive compared with my white shirt, necktie, and dress shoes. Also, I expected that my fairly quick but careful description of his store was probably different from anything else he might have gotten from previous applicants.

So why didn't he ask me to fill out an application form? Was it because he really was lazy and did things by the seat of his pants? His office was a bit of a jumble, and so I concluded that was the case.

Still, I felt a twinge of uneasiness. What if Alicia and I didn't get along? I guessed she was thorough and organized, maybe to a fault. If so, she could very easily raise red flags about hiring me. I expected her to be hesitant, even resistant, if Dick was prone to making rash judgments about people. I felt so uncertain about what would happen with the Thanes that I decided to apply for more jobs that afternoon.

It was just a little past one o'clock when I left the Thane-McDuff store. I had more than four hours to make my way up to Thane-North to meet with Alicia. I walked along Beaver Street toward downtown, and whenever I passed any business that looked remotely interesting, I went in and asked if I could apply for a job.

For the most part I was told they weren't hiring. A printing shop asked if I had any experience in a print shop, but the best I could offer was that I had used a copier on one of my previous jobs. I filled out application forms at a couple of fast food places, but they didn't seem very encouraging. An auto parts supplier seemed interested until they learned I couldn't drive to deliver parts to various auto repair shops.

By the time I had crossed the tracks and gone under the interstate, I was on the western outskirts of downtown and it was nearly 2:30. It looked as if I had only another two or three miles to go, and so I ambled up Pearl Street and stopped at the college, where I refilled my water bottle and rested in a comfortable chair in a lounge area. I set my watch alarm for 4:00 to allow myself plenty of time to get to Thane-North by 5:30, and I dozed off.

A college security officer awakened me half an hour later.

"Excuse me, sir, but are you a student here?" asked the polite, uniformed woman.

"No, I'm not," I answered, "but I'm thinking of taking some courses. I walked here and got tired. I hope it's okay that I sat here to rest a bit."

That lie, plus my dress shoes and necktie probably were convincing. Convincing enough anyway.

"Okay," she said, not at all skeptically. "But you seemed to be trying to shout in your sleep."

"I think I had been dreaming." I wondered how often the nightmares from 9-11 would recur.

"You will be moving on again soon?"

I looked at my watch. 3:45.

"Perfect timing. I need to leave in just a few minutes for my next appointment."

She smiled and said, "Have a good day, sir."

"Thanks," I said as I rose and made my way to the men's restroom.

I'd been trying to shout at Ben in my sleep. He was on a subway car in New York City, and I was warning him not to go to the World Trade Center.

The security woman was still in the area when I came out a few minutes later, undoubtedly to keep tabs on me. I nodded in her direction and walked out the door, and on up Pearl Street.

As I neared the Brentwood Library Branch, I remembered that I wanted to have some reading material. I checked out Defoe's **Robinson Crusoe** for no good reason other than that I felt stranded on an island. An island of isolation in a city awash with people. Weird. An island of my own making. What was all that nonsense about "No man is an island"? So much touchy-feely Pollyanna nonsense. I was an island in so many different ways.

I also checked out a Rex Stout mystery, a Zane Grey western, and a P.G. Wodehouse novel, knowing those would be the books I would read before I even considered opening Defoe.

I got to Thane-North about 5:20 and spent some time looking around and considering the place. Why put it here? Why put it at an intersection that had considerably less traffic than other streets? They had six gas pumps, four on the side and two on Pearl Street. It seemed a bit like overkill in this neighborhood.

During the few minutes that I was looking, though, there was a steady flow of cars in and out of the gas station; it was never full, but it was getting steady business. I decided that in the long term, it might be ok. It was three blocks west of Main Street and two blocks east of Boulevard Street. It would have a local draw for sure, and it might be more convenient for drivers to come here for gas than trying to get in and out of a convenience store on one of the major thoroughfares. Also I was sure the rent was lower here, allowing the Thane-Mart to slightly undercut the major gas station prices on the major streets.

I straightened my tie, rolled down my sleeves, and rubbed my hand over my head to straighten my hair. Oops. I didn't have any hair.

I had a lot of habits to break.

It was 5:25 when I entered. The woman behind the cash register was a dye-job redhead about my age.

"Hello," I said. "I'm Carl Jacobs." Pause. No sign of recognition. Oh, oh.

I continued, "I believe Mr. Thane called and said I would be here about a job this evening at 5:30."

I hoped I hadn't made a serious gaff already.

"Oh, you're looking for Alicia," she said.

Her nametag said she was Maggy. I should have seen that.

Maggy continued, "She'll be here in a few minutes, then, I'm sure."

"Okay, thanks." And I began to wander around and look at the store carefully. The layout was similar to that at Thane-McDuff, but this store seemed a bit bigger with a wider variety of merchandise. Everything was new, but the shelves were not as neat as Dick was keeping them at Thane-McDuff. I reflected briefly: Dick knew the importance of keeping the store and its shelves neat and tidy, but he seemed less concerned about his office.

There were two cash registers here, but it was only Maggy on duty, and she had a steady stream of customers buying gas and snacks on their way home from work.

Finally Alicia arrived. She breezed in a few minutes after 5:30 and was promptly addressed by Maggy: "This guy is here to see you about a job, Alicia!" Maggy certainly seemed enthusiastic. I inferred that she was working longer and busier hours than she wanted, which fit with all the ads for clerks that I had seen in the classifieds.

Alicia turned and studied me for no more than a second or two. She hinted at a smile and walked toward me with her hand out.

"Carl? I'm Alicia Thane."

I shook her hand and smiled. "Hi. Yes, I'm Carl. Thanks for meeting me early."

"Carl, Dick seems to think pretty highly of you, so let's go back into the office and talk a bit." And she led me to a tiny room with a desk and two chairs. Unlike Dick's office, the desk was neat, with a few things on it, but no clutter.

Alicia sat down and turned on her computer. She was a wiry woman with short hair, dressed for work in slacks and a neat shirt-type blouse. She appeared to be in her late 30s or early 40s, maybe older – she had some lines showing on her face. She had a pleasant enough manner, but I was on edge, wondering what she was thinking and what she would be like.

"Carl, where are you from?" Alicia started.

"West Texas, then Houston," I answered.

"What brings you to Jacksonville?" So far no skeptical tone, just questions.

"To be honest, I'm not really sure why I chose Jacksonville. But it seems like a thriving, growing city, a good place to be." I almost went into a description of my quest for a new beginning, restarting my life, and all that, but stopped myself. "Don't say more than you have to," I reminded myself.

"Dick says you have no experience but seem pretty sharp. Tell me what you think about this operation here, Carl."

"The location puzzled me at first, not being on Main or Boulevard, but I see you're getting constant business anyway, and so I'm guessing people from the neighborhood find this location convenient and that people from farther out prefer coming here rather than having to negotiate the traffic on those busier streets, especially since your gas prices seem to be a shade lower than the prices along the major streets.

"You have a somewhat broader selection of merchandise here than at Thane-McDuff, but I noticed the shelves here are in slightly more disarray than the shelves there." I quickly added, "But then I walked in there just as Mr. Thane was finishing straightening the racks and shelves.

"I was surprised to see more gas pumps but fewer tills here. I'm guessing you would like more gas pumps in the southern store and that you'll put in another till here as business picks up."

"Bingo," said Alicia. "You're as good as Dick said you were. But cut the Mr. Thane nonsense. It's Dick and Alicia."

"Thanks."

"We want to offer you a job, Carl..."

I breathed a sigh of relief inside myself. I hoped it showed but only slightly.

A marimba tone on my phone interrupted her. Oh, no. I hoped Evelyn wasn't calling me again.

Alicia said "Go ahead and answer it. I've got several things to do here and then we'll talk some more," and with that she turned to her computer screen.

So I answered it.

"Hello?"

A man's voice. "Carl Jacobs," he demanded.

"Yes, this is Carl."

"This is Jack Fry. We're gonna take a chance on you. Get yourself here by seven pm and be wearing steel-toed shoes."

"Excuse me," I said. "Do I know you? Where are you calling from? And what is this about?"

"Yeah! Jack Fry. Wharfhousers. We need people and we'll take a chance on you."

"Okay....." I dragged out the okay very hesitantly. "Tell me more. You know. Pay, hours, benefits, length of the contract..."

"Listen, Carl. We're offering top dollar. Eight seventy-five an hour. No benefits. Night shift from 7 until we're done but no more than 10 hours a night. Guaranteed work for a week if you work out."

Alicia looked up. Clearly she was listening.

"Eight seventy-five is good, but what do I do for work after a week or a month or whenever the work runs out?"

Alicia smiled ever so slightly.

"This is the best we can offer Carl," said Jack.

"Jack, I appreciate this, and if you had offered me this job when we first talked this morning, I would undoubtedly have accepted it. But I'm in the middle of another job interview now. What's your number? I'll call you in half an hour. And there's no way I can get steel-toed shoes and get there in an hour without paying cab fare."

"We'll pay the cab fare. Twenty minutes." Jack was trying to negotiate. I didn't care.

"I'll get back to you as soon as I can. Thanks again, Jack." And I hung up.

Alicia looked at me and scowled a bit. I was on alert – it looked like a negotiating scowl. I didn't want to have to play games, but I would. I just looked at her blankly.

"Carl, it sounds as if you already have a good job offer. What are you doing here?"

"It's good hourly pay for that job, but it seems temporary. I'm looking for something a bit more stable. I'm still here because it looks to me as if Thane-marts are well-designed and ready to continue to grow. Also I get the sense that you and … Dick… would like to consider me for a store manager position at some point. I see a chance here to develop a career."

"You've gotten a pretty good read on us pretty quickly, Carl. Here's what we have in mind. Have a seat." She gestured to the chair at the side of her desk."

"We'll start you at only $5.50 an hour for the first month. During that month we'll train you and work with you. I'll be on the night shift with you part of the time for the first week, and we'll be available by phone if you have any questions after that.

"After a month, if we both want you to stay and if you want to stay, we'll give you a $50 bonus right then and a raise to $6.00 an hour for the next two months, and from then on, time-and-a-half for statutory holidays. If things are still working out by New Years, you'll get another fifty-dollar bonus and a raise to $6.50 an hour. Another raise to $7.00 after six months, and after a year we can talk about putting you on salary with benefits.

"How does that sound? It's not $8.75, but it's stable and steady with growth potential."

"I like it, Alicia…."

My phone rang again.

Alicia smiled, and sighed an exaggerated sarcastic sigh. "The deal's off, Carl, if you're going to be on your phone all the time."

I laughed a bit. I hoped it wasn't Jack, but if it was I'd be happy to tell him I was declining his offer.

"Hello?"

"Is this Carl Jacobs?" a different man's voice.

"Yes....?" Again I was hesitant.

"This is Bill Smiley from Arby's, Carl. Is there a chance you can come in tomorrow to talk about working here?"

"Well, I'm about to take a job working the night shift in a convenience store, Bill. What did you have in mind?"

"Oh no," said Bill. "We need people for nights, too. If it doesn't work there, let me know."

"Okay, I will. Thanks a lot, Bill." And I hung up.

I looked at Alicia and smiled sheepishly. "Maybe it's the necktie?"

She snorted.

"What hours would you like me to work, Alicia?"

"When you're training in the first week, we'll want you here ten hours a night, starting at nine. I'll work with you for at least three hours each night, probably a lot longer to start, but you'll be on your own for sure between one and seven. After that, you'll be working eight-hour shifts from eleven to seven. How many nights do you want to work?"

I gulped a bit. I didn't want to give away how pleased I was.

"To start, I'd like to work every night," I replied, "but after a month I will probably want to be spelled off now and then."

"Perfect," Alicia smiled. "Let's get the paperwork done. Can you start tonight?"

"Sure! But I think double time is more appropriate for Christmas Eve, Christmas, New Year's Eve, and the Fourth of July. Time and a half is okay for other statutory holidays."

"You're probably right. Okay."

I was so pleased. I couldn't believe my luck. I expected I'd have no better things to do with my time on those holidays anyway, so the extra pay would just be a bonus.

"I'd like to go home and have some supper and wash up," I added. "How about I come back at 7:30? We can do the paperwork and I can observe and learn, off the clock, for a couple of hours."

Alicia stared at me in disbelief. "Carl, that's so different from most people we end up with. I hope we can hang onto you and that you're not conning us."

"It'll work, Alicia, but just to make sure would you mind writing out the offer for me? Just so there's no misunderstanding?"

This time Alicia sighed for real. "Okay. I can see why you'd like that. You don't know me from Eve."

I smiled inwardly that she said "Eve" and not "Adam", but said "Thanks. I'll be back at 7:30."

I distinctly remember that I very nearly danced my way back to the trailer. All five blocks.

* * *
**

Chapter 30 -- **Training**

I called Jack Fry during my near-dance home. He sounded tough and gruff and furious when I told him I wouldn't be accepting his job offer, which made me even happier that he hadn't offered me the job that morning. I really didn't want to work for a guy with macho-bully tendencies.

I was famished when I got back to the trailer shortly after six, and so I heated up some of my leftover pork roast in the microwave. While it was heating, I ate some celery with peanut butter.

Man, that roast tasted good! I really wanted to celebrate, and I think that helped me enjoy the roast even more. I made some coffee and rinsed out my newly acquired thermos, showered, changed my socks, and put on my running shoes. I poured the coffee into my thermos, checked my pocket for keys, and left. On the way back to Thane North, I looked to make sure of the street address for The Palm's Trailer Park. I also noticed that the laneway that lot 27 was on was called East 41st Street, but I wasn't sure of the exact address. Oh well, I could work it out later.

I got back to Thane-North before 7:30. Business was steady, but slower than it had been at rush hour. Maggy was still working on the till. She smiled at me and nodded toward the office.

Alicia's paperwork was perfect. It set out what she had said about the job, making clear that it was not a contract but an expectation on the part of both of us, whatever that meant. She also had added that I would be guaranteed a minimum of forty hours per week but would likely be offered forty-eight or more.

She had an employment form that asked for my name, address, telephone number, next of kin, and social security number. They also wanted my bank account number so they could do direct deposit.

"Alicia, is it okay if I bring in a voided check tomorrow for the direct deposit?"

"Yeah, sure." She seemed distracted.

"Also, I'm not sure of my address. I'm renting a trailer just a few blocks from here over on Main Street. Should I put in the lot number and the street address of the trailer park?"

"Yeah, sure," she replied, as if to say, "Whatever. It doesn't matter."

"And for next of kin, I don't really have any. How about I ask my landlady if I can list her?"

"Yeah, sure," again. She clearly didn't care. And yet so much about her seemed quite precise. I wondered if maybe she was precise about some things and not others.

"Go on out to the floor, Carl. I'll be out in a few minutes and we can get started."

So I went back out into the store and began straightening the shelves as I familiarized myself with the products. I wanted to know what we carried and where it was in the store. In addition to all the snacks, there were the basics: facial tissues, toilet paper, feminine hygiene products, condoms, soup, crackers, canned spaghetti and other canned goods. No hot dogs or buns. I wondered why.

When Alicia came out, she showed me how to log in and operate the till, how to take credit cards, and how to use bankcards. She also made a point that anytime the cash in the till got over two hundred dollars, I was to deposit fifty dollars through a slot into a bolted down safe to which I would not have the combination. The computerized till would alert me to do that. "Good security," I thought.

"No checks," she added, "and no hundred dollar bills."

"What if they buy gas and that's all they have?"

"Take something valuable from them and hold it until they come back with something smaller than a hundred."

"How about putting in a cash machine?" Left hand to the neck. I had to stop making managerial suggestions. I hadn't even started the job yet.

"Great idea, Carl. You're on our wavelength. We're looking into it now."

She continued, "There shouldn't be any deliveries after midnight. .... With one exception. The scheduling folks at the gasoline depot usually try to have their driver come in with gas during the wee hours of the morning. That's good for us because it doesn't disrupt our business then, so we don't really mind except we don't know exactly when they'll be here. But that's not a problem for you. They come in, they dump a load of gas, we give 'em a coffee and a cookie, and that's that. Nothing for you to worry about."

"Well, I hope they don't come tonight. I'd really like to have a firmer grip on the job before that."

Then Alicia looked at me quite sternly. "Another thing, Carl. We have insurance. If someone tries to hold you up, ***do not resist!*** Give 'em the cash." Pause. "You got that?"

"Yes ma'am. I have no interest in being a hero." More thought-stopping as I put my left hand to my neck. Again too many words. When would I ever learn to shut up?

The training period went smoothly that evening. Maggy logged out from the till at eleven, and it was just Alicia and me. During the next two hours, she told me about ordering supplies for the store and about ordering merchandise.

"Most of the time the distributors look after the shelves, freezers, and coolers," she said. "Frito-Lay has a route driver who checks the dates on our chips. He takes out the older stock and replenishes our supply. Same with the candy, dairy, Coke, and Pepsi distributors. We do need to keep an eye on the household supplies and a few other things, though, because we have to pick those up at Costco whenever we run low."

That was weird, I thought, but then I realized it made sense. Dick and Alicia bought things like soups and canned spaghetti and paper products in bulk at Costco and essentially were paid for doing that in the form of the higher prices they charged at the Thane Marts. For small inventories in a couple of stores, it was probably just as cheap and just as convenient to pick things up at Costco as to order small amounts from suppliers.

I got a notepad from Alicia and wrote down the various instructions she had given me and checked them with her to make sure I understood them correctly.

"Two more things, Carl. Since you're working the night shift, help yourself to coffee and cookies. Oh, here's the coffee machine." And she showed me how to use it. "Be sure to make a new pot every hour. Anything older than an hour begins to taste a bit off. The cookies and pastries are usually brought in around 5am. Just check the order and sign for it.

"The other thing is that you look nice and professional in a white shirt and tie. They aren't necessary, but they do look nice." The clear implication was that it would be really important to my future there if I continued to wear a dress shirt and necktie.

She wished me luck and left.

Things went well that night. Sales were spotty after about midnight. I drank my coffee, but didn't have a cookie or anything else, proudly reassuring myself that working in a convenience store would be one heck of a test of my will power.

I realized I wouldn't need to bring coffee to work any more. I also realized my entire sleep patterns would be messed up. But I wanted to work every night I could and stay on this schedule.

For the first few months I would probably net over $250 a week, and after six months I'd be netting over $300. I wouldn't want to raise a family on it, but it would be more than enough for me. I could probably save nearly half of it and begin replenishing my nest egg…. After I bought a new laptop and signed up for internet service.

About 4:30, as I was struggling to stay awake and upright, the gasoline tanker arrived. The driver didn't come in right away, but got to work, hooking up a hose and filling the underground tanks. While the tanks were filling, he came in and without looking at me said, "I probably should stay with the hose. Ok if I just grab a cookie and coffee before I go back out?"

"Sure," I said while thinking, "As opposed to doing what, exactly?" Or was that just his usual patter. I poured the coffee and he took a cookie, looking at me a bit strangely.

"You new?"

"Sorta, I guess," I replied.

"Hope you like it." And with that he was back out the door.

At about 6:50, someone who looked about 17 came in. I later learned he was closer to 27.

"Hi," he said. "I'm the 7 to 3 shift. You new?"

"Hi," I replied. "Yes, I'm new. I'm Carl Jacobs. What's your name?"

"Jerry Muller. I've been working here for three months now. I like the Thanes. You know, this is the best job I've ever had. I deal with all the suppliers who come in to check the stock."

"I've only met the Thanes recently, but I think I will like them, too," I agreed.

"Are you about to log in?" I asked, referring his to entering his own identification number into the computerized cash register.

"I'll be right there," he said, and then he disappeared into the restroom for a few minutes. When he re-emerged, he was wearing a clean dress shirt and had his hair slicked back. He came around the counter to the till and entered his identification number, making sure his body was between me and his fingers.

"Smart guy," I thought. "Or at least smart enough to be careful."

I mimicked his actions, logged out, and with just a hint of relief said, "See you tomorrow." I picked up my thermos bottle, and left. There was no time card and no punch clock; the logging in and out was designed to compute our hours. I liked that. I wondered if it would compute my pay each week and send it to my bank.

On the way home that morning, I took a detour via the discount store for yet another visit, hoping they'd be open by 7:30 so I could buy some more dress shirts, but they weren't. Oh well, extra exercise.

I was totally exhausted by the time I got home, but I pulled down the crockpot and started another pork roast with whatever cut up vegetables I still had in the fridge. Then I heated up some more of the leftover pork roast from the fridge because I was too tired to fry up some eggs and vegetables. I set my watch alarm for 4:30pm and collapsed into bed.

When the alarm woke me up, I groaned. I was still tired even though I'd had nearly eight hours of sleep. A shower and some of the fresh pork roast from the crockpot fixed that. I prepared the rest of the roast for the fridge and freezer and took some of the old roast out of the freezer to have for my lunch at work. I cut up some more vegetables and put them in bags in the fridge.

I decided to go up to the discount store, where I bought two more white shirts and two conservative neckties. On the way home, I stopped at the grocery store to buy more vegetables. I also looked in at one of the other laundromats. It seemed somewhat better than the one at the trailer park, but not enough better to walk to all the time.

I finally admitted to myself with a smile that eventually I would have start washing clothes and stop buying clothes.

- - -

Over the next few days at Thane-North, Alicia went through more details with me.

- Power outage? Initially, just use cash or the old hand-push charge-card gadget. The pumps would shut off, but get the totals from the customers who were in the middle of pumping gas and trust them – don't leave the store. If it's more than thirty minutes, shut the store and call us. Don't open the coolers.
- Shoplifters? Gas-and-go? Try to get the license plate numbers. Don't try to stop them.
- Job applicants? Give them a form to complete and size them up. Chat with them a bit and see what you think.
- Can't make it to work for some reason? Make sure you let us know well in advance; otherwise be here.
- Pay? The first month we'll pay you at the end of each week by check. After that, we'll set up a bi-weekly direct deposit.
- Bathroom breaks? Use it before you start, and later in your shift make sure there's no one in the store and the till is locked.
- Supplies and merchandise re-ordering? Add the item here on this pad on the counter behind the cash register.
- Cigarette sales? Make sure they're 18. We set an age policy of 21, but allow for it to be shaded down to 18 without telling the customers.
- Beer and wine sales? Check their I.D. if they don't look at least 30.
- If Jerry or a replacement don't show up at 7am? Stay and we'll pay time and half, but call us. We'll have someone here in under two hours.

And of course we went through everything several times to make sure I had it all.

My third night there, some smart-alec young teen decided to try to shoplift some candy bars while Alicia was still there. Just as he was getting to the door I called out, "Would you like me to hold those candy bars for you here at the cash register while you continue shopping?"

He dropped them and ran.

"Where on earth did you learn that?" Alicia asked.

"I don't know. I didn't want to confront him, but didn't want to let him just sneak out. That was the first thing that occurred to me."

"Well, it won't always work, but that was good!" she said.

- - -

After just a few nights, I decided I wanted food ready for me when I got home from work, not after I slept. And so I had my veggie omelettes after I got up in the late afternoon and set the crockpot going when I left for work whenever I wanted to use it.

On the way home one morning, I called Evelyn.

"Hi, Evelyn. It's Carl Jacobs. I thought I'd give you a call to let you know how things are going."

"Oh!" she exclaimed. "Carl! I'm glad you called. How **are** you? I didn't want to bother you, but I'm dying to hear how you're doing."

"Well, things are going pretty well. I have a job and I seem to be adjusting okay to working nights."

"That's great, Carl. What's the job?"

"I'm working nights at a convenience store. They seem to have a fair amount of confidence in me. I expect I'll be a night manager in a few months, but that won't mean doing anything different than I'm doing already --- just higher pay."

"Wonderful! Where is it?"

"It's the new Thane Q-Mart over on Pearl and Beechwood."

"Oh, I think I've seen it. Would it be okay if stop in to say hello now and then?"

"Sure…" but I wasn't sure. I hoped it wouldn't be often or that she wouldn't be distractive if she came by.

She must have sensed my feelings from my tone. "Oh, don't worry, Carl. I know, I know. I'll just stop in for gas and tonic or something."

"Gas and tonic!" I laughed.

"Evelyn, I'm loving the trailer…."

"I'm so glad," she interrupted.

"But I have a couple of really basic questions."

"Okay…." She stretched out the …kay part of okay, sounding just a bit concerned.

"Oh there are no problems at all," I hastened to reassure her. "I just wanted to know what the mailing address is for the trailer, or what I do about mail."

"Oh," she said using three different notes for the one syllable, and giggled a bit out of relief. "Just give people the address of the Trailer Park and add 'suite 27'. That's what the Bunters across the lane from you do, and I think it's so terribly clever. I think the folks running the park do, too. There's a jumbo box for mail next to the trailer park office. Oh! I need to give you a key for that. I'll stop by soon with it." And she gave me the postal code.

I laughed. "I like that version of the address. Evelyn, another thing. They want to know my next of kin for the job, but there's not really anyone I can list. I was wondering if I could list you and Don on the forms."

"Why, Carl! I'd love to be listed. Feel free."

"And, Evelyn, if this job doesn't work out, would it be okay for me to list you as a reference? I know we don't really know each other very well, but I might need a reference from someone here in Jacksonville."

"I know, I know. And of course."

"Well, thanks, Evelyn. I really appreciate it."

We said our good-byes and hung up.

* * *
**

Chapter 31 – *Settling In*

The Thanes did their payroll every Thursday night, as of midnight, and paid their employees on Fridays by noon. So when I arrived at work my first Friday, there was a check waiting for me for $162. I did the math quickly and realized they had deducted $19.50 for various taxes, but I still felt rich. I couldn't wait to deposit the check into my Everbank account and at the same time move more money from my Omaha account. I did all that on Saturday morning. I also treated myself to breakfast out that day --- still just a veggie omelette with no potatoes and no toast, but it was a treat because I didn't have to prepare it or clean up afterward.

Sunday morning, as I was ready to go off my shift, Evelyn stopped in. I offered her some coffee and one of the cookies that I never ate even though Alicia had said I could have some. We stood outside the store and chatted a bit after she moved her car from one of the gas pumps. It was good to see her.

"Would you like a ride home, Carl?" she asked.

"How about up to the grocery store?" I replied. "I need to pick up a few things. I thought maybe I'd try some chicken in the crockpot this week, and I'm about to run out of eggs."

As we drove there, I laughed at myself as I told her I had finally figured out that setting the crockpot up before I went to work would be more sensible than counting on doing that when I got home. I was tired when I got off work and just didn't feel like doing all that work then.

"Oh, how's Don doing?" I asked.

"About the same," she answered matter-of-factly, "but going downhill slowly. We've had to hire some home care workers to come in a couple of hours each day to help look after him and to make sure he does some exercises while I'm out at work. I count on having some time to myself. I wouldn't be able to stay home all the time. I know, I know, but it's just not in me. I go to church off and on, too, just to get out some. I'm on my way there now, but I can wait while you shop and drive you home..."

"Oh don't do that, Evelyn. I'd feel rushed just because I wouldn't want to keep you waiting, and I'd really like to take my time."

"Well.... Okay." She sounded what? Skeptical? Disappointed? I wasn't sure.

Then she reached over and took my hand. A firm grip.

"Carl, I know this sounds odd, but you have been a very important person to have suddenly come into my life. I don't understand it, but I'm glad."

I squeezed her hand and said, "Well, thanks. I don't know where I'd be if it weren't for you. Probably living at some mission, eating scraps from a dumpster behind a diner." and I smiled a bit, squeezed her hand again, and got out. "Thanks for the lift," I waved as I closed the door.

As I carried my groceries home I wondered about Evelyn. What was the connection between us? I had never felt anything like a "connection" with anyone before in my entire life, not even with Susan. Was this one of the things I had been looking for and that had been missing from my life? It made me feel uneasy. I didn't trust it or like it, but still I liked it. I felt so conflicted. I wondered if maybe it was just her positive "vibes" toward me that made me feel the connection. I didn't understand it. And it didn't help that she was married. That added to the guilt I felt for liking the sense of a connection.

When I got home, I distracted myself with household chores, eating, and sleeping. Late that afternoon I finally tackled my laundry. Two loads in the washers, one in a dryer, and I read some Rex Stout while doing the laundry.

- - -

No one else at Thane-North worked seven days, but I was tickled to have all the shifts I could get. I was netting over $270/week that first month, and I realized I had found a resting place, a respite of sorts.

I settled in and began thinking more deeply about my future and who I wanted to become. My mind spun, and I made little-to-no progress. The process was so new to me. I had no idea how to begin. I had never been forced to contemplate my life before; somehow I had managed to avoid what must have been the identity crisis.

- - -

A month or so later Maggy showed up at 7am to begin the early day shift.

"Hi Maggy! I usually see you when I start, not when I quit."

"You got that, Carl," she said, "but I'm on the day shift starting today. We have enough business now that they have Jerry coming in from eleven to seven during the days. He likes to sleep late, and I get to go home earlier to be there with my kids. Win, win!"

"That's great!"

We talked a bit about her children. She had two, a bit younger than mine. She said that with her new work hours she could set out breakfast for them before coming to work, and then be there when they got home from school. I could see why that would be important for a parent. I almost started telling her about Timothy and Liz, but stopped, reminding myself, "You have no history, Carl!"

I guessed from our conversation that Maggy was a single mom. We hadn't chatted much before. When I had showed up about quarter to 11 for my shift, she was always eager to log out and leave, often a few minutes early. I didn't mind taking over a few minutes early then, and now I understood why she was so eager to get going. I wouldn't want to leave young teens or preteens alone five evenings a week either if I could avoid it.

"You gonna work Thanksgiving, Carl?"

"Geez, I hadn't thought about it. Yeah, I guess so. Will we even be open then?"

"Oh yeah, for sure we'll be open. So ya got no one to spend it with?"

I didn't want to answer. So I sidestepped the question.

"It's just that I want to work as much as possible. Do we get paid extra for working holidays?" I knew that I had been promised time-and-a-half for most holidays and double time for a few major holidays, but I didn't think I should mention it in case it wasn't standard policy.

"You betcha we do. Time-and-a-half."

"Oh! That'll sure come in handy."

"Carl, I asked about Thanksgiving cuz it's hard to find replacements for the holiday. The Thanes can usually find temps for most days, but I'd really like some time off then when the kids aren't in school. I'm wondering if you'd be interested in working a coupla shifts for me that Thursday and Friday."

I thought about it for a few seconds. I could sure use the money because the laptop and software I wanted would not be cheap. I knew working 16-hour days would be exhausting, but figured I could do it if it was only for a couple of days.

"Well, I think so," I hesitated. "I think I can handle the work, but do you think the Thanes would go for it? What if we talk to Jerry or to whoever takes over your evening shift to see if I can split with them and do only 12-hour shifts?"

"Carl," Maggy said, "That...is... brilliant. I'll talk to Alicia and Jerry about it later this week. I don't wanna press my luck with them right now cuz I just got put on this early day shift. I'm so happy with it. But I'll ask in a few days."

"Okay!" I agreed with her plan.

I logged out and thought about getting a laptop as I walked home. I knew I had enough money to buy one then, but I wanted more of a cushion. I had already moved all my money from Omaha to Everbank, and I had put all of it plus some leftovers from my paychecks into a savings account there. I had even set up internet banking, despite not having a computer, and I now had a credit card with a $1000 credit limit! "Woohoo!" I muttered sarcastically! It felt so strange to be happy with minor things like that. It was also annoying to be earning so little interest on my savings account. I knew that at some point I would have to reconsider what to do with my savings.

Maggie and I chatted frequently after that. She didn't want to work weekends, but that was fine with Alicia and Dick; they had hired students to work those shifts from the beginning of Thane-North.

About a week later, Alicia stopped in before my shift was over but before Maggy checked in.

"Carl, are you still okay working every night shift?"

"Sure," I said. And then I became a bit concerned. "Why do you ask? Is everything all right?"

"Oh, we're delighted that you're willing to do this. Just be sure to give us plenty of notice if you ever feel you want a shift or two off."

I breathed a sigh of relief.

"There are two other things I want to talk about with you, though, Carl."

"Hmmm," I thought, still worried, but I just said, "Sure. What are they?"

"First, we don't want to lose you as long as you're happy here, and we want to keep you happy here. We're bumping your pay up to $6.50 now instead of later, and giving you your second fifty-dollar bonus now."

I tried to take that in. I'd be netting more than $320/week. I tried to hide my pleasure, but I did smile.

"Geez, thanks, Alicia. That'll all sure come in handy."

"The other thing is that Maggy has asked about getting some time off at Thanksgiving. She said you mentioned the idea of maybe splitting her shifts with Jerry, and he's okay with it, but he'd like to work 9-'til-9 if that's okay with you. Would you be willing to work the other 9-'til-9 on Wednesday, Thursday, and Friday nights over Thanksgiving weekend? The pay, as I promised is time-and-a-half for all your Thursday hours on Thanksgiving."

"That'll work great for me, Alicia. I know I could go the full 16 hours if I took over her shifts, but it's better not to have to work that long, especially since I always feel uncertain about taking bathroom breaks."

Alicia smiled. "I know what you mean. Just make sure you lock the till and don't dawdle."

"That's what I do," I said, and I smiled back.

- - -

At one point that fall, probably mid-October, about 4am a young teen came into the store wearing a hoodie up over his head with his hands in his hoodie pockets. He walked straight up to me at the till and said, "Have a gun. Give your money."

I thought maybe I had seen him a couple of times around one of the less-well-maintained trailers. I was surprised he didn't recognize me, but I'd always had my bucket hat on at the trailer park.

I looked at his pupils. Not dilated; not pinpoint; eyes not bloodshot. It was unlikely he was strung out on drugs.

I took a chance that in retrospect was probably stupid, but I said, "Show it to me. I'm not giving you a thing until I see your gun."

He turned around and walked slowly toward the door.

"Wait!" I shouted. "You want some money? I'll hire you."

What on earth had prompted me to say that? "Oh well, here goes..." I thought.

He turned and looked at me with a sad pleading look.

"Don't know how to do nothin'."

"I'll teach you a few things. You come in for one hour during my shift every night and I'll give you five dollars cash each time you're here."

Sigh. It would have to come out of my pocket, but oh well. Time for a new beginning.

"It's not much, but it's all I can afford. I'll pay you out of my own pocket, but you have to be reliable and willing to work."

"What time?" he asked.

"How about you come in a little after 11? That's when I start. Just come in after the person I replace leaves."

He looked at me suspiciously. "What I gotta do?"

"Clean the restroom, make sure the paper supplies there are good, empty wastebaskets, mop the floors there and out here, help neaten the shelves and racks, and wash the windows."

He looked shocked. "That sound like a lot. Don't know how to do any that."

I quickly learned that he often left off letters and left out words when he spoke.

"If you work steady, you'll get it done. And I'll teach you how to do each job."

"Can I start now?"

"Okay. As soon as we're done talking here, we'll start the clock. What's your name?"

"Ronnie.

"Ronnie what?" I asked.

 Ronnie Day."

"Where do you live, Ronnie?" I thought I knew the answer.

"My ma's in trailer park, but she not there much."

"Okay. My name is Mr. Jacobs. Now, let's start with washing the windows. Come with me."

I got some window washing fluid in a spray bottle and some paper towels and handed them to him. "You use this on the inside. Outside you use a bucket and a squeegee."

He just stood there. I had to explain each step carefully. He left huge smears and streaks, but I complimented him anyway. Then I got him to mop the floors. Explaining each step was painful, but he was a willing learner. I had him start out in the store so I could watch and be available in case he had questions. I wasn't going to criticize him no matter what he did, but I'd be ready if he had questions.

"Whatever you do," I cautioned him after he finished mopping the restroom floor, "don't forget to put out the wet floor sign before you mop. And since I'll want you to put the sign away when you're finished, maybe you should do the floors first thing when you get here from now on."

"Every night?" he asked incredulously.

"That's right. Now let me show you where the spare toilet paper is. I'm not going to show you how to change it, but I'll explain it if you need help."

"That okay, Mr. Jacobs, I can do that."

"Good. Now, did you see where I got the paper towels for doing the windows? Go get a stack about two inches thick."

When he came back with the towels, I explained how to open the paper towel holder in the restroom and asked him to top them up there. He went in and fussed about for a minute or two and then came back out empty handed. I assumed he was done, but instead he went to the storage closet and got another two inches or so.

"It pretty low so I got more," he said.

"Thanks."

I took that as an indication that I had made a good decision; at least it seemed that way. I sure hoped so.

When he came out, I said, "Thanks, Ronnie. It turns you DO know how to do stuff after all. If you could empty the wastebasket there in the restroom and back here, that'll just about do it for tonight."

"Where?" is all he asked.

"It's right here under the counter," I said, pulling it out. And then I saw the blank look on his face.

"Oh. There's a dumpster out back. Empty them there," and I handed him the undercounter wastebasket.

When he came back with the empty undercounter wastebasket, I had a five-dollar bill waiting in my shirt pocket for him.

"Here you go, Ronnie. See you tomorrow night?"

He didn't leave though. Instead he picked up a carton of milk and a box of cereal and brought them to me.

"You get an employee discount," I said.

I had never remembered to ask about the employee discount, but I assumed there was one. "With the discount, it comes to $4.25. If you can wait to buy groceries, though, they're a lot cheaper up at the supermarket."

"Want these now, but will next time."

"Okay. See you tomorrow."

"Yeah, I guess."

No "thank you", no anything. He just shuffled out the door, head down.

He'd been trying to rob the store to get money for food. Poor kid must have been desperate.

I just shook my head. I knew that I could barely imagine what his life must have been like. I hoped that if he worked out okay for this cleaning job, eventually I could get him hired formally by the Thanes so that he would have a work history he could use in the future. I hoped, but I worried.

* * *
**

Chapter 32 – *Ronnie*

Ronnie showed up the next night. And the next night, and every night. I taught him how to clean toilets, how to sweep floors and how to sweep the walk in front of the store, how to wash the outsides of the windows, how to clean the gas pumps, how to polish the doorframes and handles. He never said much, but he never had to be told twice how to do anything. The place was looking subtly but surely nicer all the time. Within a week or two, he just started looking around to see what needed doing, including straightening the shelves and neatening the items in the coolers and freezers; I didn't have to make many suggestions or answer many questions.

After a couple of weeks, it became clear that Ronnie was not spending the money he was earning on drugs or cigarettes or beer or anything like that. One night I asked him why he had come in and tried to rob the store.

"Got two little sisters. Wasn't no food," he said.

"Does anyone know you're doing this? Does anyone know about your sisters' not having enough food?"

"Nah. They'd just split us up and put us in different homes. Don't want that."

"Okay," I nodded. "I understand."

I didn't really understand. I had no clue. How could I understand, given my background? But I wasn't going to press him any more.

After another week or so, Alicia stopped by about midnight while Ronnie was still there.

"Oh, oh," I thought.

"Alright, you two." She said somewhat sternly. "What's going on here?"

"What do you mean?" I tried to play innocent. It didn't work.

"You know very well what I mean. This kid's been hanging out here every night doing little chores, and the place looks cleaner and better maintained than it ever did, something I didn't think was possible."

In that instant I decided not to tell her too much about how Ronnie and I had met.

"Ronnie lives in the trailer park and he wanted to earn a little money, so I've been paying him five bucks to come in each night and do some of the cleaning."

"Five bucks? Where are you getting this money?" She really sounded suspicious.

"I pay him out of my own pocket."

She turned to Ronnie, "What's your name, young man?"

"Ronnie Day."

"From now on, it's 'Ronnie Day, **Ma'am'**. Do you understand?"

"Yeah..." he said in a dejected-sounding voice.

"What?" She didn't scream. She just asked "What?" very forcefully.

Ronnie looked scared and confused.

Alicia caught on and said calmly "You don't say 'Yeah' in a situation like this, Ronnie Day. You say, 'Yes, ma'am'."

"Yes, ...ma'am."

"How long have you been doing this, Ronnie Day?"

"'bout a few weeks........ Ma'am."

He was learning quickly and willing to show respect. Another good sign.

Alicia glared at me and then turned back to Ronnie. "What's the agreement between you two?"

"I clean an hour.... Ma'am... and he give me five dollar cash."

"Do you two see each other outside work?"

I was stunned. She thought I was procuring young men.

"No, ma'am. I seen him walking sometimes but that all."

Whew.

"Carl, this better be on the up-and-up."

"Believe me, it is. I just wanted to help him out."

"Well this can't go on like this," and she looked at Ronnie again.

"Ronnie, how old are you?"

"Fifteen. " Pause. He looked at me and then at her and hastily added, "Ma'am."

"Do you have a social security number?"

"No, ma'am."

"You go get one, and we will hire you officially. And we'll pay you minimum wage, which is five-fifteen an hour. Carl, you owe Ronnie fifteen cents an hour for every hour he worked for you."

I hid my smile. I liked the way this was going.

"Let me make sure you understand this, Ronnie," she said. "I want you to keep working here, but you will be working for me. Mr. Jacobs will still be your manager, even though I'm the one who is giving you the job. But I can't give you any of the pay you will earn after tonight until you give me your social security number. Okay?"

"Yes, ma'am."

"Good. Carl, give him the money you owe him for the past and pay him for tonight now."

I gave him ten dollars.

"Now. What hour do you want to come in each day? You don't have to come in this late if some other time would suit you better."

He looked at me. "I like this, ma'am. Comfortable here this time of night."

I knew one reason he liked coming in late was that his sisters would be asleep, but I thought, too, that he was contented working with me and didn't want that to change.

"Okay. You just keep coming in. Carl, I'll leave it to you to keep track of his hours."

"Ronnie," she continued, "Take off now. You don't have to do any more work tonight. I need to speak with Mr. Jacobs for awhile."

"Yes, ma'am....." and he put his head down and mumbled, "Thanks."

I almost wept. I'd never heard him say "Thanks" and so I knew this was important to him. It was important for me, too. I was elated that it seemed to be working out.

When he was gone, I burst into laughter. A laughter of relief; a laughter of happiness.

"Alright, Carl, what's going on?"

"Ronnie is pretty much looking after his two younger sisters at the trailer park. His mom isn't there very much and there isn't much food in the house very often. He's working to get money to help feed his sisters. That's all I know.

"Well," I continued, "that, and he seems like he'll be a decent worker. He picked up on things pretty quickly. You should have seen his first attempt at cleaning the windows. The fact that he feels an obligation toward his sisters is a big plus, and he has shown up on time every night ever since I hired him. Thanks for your confidence and trust."

"Carl, don't ever do that again. As you know, we're hoping eventually to make you a manager. When that happens, you hire people the right way, on the books. You pay minimum wage, and you make sure everything is on the up-and-up. You got that?"

"Yes...........ma'am," emphasizing 'ma'am'.

She scowled at me. I smiled at her. And then we both laughed.

"I came by for another reason, too, Carl. We know you're working 9-to-9 over Thanksgiving, but we were wondering if you would like to come to our place for Thanksgiving dinner before you come to work that evening. We've also invited Maggy and her kids. Dick can pick everyone up about 5:30, then drive you back here for work by 9 and drop Maggy and her kids back home."

That sounded quite nice and quite welcoming. I was almost overcome. Almost. I just hoped they weren't trying to set me up with Maggy, who had become increasingly chatty during the morning switchover.

"I would really like that!" I enthused, and I meant it. "I was just going to stay home and read when I wasn't sleeping, but this sounds much, much better. Thank you so much!"

"I know you live at the trailer park, but where exactly?"

"It's lot 27. It's way at the back along 41ˢᵗ Street, backing onto the cemetery," I almost smirked but not quite. I was feeling giddy from happiness about the way things had worked out with Ronnie.

"Can I bring anything?" I was always taught to ask that.

"How about some dinner rolls." Alicia replied. A statement, not a question.

"That'll be fine," I said continuing to use my replacement phrase for "No prob, Bob." In fact I didn't even think about my old phrase anymore. "That'll be fine" had become natural for me."

Truth be told: In all my life, I had never had anyone tell me I could bring something when I asked, and I was somewhat taken aback by Alicia's response. I laughed at myself after she left. I contemplated trying to make some rolls from scratch but then said out loud, "Too much bother for that!" I decided I'd look for some "thaw'n bake" rolls in the freezer section when it came closer to the date. I also determined to pick up a decent chardonnay to take, too – decent meaning priced over ten dollars and probably from California.

Ronnie showed up right on time the next night, and he already had a social security number. Quite clearly this job was important enough that he figured out how to get his SSN in one day. That was yet another reason to think he could become something more than a street kid.

I wrote his name and social security number on the top of a sheet of lined paper and taped it to the inside of the storage closet door.

"Ronnie," I said, "just write the date, the time you arrive, and the time you leave on each row here, okay?"

"Where do I get date and time?"

I had a lot to learn about Ronnie. I was so far removed from his life.

He didn't have a watch and probably didn't really pay all that much attention to times or dates most of the time. And yet he somehow managed to show up on time for work every night. I wondered how he did that. I found out later that he watched television and left for work just before a show was ending at 11pm and made it to Thane-North by about 11:10 each night.

"Here on the screen," I answered and showed him where to find the date and time on the cash register screen. I knew I could tell him the date and time instead of having him look at the screen, but I wanted him to do things for himself every time he could. I would get him a digital watch for Christmas... if he was still around.

- - -

Thanksgiving was very significant for me that year. I had so much to be thankful for, and I really had to work hard to control my emotions that day: I was alive, I had a place to live that suited me perfectly, I had a job I actually liked -- a lot, and I was helping someone else get on with his life productively. I even had some friends, sort of. They were different from my friends in Omaha, but they were all I had for now.

By Thanksgiving I had dropped another twenty-odd pounds and was down to 180. I still had a long way to go to reach my goal weight of 150, but I already felt better. My clothes were getting a bit loose, but they weren't too obviously loose. I would wait to buy more until I lost at least ten more pounds. The one problem with working seven days a week was that I couldn't get to thrift shops to buy "new" clothes very easily when those shops were open. I would make time, though, when I got down to a 34-inch waist, which would likely be soon.

I worked until 9am on Thanksgiving morning and then scurried home after that twelve-hour shift. I needed to get some sleep and then get up by 3:30 to bake the Thaw'n'Bake buns, shower, shave, and be ready for Dick to pick me up. I decided to wear my sweater from the thrift shop over my striped dress shirt; it fit me perfectly now, and it looked both more casual and more dressy at the same time.

Dick arrived a little after 5:30, driving a Dodge minivan. When I got in the front passenger seat, Maggy and her children were already in the back, and we made our introductions. The kids seemed like normal kids. A bit shy and a bit giggly. The giggly part suggested to me that Maggy had talked about me at home, but perhaps I was being both too self-centered and too paranoid. Anyway, whether it was necessary or not, I got my guard up a bit. At the same time, it was hard not to feel an immediate attachment to the kids because I missed mine so much. I sighed silently and reminded myself that the last thing I wanted to do was trade in my Omaha life, wife, and kids for a replacement set down here in Jacksonville. I tried just to enjoy the time with them that evening.

The back of the minivan had boxes of supplies for the Thane Marts. It looked as if the minivan was an important storage facility for them. That helped explain how they could keep the shelves restocked fairly quickly. I wondered what portion of the minivan expenses they wrote off as business expenses. I hoped it was a lot.

The Thanes' house was a modest ranch in the western suburbs. Jerry Muller wasn't there because he was still working, but others from our store were there and so were a few people from the Thane-McDuff store. When I saw how many people were there, I wished I had brought more than just one bottle of wine, but at least I had made 24 dinner rolls. There was a turkey and a ham, already carved, plus all the fixin's. It reminded me of Thanksgivings on the farm as I was growing up, with all the family there. The food was put out on the table buffet style, and we had to eat from plates balanced on our laps, but it was all pleasant. There was constant commotion and hubbub, and I loved it. I turned down the wine, pleading that I would have to work all night and didn't want to be too groggy. There were pecan, pumpkin, and lemon meringue pies for dessert, though, and I broke down and had small pieces of each one.

At about 8:20, Dick said he'd have to round us up to drive Maggy and her kids home and me to work. As we were leaving, Alicia handed me two boxes of food.

"Here. One of these is for Jerry. You can give it to him when you get there. The other is for Ronnie when he comes in."

"How kind and thoughtful!" I said.

On the way back from the Thanes' home, Maggy asked, "Who is this Ronnie? I've seen a separate time sheet for him on the storage closet door, but I've never met him. He seems to work only an hour, but comes in every night while you're working, Carl."

"Yeah," I said. "He's a young kid from the area who is trying to help with expenses for his sisters, so Dick and Alicia have him come in to do some general cleaning and maintenance for an hour every night. Pretty nice, isn't it."

Dick turned his head sharply to scowl at me briefly. I'd given them the credit and not told the whole story. I could see he would file that away.

We dropped Maggy and her kids at a walk-up apartment building and then went to the store. On the way there, Dick confronted me.

"Carl, you made it sound as if hiring Ronnie was our idea, but you know very well it wasn't. Why'd you do that?"

"I don't know. I just didn't want to go into details about him, I guess."

"Or about you, obviously. We're not idiots, Carl. Alicia and I can see that you're not who you appear to be. You have both a toughness and a softness about you, but there's a darkness there, too. It concerns me. I need to know more about you."

I didn't want to go into anything about me, but I threw him some scraps, hoping he wouldn't press me too hard.

"Well, I was raised in a Methodist church. I sang in the choir. I tried playing football in high school, but I wasn't very good and I hated the violence. After that I had trouble finding any meaning in my life. I think landing here in Jacksonville and getting this job with you has really helped me."

"That's not much, but it's a start. We need to talk more."

And with that he pulled up in front of Thane-North and dropped me off.

Both Jerry and Ronnie were delighted with the food Alicia had sent for them. She'd even had the foresight to include plastic eating utensils. Jerry took his food with him when he left, but Ronnie ate his right away when he got there for work. I think I got another tear in my eye watching him eat. How could a mom abandon her kids the way his mom had.

What was I thinking? How could I abandon my kids the way I had? What a hypocrite I was!

Well, I consoled myself, at least I didn't leave my kids alone and hungry. But the comparison hurt. I wondered if my trying to help Ronnie find a better life was a way of trying to compensate.

* * *
**

Chapter 33 – *Weekend Feature*

I put off buying a computer. After all, the Brentwood Library Branch was just a few blocks south of Thane-North. It took only a few days after my week-long training period for my body to adjust to the fact that I didn't really need to go to bed right after work because I didn't need to leave for work until 10:30pm. Back then the library opened at 8am so that people in the neighborhood could go in before they went to school or work.

I went in to read papers and to exchange books and didn't always use their computers. I started Robinson Crusoe twice, but just couldn't handle it. Not because of the story but because it was so boringly written. I pretty much stuck with Rex Stout and other mystery writers.

When I did use their computers, I tried to check various newspapers randomly, and sometimes I even skipped reading the Omaha paper at all. But I made sure I looked at every issue of it eventually.

After the first week, there wasn't much in the Omaha paper about 9-11 or about me. However, the October 11th weekend edition of the Omaha paper had a full-page feature about me on the one-month anniversary of the attack on the twin towers. It was so extensive, I had to block-copy it in sections to get it into my email to send it to myself.

Once that was done, I sat back and read it. I was in much better shape emotionally after having worked for a few weeks, and I was beginning to realize that this new life might very well work for me. I was no longer prone to breaking into tears every single time I read something about Susan or the kids... Not every time, just some of the time.

The feature began with a summary of what they knew about what had happened to me on 9-11:

- I had gone to New York City on September 10th for a meeting with Jordan Singer from Cantor Fitzgerald at 9am the next morning at their offices on the 101st floor of the World Trade Center.
- I had emailed Susan over an hour before the meeting that I was leaving the hotel to attend the meeting.
- My cellphone went dead about the time of the crash.
- I had not returned to my hotel room.
- No one had seen me or heard from me since then.
- There had been no use of my credit card or bankcard after the crash.
- I was missing and presumed dead.

The next section summarized my life: my schooling, my parents, my background on the farm in Western Kansas, my participation in various organizations in Omaha, and (very briefly) my career at Klein-Staily.

The third section was about Susan and the kids and the impact on them.

It was a terrible shock to us when we learned the first plane had hit the very offices where Fred was meeting with Cantor Fitzgerald," Susan said. "We feared for the worst from that moment on. I tried to call him immediately, but of course I couldn't get through to him, and the folks at Klein couldn't reach him either. After just a few minutes of trying to reach him, I broke down in tears.

Then I washed my face and drove to the children's schools and took them out of their classes. They had both already heard about the attack on the North Tower, but they hadn't figured out the significance for our family. When they saw my face, each of them collapsed in tears. They knew. At each school, we stood in the school parking lot and hugged and cried together.

I told them what little I knew, and we drove home. A friend from the neighborhood was already there to help, and as the news

got out that Fred was there when the plane hit, all our friends
started calling and stopping by, offering emotional support and
wanting to know what had happened with Fred. The first two
friends who stopped by stayed with us all that day, answering
the phone for us and turning reporters away at the door.

The people were all so kind and helpful, sending food, offering
to run errands for us, fending off the nosy people we didn't
know but who wanted a piece of our sadness.

That section went on to describe the lives of Timothy and Liz but had
no direct quotations from them. It did however have indirect quotes
from their friends, who generally said they seemed very upset at
first, but after a few weeks were mostly back to being themselves in
public, participating in school activities, but a bit more withdrawn at
times.

The fourth section must have been written with considerable input
from Ben Gruvel, chronicling my history at Klein-Staily. It was
carefully worded with only a hint of problems.

I had joined the firm right out of college, working as a farm mortgage
appraiser and later and more generally as an agricultural mortgage
analyst, according to the article. I had no idea what an "agricultural
mortgage analyst" was, and I assumed it was some title they just
made up to show I had made some progress in the firm and had
begun traveling to specific farms less frequently.

And then the MBBs:

Fred Young moved to the financial side of agricultural mortgages
six years ago. It was there that he pioneered the use of
Mortgage-Backed Bonds [MBBs] that moved Klein-Staily into a
position of national prominence.

"Fred was a financial genius," related Ben Gruvel, senior partner
at Klein-Staily. "He found a way for lenders to reduce the risks of
lending for agricultural real estate and businesses while at the
same time increasing the amount of funding available for

farmers and the entire agricultural sector. When a few problems
emerged last year, it was clear that Fred's MBB plans were not
the source of the problems. It was instead the fact that
mortgage appraisers were misjudging the markets for crops and
real estate."

Put that in your pipe and smoke it, Lester Johnson.

That section concluded quoting Joshua Klein, the President and CEO
of Klein-Staily,

Fred Young was a treasured member of our firm. He was
creative and innovative. Even as he died, he was developing new
markets and new financial instruments that would benefit
lenders and agricultural borrowers alike. He will be greatly
missed.

Whatever. Ben probably wrote that. But I was more than a little
relieved to read it because the phrase, "Even as he died…" meant
everyone was accepting that I had been killed; and I was even more
relieved because it meant that my children would not be tarnished
by the attacks on my reputation that had been launched both from
within the firm by Johnson and his cronies and from outside by
unhappy investor-lenders who had bought the lower-level-tranches
of our MBBs.

The final section of the feature covered the insurance payouts to
Susan. The insurance companies had paid up with almost no
hesitation; Ben had done a terrific job. Fortunately there was no
mention of the amount of the payments Susan would receive, but I
knew from the experiences of friends and past clients that the blood-
sucking vultures would begin circling overhead within weeks or
even days with pleas for money and sales pitches for cars, cottages,
and can't miss investment opportunities. I cringed.

Ben tried to head off the vultures.

"The Young family will receive enough money to allow them to
stay in their home and to provide for the education of Timothy

and Elizabeth," said Gruvel. "But the rest of the funds have been locked into an inaccessible trust by Mrs. Young."

Well, good luck with that. There were dozens of firms that encouraged people to borrow against so-called inaccessible trusts. But it sounded nice.

The kicker, though, made me smile:

> "Klein-Staily will continue to be the financial managers for the Young family and will be prudent in assessing all investment options.

In other words, people trying to approach Susan now and the kids later would all be referred to Ben and others he trusted at Klein-Staily. I hoped that would cut down on the hassles Susan would have to face.

- - -

Several weeks later, I saw a notice in the paper that Susan had been made a deacon of the church. And later she was named a member of the board of directors of the Omaha United Way.

The vultures had struck. I didn't fret too much though; I knew Susan was strong-willed, and so I knew she wouldn't take on anything that didn't suit her. And what the heck, she had the money so there was no reason for her not to support causes she cared about.

One thing I had not anticipated … well, let's face it, there were tons of things I hadn't anticipated… was that people sent money. Thousands of dollars were sent to Susan, ostensibly to help her and the children and to contribute to some sort of Fred Young Memorial Fund. I had no idea this was going on until a few weeks later when the creation of Fred Young Foundation was announced by Susan, with Timothy and Liz by her side and Ben next to them.

> Today we are pleased to announce the creation of the Frederick Robert Young Foundation to honor the memory of my husband,

our children's father, who died during the terrorist attacks on September 11th. We are grateful to everyone who has contributed to the Frederick Young Memorial Fund. Those contributions, along with a sizable portion of the insurance proceeds, and with pledges from Fred's friends and colleagues at Klein-Staily, will provide an endowment that will fund the Foundation's activities for the foreseeable future.

The primary goal of the Foundation is to provide academic assistance for young people from rural and agricultural backgrounds. Both Fred and I grew up in rural areas, and we were deeply indebted to those who helped us along the way. It is the hope of our children and me that others will be similarly helped with assistance from this foundation.

Several reporters, interestingly *not* including Jeremy Rat-face Hall, tried to press her on the mechanics of the Foundation: how big was the endowment? How would the funds be administered? Who was on the board of directors of the foundation?

Susan responded by implying they should mind their own business:

"We are in the early stages of establishing the legal framework for the Foundation. We wanted to make this announcement now to reassure everyone who has contributed to Fred's Memorial Fund that every penny of their contributions and much, much more will be put to good use and that a lasting memorial will be created in Fred's name."

When I read that, I just sat there, overwhelmed. I had no idea how much the Foundation had been Susan's idea and what role Ben had played, but I was impressed. She had both savvy and care. I loved her. I missed her.

* * *
**

Chapter 34 – *Management*

One night in early December I left the trailer a little before 10:30 as usual to stroll to work. This time, though, Ronnie met me at the gates of the trailer park.

"Okay if I walk with you Mr. Jacobs?"

"Sure, Ronnie. It looks like you're going to get to work a bit early tonight."

"Yeah…. Can I ask you something?"

"Of course. What is it?"

"I want to keep working there, and I like being there when you there, but I wonder if maybe I could start at 10 and then leave when you get there. You can still check my work then and let me know how I'm doing."

That was by far the most he had ever said to me. I thought to myself "This must be important."

"I don't think there should be a problem with that. What's up?"

"I don't need to stay home so late. The girls sleep earlier. And I need more sleep."

"Well, the only reason I had you coming in that late was because I was doing that on my own at first and didn't want anyone else to know about it. But now that you are working for the Thanes and everyone knows about you, it should be fine."

"Good. Thanks," he mumbled.

"When we get there tonight, I'll introduce you to Donna and we can explain it all to her. She's the woman working 'til eleven. Then we'll do the same thing with the people who work on weekends. It'll be fine."

We walked on in silence for a block or so.

"You go to school, Ronnie?"

"Yeah. That why I need more sleep."

"I see," and we walked on in more silence for another half block.

"Ronnie, do you ever use a computer?"

Where on earth had that come from? Why did I ask him that? I guess because I thought knowing some of the basics for using a computer would be important for him.

"No, sir. Don't know how."

I almost fainted. He said, "No sir," not "Nah."

"Do you have a library card?"

"Why I want that?" He was still prone to leaving out words, and it always caught me off guard.

"During your Christmas break from school, we can go to the Brentwood Library. It's only a few blocks south of the store." I turned to him and added hastily, "Only if you want to. We can get you set up with a library card, and you can learn how to use the computers there. I don't have a computer myself. I just go there and use theirs. Do you know where that library branch is?"

"Been there once."

He didn't seem all that interested in my suggestion, and since we were almost at the store, I let it go. There was so much advice I wanted to give him, but I had no idea how to do it. And I was afraid I could too easily become a meddling busybody. I also had a fear of becoming too involved. I didn't want any entanglements. Not yet anyway.

We went in and I introduced Ronnie and Donna.

"Oh!" Donna exclaimed. "I've seen your time sheet on the storage room door and always wondered about it. I'm glad to finally put a face with your name," and she smiled at Ronnie.

I explained that Ronnie would be coming in to clean around 10 or 10:30, during her shift.

"Wonderful," she enthused.

Donna was about 30 or so. Maybe late 20s. She and I hadn't talked much, and I had never seen her display much warmth or anything like it. Her warm reception to having Ronnie come in during her shift seemed to put him at ease a bit. I had never seen her like that, but then it occurred to me...

"It'll be nice for you to have someone else here in the store with you during that last hour of your shift, won't it," I suggested.

"It sure will! Just having two people here makes me feel a lot safer. I never feel quite so safe after Jerry leaves at seven."

I knew what she meant, and I actually was not looking forward to losing Ronnie during first hour of my shift for that very reason. I smiled, acknowledging her thought. Ronnie was small for his age, and I knew he had lied about being fifteen. He wouldn't be fifteen for a few months yet. He wasn't going to take on any criminals at his size, but his very presence could serve as a deterrent to robbers.

- - -

A few days later, Dick called me and asked me to meet him at the store an hour early so we could go over a few things. I wasn't looking forward to it. I feared he would want more information about me and about my background. But I agreed to meet him and met up with Ronnie on the way there.

"Mr. Jacobs, you going to work early?" Ronnie asked.

"Yes. Mr. Thane wants to meet with me."

"Good. It always seem to me you the boss not them."

Dick was waiting for me when we arrived. He pleasantly acknowledged Ronnie and then gestured for me to join him in the office.

I was nervous. I hoped it didn't show too much. So I babbled. "Ronnie's a good kid, I think. He seems to be working out well, don't you think? Thanks for taking him on."

"You got lucky that time, Carl, and I'm glad it worked out. But as Alicia told you, we have to do things on the up-and-up. We can't have labor standards people down our throats."

"I understand."

"Carl, I wanted to meet with you because we're ready to move you up to the manager position now, beginning January first."

I was surprised. It was too early. "Thanks, Dick. I really appreciate your confidence and trust." I wondered if he sensed the hesitation in my response.

"The job will pay 28 thousand a year, a lot more than you're making now, and you'll have some other benefits, including a small contribution to a 401K for some retirement savings. How would that suit you?"

"What all would be involved? I do a lot of the day-to-day stuff already. What else would you want?"

"The store would be under your control. You would let us know about supplies and merchandise you need, and we'd take care of it."

"I pretty much do that now, I think, Dick, don't I?"

"Yes, of course. You'd also be responsible for all the hiring and firing and making sure all the shifts are covered."

Oh, oh. Now I saw what was happening. Make me responsible and if I couldn't find people to fill the shifts I'd have to cover them myself.

"Dick, I don't think I'd want to have to look after filling my shift at night. I've seen the help-wanted ads, and I know how hard it is to find people to do the graveyard shift at a convenience store."

"Well, you could still manage the store and work the night shift couldn't you?"

"Hmmm." I hesitated. "How would I hire people if I'm working nights?"

While we were talking I did some rough math in my head. During the next year I would be making a little over twenty thousand dollars without benefits, and the Thanes were offering me nearly eight thousand dollars more plus benefits to take on the headaches of filling shifts.

"I like the sounds of getting a raise and of having benefits, Dick, but I'm not sure I'm ready for that much responsibility."

He looked both upset and disappointed.

"With me here reliably on the overnight shift, Dick, you and Alicia have been able to relax a lot. You never have to cover a missed shift overnight at Thane-North. I know I'm a valuable and valued employee as a result, and I have every intention of continuing to be. I've gotten used to the night shift, and I like it. I would like very much to ease into this management arrangement you're offering me, though, so is there some way we can work out something to ease my transition?"

"What do you have in mind?"

"Nothing in particular." ... Pause... Pause... "Here's a thought: Aside from the overnight shift, which shifts are the most difficult to fill reliably? Which ones do you and Alicia have to cover yourselves most often when you don't have someone to fill them?"

"It's pretty even," Dick replied. "We get stuck for the morning or day shifts sometimes when a mom has to stay home with a sick kid. And sometimes if we hire teens, they just won't show up for the evening shift if some social event comes up."

"How about as people leave, we replace them with part-timers? If we have a large group of part-timers working in the stores, maybe they can be called on at the last minute to fill in when someone doesn't show up."

"That's pretty much what we do now at the McDuff store," Dick said. "It works, but it's a management nightmare," and he grimaced, realizing he had just admitted that he was trying to hire me to take over a nightmare.

"How about we make me an assistant manager for maybe a year?" I suggested, "and then see how things are going?"

"Well, that's a name change from what you're called now, but what would you be doing here and how much pay would you want?"

I touched my left hand to my neck under my ear. "We're lucky here. You and Alicia have hired reliable people. The weekends can be a mess at times I guess, with the weekend replacements, but overall staffing here has gone pretty smoothly in the few months I've worked here."

I went on, "Maybe I could screen all the job applicant information before passing that information on to you. I could more explicitly take on stock and supply management. And I could begin to make arrangements for increased security to cut down on shoplifting and gas-and-goes."

"That sounds expensive. I'm not sure I like it. What do you have in mind?"

"Oh as an assistant manager, I would discuss everything with you. If I were manager, I would decide for myself what to do." That last part was a dig at him, and I knew it would make him cringe.

"Do you have any specific things in mind?

"Well, one thing for sure. We need a couple of those big convex mirrors well placed so the cashiers can keep tabs on what's happening in the aisles. I don't think there's a lot of shoplifting going on at night, but during the afternoon and evening when it's busy here, I can imagine a fair amount of stuff leaves the store in people's pockets. You have one at the McDuff store. It must be reasonably cost-effective."

"We do have an 'inventory shrinkage' problem," Dick agreed, actually using the air quotes. "The mirrors are probably a good idea."

"And all the cashiers need to be trained in how to deal with shoplifting," I added. "Shoplifters lie, but the goal isn't to catch them because confrontations are messy. The idea is to deter them, isn't it?"

Dick chewed on his pencil. "I like that approach. Anything else?"

"Not really. But I'll think about it some more if you like."

"Okay, yes. Do that. Now, about pay…"

"Yes?" I was beginning to learn to keep my mouth shut.

"How's seven twenty-five sound for the next six months after New Years?"

"It sounds good, Dick. At some point, though, I'd like to have some health benefits and maybe some minor contributions to a pension plan. Those benefits would be tax free for me, so they'd help me out without raising my taxes. How about we talk again in mid-April?"

"Okay, let's do that," Dick said as he stood up. I guessed the meeting was over.

"Oh. Just one more thing," he said.

Oh, oh. I wondered what was next. But at the same time I smiled inwardly at his use of the Colombo phrase. I just stood there and waited for the hammer to fall.

"Do you know much about computers?"

I quietly breathed a sigh of relief. "I use one at the library now and then, but that's about it. Why do you ask?"

"We're going to upgrade our systems, including the cash registers. If you have any suggestions there, let us know, okay?"

I had thought about their system quite a bit in my long hours during the overnight shift, but I decided to wait to say anything. "Sure. I'll give that some thought, too," emphasizing that he was asking me to think about several things.

I did give these things some thought, and over the next few months I gradually suggested combining security and the computer system. I had no idea how much things would cost; I'd leave the financial considerations up to Dick and Alicia.

The overall recommendation was for security cameras both outside the store and inside, covering all the gas pumps and the aisles in the store. I also recommended that they be connected to the computer system so cashiers could watch them in real time and that they feed a separate computer drive on rotating intervals. And since things were being fed to the computer, I suggested that the pay-at-the-pump system be jiggled slightly so that after 7pm, no one could start pumping gas unless they paid in advance inside or got preauthorized with a credit card or bank card.

They loved the suggestions. They were so enthusiastic that they had Laurence Ruggles, the regional manager for Q-Marts come by to discuss the ideas over a dinner, the likes of which I hadn't seen since I'd been on an expense account at Klein-Staily. The only problem for all of them was what they called the "make or buy" decision: should they develop the system themselves or should they shop around to find someone else who had a lot of experience in the field.

At that point I tried to keep my mouth shut. I had never seen an in-house computer system that was homegrown and that didn't have massive problems initially, but I couldn't say that. Instead, I rambled a bit.

"If you do a good job of developing it in-house, maybe you can sell it to other convenience stores? Or maybe some of them have already done it and you can buy it from them?"

It was a trivial observation, the kind a bright but inexperienced person might make. Perfect for Carl Jacobs.

* * *
**

Chapter 35 – *Christmas*

Christmas, 2001, would be my first Christmas alone... ever. I wasn't looking forward to it, and I was glad I would be working over Christmas Eve and Christmas Day. At the same time, I was happy to get pay for double time on Christmas Eve and Christmas Day as Maggy, Jerry, Donna, and I worked out ways for me to take on more of their hours so that they could spend more time with their families.

"Don't you have family you want to spend some time with?" asked Donna.

"Not really," I answered. "Besides, I need the hours."

Yes, I did have a family I wanted to spend time with. I desperately missed them. I wanted to share all the moments with them. I thought about putting up and decorating the tree with them. I thought about opening stockings – that, more than opening gifts for some reason, maybe because it was the first thing we did each Christmas morning and the stockings always included some fun surprises. I thought about going to church and singing Christmas carols lustily. I even contemplated going to a church or two in Jacksonville just to recapture the experience. Or maybe I wanted to go to a church in Jacksonville to push all those past family experiences out of my mind.

I was beginning to be happy with my weight and size. My weight was down below 170 and 34" pants would fit me well. So one morning after work, I went back to the thrift stores south of the river and loaded up on new shirts, pants, and a new belt. The next day after work, I bundled up all my old clothes that I had shrunk out of and dropped them in a donation box next to the discount store.

I decided to buy a new white shirt, too, just in case the ones from the thrift shops weren't as good as I had hoped. I wanted a backup to keep in bottom drawer in my bedroom. I needed all new briefs, too. And while I was there, I bought a new pair of Excell running shoes. I tried on two different sizes and decided that with less weight on my feet, I might do better with a half-size smaller. The new ones fit well, but I put them aside, to have as backups.

On the way back to the trailer, I gently chastised myself. I was beginning to stock up on things I didn't need and wouldn't use right away. I had to stop doing that. I loved my Spartan lifestyle in the trailer, and I wanted to figure out how to cope with having less stuff. Stocking up and having backups was part of the old me, a person I was trying not to become all over again.

This was a lesson I had to work on. It wasn't horrible that I had a backup shirt and a backup pair of running shoes, but I didn't want to fill the trailer. I had to be careful.

About a week before Christmas, Dick and Alicia dropped off wrapped gifts for every single one of their employees at Thane North. Part-timers and full-timers alike, we all got the same thing: Two white shirts with "Thane-Mart" embroidered over the pockets. There was a note in each package:

> Dear _____
> Merry Christmas, Happy Hanukah, Happy New Year. We are so pleased that you are working here as part of our growing Thane-Mart family, and we hope to have a long, growing relationship with all of you.
>
> Don't panic about this gift. We will not be requiring you to wear company shirts on the job. We are giving you these shirts to wear when you're working so you won't have to wear your own shirts to work. We'd like you to wear one of these shirts when you can, but we know that shirts get ruined, stuck in the laundry, etc.
>
> Merry Christmas, and best wishes!

Two shirts. Well, I would certainly need more than two. I'd be wearing my own much of the time between loads of laundry, which I generally put off far too long and then did in big batches at the laundromat. It was a really nice thought on their part, though, and it did mean that I wouldn't need as many shirts of my own for work. I generally went through one shirt every two days, but didn't like to do my laundry more than once a week. With that schedule, I'd be wearing my own shirts nearly half the time. Still, it was a nice job-related gift from them that would help all of us out in some way.

I had seen two other approaches to company shirts. One place back in Manhattan, Kansas, had provided company shirts for people to change into at work; lots of those shirts disappeared fairly quickly as people stole them for some reason. The other approach required employees to buy their own uniforms, pretty much at cost, but the cost was deducted from their pay. This latter system encouraged people to look after their shirts more carefully, but caused some resentment, especially among part-timers.

The Thanes' approach was interesting. They gave us the shirts but didn't require us to wear them. I was skeptical, at first, but it seemed like a decent gesture on their part, and in the end it worked out pretty well.

- - -

Over the holidays, I spent several days trying to track my family in Omaha, but there was no more news about them or about me. I figured they were adapting. They would miss me, but there would be others in their lives. I hoped they would find some genuine friends, not just sycophants who were after their money. And that made me wonder if I had been right to escape like this, leaving them with so much money.

Left hand to the neck to stop that thought. I knew that Susan was both wise and strong. And I knew she would have a good influence on Timothy and Liz. Even though I worried about them, I knew they would be okay in the long run.

- - -

The day after we received our shirts from the Thanes, I went to the discount store and bought a watch for Ronnie. It was pretty much like mine. I hoped he would like it, use it, and not be insulted by it.

On the way home, I bought two large pork loin roasts, a bag of onions, a bag of garlic, two liters of half-and-half, some large green and red peppers, more instant flour, and a half dozen more plastic food storage boxes. Over the next several days, I cooked the roasts in the crockpot, and as each one was done, I sliced it up and put the slices with some sauce into a plastic storage box in the freezer. I ended up with six boxes of sliced pork roast. I put names on each one, along with stick-on bows, and took five of them into work: one for the Thanes, one for Maggy, one for Donna, one for Jerry, and one for Ronnie. I saved the sixth one for Evelyn.

Everyone at Thane-North seemed, or at least acted, pleased to receive the gifts. They all had a sense that I was up against it financially, which I wasn't really I guess. I was working and saving money. But they didn't know that; they saw my having made these gifts for them as a sign that I cared and liked them, which was definitely true.

On Friday night, three nights before Christmas Eve, after Donna had left, I called Ronnie over and gave him his container of pork roast. His eyes lit up. He was ready to eat it right then, but couldn't because it was frozen. He paused for a moment and then smiled. He walked over to the microwave and turned to me, "Mr. Jacobs, how this work?"

So I explained about setting the power low to defrost things in the microwave. As it was reheating, I said, "Ronnie, here's something else for you," and I gave him the watch. It was a nothing-special-but-probably-durable watch not unlike mine.

He seemed overcome. "Why you do this?"

"It's Christmas, Ronnie. Merry Christmas."

He just looked down. Then he looked at the food. Then he looked at the watch. Then he looked at me.

"Thanks Mr. Jacobs."

"Ron," I said instead of 'Ronnie', trying to let him know I was beginning to think of him as a young man, and not a lost kid, "You've never been late for work, so I know you don't need this, but it might come in handy now and then."

At the end of that shift, on Saturday morning, Evelyn stopped by to chat and have coffee with me at the store after I logged out. I loved the timing of her visit because I had some pork roast for her in the freezer at home, and so I suggested maybe she drive me home and I'd make coffee for the two of us there.

She laughed -- actually laughed -- and said, "Carl, I would **love** that." Oops. I wondered what I was getting into. She was smiling the whole way back to the trailer.

When we got to the trailer, she was chuckling, but instead of following me to the door, she popped the trunk of her car and brought out a large gift-wrapped package.

"Carl, I had no idea how to get you to let me give this to you. I couldn't believe it when you asked me to drive you here to have coffee with you," and she kept laughing the whole time as we went in.

She set the package on the table and said, "Why don't you open it right now!" Not a question, a strong suggestion.

"Sure, but let me get the water started for coffee."

Evelyn giggled. "Go ahead," and she burst out laughing.

I was dumbfounded, but then it hit me what was going on.

"Okay. I'm really curious about what's in this box; maybe I will open it first after all," and I smiled at her. Then we both laughed and hugged each other.

I had guessed right. She had bought me a coffee maker. It was a very touching, thoughtful gift. We set it up on the counter, next to the microwave and didn't bother to run water through it to clean it out. We just made coffee, first run. And it smelled great.

And I told her what a thoughtful, generous gift it was. "I really appreciate this, Evelyn. Thank you so much."

While we were waiting for the coffee to finish brewing, Evelyn looked around.

"Carl, you are really keeping the place neat and tidy," and she walked toward the back of the trailer as if she owned the place. Well, I guess she did. I was glad I hadn't left much stuff lying around; there was virtually no clutter other than some library books on one of the night tables. I followed her back toward the bathroom and bedroom.

"Wow, you even keep the mirror and the toilet clean! And you make your bed every day!"

"Yeah, I'll make someone a good wife some day." I laughed at my male chauvinistic attempt at humor, but Evelyn didn't laugh at all. Instead she turned and looked at me sharply.

"Carl, are you gay?" She had a shocked look on her face.

That was a dumb joke for me to have blurted out. I really would have to be more circumspect.

"Not at all. That was just a bad joke about my homemaking skills."

"Speaking of which," I continued, trying to avoid any more discussions about my sexual preferences, "I have a gift for you, too. That's why I asked you to drive me home. So I could give it to you."

She seemed to sigh a slight sigh of relief and then her manner changed abruptly as she laughed. "What is it? Where is it?"

She was like a kid. "I know, I know," she began babbling, "I have to be patient. I'm so excited, Carl! What is it? I can't wait to see it!"

"C'mon." I led the way back to the kitchen. "The coffee's ready," and I poured us each a cup.

"And I'll get some cream for you," I added. That's how you take it, right?"

I knew very well that was how she took it, but I wanted to let her know I had paid attention.

"Right," she almost cooed. Hmmm. Maybe it would have been better if I had asked after all.

I opened the fridge and took out the container of frozen pork roast and the carton of half-and-half at the same time.

I set the carton of half-and-half on the table and handed her the container of roast pork, "Here. I made this for you and Don using your crockpot. I hope you like it." I was suddenly overcome with shyness and uncertainty. It seemed so cheap compared with her thoughtful gift of the coffee maker.

She jumped up from her chair and threw her arms around my neck.

"Oh Carl, how thoughtful!" and she held on tight for a few seconds. It felt good.

Then she turned away and tried to disguise wiping her eyes as she looked down at the table.

"The coffee smells good, Carl."

We sipped our coffee and chatted. I told her about being offered a manager position and why I was hesitant. She agreed with my skepticism, but she also understood why I wanted benefits and pension contributions.

"So what will you say in April?"

"I'll probably take the job. After a year or two, if it goes well, I may want something bigger, maybe not in the convenience store business, but I don't know. I'm still trying to find myself."

I smiled, a bit embarrassed. "I guess I'm a bit old to be going through the identity crisis?"

"I think we all go through that crisis all the time," Evelyn replied. "It just hits each of us differently at different times."

It sounded significant, the way she said it. I nodded.

She was only half right about me, though. The self-questioning identity crisis hadn't hit me until a few years ago. I'd been drifting through life sublimely uncritically until then.

"I'm not sure I really want a different life from what I have now, though, Evelyn. I like my job, and I love my home here," I smiled, gesturing vaguely toward the rest of the trailer. "I may just try to get some health benefits and keep my job as an assistant manager."

I had been thinking that wanting too much was one of the reasons I had worked so hard and tried to earn so much at Klein-Staily. I didn't want to have those goals any more, but I had to keep reminding myself of that.

At the same time, I had loved the challenge of creating and marketing the Mortgage-Backed Bonds. I loved the puzzle, working on the puzzle, and explaining the solution to everyone.

"I guess I'm still groping, wondering," I said. And I changed the subject.

"Evelyn, does your church have anything special planned for tomorrow evening? Like a carol sing or a pageant or something?" I hoped she wouldn't think I was religious at all.

"Do we ever! We have three different choirs, and they all sing different Christmas songs; and kids re-enact the Luke 2 Birth of Jesus story. The music is wonderful, and the kids are *so* cute. Would you like to come with me?"

I hesitated. "I'm not all that religious," I said, "but I like the Christmas pageantry and music."

"I know, I know. I'm the same way. The program starts at 7pm but we have to get there before 6:30 to get a decent seat. Why don't I pick you up at 6?""

"That'll be fine," I said. "I don't have a suit or sport coat to wear, but I can wear my sweater. What do you think?"

"A sweater over a dress shirt will be great. People are not dressing up so much for church these days."

- - -

The church was way out west of town. On the way there, I asked about Don.

"He's slowly going downhill," Evelyn said. "We have someone in much of the time now to look after him there. I know, I know. He probably belongs in a home somewhere, but I just can't bring myself to suggest it even, and I know he wants to stay in our home as long as possible."

I nodded. I understood... sort of. I missed my home and family in Omaha.

We cheered up when we got to the church. The Sunday evening church service was everything I had hoped for: choirs, carols, and pageantry. Too bad about the praying and preaching, though. I

enjoyed singing all the verses of all the Christmas carols in a large
group like the congregation there. I think Evelyn enjoyed it, but she
also enjoyed having me there with her, singing out and smiling at the
kids. It was fun.

By the time we left the church it was after 9pm, and I didn't have to
be at work until 11. I was reluctant to invite Evelyn back to the
trailer, and so I suggested we go someplace for coffee.

"What a great idea, Carl! I know just the place and it's right on the
way back."

She took me to an upscale coffee shop called Starbucks. There
weren't all that many Starbucks locations back then, and it really did
have some appeal.

"Evelyn, tell me about your job," I suggested while we sat there.

"Sure. I'm an account administrator with Allstate Insurance. I know, I
know, what does that mean? I look at all the contracts that come in
to make sure that all the i's have been crossed and the t's dotted,"
and we both laughed at her having switched the words. I think she
probably did that often and on purpose, as a joke.

"That's where Don and I met many years ago..." and she got a
pensive look, remembering past joys and pleasures, I assumed.

"How long have you two been together?" If I kept asking questions,
she wouldn't ask me about my past.

"Well, we met back in the wild, free days of the late 1960s," she said
with a smile and a devilish glint in her eye. But then she turned
pensive, "and we've been together ever since. It's hard to see him
deteriorating so rapidly, so inevitably."

I wanted to hold her hand or something. I think my look conveyed
that.

"Thanks, Carl."

When we got back to Thane-North, I already had my left hand on the seatbelt buckle and my right hand on the door handle. Before we stopped I said, "Thank you so much for taking me with you tonight, Evelyn. It was really nice."

She touched my arm as I left the car, and that seemed to be typical now. I just didn't want her to hug me or anything like that, where others working there might see it. For some reason, I had no desire to have to answer questions about her.

As it was, Donna said, "Hi, Carl. Who was that who dropped you off?"

"My landlady," I smiled. "She took me to church with her tonight. It was nice. I liked watching the pageant and belting out the traditional Christmas carols."

"That's nice. By the way, thanks for the pork roast. It was real good. How'd you cook it?"

"I just threw a few things into the crockpot. I really like using the crockpot to prepare meals while I'm working." I stopped myself from explaining that the landlady had left the crockpot in the trailer for me to use.... And had just given me a coffee maker.

"That's a great idea! I'll have to give it a try."

- - -

Christmas came and went. So did New Year's Eve. We sold gallons of tonic, beer, and sparkling wine during the afternoons and evenings, and we sold tons of frozen meals, chips, and cookies between midnight and 7am throughout the holiday season. People seemed to love stepping out "to pick up a little something" then.

Everyone at Thane-North wore their new shirts on the job whenever the shirts weren't in the laundry. The holiday spirit seemed to infuse us all with cheer and good will. I noticed it, and I think our regular customers noticed it, too. I liked being busy, and I earned a lot of extra money working the extra hours and getting the extra pay for holidays.

Because I was working New Year's Eve, Donna wished me a Happy New Year when I arrived for my twelve-hour shift at 9pm. Ronnie came in about 10pm and seemed to be in good spirits. As he left at 11pm, I said, "Happy New Year Ron. And here's to an even better year, right?"

He smiled shyly and nodded, "Right."

Just before midnight, Evelyn came in. I groaned inwardly because there were a lot of customers milling about, and I needed to keep an eye on all of them. Ordinarily I'd have welcomed her company at midnight, but with so many people there, I didn't want the distraction of chatting with her. She took the situation in right away and pretended to be shopping, looking at various cans of soup.

The sirens everywhere sounded at midnight, and I nearly freaked out. It was a bit of a flashback to New York City. I panicked for a few seconds, and my pulse shot up.

Evelyn came over to the counter and then suddenly came through the gap for cashiers.

"I know, I know. I'm not supposed to do this. But it's New Year's Eve!" She smiled up at me, stood on her tiptoes, reached up and kissed me. It was better than nice.

"Happy New Year, Carl. Oh, wow! Your pulse is racing! Did my kiss have that effect on you?" and she laughed.

"I'm sure that was part of it, but the sirens startled me, too."

"Well, I'll let you get back to work," she said as she went back from behind the counter, "but I couldn't let New Year's Eve go by without seeing you and letting you know again how glad I am that you are living in the trailer. Thank you so much!"

"Thank you, too, Evelyn. And Happy New Year to you, too!" and we hugged each other.

After that, I had to look after the various customers who had celebrated New Year's Eve at Thane-North. I had never heard of celebrating New Year's Eve at a convenience store, but they all seemed to be having a good time, and it was a lot cheaper than going to some club or restaurant. We made a lot of money in extra sales that night; I made a note to talk with the Thanes about it.

* * *
**

Chapter 36 – *Winona Trail*

I continued with my determination to eat only healthy food and to lose weight. My weight was down to 165 by January 1st, and I could tell my overall fitness level was increasing. I was on my feet at least nine hours a day, including walking to and from work, and that didn't include shopping, household tasks, and walking around in general.

The trouble with all that type of exercise was that it was all in my legs, feet, and lower body in general. I had nowhere near the same level of upper body fitness to balance my lower body, and it looked as if I wasn't going to get much upper body work without doing something about it.

I had joined a gym in Omaha along with some of the other people from Klein-Staily. It didn't help very much primarily because I didn't go very often and I didn't do much when I was there. Even so, I shuddered to think what shape I'd have been in if I hadn't at least tried. But there was no way I was going to join a gym in Jacksonville. Too expensive and too inconvenient. I decided to develop my own workout program instead.

There wasn't enough room in the trailer to do much exercising. I did leaning pushes, sort of like vertical pushups, using the doorframe to the bathroom, placing my hands high, then lower as I did more pushes, but that was about it.

I hated doing exercise for the sake of doing exercise. I had been fit as a young man because I had worked hard on the farm, and I just couldn't get into making myself sweat without accomplishing something.

My compromise solution was to carry my backpack and my shoulder bag with me to and from work... but not on my shoulder or back. I carried them in my hands, one down on each side, with a can of soup in each one. As I walked along, I lifted my arms out to each side, keeping my elbows and wrists as straight as I could. It hurt a lot more than I had expected, and I couldn't lift the bags very high or very many times. In between, I would do wrist and elbow curls. They hurt, too.

I had tried to do too much too quickly, and so I took the soup cans out for a few weeks. That helped. I did these exercises every day, carrying my lunch to work in one of the bags, and eventually I put the cans of soup back in the bags.

Soon I expanded the exercise regime by walking along the Winona Trail, which went right past Thane-North. Well, Winona Trail was my name for it because it went alongside Winona Drive for part of the way. It was an abandoned rail line that had been turned into a bicycle and walking trail. I walked along the trail doing my shoulder and arm lifts out to each side of my body.

The trail couldn't have been much more than a mile or two long in total. Some days I started from Thane-North and walked northwest on the trail up to where it ended at Norwood Plaza. Other days I walked southeast on the trail down to 21st Street and went back home through Evergreen Cemetery.

Even though I had been on my feet all night, I walked up and down the trail every morning when I got off work, doing my arm and shoulder exercises.

At times I imagined I was talking with my family, asking for forgiveness and yet knowing I had provided for them very well. I had clearly been a failure – well, something considerably less than a success anyway – on the relationship side of things, and I deeply missed them. I missed the history we had built up together, and I missed the regularity and stability they had provided, even though those were some of the things that also contributed to my sense of emptiness in my old life.

This contemplation of what had led me to escape was an important part of my rebirth. I had been free back then, and yet I had felt trapped. I had an opportunity to change all that now. I didn't know how, though.

Yes, I felt trapped in my current life, too, by my lack of income and by my financial uncertainties, but it was a different kind of feeling trapped. I didn't feel the need to compete in the testosterone-driven world of high finance. I didn't feel the need to get more stuff or have more experiences. I had already developed a type of inner contentment that I had never experienced. I was determined not to lose it.

I began to speculate: what if I had quit my job at Klein-Staily? We had a couple of million dollars saved up for retirement. We could have moved to a three-bedroom tract home, scaled back to one car maybe, done family things in Omaha without traveling, and I could have found a night shift job as a clerk in a convenience store... Or even a day shift job somewhere. We didn't **need** the money. I wondered how the family would have reacted to that alternative. What if I had just gone home from New York after 9-11 and told them I was quitting my job and we'd all have to change our lifestyles.

I wept openly as I was walking along the trail. I knew Susan would have gone along with my decision. She might even have been enthusiastic about it. After all, she had been, what was it: hesitant? reluctant? uncomfortable? with my career moves into the go-go world of finance. The children would have whined about not having so much stuff, but in the end they might have been just as happy (or mentally healthy anyway) if we had had more family time and less "stuff time".

What if I had realized I had been living a pretense, shaped by everyone's expectations about the Great Mid-American Dream? The adjustment would have been difficult for the whole family. In all likelihood, people would have said I suffered from chronic post-traumatic stress disorder after 9-11; they would have expressed sympathy to Susan and the children and would have said they understood.

They would not have understood.

I could have explained to the family that, yes, the events that day were like an epiphany for me: I saw a flash of light in the skies not unlike the flash Paul saw on the road to Damascus. But that wouldn't have been the entire story. And I don't know that I could have faced them and told them I'd been unhappy with much of my life for the previous five years. I had loved my work, but clearly it had sapped my energy from other things that were important. I don't think I could have explained all that to them. Not to their faces.

And I don't know that I could have just walked away from Klein-Staily. My doing so would have been taken as an admission of wrongdoing by too many people. I, and especially my family, would have become pariahs and would have experienced all the things I had hoped to save them from by disappearing as I had.

But dammit, I missed them. I wanted to be with them. I wanted to talk with them and be a richer part of their lives. Even more, I wanted them to be a richer part of my life. I felt like a miserable failure for not having understood things better back then. I had just been so wrapped up in the strategies and planning at work that I was missing out on much of the rest of life. And yet I knew that those very things had also given me a really strong sense of accomplishment and achievement: I had devised and worked out the details of a really important financial tool that could have helped and probably still would help revolutionize financial markets.

Trade-offs and choices. I was glad I had made the choices I'd made, and yet I regretted them. What a mess.

- - -

When you're walking on public trails, you tend to smile at the people you meet; maybe even nod or say "hello". Most of the time the smile is designed to reassure the others that you're not a mugger or a rapist, but it also conveys a friendliness, a sense of "Hello! I'm out walking on the trails, just like you. We have this interest in common. We're part of the same group."

I wasn't really a trail-walker, much less a hiker, but I liked that sense of being a member of the trail-walking community, albeit as a totally anonymous member. I didn't know these people and, truth be told, I didn't want to know them. I just wanted to walk and get some exercise; along the way I was happy to be on the trail walking with others who were there enjoying it, too.

Whenever I saw someone coming, I lowered my arms with the bags and switched to trying to do subtle wrist curls. When they got near me, so as not to take up too much room on the trail, I put one arm in front of me with one bag and the other behind me with the other bag.

After a month or so of this self-designed workout regimen, I began to recognize some familiar faces – others who were out walking as part of their morning routine or who were using the trail to walk to or from work.

There were two guys who jogged together that I saw nearly every morning. They were young and fit.

There was a young woman who was pushing a stroller with two children in it. After we had seen each other several times, I smiled more and then began saying hello to the kids, too.

After a few weeks, she asked, "Why do you always carry your bags like that instead of on your back or over your shoulder?"

I explained I didn't want to join a gym and was doing shoulder, bicep, tricep, and wrist exercises; and I showed her the various exercises I did. She smiled and nodded, "Makes sense, I guess." And she kept walking. The upshot? Every time I saw her coming I kept doing the exercises right up until I needed to make room for her to get by me.

Later I learned that she worked up at Northwood Plaza and was taking her kids to a daycare center on the way.

Eventually I learned to check on Saturdays and Sundays before I counted on using the trail. There were all sorts of walking and running events that took place on the Jacksonville trail system, and the trail was reserved for their use on those days. Sometimes on those days, I was able to complete my walk before the events started, but there were so many people around that I didn't do many upper body exercises. In the end, I just avoided the trail on event days.

Frequently on my walks, about 7:30 each morning, I would meet and pass a woman in her late 30s who was walking the opposite direction. She wasn't power walking, but she wasn't ambling or strolling either; she was just walking.

As with everyone else, I smiled at her as we met. After passing each other for a couple of weeks, I began to say "Hi" or "Good morning" to her. She smiled back at me and I saw her eyes! She had intriguing deep bronze-colored eyes, shaded with hints of blue and green. I couldn't **not** stare at them as we passed each other after that. But I tried not to be too obvious about it.

One mid-April day after a couple of months, we passed each other as usual. I tried not to stare at her eyes too obviously as we said our hellos. And then from behind me, as I started lifting my bags I heard her voice say, "I thought so!"

I froze, and then I slowly lowered my arms.

I was afraid I had been recognized. I slowly turned around, and she was standing there smiling at me.

I tried to control my emotions. I was relieved that she was smiling, but I was still concerned. I didn't recognize her aside from seeing her there on the Winona Trail, but who knew? Maybe she was an insurance investigator.

She must have seen my expression and assumed that I was confused or something

She laughed. A pleasant laugh.

"Ever since we began passing each other here on the trail," she said, "I've been wondering about the backpack and shoulder bag. I kept asking myself, 'What's up with that guy? Why is he carrying those bags like that? At first I was worried that you had weapons in them."

I relaxed a bit.

"Nope. No guns or knives. Just two cans of soup that I carry for a little extra weight when I do my arm exercises." I laughed slightly, and shrugged as if to mock myself, trying to make sure it was clear I was laughing at myself for using cans of soup as light weights, and not laughing at her for having worried that I might be carrying weapons.

I pulled out the cans of soup to show her.

"Tomato in one," I said as I held it up, looking at it to remind myself what they were. It had been so long since I had looked at them that I couldn't remember.

".... And..... tomato in the other one, too. I'd forgotten what I had!" and I tried to smile a somewhat embarrassed smile.

"You use soup as weights for doing arm exercises?"

"Yeah," I half-grinned a bit shyly. "I do this most mornings when I get off work. I guess I'm not too keen on the idea of joining a gym. This isn't Nautilus, but it's something at least."

"Mornings when you get off work?"

"Yeah, I'm sort of the night manager at the Thane-Qmart just up there at Pearl Street. I'm on my feet all night, so I think my legs and feet are in ok shape, but the job doesn't do much for my arms and shoulders."

She smiled. I loved that smile. And I kept staring at her eyes.

"I guess that makes some sense."

She didn't turn or move to keep walking away.

I asked, "What about you? I see you walking here quite a bit."

"I just like walking. I get out and away to contemplate. I like nature, too. Sometimes on weekends I walk out at the Jackson-Baldwin Trail. Have you ever been there?"

It almost sounded like an invitation, but I wasn't sure. "No. Where is it?"

"It's only a few miles west of town -- another reclaimed railroad bed. There are some beautiful natural places along the trail. You should join us."

"Us?"

"I go walking with a trail conservancy group sometimes. And sometimes with bird watchers."

"Oh." And then I added, "But what about you? Where are you going every day when you're on this trail?"

"Oh, I just walk up and down the trail in the morning. I'm a physical therapist at the college clinic."

"I see," I replied. But I didn't really. "What about in the hot, muggy summer? It must get pretty unpleasant on the trails, especially out on that other trail you mentioned?"

She smiled. "It is! So we don't go out there much in the summer. Still the birds and scenery are quite different then, so we try to go there every once in awhile. The bugs can be a bother, so we load up with deet. And we wear sunhats."

"I can imagine," and I could.

"But sometimes in the summer we go the ocean. It's cooler there and everything is so different..."

"That sounds pleasant." She was easy to talk with.

I decided to end my exercise. I turned and walked with her back toward Main Street.

"Okay if I walk with you for awhile? I'll turn off when we get to the cemetery. I go through there to get home when I come from this direction."

"Sure. I'd like that." And she smiled again.

"I'm Carl Jacobs," I offered.

"Steffanie Niles," she said. "Steffanie with two 'ff's instead of a 'ph'. My parents wanted me to be a bit different," she smiled again and laughed a bit, "and I guess they got their wish."

We chatted a bit more about our jobs, but then said our goodbyes as I turned off the trail to go through the cemetery back to the trailer. I think we both looked forward to seeing each other again on the trail.

* * *
**

Chapter 37 – *Evelyn*

After New Year's Eve, Evelyn began stopping by the store now and then. I was happy to see her every time she was there. Sometimes she stopped just before seven for coffee on her way to work. On those days we mostly just said "hi" to each other and exchanged maybe a sentence or two.

Weekends were different, though. She didn't' have to go to work, and I wasn't trail-walking on walk-event days.

She didn't often stop by on Saturdays because she had shopping to do and errands to run then. Sundays were different, though. She stopped on her way to church. We picked up a couple of cookies, she gave me a ride home, and we had coffee together for half an hour or so before she went on her way to church. We both liked the time together and were becoming closer as time went on.

One Sunday morning in February while we were sitting at the table, Evelyn hesitated and seemed embarrassed about something.

"What is it?" I asked.

"Carl, I know you looked at me very sternly and said, 'I have no past' when I asked you about your background back in September when we first met, but even though I feel as if I know you, I know nothing about you. Who are you, really?"

"I do have a past, Evelyn. I won't talk about it, though. I will tell you the same thing I told the Thanes when they hired me: I never committed a crime; I was never investigated for anything illegal or even wrong. I could make up a story about my past, but I won't insult your intelligence by doing that."

"But then why? What happened to make you come here and start fresh?"

"All I'll tell you is that I was struggling, searching. But if you ask me any more, I'll say ...... 'parsnips.....', and if you press me on this, we'll have to stop these visits."

Evelyn looked down at her hands on the table. She seemed very sad.

"I know, I know. I'll try not to ask any more."

I think she started to tear up just a bit. Then she reached out and took my hand and gave it a squeeze.

Evelyn gave me an extra-strong, extra-long hug that morning when she left for church. It felt good, as usual. I looked down at her, smiled, and hugged her back. And then I kissed her. We both smiled at each other, and I walked her to her car.

What was I doing? Did I really want this relationship to go in this direction? Evelyn was married to a dying man. Did I want even more of a relationship with her? She was my landlady and she was thirteen years my senior. This could get messy.

"I know, I know," I said to myself, mimicking her after she left. I could see where we were headed despite my concerns. I knew it was dangerous, but I wanted more, too.

I didn't see Evelyn all the next week. When she came in on Sunday, she was noticeably less effervescent than usual. She seemed unenthused about getting the cookies from Thane-Mart, and she was less chatty than usual on the five-block drive to the trailer.

When we got to the trailer, she turned around just as I closed the door and looked up at me. She put her arms around my neck and hugged me tight.

"Take me to bed, Carl," she said quietly. "No strings, no commitments. Just make love to me."

I had half-anticipated that something like this would happen eventually, but not like this.

"I would love to, Evelyn. I've thought about it often."

I steered her to the chair in the living room, and I sat on the loveseat. I wanted to keep my wits about me if I possibly could.

"I'm worried, though," I added. "You're my landlady, you're married, and you're older than I am. I don't see a future for us, and so I don't want to get too involved."

She laughed, got up from the chair, and came over to the loveseat, where she snuggled next to me.

She was both laughing and crying as she said, "Carl, I didn't say anything about a future! I didn't say anything about getting involved. I said, 'No strings, no commitments.'"

"I'm not sure that's possible," I answered. "We have a good friendship. I don't want to jeopardize it."

She pushed herself away from me and smiled. "Carl, there has been a sexual tension between us almost from the beginning. All of our time together, beyond just enjoying the friendship part of it, has been sexual. It just hasn't been actual, physical sex."

I was nonplussed. She was right. What I had seen as friendship was really more courtship than friendship.

She got up on her knees on the loveseat and leaned over and kissed me gently.

"It's been sexual all along. And now that I have raised it, things have changed between us, no matter what we do. So we might as well go ahead!" She smiled and kissed me again.

"I'm still concerned.... apprehensive, Evelyn. I'm very inexperienced both emotionally and physically."

"A man like you? I find that hard to believe. Just keep reminding yourself that you want to enjoy yourself, but it is not a lifetime or even a one-year commitment. It's not even a one-week commitment. It's a chance to be together ...for now." And she kissed me again. Long and exciting.

We made love that morning.

And again the next Sunday morning.

After that I tried to convince myself I wouldn't get attached to her. But I knew I was enjoying making love with Evelyn. There was a physical and emotional closeness with her that was overwhelming even though we had little else going for us.

The fourth Sunday, there were no walking events on the trails, and so I begged off going back to the trailer with Evelyn to go walking instead. I didn't want to begin to count on her for a sexual relationship.

She didn't seem disappointed, and that disappointed me. It also confirmed for me that I had to guard my feelings. "No strings, no commitment," she had said. Maybe that was easy for her. It wasn't easy for me.

By mid-March, it was clear to both of us that our relationship, such as it was, was empty. We had enjoyed each other's company up until then because of the sexual tension, the unrequited physical desire. Once we began talking about it and were sleeping together, we should have become more comfortable together, but we weren't. We felt like strangers.

We never acknowledged this change to each other, not verbally. We began to sense it though. Evelyn stopped coming by for coffee much during the week, and we didn't feel the closeness with each other emotionally that had been there earlier.

By the end of March she stopped coming by the store on Sunday mornings. I felt sad. I missed her. I missed the closeness we had had, and I missed having sex with her. I felt a loss that confirmed for me that I was right to have been reluctant to have a sexual relationship with her. But it also confirmed for me that she was right in saying that the physical act itself didn't really affect our relationship; for me, it just made things clearer sooner.

One Sunday in August, Evelyn stopped by the store. I was even more pleased than I expected to see her.

"Evelyn! What a wonderful surprise!"

She came around the counter and gave me a big hug. It felt good, and at the same time it felt all right. It made me want to make love with her again as it stirred some really nice memories, but it was okay and I was okay without it. I hadn't developed the attachment issues I had been afraid of. Or, more likely, I had gotten over them.

"Let's go for coffee when you get off, Carl. I have next year's lease with me."

I cocked my eyebrow slightly. I hoped she wouldn't jack up the rent too much on me.

"Oh, relax, Carl," she laughed almost condescendingly as she went back out from behind the counter. "I haven't changed anything except the dates."

I thought about inviting her back to the trailer but decided against it. Instead we went up to the coffee shop at the plaza and signed the copies of the lease. We were locked in until September, 2003.

"Now you can relax, Carl," and Evelyn laughed. She seemed to understand what I had been worrying about.

She offered to drive me back to the trailer, but I declined. "No, thanks," I said. "I have some shopping to do. I'll be fine."

I walked back to her car with her.

"How's Don?" I asked.

"It won't be long, now."

I hugged her, opened the car door for her, and leaned down to give her a quick kiss. Evelyn had been an important chapter in my life. I think I had been important for her, too.

In December, 2002, Evelyn called to invite me to go with her to her church's Christmas Sunday service.

"I'd love that, Evelyn. Would it be okay if I bring Ron with us?"

Pause. Silence.

"No, Evelyn, I'm not gay! And I'm not a pedophile. Ron needs some more exposure to some nice things in life, though. I think the Christmas service at your church would be great for him."

"Well... sure!" She had hesitated at first, but then sounded enthusiastic. I wasn't sure whether she had adjusted on the fly or just pretended to. I didn't care. I was looking forward to it.

She picked us up a little after 6pm, and we had a wonderful time. I had told Ron pretty much what to expect, and his smile beamed as the pageant unfolded in front of him. He even tried to sing along with some of the traditional carols, but it seemed he hadn't heard most of the later verses.

As we drove away from the church, Ron said somewhat carefully, "Thank you for taking me. Can you drop me at work now?"

We dropped Ron at Thane-North and went on to a coffee shop for a repeat of the previous year. The atmosphere between us was pleasant, but then Evelyn looked pensive.

"Don is going to die any day, now."

"I'm sorry," and I reached out and touched her hand.

"It's ok. I'll miss him, but I'll be relieved, too. This last year hasn't been easy for him. I think he's ready. Will you come to be with me during the visitation and memorial?"

"Of course. Whatever you need."

The services went pretty much as expected. I had never been to Evelyn and Don's home before. It was a larger-than-standard ranch home in the northwest. I was introduced as their tenant and friend.

Over those few days, it became clear that Evelyn was ready to move on and live a more exciting life. She talked about going line-dancing and she had a beer in her hand much of the time.

A few months later she came into the store in very tight pants and fancy cowgirl boots.

"Jimmy, this is Carl. He lives in the trailer. Carl, this is my friend Jimmy. He runs Cowgirls, a country bar on the south end of town. We have so much fun together there!"

Jimmy seemed about her age and had a bit of a paunch. I took an instant dislike to him but tried not to show it. I didn't have to worry, though. The next time I saw Evelyn she was wearing a similar outfit but with a different man in tow. Our sense that first winter that we were not well-suited was right. I couldn't imagine a life with her, but I was happy for her that she was finding herself, just as I had been working on rediscovering myself.

Evelyn stopped in every once in awhile after that -- sometimes with a man in tow, sometimes on her way to work. It was always nice seeing her. At the same time, though, she seemed like a stranger.

In August 2004, nearly three years after I had moved to Jacksonville, Evelyn stopped by the store on a Sunday. That it was a Sunday took me by surprise.

"Hi Carl," she said. She was dressed a bit more modestly than when she hung out with the various cowboys.

"Can we go for coffee again? I need to talk."

Oh, oh. Those men I had seen her with looked as if they could have been abusive. I looked at her carefully but saw no signs of bruises or even of makeup covering bruises. I privately breathed a sigh of relief.

The way Evelyn had said it, I knew she didn't want to talk right there in the store, and I quickly agreed to go up to the coffee shop at the plaza with her.

When we sat down with our coffees, Evelyn said, "I'm going to sell the trailer Carl."

And before I could react, she smiled slightly and added, "Would you like to buy it? I can give you easy terms if you don't have enough money."

"Evelyn, I'll be very straight with you. I love the trailer, I love my life there and I love living here in Jacksonville. I know it's not usually good to start a negotiation by saying how much I like something, but it's all true, and I'm sure you know it. How much do you want for the trailer?"

By living frugally, I had managed to save over thirty thousand dollars in the past two and half years. I was just beginning to consider using some of the savings to buy some stocks, but maybe I could buy the trailer too.

"Well, old trailers like this don't go for much, especially in parks like "The Palm's" and especially if they haven't been moved for a few years. How's three thousand dollars?"

I gulped. She thought I was gulping because it was too much, but actually I was gulping because it wasn't very much at all. I figured she had been clearing at least a hundred dollars a month after paying taxes, park fees, and utilities…. More than a thousand dollars a year, clear and free. To get that kind of return I'd have to invest ten thousand dollars, assuming a ten percent return was even possible. To get a thousand dollars a year at three and a third percent, I'd need thirty thousand dollars! Yet she was offering me that kind of return for only three thousand dollars.

Once again, Evelyn was more generous than she needed to be. In response to my gulp, she said, "Okay. How about twenty-five hundred dollars?"

I was reminded of the first time we met, when she offered to rent me the contents of the trailer for an extra ten dollars a month. Again she was being overly generous.

I put my hand up to stop her from talking and to stop her from lowering the price any more. "Evelyn, twenty-five hundred will be fine. I'll pay all the legal fees and transaction costs, though."

I continued, "Are you going to be okay with this, financially? I mean, the trailer has been an okay source of extra income for you, hasn't it?"

"Oh, I have plenty of money from Don's insurance and our savings, so I don't need the money. And the income and expenses from the trailer are just an accounting headache for taxes now."

We closed the deal in September.

I almost cried. Right there in the lawyer's office.

I felt as if my buying the trailer meant I wouldn't see Evelyn again, and she had been so very important to me during my first six months in Jacksonville.

Out in the hallway, I couldn't help crying, even though I was getting one heck of a deal and even though I had moved on with my life. I hugged her, and kissed her, and hugged her again.

Evelyn cried, too. "I know, I know," she said. "Carl, you have been very special to me. You looked like an angel dropped into my life when you first came to the trailer. I've never understood it, but I know that being with you and thinking about you helped me through some of the most difficult periods of my life.

"You were my first," she murmured, "and by far the best. For someone claiming inexperience, you were so sensitive and caring."

"Evelyn," I replied, holding both her hands, "you were so special to me. I cared for you and I cared about what happened with you. My tears now are so confusing. I missed you so much when we drifted apart, but I knew it had to happen. I accepted all that."

I went on. "Now though, we're saying goodbye to such an important part of my life. You were so generous; you were so kind and caring. I will always be grateful to you for everything you did to help me get back on my feet."

Evelyn hugged me again. A long, caring hug. "I know, I know. Carl," she half-sobbed and choked back some tears, "Let's do Christmas Sunday service every year together if we can. I can't bear the thought of going on without you in my life, at least to that extent. "

"Absolutely!" I enthused. And I meant it.

* * *
**

Chapter 38 – Spring and Summer in Jacksonville

All through the winter of 2002 I continued to visit the Brentwood Library once or twice a week to exchange books but mostly to try to keep up with the Omaha news. So far as I could tell, there was no more news about Fred Young. He was dead and forgotten.

Well, that was something.... I was thinking about Fred Young in the third person, which surprised and pleased me.

There was no mention of Timothy or Liz, either.

Susan was a whole 'nother story, though. In the first six months after 9-11, she became increasingly active. In addition to her church work and joining the Board of Directors of the United Way, Susan was Chair of the Fredrick Robert Young Foundation; and all of that had happened within the first two months. Over the next few months, her name was also included among people who were visiting bereaved children whose parents had died in an automobile accident. And she was appointed to the citizen review board for the Omaha Police Department.

This was a side of Susan that I had never paid attention to. Had I stifled her ambitions? Had I "kept her down on the farm"? Had our traditional marriage and our desire for the Great Mid-American Dream inhibited her? Or had I just been too self-centered and too ignorant to see that side of her?

I knew Susan had administrative skills; that was what she had been hired for when we first moved to Omaha. And I had seen constant reminders of her skills as a homemaker after she became a stay-at-home mom.

When she became pregnant with Timothy, Susan took my hand across the table and told me in a very determined tone, "I am choosing to be a homemaker and a mother. I have even studied for this career. I will devote myself to it. You do your work, I'll do mine, and we will be true, sharing partners. When the children are older, I might consider re-entering the workforce, but not until then."

Susan did, indeed, devote herself to her career as a homemaker and a mother. The kids were nurtured emotionally as well as physically. She took an interest in their lives and their activities. She had many skills going into her "career" choice, and she developed many more over the next sixteen years. I knew it, but I took it for granted. She was a scout-leader, president of the PTA, a chief fund-raising soccer mom, and a leader at the local children's museum; I was pleased and proud of her, but I think I under-rated her skills if I even thought about them at all.

At the same time, I wondered what role the insurance money played in her recent activities. Clearly organizations had sought her out to be a "director" or "consultant" or "advisor", all the while seeking donations from her as well, of course. She had the money, and she could pick and choose her causes. I rationalized: My "death" provided her with opportunities she would never have had otherwise.

Susan was clearly talented and wealthy. She would likely become a very different person from the one who had devoted herself to home and family. I could see most of this coming.

Nevertheless, I was more than a little surprised when I read in May that Susan was going to run for the U.S. Senate on the Republican ticket. Wow!

I knew she would win. She had talent, brains, a careful and cautious manner, and a husband who had died a hero – of sorts.

I was jealous, ashamed that I hadn't seen and encouraged this side of her, proud of her and proud to have been married to her, emotionally wrapped up, ... a wide spectrum of emotions. I wondered if she was glad I had died. I knew that I felt like a stranger as I read about her and her life style. And I wondered whether perhaps we hadn't been as close as we had pretended we were.

- - -

In April 2002, as promised, the Thanes and I had our meeting to talk about my future with Thane-Mart. They took me to dinner at a very nice restaurant and engaged in tentative small talk for nearly half an hour before getting down to business.

"Carl," Alicia said, taking charge of the get-together, "We are not going to push you to do any more than you want, but I hope you understand that you have managerial talent and skills. We would like you to manage Thane-North. We will do what we can to make it work. We know that if you want to move up in the organization, the regional office for Q-Mart will be eager to hire you in a year if not tomorrow."

I was dumbfounded. What had they seen? I got along with my co-workers. I didn't screw up. I kept things working smoothly. I had worked every night since they had hired me. I had helped others by taking on portions of their shifts. I had reasonable ideas about possible changes. I guess those things made me management material in the convenience-store business.

Deep down, I knew better than that. After all, I had been a partner in a major finance firm and I had developed innovative finance tools. Maybe those skills showed through somehow.

I took a deep breath.

"Alicia, Dick," I said, looking at them in turn, "I really appreciate your confidence in me. You took a chance on me when I was down and out and had nothing. You two, and Evelyn, my landlady, provided me with a safety net that has helped me get on my feet over these past eight or so months. I don't know how to thank you."

"Become a manager!" Dick intervened with a smile.

"Okay," I returned his smile, paused for effect, and nodded in assent. "Let's see what we can work out."

Alicia and Dick let out a small cheer, causing the others in the restaurant to look over at us.

"What do you want?" Dick asked.

"I have become accustomed to working nights," I answered. "I don't want to give that up, but even more I don't want the headaches of trying to replace me on nights."

I smiled, knowingly, as I said that, recalling my earlier conversation with Dick and recalling all the ads for people to work the night shift in convenience stores. "We'll have to work around that for now."

"We understand that," said Alicia. "Finding reliable people to work overnight shifts isn't easy. We can cover the evening shifts with part-timers usually, but we know we got lucky with you for the night shift." She squeezed Dick's hand a bit to acknowledge that he had been the one to recommend hiring me despite my lack of any background.

"I have some ideas that might help us and still allow me to work the night shift," I said. "How about we ask job applicants to come in for interviews either at 8am or at 10pm? I could screen the applications during the night shift and then either work an hour or two later or start an hour earlier to meet with them."

I paused a moment to let them think about that before continuing.

"I would mostly be interviewing applicants for the day or evening shifts, and they should be able to make it to interviews at one of those times. That way I could keep working the night shift and still manage the hiring decisions at Thane-North."

"Amazing," said Alicia. "We knew this was the right thing to do."

"Beyond that, I would like a rotating two-week schedule posted on the inside of the storage room door. You two have done an amazing job, hiring Maggy, Jerry, and Donna, and the four of us pretty much fill up the bulk of the hiring needs. But we rely heavily on students and other part-time employees to fill in during rush periods and on the weekends. I'm sure there is scheduling software available to help look after this."

"We sort of do that by hand, now," said Dick, "but only a week ahead and doing it by hand is drudge work. Good suggestion."

"So that would be okay with you, then?"

They both nodded.

"Let me let my hair down, now, so to speak," I said and smiled.

They laughed and then became extremely interested in what I had to say, undoubtedly expecting more details about my past.

"As you both readily guessed,..." I paused and looked down at the table.

Then I looked up with determination. "I don't have a past. That is firm with me. I will say, though, that it is with some trepidation that I take on any kind of management position. I have enjoyed my steady, quiet life. I am not at all sure I want any more than what I have now, both in terms of excitement and stress on the job and elsewhere in my life."

I didn't tell them about having to adjust to having had Evelyn in my life and then having spent the past month grieving and learning to accept that she wouldn't be there very much anymore. It was an emotional pain that I hoped wasn't affecting the rest of my life.

"What kind of compensation are you looking for, Carl?" Alicia asked. She really did seem to be the management brains of the Thane enterprise.

"I hope you'll go along with this," I replied. "Sooner or later labor law is going to change, and it would be a great public relations move both within the Qmart chain and with the public for Thane-QMarts to be at the forefront. I think everyone working full-time, by which I mean at least 35 hours/week, should receive some bare-bones medical benefits. Both stores. I also would like to have ATMs in the stores. Alicia, you and I talked about that last fall."

They flinched slightly. Well figuratively, anyway.

"We're still looking into the ATMs," Dick said, somewhat sheepishly. Clearly he had been responsible for that and hadn't done it.

"What do you have in mind for medical benefits?" asked Alicia.

"Not a drug plan and not a dental plan, mostly just a hospitalization and catastrophic health plan with maybe a 20% co-pay for anything up to $2000 and full coverage after that?"

Dick said, "We haven't even considered looking into that, Carl. Do you know anything about those things?"

I lied. "Not really. Just what I see in newspaper columns and ads." I almost slipped but it wasn't noticeable. I didn't want them to know anything about my past, including the fact that I had been on the benefits committee at Klein-Staily.

"I'm sure we could meet with account representatives of major insurers to get proposals and quotes," I suggested.

"We can certainly look into it," Alicia said, "but what about you? What do you want for yourself?"

I was firm: "I want a commitment that you will more than look into it. I want a commitment that health benefits like what I've outlined, or better, will be in place within six months, preferably before fall. That is a requirement for me to become a manager. In return I won't ask for a super big raise."

"Why are you doing this, Carl?" Dick asked.

"I see it in the papers all the time, Dick. People with jobs like mine get hammered when it comes to major medical expenses. We feel that can't afford health insurance on our wages, and it would be a great tax-free benefit for us. The one thing that scares me about my future is my health. I really want some form of health insurance, but I'm not in a position to pay for it myself. Also it will be a tremendous plus when we're trying to hire people. We'll get better, more reliable people."

"All I can promise at this point," said Alicia, "is that we'll look into it…. Seriously. We will if that's what it takes to keep you as a manager."

"I understand. We'll also need reassurances for everyone that you won't be assigning 34-hour workweeks to avoid paying the health benefits. But we can work out those details later, after you get an idea what the benefits will cost you."

"You'd be assigning the hours," Dick said. "You can make sure that doesn't happen."

I couldn't help smiling again. Dick was no slouch intellectually either. They were a good team.

Alicia asked, "If you don't want a super-big raise, Carl, what kind of raise do you want?"

"Dick offered me $28 thousand plus some benefits. I'll be happy for the next six months to be at just $8 an hour with the understanding that I'll be averaging at least one extra hour each day on management items like staffing, security, and assisting you with planning. That works out to just a bit over $26 thousand a year. After six months, I will probably want more, but we'll see."

"Why not a salary, Carl?"

"I've read about it before, Dick. People on salary in management positions like this one are expected to cover when people don't show up for work. When that happens, the owners make money because they don't have to pay the so-called manager anything extra but the manager has to work extra. I just want to be paid for the work I do."

"Okay," Alicia said. "Anything else?"

"Well, now that you mention it...." I half-laughed and half-smiled as they became apprehensive again.

"I want full access to the store's computer network for payrolls, scheduling, and eventually benefits, in addition to the store's video surveillance that would be monitoring the tills and gas pumps. I don't need or even want access to the overall company data, but I do need access to everything to do with the Thane-North store."

"Okay..." Alicia seemed hesitant. "I think we can get that done. Not tomorrow but probably within a month or two."

"Good. Two other things."

Pause. Alicia nodded for me to go ahead.

"I'd like to have access to the office computer for my personal use as well.... Reading news, internet banking, etc. That, or, better yet, provide me with internet access at the store and buy me a laptop that I would mostly leave there."

"We can get you a laptop and internet, no problem," Dick said. "And the second thing?"

"The other thing I know you'll also have no problem with. I'd like to hire Ron to do more than clean one hour a day. Perhaps we can hire him to come in to clean and help out at the tills from 6 – 9am. It gets pretty busy sometimes during that period. I know he's not really old enough to be working the tills yet, but I'd like to have your permission to do that when I think he's ready."

Alicia smiled. "Carl, you'll be the manager. It's your choice."

And then with a fake, extreme bossy firmness, she added, "Just be sure to pay him at least the minimum wage and don't mess around with child labor laws! You got that?"

We all laughed and smiled together at that.

I was pleased with the outcome of the meeting. I'd have health benefits soon, I'd be making lots more per month, I wouldn't have to buy a computer, and I'd be able to put some of my ideas into operation.

I was nervous, too. I didn't want to jump back onto the treadmill. So far it had mostly been fun. I had to keep it that way and not let it control me. I was beginning to have a deeper understanding of who I was and what I wanted, and I was realizing that I didn't want a high-powered career.

By September of 2002, things were going as planned. I had a laptop with internet access, and we had an ATM in the store. Even better, Maggy, Jerry, Donna, and I all had major medical and hospitalization benefits. I know it wasn't inexpensive for the Thanes, but I was happy to forego some pay so we could all have those benefits. I think the others were, too, especially when I pointed out that even the barebones insurance would have cost us well over a thousand dollars each.

The Thanes and I agreed to an arrangement that I would do much of the management work during my eight-hour shift but would clock at least an extra half hour each day during which I finished up store business, read news or did banking. The Thanes were happy with the arrangement. I generally clocked only a half hour extra unless I had to meet with people later that morning; in those cases I clocked the actual time I was in the store, which sometimes was two hours or longer.

The overall positive atmosphere among us regulars carried over to the part-timers. Everyone seemed to enjoy working at Thane-North. Both sales and net revenues grew steadily. In September, the Thanes and I met again to review the situation. I knew I had pushed them to provide benefits and other things back in the spring, and I told them I was happy with my wages as things were, but maybe another twenty-five cent raise would be nice after Thanksgiving. They readily agreed.

- - -

One problem with my new job and responsibilities was that I wasn't always able to walk and exercise on the Winona Trail. When I left the store at 7:30, it was no problem, but when I had to stay until 8 or even 9am to meet with applicants or suppliers, I didn't much feel like walking on the trail very far.

Off and on, I still met Steffanie on the trail. Sometimes we just said "Hi". Other times we walked together for a while. She had a quick, long stride, and I had to push myself to keep up with her. As we walked, we talked about the weather, about our jobs, about local events. And of course she described the natural phenomena we passed and pointed out various birds.

In late May, 2002, she suggested, "Carl, why don't you come on one of our longer nature hikes this Saturday out on the Jacksonville-Baldwin Trail? That's the one I told you about earlier."

"That sounds nice," I said. "I'd like that. What time does it start?"

"We usually get together for the walk about 8am. Is that too early for you?"

"Well," I hesitated. "I usually work until 7:30, but I guess I can get off at 7 that day. I'll check to see when there might be bus service to the trail."

"What? Don't do that. I'll pick you up at your store. If I pick you up about 7:15, we can get there early and you can meet some of the other people we'll be walking with."

I liked the idea.

I enjoyed the drive and the walk, and I liked what little I knew about Steffanie. She had a directness to her that was disarming and refreshing.

We met on the trail frequently that summer. Eventually Steffanie sometimes stopped at the store to wait for me to go walking. It was an easy, comfortable friendship.

During one of our walks, Steffanie suggested, "We're going to Timucuan on Sunday morning. Would you like to come along?"

"Sure!" I paused and looked at her. " Timu…. What's that? "

My priorities were made clear in those three-plus words. They said: "Yes, I'd like to do something with you no matter what it is."

She looked down momentarily and then looked up at me and smiled. I think she caught the implications without my having to be explicit.

"Timucuan. It's an historic preserve over on the ocean. It's well away from any tourist condos, and so it isn't crowded. We tend to walk nearer the ocean where it's cooler in the summer, but you'll need sunscreen and a hat," she said.

Steffanie knew I shaved my head because she had seen me in the store, but she had only rarely seen me outside without my bucket hat. It was a no-brainer for me, and I was puzzled as to why she said that. She didn't ordinarily talk just for the sake of filling the silence. I inferred that she wanted to say something caring, and that was what came out.

"Will running shoes be okay?" I was still on my first pair of Excells from the discount store, but I was about to have to move to my newer pair. I resolved that I would buy another backup pair soon and retire the pair I had been wearing all the time.

"Sure. We don't walk in the sand much, and if we do, we just take off our shoes and socks. You've already met many of the people who will be going. Some of those keeners wear hiking boots, even on the beach," she laughed.

It was an organized group walk with lectures along the way by some guy who seemed to know everything about everything. After the walk-and-talk, I suggested to Steffanie that I take her somewhere for lunch to thank her for driving me around.

Over lunch she told me she had been in an abusive relationship for over ten years.

"It was more emotionally abusive than physically abusive," she said. She had left the relationship five years before we met. All she had when she left was her job, some of her clothing, and a few personal effects, but not much else.

"I was lucky, Carl. I have a good job, and I have been able to get back on my feet slowly. But walking on the trails and joining these nature groups really helped keep me sane. I think I'll always be damaged from those experiences. But things are always looking up," she smiled and I could see she felt uncertain about the future but didn't want to admit it.

And then what I dreaded.

"What about you? Tell me about yourself."

"I came to Jacksonville last fall with practically nothing. I had some meager savings and the clothes on my back and nothing else. I struggled for a few days, but I was fortunate that a trailer nobody else seemed to want to rent was available and was perfect for me; the rent is so low, it embarrasses me. Also the job is working out well, too."

She looked at me somewhat seriously. "Before you came here, Carl. Tell me about your life before Jacksonville."

I let out a sigh that I hoped was imperceptible. I wouldn't tell her a thing. But I hated turning her down.

"BJ.... Before Jacksonville," I chuckled. "I'll try to remember that."

She just looked at me, expecting me to continue.

I looked her straight in the eyes. "Steffanie, I will tell you what I told the Thanes. I have no past."

I paused to let that sink in and then continued, "I did nothing illegal. I was never even investigated for any wrongdoing or anything criminal. I was searching for something and had no idea what I was searching for. So far, here in Jacksonville, I've found a kind of contentment I never had before."

I loved looking at her eyes.

"Well, Carl Jacobs, I've tried to track you down on the internet. According to the internet you don't exist. Are you in witness protection?"

I grimaced. "Well, Steffanie Niles, I'm not." Using our first and last names like that seemed to signify that something meaningful was developing between us. "But if I were I'd have to tell you I'm not." I didn't smirk. I wanted to be serious, even though the logic of that statement amused me.

I hoped that would work. It did. Sorta.

"Your not having a past makes me uncomfortable, Carl. After what I've been through I feel uneasy about it."

Well, that was poignant. She had been checking me out on the internet and she was uneasy about having a relationship or even a friendship with me. It felt good to know all that. At the same time, I didn't think I could handle another relationship like the one I'd had with Evelyn.

"Slow and easy," I told myself. "Slow and easy."

"All I can say is that I like spending time with you, Steffanie. I like walking with you and talking with you, I like hearing you talk about birds and kudzu and rivers and oceans and hurricanes. I like looking into your eyes. I like hearing the details of some of your physiotherapy work. I hope we can keep doing these things together. Over time you'll get to know the real me as I am and as I am becoming."

She smiled. Whew.

"Becoming," she said. " ...Me, too. It's a touchy-feely word but it describes me. I guess you think it describes you pretty well, too."

- - -

We didn't go to bed together right then, even though we both felt as if we wanted to. We held each other tightly and longingly before we got into her car. I kissed her softly and gently. We both knew where we were headed.

Steffanie and I continued to enjoy each other's company that summer and into the fall. My being the manager of Thane-North cut into our morning walks often, but that meant we both had our own lives and weren't unduly attached to each other, something that appealed to me.

On weekend mornings, though, we often spent a few hours walking on some of the trails and beaches in and around Jacksonville. Steffanie pushed me often, not about my past and not about day-to-day things so much, but more about who I wanted to be. Her directness bordered on bluntness sometimes and made me uncomfortable at times, too. And yet I valued her company and the insights her questions forced me to consider.

I was never sure what she saw in me, other than determination and a sense of integrity. That made me smile and frown. I was determined about a lot of things, including that I wanted to learn more about myself and didn't want to slip back into my old life, where I had been pretending about relationships.

During one of our conversations, Steffanie said, "I learned from my marriage that the only way to be true to yourself is to be willing to live alone. I wasn't true to myself because I didn't want him to leave me. I was afraid of being alone. I gave in to him and to social pressures. I became inwardly angry, even passively aggressive, and that would provoke him even more."

I nodded earnestly. It struck a chord with me. I had been raised to live a life of pretending, of not questioning, of not thinking about what I wanted. I had been trained to try to live the Great Mid-American Dream, and it had left me feeling empty.

Steffanie looked at me questioningly.

"I think that's probably what happened to me in a way, too. I came to Jacksonville and left everything behind me. It was an enormous risk, but the way you put it rings true for me. I wanted to be true to myself. I wanted to stop pretending."

"Carl Jacobs," she said, using my first and last names as she did when she was feeling close to me. "I don't want to pretend any more."

By early fall, we had begun having Sunday breakfast at either her place or mine: we spent a few hours together, lolling about or dozing together in bed, and we truly enjoyed each other's company. Steffanie thought my trailer was "quaint"; I thought her apartment was "nice" which was my personal euphemism for "adequate but uninspiring".

"You don't have a television, Carl?"

"Nah... I keep up on the news at work. I read papers there when there aren't any customers. I suppose there are some programs I might like, but I'm happy not to have a television. Besides, where would I put it?"

"I guess you could have one on your bedroom dresser..." Steffanie suggested hesitantly. And then she added hastily, "If you wanted one."

She clearly didn't want to seem too pushy. I appreciated that. I tried to let her know how much I appreciated it.

We enjoyed being together, and we shared lots of experiences and thoughts. Aside from my silence about my past, we had a very open, honest relationship. With Steffanie, I had no problems opening up about my feelings. It felt good.

My co-workers at Thane-North were well aware of my relationship with Steffanie. Unlike my brief relationship with Evelyn, I was pleased and happy to have them all know about Steffanie. I made sure I introduced her to all of them when she first started coming into the store.

* * *
**

Chapter 39 – *Ron(nie)*

Steffanie didn't have a chance to meet Ron right away. In the spring and early summer, he came in at 10pm and left a little after 11pm, when I started my shift. Later in the summer, I suggested he might be able to work more and earn more if he was willing to come in first thing in the morning. He could come in for two hours each morning, arriving at 7am, and during the two hours he could clean and also help out on the second cash register when things got busy.

"I don't know how," Ron said. He seemed almost panicked.

"Ron," I said, "Maggy will be here, and I'll be here the entire two hours the first few days you're here. I'll teach you everything you need to know, and you'll be fine."

Indeed, he was fine. He learned all the ins and outs of the cash register in no time flat. He was very perceptive, and seemed to have a natural intuition about the logic of how the store worked. He quickly learned to open the second till any time there were more than two people waiting for Maggy to wait on them, and in the meantime he did the cleaning and minor maintenance chores perfectly.

Ron was a bit embarrassed at first when he started looking at the store windows in the daylight. They weren't perfect when he finished washing them at night, but they were ok. In the daylight, though, he saw the streaks and within a few days he had perfected methods for making sure the streaks were gone.

Initially the customers were somewhat nonplussed, maybe discriminatory in their outlook, to have a young person waiting on them. But he compensated by calling them "Ma'am" or "Sir" and by adopting a very professional demeanor. After two weeks, I gave him a raise to $5.50 an hour. It was less than Maggy, Jerry, and Donna were making, but it was in line with the weekend part-timers.

Ron beamed. I beamed. He was netting over $60 a week. Things were working out well for him.

One Saturday morning in late August while Steffanie and I were walking, she asked me about Ron.

I told her what I knew, including how we had met.

"He came in at 4am with his hands in his hoodie pockets, told me he had a gun, and told me to give him money. I had an inkling he didn't have a gun, and so I challenged him. For some reason, I could see something in his desperation and offered him a job right then. That night. It wasn't for me to do, and I knew it. I had him come in to clean when there was no one else working at the store so that no one would know what I was doing, and I had to pay him out of my own pocket."

"Do you know what he did with his pay that first night?" I asked rhetorically. "He used it to buy milk and cereal. I felt so bad for the kid. But he was determined he would continue working for me. After only a few weeks, the Thanes caught on and insisted on hiring him themselves. It turned out that he was providing much of the food for himself and his two little sisters. Apparently his mother is on the streets most of the time."

"He doesn't talk right, but he's improving. He's a quick learner. He's reliable; he hasn't missed a day of work since I hired him. And he has an insight that most young adults don't have, looking for things that need doing and striving to do things better, not just adequately."

"Does he go to school?" Steffanie asked.

"He says he does. I haven't pressed him on it, but recently he suggested that in the fall he might want to come in at 6:30am and leave at 8:30 so he could get to school on time. Of course I agreed."

Steffanie stopped. When I stopped to see why, her eyes were teary. She said, "Carl, what you've done for that young man is so special." And she put her arms around my neck and held me tight.

I didn't know how to respond. I thought of the foolish things I might have said in my past life, but I just mumbled, "Thanks," and let it go at that. And then she kissed me. It certainly wasn't our first kiss, but it felt very special. We both had tears in our eyes….

On Wednesday, September 25, 2002, just a couple of weeks more than a year since I had moved into the trailer, Ron didn't show up for work. It puzzled me. I figured there was a good explanation, but I was a bit miffed, too, since he had been so reliable up until then. I hoped he hadn't gotten involved with the drug culture at school.

I was mulling it over while walking home through the cemetery after my walk with Steffanie, when I saw Ron lying on the ground, somewhat concealed by two large gravestones.

I walked over to him to see if he was okay.

He looked up at me and seemed quite embarrassed. And then he broke down in tears, burying his face in the ground.

I took his hands and helped him up and hugged him. I actually cooed a bit as I said, "There, there. What's the problem? What's wrong, Ron?"

He sobbed and choked. He finally was able to spit out a few words.

"Ma arrested yesterday. Family cops took Janie and Abby. I saw 'em waiting for me. Came back here to hide."

"We'll sort it out," I said. "Let's go to my trailer and you can tell me what happened."

Ron had never been in my trailer. I think he was surprised by my Spartan lifestyle. The trailer was considerably smaller than his mother's, and I didn't have any large appliances or much else.

"C'mon," I urged and pointed to a chair at the table. "Have a seat. I'll make some coffee and breakfast."

"What about school?" Ron asked.

"You can go in awhile. I'll go with you, and we'll make sure your counselors know what's going on. Do you drink coffee? Or maybe I have some milk here." I opened the fridge to see if I had any milk.

"No, Mr. Jacobs. We drink Kool-Aid mostly," he said.

"I don't have any Kool-Aid, Ron,…. and I appear to be out of milk. How about a glass of water?"

"Okay."

Ron sat at the table while I fixed breakfast. I always had a fresh container of cut up vegetables on hand, along with shredded cheese and plenty of butter and eggs. I guessed Ron might be hungry, and so I made a six-egg scrambled egg type of omelette.

I was right. Ron devoured the lion's share of the omelette. After he finished eating, I asked him to help me with the dishes. I washed, he dried. Then I poured myself another cup of coffee and said, "Let's go sit in the living room," referring the area with a chair and loveseat.

"Ron, where will you stay tonight?" I didn't know how to broach the subject, but this seemed as good a way as any.

"Dunno. Can't go back home. They find me and take me."

"Well, they might put you in an ok foster home, Ron…" I suggested.

He shuddered.

"At any rate, you can't count on sleeping in the cemetery every night. You need a place to store clothes and to wash up."

"Been in foster homes. Most don't care 'bout school. Beat me. Work me. You pay me for work."

"Ron," I offered hesitantly, "You can stay here for awhile, maybe longer, if you want. I can't formally become a foster parent, but we can let your school know this is your new address for now."

I knew this would be the result, the minute I saw him lying on the ground in the cemetery. I just didn't want to push it, in case he didn't want to live here.

He looked around. "What I gotta do?"

I thought for a few minutes. I sipped my coffee. He got nervous.

Finally, I said, "Ron, for now you pay me ten dollars a week for room and board. I'll provide the food. This weekend we'll go to some thrift stores where I will buy you some clothes. I will want you to keep your room neat and to help out with cleaning the trailer and doing the dishes."

"Okay." He didn't seem enthused.

To be honest, neither was I. I had just taken on responsibility for a 15-year-old boy. He'd be alone in my trailer every night while I was working, my sleep patterns would be completely messed up. And my relationship with Steffanie would be in jeopardy.

"Carl," I thought to myself. "What are you doing?"

I honestly felt as if I had no choice. I liked Ron, and I saw potential in him. I couldn't push him away. But if he wasn't sure, I wasn't about to push it.

"Ron, I don't want to push you into this. It's just a suggestion. What would you like to do?"

"I wahn stay here."

He started crying again. Through his tears he asked, "Why you do this, Mr. Jacobs?"

"Ron, I like you, and I respect you. You are a really nice person who deserves a break. I've seen you work. I've seen you solve problems. You are always on the ball and reliable at work. If I can help you along your way for awhile until things improve for you, I think you deserve a chance."

He broke down and couldn't stop crying. He curled up into a fetal position on the chair, still crying. I wanted to hug him again, but I didn't do it. I didn't want there to be any sense of impropriety between us.

As he was settling down, I thought of a few more things.

"Ron, you'll be on your own at night while I'm working. Will you be okay with that?"

He nodded. Of course he would. I was a dumb question. He had been on his own at night a lot and had had to look after his little sisters.

I tried to consider other problems and was concerned.

"But listen. I need to sleep during the day. What time do you usually get home from school?"

"'bout three."

"If you come in here at three, that will really mess up my sleep. I can't have that. I need you to stay at school, if you can, to do homework or get help from teachers. And I need you to spend time at the library or someplace. Mostly, I need you not to come home before five. Will that be okay with you?"

"Yes, sir," he said in a monotone that reminded me of Ellen Smith at The Alameda Motel.

I tried not to take the monotone as a sign of a lack of enthusiasm.

"Okay," I stood up. "Come over here and lie down on this loveseat. Let's see if you fit here."

He didn't. He was about six inches too long, and who knew how much more he might grow.

"It okay, Mr. Jacobs. I can still sleep here."

It bothered me that he sounded desperate, pleading.

"Well, before we settle on that, let's see what other options we might have. You haven't seen the rest of the trailer, have you?"

I led the way to the storage room. I had been using it as a dressing room, but I had plenty of room in the dresser drawers in my bedroom, and I could put up a rod over my dresser for my hanging clothes.

"This can work," I thought to myself.

"Ron, I think this room can become yours. I'll move my things to my bedroom, and I think we can just barely fit a bed in here. You'll have this dresser, and eventually we can get a small desk to put next to it"

It was as if he was in a daze. Had I been moving too quickly?

"Never had space my own," he said. He was dropping more words.

We moved on. "Here's the bathroom. We'll put out a separate set of towels for you, and I'll make space in the medicine cabinet for you to keep some things. We can share the soap and toothpaste."

I looked at him expectantly, but he just stood there.

And so I went on, "A couple of minor things that I'll ask, Ron. Use your facecloth to wipe the faucets and sink to keep them looking good, and wipe off any toothpaste splatters from the mirror. And always make sure there's spare toilet paper on the back of the toilet. Okay?"

Pause.

"Don't have no toothbrush," was all he could say.

"Well, I think our next step should be to go up to the discount store to get you a set of clothes, a toothbrush, and anything else you might need. It'll take awhile to get a bed, so you'll have to sleep in the living room at first. And I can see from the way you ate those eggs, we'll need a lot more food. Let's go."

Ron just looked around. It was a small trailer with a small space for him, but it would be his space. I could see that would be important.

As we walked up to the discount store, I asked him, "What do you do for lunch?"

"Nothin'. We don't get much food. Mostly what I can buy."

"You need some sustenance during the day, Ron. I'd rather not have bread or things like bread in the place, but we can get you some of the healthier types of granola bars and some juice boxes for lunch. Or you can make rice cakes with peanut butter or cheese. That's what I do."

I was relieved that I had gotten all those raises. Saving a lot of money for my retirement wouldn't be so easy now. I could still save some, though, and I was determined to do it.

We bought Ron a pair of pants, a sport shirt, a dozen briefs, and a dozen pairs of socks. His eyes were wide. I think he had never had that many new clothes all at once. I looked at his shoes and decided shoes could wait. Then I looked at his face.

"Ron, I'm not keen on sharing razors, but I can see you're likely to want to use one pretty soon. I hope it's okay if we buy you a different brand than the one I use so we can tell them apart."

He smiled. "Okay."

We bought two toothbrushes, one for him and one for me. He liked the idea of purple, so that's what he got; mine was green. And we bought the same brand of toothpaste that I'd been using.

The discount store had elevated air beds, so we bought one of those for him, along with some single bed sheets.

"All you really need is one set of sheets for now. When you do your laundry, you can wash the sheets then, too."

He looked panicked again.

"Never done laundry."

That surprised me. I guess his mother had at least looked after that for him. "It's easy. I'll show you. It can become one of your weekend chores."

I got Ron to choose a towel set, and then we picked up some boxes of granola bars and a dozen juice boxes.

"Anything else you need, Ron?"

His eyes were glazed over. He seemed to be in shock. "No, sir."

"Ron, can you carry that bed? It's pretty heavy."

"Yes, sir." And he did.

Along the way home, I told him we'd go to the thrift stores to buy him some more clothes on Saturday after we got off work.

"We'll need to pick up a bunch more groceries soon, too."

And then I had a bit of a panic. I'd have to let Steffanie know about all this right away.

He was exhausted when we got to the trailer.

358

"Ron," I suggested, "Why don't you take a shower now, put on your new clothes, and then we'll go to your school?"

He was shy. I didn't blame him. He took his towel set and his new clothes with him into the bathroom.

I lay down and let my mind wander. While I was lying on my bed, I heard him brushing his teeth. And then the shower.

I called Steffanie's cell phone. I knew she couldn't answer it while she was at work. I left a message:

> Steffanie, Ron's mother was arrested yesterday. His sisters have been taken by Family Services and Ron ran away. He's staying with me for now and might move in. I think there's a good chance I'll become his unofficial foster parent. It will change how and when you and I can get together, I'm afraid. I hope you understand.

At noon, I had Ron take two granola bars with him, and we walked to his school. When we got there, I stood at the main office desk with Ron and asked to speak with the school counselor or principal. Fifteen minutes later we were ushered into the office of Mr. Vance Hartman, the vice-principal.

"Well, Ronnie," his smile almost menacing, "What have you been up to? You missed school this morning."

"Mr. Hartman," I interrupted. I wasn't going to let a bully push Ron around if I could step in. "Ron has had some issues at home, and so he's living with me now."

"And who are you?" Hartman asked pointedly.

"I apologize." Ugh. I sounded like a pretentious jerk.

I started again. "I'm sorry, I should have introduced myself. I'm Carl Jacobs. I'm the manager at Thane's Q-mart on Pearl Street. Ron has been working there part time for nearly a year, and during that time he has been using most of his pay to help feed his sisters. His mother has been arrested, and his sisters have been taken into foster care."

"I see."

"Ron has pretty much been left to fend for himself," I said as I stretched the truth. "I offered to let him stay with me while things are being sorted out."

"That's very kind of you, Mr. Jacobs." He was abrupt and formal, but seemed to be softening somewhat. "What does that mean for us here at the school?"

"It means that until Ron tells you otherwise, he will unofficially be under my care. I will be making sure he is well-fed and well-clothed, and I will be trying to make sure he keeps up with his schoolwork."

Hartman still had a smirky skeptical smile.

I continued. "As I said, Ron has worked for us for nearly a year. He never missed a single day of work until this morning, when I learned of his home situation. He is reliable and careful, and he has shown considerable initiative. I hope he'll be treated with respect and will receive some consideration when he needs help."

Hartman began to blubber some administrative babble about how the school cares for all its students. I didn't blame him. I was coming off as a pompous, pushy outsider, and he was put on the defensive by my manner.

I interrupted again, "What I mean is that Ron should be given help with learning. That's all I'm asking." And I added to make sure both he and Ron knew what I was asking for, "No concessions, no leniency. Just help with learning."

"I don't know a thing about you, Mr. Jacobs," Hartman said somewhat stuffily, "but you can be assured that is exactly what we provide all our students."

"Wonderful," I smiled. "We're on the same page then."

On the way out I left my name, address, and telephone number at the front desk.

Before Ron went to class, I spoke with him. "Mr. Hartman seems stern, but as long as you show respect for your teachers and him and work hard, he'll come around. Don't worry, Ron. I've met lots of people like him before."

"You the only one calls me Ron."

"I changed last winter when I realized you are a young man who has had many responsibilities. If you like I'll call you whatever you want though."

He almost puffed out his chest. "Ron," was all he said.

"Ron, I forgot to give you a key. I'll prop the door open when I get back. When you come in, please come in quietly and don't wake me before 7pm today. Okay?"

"Sure."

He was beaming as he went to class.

* * *

**

Chapter 40 – *Rescheduling Everything*

Ron came in so quietly and carefully that evening that I was afraid he hadn't come back. When I awoke, it was almost eight o'clock, and I had a sudden fear that something had gone wrong. I rushed to the living room, and there was Ron, sitting in the chair, looking at his schoolbooks.

"Thanks for being so quiet Ron. I really needed that extra sleep."

He just smiled.

Then he said, "I wanted to put my bed up but didn't want to wake you, Mr. Jacobs."

"Thanks, Ron. Let's get something to eat first, and then we can get things organized in your room ... and mine."

We heated up some chicken stew I'd made in the crockpot the night before. "Man, is that thing ever going to get a workout now!" I thought.

We rushed through supper.

As we started to do the dishes, Ron said, "I'll do this if you want some time to rearrange your stuff."

Crafty kid. He wanted my things out of his room, and he was offering to do the dishes to speed the process.

"Great idea!" I enthused.

I moved my clothes from the small dresser into the empty drawers in my dresser. I kicked myself for not having bought something at the discount store that I could use to hang clothes over the dresser, but I folded some of my hanging clothes and put those in my bedroom dresser along with my other clothes. I left a few clothes hanging in Ron's room, too, and hoped Ron would be ok with that. The vacuum was the major problem... where to store it.

When Ron came into his room I was just moving the vacuum out.

"That ok. Leave it where desk going," he said. "And if you wahn leave some clothes here, too, that good. Can we put up my bed?" He was so eager! So transparently eager!

We put up his bed. It barely fit, but it would do.

Ron had apparently never seen sheets before. I showed him how to put the fitted sheet on the bottom, which wasn't easy. The bed was tight against walls on the side and at both ends, and it had a frame that blocked hooking the bottom sheet on very well.

I got a blanket from my room for him.

"Why you use sheets?" Ron asked.

"I'm not sure," I answered, "but I think it's to keep sweat and body odors off the mattress and the blankets so they don't need to be cleaned much."

"Ron, this may seem picky on my part, but I want you to make your bed every morning."

He looked completely confused. "You mean gotta take all this apart and then put it back up at night?"

"No," I tried not to smile at his ignorance, "Making your bed means pulling up the sheets and covers and neatening them. This weekend we'll get you a pillow when we go for groceries. Until then, you can use one of mine."

Next I went back to the kitchen and took out the extra key for the trailer.

"You've probably noticed that the trailer door locks when it closes. That's why I had to prop it open for you today. But from now on we'll close the door and make sure it's locked when we leave, right?"

"Yes, sir." He was smiling. He knew I was giving him orders, but he didn't seem to mind. He even seemed to enjoy the structure.

"Ron, here's a key to the trailer. Please don't lend it to anyone else, and please don't lose it. We'll get a backup key or two made in addition to everything else we're planning to do this weekend."

"Okay." He seemed pleased.

At about nine o'clock, Steffanie called.

"Carl Jacobs, you are a wonderful man!"

Well! I guess that settled how she was going to like my having Ron move in with me. I was a bit taken aback.

I looked at Ron and said, "It's Steffanie." I took the phone to my bedroom. Not "the" bedroom anymore, but "my" bedroom; big difference.

I told Steffanie the details of this morning, about buying "a few things" for Ron, the visit to the school, and my concerns.

"I hate going off and leaving him alone when I go to work," I said. "I don't think he'll get into trouble, but I still worry since I don't know him very well really. And weekends! We can take him walking with us sometimes, but we'll need our time alone, too. I gotta figure how to arrange that."

"Don't worry," Steffanie said. "We'll work things out together."

And we did. The three of us had breakfast together that Sunday. Ron and Steffanie had met each other at Thane-North several times, but it was still a bit awkward. After breakfast, Steffanie suggested that Ron stay at the trailer to do his schoolwork while she and I went back to her place. That was no problem for Ron; his mom had left him alone often; he was used to it.

I gave Ron the next available weekend morning shifts at Thane-North in addition to his daily morning job, leaving time for Steffanie and me to walk and talk and spend more comfort time, relaxing together.

Our co-workers didn't know that Ron had moved in with me. And he always called me "Mr. Jacobs" in front of them. In fact he always called me "Mr. Jacobs" everywhere.

After my initial splurge for him at the thrift shops to buy more clothing, Ron used his own increased income to buy his own clothing. He also started buying cereal and milk to keep in the trailer for his breakfast. He was proud of being able to do those things.

"Ron," I scolded him, "the deal was that you pay me ten dollars a week to cover room and board. That means you get a room, and I provide the food, do you understand?"

He nodded slightly, putting on his somewhat vacant look that seemed to mean he didn't much care what was being said.

"So from now on, I'll buy the cereal and milk when I go shopping. You got that?"

"No, sir."

What??? I just about fell over. Calmly I asked, "I beg your pardon?"

"You providing evening meal and lunch things and laundry things. I'll buy cereal and milk."

"Well...." I hesitated. I knew it was important for him to continue to take what responsibility he could. "Okay.... But if you change your mind, ever, let me know."

So my patterns changed. Ron ate cereal with milk before coming to work in the morning. Then, when I got home from work in the morning, I started the crockpot whenever we needed more food for dinner. I had my eggs in the morning before going to bed for the day.

It all worked pretty well.

- - -

Ron began making noticeable changes. His speech was becoming more complete, his schoolwork was improving, and he started growing physically. It was a pleasure being able to foster his growth. When I first met him, his language skills seemed to be at about a third grade level, if that, but within a couple of years, he was almost up to his grade level.

There were never any problems with Ron in school during the four years that it took him to finish high school. I didn't know what he had been like before that, and I didn't ask. Ron made a point of going to his sisters' school at least twice a week to visit with them after they got out of school. He made sure they knew he cared about them and would do what he could to help them. I was certain he was slipping them a couple of dollars each week, too, for spending money.

A few things the teachers told me during the next few years led me to believe that Ron hadn't done much of anything in school, hadn't even tried to do much, and, in fact, hadn't bothered to show up at school a lot of the time. I knew from that first day when I hired him that he had problem-solving skills and was able to take initiative in some areas. I was cautiously pleased with myself.

One reason for my cautious take on the situation was that I kept asking myself, "What are you doing? Here? Looking after this lost young man? You have a family in Omaha that could probably use your guidance and love!" And yet I felt real now, even though I was lying about who I was. I felt an inner authenticity I had never imagined before.

A month or so after Ron moved in, the U.S. elections were held. I was glued to my laptop at the store that Tuesday night, following the election returns. By midnight, Jacksonville time, it was clear that Susan had won the Senate seat. There were photos of her smiling and waving, with Timothy on one side, Liz on the other side, and a large portrait of me in front of her somewhere. Ben was in the background along with numerous hangers-on. After the usual thanks and congratulations, Susan went on:

> My family and I will always maintain our home in Omaha. This is where we live. But with Fred gone, I also need to have my children with me so we can share our love and lives together. We will soon be looking for accommodations in Georgetown, and the children will transfer schools at the end of the semester.

None of that could have happened had I lived. I hoped it would work out well for the children. They would be popular as the children of a woman who was clearly going to be a success as a politician. And I knew Susan would continue to help them keep their own identities.

Susan had been a somewhat protective mother, and so this move would upset their routines, for sure. But I guessed Timothy and Liz had eased into new patterns over the past fourteen months as Susan became more involved in her various charitable and social organization work, and especially when she decided to run for the Senate.

I was actually embarrassed when I realized how much she was blossoming. I wondered if I had somehow inhibited her. And yet, I hadn't said or done anything explicitly to keep her from doing these things. At least I didn't think I had. The more I reflected about how she had changed, the more I was sure that like me, Susan had been pretending to enjoy our pursuit of the Great Mid-American Dream. I was fairly confident now that we had both been pretending, and that made me think it wasn't just I who had escaped. Susan had escaped, too.

- - -

Steffanie was true to her word. "Don't worry," she had said. "We'll work things out together." She and I still did our morning walks together three or four times a week, and often on Saturdays we went on expeditions with a nature or bird-spotting group. Sunday mornings we spent together almost exclusively at her place, where we could relax together.

We slowly and gradually fell in love. It was a deep, close love that lacked the heat and sexual tension I had felt with Evelyn. But it was also a more open and honest love than I had ever imagined. It was nothing like what Susan and I had had. I liked it.

Sometimes on a weekday night, Steffanie would have Ron and me over for dinner; other times, we tried inviting her to the trailer for crockpot miscellany, but seating was awkward in the trailer, so mostly we tried to contribute by taking our crockpot meals to her place now and then.

Steffanie balked when I suggested that she join Ron, Evelyn, and me for the Christmas Sunday evening service.

"No thanks," she said emphatically. "My ex was religious and used his religion to abuse me. I don't know if I'll ever get over it."

And so that year, and the next, Ron and I went to the service with Evelyn without Steffanie.

In December 2004 after Evelyn had sold me the trailer, I kept calling her, leaving messages, hoping to go to the Christmas service, as we had promised each other we would. Finally I got through to her.

She sounded different when she picked up the phone.

"Yessssss?" She dragged out the sssssss.

Was that the Evelyn I had liked and cared about so much?

"Evelyn, it's Carl."

"Oh. Hi, Carl." She seemed to slur even those three syllables, and her tone implied she wasn't interested in talking.

I tried anyway.

"Evelyn, I just called to see if you're going the Christmas Sunday service at your church this year."

"No," she drawled. "I don't much feel like it this year. Sorry."

"Okay. Well, Merry Christmas, then," I said and got off the phone quickly.

I sat down and put my head in my hands.

"What is it, Carl?" Steffanie asked.

"I think she's become an alcoholic. That really makes me sad. She was so nice to me, and so helpful. But shortly after Don died, she took up with a number of different men she seemed to pick up at country bars. She must have been terribly inhibited and controlled by Don. I actually feel a sense of loss."

Steffanie came and sat beside me and hugged me. She had no idea that Evelyn and I had been lovers briefly, but that wasn't really relevant at this point. I was forcing myself to say goodbye to some very important memories.

"Carl, if you like, I'll go to the Christmas church services with you and Ron this year. I can drive us."

I hugged her back.

"That would be wonderful, Steffanie. Maybe just this once anyway."

It wasn't the same without Evelyn, but we all enjoyed ourselves. Steffanie even seemed amused by how Ron and I belted out the traditional Christmas carols. We were all laughing and smiling and hugging as we left the church that evening.

- - -

Evelyn died in January, 2005. Her estate lawyer called me the next day to tell me about it.

"We'll need some people for the funeral, he said. I think you should be one of them."

"Well, who else will be there?" I wasn't eager to meet up with more cowboys.

"You, me, and whoever walks in off the street. We may have to hire some folks from the funeral chapel to help bear the coffin."

I sucked in my breath. She had died alone. That added to my sadness.

"Carl, would you say a few words?"

"I'd love to. When is the funeral?"

I didn't have a suit. I'd have to get one the next day.

"Three days from now," and he gave me the name of the funeral home and the scheduled time for the service. The funeral home was Evergreen, just a few blocks from the trailer park.

"Carl, there is one more thing I should probably tell you."

"Yes?" I wasn't sure I wanted to hear whatever it was.

"She left half her estate to the church and half to you."

"Oh ... my...," I stammered.

"I'm to be the executor," he said. "Roughly it looks as if you'll inherit about three hundred thousand dollars after we sell the house and its contents. The house alone is worth over four hundred thousand."

"Well." I said and paused. "I'm truly stunned. Evelyn and I developed a close relationship briefly after I moved to Jacksonville. She was very special to me."

"As you were to her," he said. "I distinctly recall her telling me about the closeness she felt for you as she had me draw up this will for her."

The funeral was sparsely attended. Steffanie and Ron went with me. There were a few folks from her church, and, much to my relief but not surprise, none of the cowboys.

The church preacher said a few meaningless things that indicated he had no idea who Evelyn was or had been; then he prayed a bit; and then he asked me to speak. I told everyone what I knew about Evelyn: about her work and about how she and Don had traveled with their trailer. Next I spoke about how special Evelyn had been to me, how she had trusted me when I was down and out and had made it possible for me to get a fresh start in Jacksonville. I gave details on how she had welcomed me to her trailer home, provided me with the essentials of life, and even taken Ron and me to the Christmas pageants at her church. Once again, I couldn't stop crying.

The funeral director drove us to the gravesite, which was only a few hundred feet from the funeral chapel and not far from the trailer. That part felt right. She would be buried near what had been her happy place.

I felt bad that she had gone the way she had, but also I was pleased to have been a part of her life before she started drinking in country bars. After the graveside interment prayers, I walked off toward the trailer to be by myself for a few moments. Steffanie and Ron, bless them, stayed at the gravesite and let me walk alone.

I remembered Evelyn's warmth, her energy, and her loving kindness. And I cried again. Not a lot… until I remembered our tearful goodbye after she had sold me the trailer. I lost it then. It was as if we had both known it was a goodbye forever.

After I composed myself, I wiped my eyes and returned to Steffanie and Ron. They hugged me in turn. I was grateful they were with me.

She hadn't been interred but about five minutes when the minister huddled with the lawyer. He was hustling money, I could see. And then he approached me and asked if I had decided whether to make a donation to the church with my inheritance.

What an insensitive leech! I could have punched the creep. There was no need to mention that I was getting an inheritance in front of others, but maybe he just assumed they knew. I hadn't told them.

"My understanding is that Evelyn left half of her estate to your church," I replied. That's pretty substantial. Also, I don't have a pension, and so what she left me will be very important as I get older."

In other words, go away, you money-grubbing blood sucker.

I realized that he had to look after funding his church, but it upset me that he couldn't wait until later to discuss the estate. This was not the right time.

I turned and started walking to the trailer. Steffanie and Ron caught up with me, and each of them put an arm around me. And I put my arms around each of them as the three of us walked off together very slowly. The closeness and love were comforting.

Later, Steffanie, Ron, and I went to dinner at a chain restaurant. There I explained to them that indeed I had inherited some money from Evelyn, but that I had no intention of spending any of it. I would use it to provide for my retirement, and I was extremely grateful to Evelyn for having done this.

Ron asked, "Why did she like you so much, Mr. Jacobs?"

I noted with pleasure that Ron had included the word "did" in his question. He was progressing.

372

"Her husband was very ill when I first met her, Ron. She and I consoled and comforted each other as I was trying to get settled here in Jacksonville. We spent a lot of time talking together about life.... But I was surprised with the changes she made after Don died. There was a side to her I didn't know."

Steffanie cleared her throat quite obviously. She knew there was a side to me that she didn't know, as well. I tried to ignore her.

* * *
**

Chapter 41 – *Steffanie*

The next time Steffanie and I were alone together, I told her more about my financial situation.

"Last fall, when Google went public, I put ten thousand dollars of my savings into their stock. I have another fifteen thousand in mutual funds."

She looked surprised. "How on earth did you save that much?"

"I live frugally. You've seen how I dress. I buy most of my shirts and pants at thrift stores. I didn't even have a suit and had to buy one for Evelyn's funeral."

"I know, but twenty-five thousand dollars in total?"

"You know how Ron and I eat. We prepare all our own meals…" and then I smiled… "Except when we eat here with you. I don't own a car. I have no debts. Also the trailer cost me very little when I was renting it from Evelyn --- even less after she sold it to me. And the Thanes provide me with a laptop and internet access at work."

"Wow!" she said and shook her head. "It's impressive."

"Steffanie, when I came here a little over three years ago, I had nothing. I had no idea what I would do for money. I was determined I would live extremely frugally and try to save, knowing I would have only my own savings to rely on in retirement."

"Well, you'd have social security, too," she said.

"Yes, and I'll need it, too, if it isn't completely ruined by then."

"Carl, why are you telling me this?"

"I want you to know that I've been careful and that I'm looking after my future. On my own. I didn't expect a thing from Evelyn. In fact we hadn't really seen much of each other after that first year or so."

"Steffanie," I added somewhat embarrassed, "I planned and intended to look after myself, by myself. I want you to understand that."

"Okay." She dragged that out as she nodded, as if to ask "And...?".

"Evelyn left me about three hundred thousand dollars."

I paused to let that sink in.

"Holy cow!"

"It's mostly for my retirement as far as I'm concerned. I'll invest most of it: some in mutual funds, some in stocks. But I'd like to use a hundred thousand of it to help provide maintenance and extension of the trail system here in Jacksonville."

I went on. "The trails are where you and I met, and even before that they were great places for me to walk on my own. Since we've known each other, we've spent so much time together on the trails, and you have taught me so much about nature and birds along the trails. So I'd like to do this, partly to make sure the trail system receives additional support and partly, just for you and me, to signify the specialness I feel about us. You do know, I hope, that I love you."

It was the first time I had said that to her even though we had been together for several years.

"Oh, Carl."

She looked down and then looked up before continuing. She looked at me quite seriously.

"I don't really believe in love anymore, Carl. ...
...But if I did,
...I know I would love you. ...

.... Oh ... what am I saying? Of course, yes, I love you, too, Carl. And I love what you're doing."

We talked for hours about us and about the trail system. We agreed, laughing together, that we were an item and had been for a couple of years. And we talked about maybe moving in together at some point, but we both felt we wanted more time.

"When Ron finishes his training," I said, "Maybe I'll give him the trailer and we can find a place together?"

"How long will that be? I'm so afraid of rushing things."

I caught both the eagerness and the reluctance and smiled.

"He'll finish high school this year. It has taken him an extra year because he really needed serious remedial work. He wants to go to x-ray technician school next year. That'll probably take him three years. How does that sound for a timeline?"

"Perfect. But if we become too eager to be together more, maybe we can shave a year off that?" She smiled a very alluring smile. I loved her smile, and I loved her eyes.

"Carl, what should be done with the money you want to provide for the trail system? It'll be your money, so you should be able to say what you want done with it."

"I don't really know. I just know I don't want to be a director or executive or anything. I just want a better, bigger, and well-maintained trail system."

"How about designating some portion for land acquisition, a portion for construction, and a portion for maintenance and repairs?"

"That sounds good." I smiled at her again. I still felt mesmerized by her eyes.

"There are lots of places where there are abandoned rail lines," Steffanie said. "The rails and ties are long gone, but the sites are perfect for expanding the trail system. I know the Trail people would love to buy those rights of way."

"Perfect. Steffanie, I'm happy to sit in on meetings for those sorts of things, but only if you're there, too. Would that be okay with you?"

"Well, okay. But I'm not an executive type myself. Let's just make sure that people we trust make the decisions."

"Good plan. I'll have to trust you, though, to help me even in that area."

- - -

That night at work, I took a few minutes to buy more Google stock with some more of my savings. When I received the inheritance from Evelyn, I put fifty thousand in a savings account at Everbank and fifty thousand in an account at a nearby credit union. Those insured savings accounts were for the Trail association.

Then I bought more Google stock and added some Apple stock, along with some PetSmart stock. The PetSmart stock tanked, but the other two were solid buy-and-hold choices. I also put the remaining half of my savings into two different index funds with very low management fees.

- - -

Sometime during the late winter of 2008, a family I recognized came into the store at about 8am. It was the Schultz family from Omaha. I happened to be there waiting to interview a job applicant when they came in.

I had known the Schultzes a bit. They lived down the street from us when I lived in Omaha. I remembered Harry as a bright but geeky guy, but I didn't remember much about any of the rest of the family. We'd been at neighborhood get-togethers now and then, but usually the guys just got together and drank and talked about the business world. Seeing the Schultzes brought back a flood of memories, most of which helped me realize I was glad to be Carl Jacobs and not Fred Young.

I was immediately nervous to the point of paralysis when I saw them, but I was pretty sure they wouldn't recognize me. I should have just retreated to the office, given that I felt some concern, but I wanted to know if people might recognize me.

To find out, I waited on them myself and answered their questions, altering my voice only slightly with a hint of a southern accent. I looked them in the eyes.

No signs of recognition! As I had expected. Not a hint of familiarity Not a questioning look. Not a question of, "Do I know you?" or a statement of "Hey, you remind me of..." Nothing.

I breathed a sigh of relief, and neither Ron nor Maggy noticed a thing. After the Schultzes left, I took my pulse. It was high, but not extreme. I relaxed.

Not three minutes later, Harry Schultz was back in the store, asking for directions to the stadium where the Jaguars play football and where the Super Bowl had been played back in 2005.

As I gave him directions, it seemed to me Harry was staring at me.

I became more than a little concerned. Had he recognized me? Did he have some sort of vague idea who I was?

He stood there looking at me after I gave him the directions. There was a brief, awkward pause.

"Anything else?" I asked.

"No,... thanks," he hesitated. And then he left the store without looking back at me.

What were the three minutes about? What was the staring about? Was he trying to imagine me with hair, a beard, and an extra sixty pounds?

Had the Schultz family discussed my resemblance to Fred Young and sent Harry back in to check me out? That seemed improbable to me. After all, I hadn't seen them for nearly seven years. But I couldn't be sure.

Why did he stare at me? And why the hesitation?

I was beginning to panic, but I controlled myself.

The Schultzes were not going to do anything right then, no matter what they might have thought. And even if they thought I looked or maybe sounded like Fred Young, they would almost surely talk themselves out of it:

- Fred Young had been declared dead.
- I didn't look at all like Fred Young without my beard or hair.
- I had altered my voice a bit when speaking with them.
- I was sixty pounds lighter than Fred Young had been.
- It had been almost seven years since they had seen Fred Young.

They would surely chalk it up to a weird sensation at most even if they did think there was a hint of similarity between Fred Young and me.

My attempts to reassure myself were not entirely successful.

- - -

By the spring of 2008, Ron was nearly finished with his training as an x-ray technician, and he had two different job possibilities.

Steffanie and I took him out for dinner in April to celebrate his moving on. After dinner, I handed him an envelope. I think he expected a graduation card and maybe some money. When he opened it, though, he saw the legal papers giving him the trailer.

Ron began crying and jumped up from the table, knocking his chair over in the process. He rushed around and pulled me up from the table to hug me. He'd had a growth spurt in high school and was nearly as tall as I was. He hugged me, and then he hugged Steffanie, and then he hugged me again.

"This is so generous. I can't believe it."

"Well, Ron," I laughed, " I'm not sure how great a gift it is. I've been staying at Steffanie's so much the past two years, it's almost your trailer anyway, and now you'll have to look after the park fees, taxes, and insurance yourself."

"I love the trailer. It's the only real home I ever had. I didn't want to move out, but I figured I would have to, once I got out of school and started earning a good salary. Now I won't have to move."

"What's more, Ron, you can move your things into the big bedroom. Your old bedroom can become your study."

"Thank you, so much, Mr. Jacobs."

He was pleased, and I was so pleased that I had done this.

"Ron, why don't you call me Carl from now on. It's up to you, though."

I quickly added, "I don't think it will take long to move my things out. I'll stop by after work tomorrow."

"One more thing. There's a spare key under the Fellows grave marker in the cemetery. I put it there just a few days after I moved in. At least I think it's still there. I meant to keep checking on it, but I haven't looked the past few years."

"That was yours?" Ron laughed. "I found it when I was wandering in the cemetery that morning. I had no idea it was for your trailer. It was still there the last time I looked."

After dinner we dropped Ron off at the trailer. Inside, it looked pretty much the same as it had the day he moved in with me.

Ron seemed pensive as we said our goodbyes.

"Now that I know I'll have a job that I'll start in June, I wonder if I can have Janie and Abby move in here with me. I know that foster homes will just hold them back and keep them miserable. Maybe I can do for them what you did for me Mr. Jacobs."

He hadn't adapted to 'Carl' right away, I guess.

"If they're anything like you, Ron, they will blossom under your influence. But don't rush into anything. Looking after two younger sisters while trying to get your feet on the ground in a new job can be a lot of work. Maybe start with having them visit now and then and increase the visits as you all become more comfortable together?"

We had goodbye hugs around. As we left, Steffanie asked if we could leave her car at Thane-North and go for a walk along the Winona Trail before I began work.

"Sure."

As we walked along the trail, Steffanie slipped her hand through my arm and said, "Carl, you've seemed a bit edgy for the past few weeks. Is there anything wrong?"

"Well, yes, there is. No, there was, but there isn't anything wrong now. Steffanie, I worry that my past might catch up with me at some point. I had an incident a couple of months ago that probably meant nothing but it bothered me. I guess you picked up on it."

I stopped and looked at her. She had tensed up. I recognized the look on her face when she was tense and unhappy.

"Look," I said. "I love you, and I love my life. I aspire to nothing more than the contentment I have found here in Jacksonville with you, Ron, and the Thanes. I love my job. I love walking the trails with you. I love being with you and sharing our lives. I love learning from you. I love seeing Ron blossom. I love everything about this life."

Steffanie seemed scared. "Why are you saying these things to me Carl?"

"When that incident occurred, I briefly considered running away. Very briefly. But then I weighed the odds that my past would catch up with me against my immense, joyful contentment with the life I have found here. I think the odds are very low that the incident could ever come back to affect me. Extremely low. Vanishingly low. Yes, I have been edgy, but my life here, including being with you, is what I was searching for before. It took a jolt from my past for me to realize this.

"I'm sorry I've been on edge. I'm sorry I can't explain it very well. All I know is that I have found here what I was looking for for so many years."

Steffanie didn't collapse into my arms. Instead she looked at me sternly. Typical of Steffanie.

I loved her no-nonsense manner. I had always believed that love should be romantic and full of bells and fireworks. I hadn't experienced romantic love with Susan but we tried to pretend we had; the closest I ever came was with Evelyn, and that turned out to be fleeting. I loved Steffanie because of who she was, not because of any Hollywood notion of love.

Steffanie was different. There was a romantic edge to our being together, for sure, but her directness and her own hesitancies brought out an honesty and depth I had never imagined possible.

"Carl, I love you, too," she said, "But I cannot take any sudden shocks in our relationship. Your past frightens me for two ... no three, reasons. It frightens me because I don't know you; your past has shaped you into who you are, and I'll never really understand you since I can't know your past. It frightens me, too, because it frightens you; I am deeply attached and in love with you, and I don't want to see you frightened or hurt. And most importantly, it frightens me because I don't know what it means for us. I don't want to live under that uncertainty."

I cautioned myself: Don't jump in. Don't try to make everything better for everyone. Don't say too much.

- - -

I wanted to make things work for Steffanie and me. We had become both comfortably close and intensely close over the six years we had known each other. But because of my silence about my past, she had reservations. I wanted to tell her the truth, but I knew I couldn't. I didn't feel I could trust anyone with the truth, but mostly I worried that she wouldn't trust me or want me in her life if I told her who I had been, what I had done, and why I had done it. So I kept my past a complete and total secret.

We drifted warily over the next few months, eager to hold our relationship together, both of us knowing that we wanted to be together. It took time, but gradually, we reestablished our sense of closeness. Over time, I think I gained her trust. I honestly believe that aside from her concerns about my past, Steffanie trusted and loved me.

Most importantly, I didn't leave.

- - -

Last week I saw a lawyer to draw up a will, leaving everything to Steffanie and Ron.

And I left this manuscript with the lawyer.

This book is for you, Steffanie Niles. With love and gratitude.

* * *
* * * *
* * * * *

Acknowledgements

I owe a great deal to everyone who read portions of **2605** as it emerged and who offered insightful comments, suggestions, corrections, and encouragement. In alphabetical order:

Jack Allingham
John Berry
Joan Clayton
John Crawford
Bev Early
Dilan Goonetilleke
John Henderson
Lissa Kuzych
Dianne van Leeuwen
Paul Merrifield
John Moore
Paula Nicholls
Matthew Palmer
Anne Quast
Brian Quast
Dale Tassi
Carolle Trembley
Vivian Trembley

The possibility of shaving to change one's appearance drastically was made evident to me some years ago when I lost a challenge with students and had to shave my head and beard. The pictures on the back cover were taken of me, a day apart. These before and after photos illustrate the effect. No one, not even my sons, recognized me the day after I shaved.

The idea for the novel formed in my mind about a year after 9-11, and I laid out the concept of Chapter One for my nephew, Brian Quast, and my late friend, Ben Singer, over coffee one morning. I started work on the novel then, but didn't like what I had written and shelved it for nearly fifteen years. Then in September 2017, it hit me how I wanted to write Chapters 1-6. The rest unfolded from there. I'm glad I waited.

About the author

John P. Palmer was born and raised in Muskegon, Michigan. By his own admission, he barely graduated from Carleton College (Northfield, Minnesota) in 1965 with a major in economics and minors in mathematics and religion.

From 1965 – 67, he was a student at The Chicago Theological Seminary, where he was active in the Civil Rights and Anti-Vietnam-War movements. While there, he realized he loved economics and wasn't at all cut out to be a church minister, and so he switched to graduate school in economics at Iowa State University (Ames, Iowa) where he received his PhD in economics in 1971. That same year he accepted a position in the Economics Department of The University of Western Ontario (London, Ontario). He retired from there forty years later, in 2011.

A self-described dilettante, he has been a photographer, an orchestra conductor, a sportscaster, and an actor. He has three children, seven grandchildren, and two great-grandchildren. He lives with his wife in London, Ontario, where he is still active in theatre, play-writing, music, and sportscasting. *2605* is his first novel.

He is currently working on a companion novel, **Susan's Story**, for which the expected publication date is sometime in the first half of 2020.